6/27/15

Antonia,

"You're a Great Catch!
Never settle for less!

Blessings,
Sonya Jenkin

Psalms 37:4

SHAYLA'S CATCH

A Novel

By Sonya Jenkins

Acknowledgements

I give thanks to God for making all things possible in my life. Thanks to my parents, Alfreda Jenkins, a former media specialist, who encouraged my creative writing and pushed me to be the best that I could be, and to my father, the late Lee Jenkins Sr., a sports enthusiast who was often the life of the party, for helping plant a solid foundation in my life. Thanks to my big brother, Lee Jenkins Jr., a minister and former draftee of the NFL, from whom I gathered much insight into the lifestyles of athletes, and who showed me - by his character and accomplishments - that athletes can be faithful, grounded and educated. Thanks to my many friends who allowed me to share my novel with them while it was in its infancy and encouraged me to continue writing *SHAYLA'S CATCH*. Thanks to all who provided information during my research and writing. You helped me to gain more knowledge and write about different scenarios and perfect certain dialogue. And to my readers, your purchase and support of my first novel, *SHAYLA'S CATCH*, has meant the world to me! YOU are a source of motivation! I truly appreciate you!

Special Thanks: Karen Ash, Andrea Barrett, Wendy Collins, Dr. James Crook, Shawn Evans, Lavoisier Fisher, Dainnese Gault, Rommie Hawkins, Kimberly Howard, Carla Johnson, Professor Bill Larsen, Coach Tee Martin, Shawn Evans Mitchell, David Michael Smith, Dr. Thanayi Smith, Dr. Thomas K. Taylor, Omar Tyree, Rosetta Perry.

Chapter One

Weak In The Knees

$\mathcal{A}$s I thumbed through the Falcon's game day program, a warm and tingly sensation rushed through my body when I saw Calvin Moore's picture. I was drawn to his Hershey bar skin, his boyish smile and deep dimples. *I would give anything to be his girl.* I read his biography like it held the winning numbers to a lottery ticket:

At 6 foot 2, 195 pounds, Calvin "CK" Moore led the Atlanta Falcons in receptions for the 2010 season with 70 catches for 1500 yards. Moore was an All-American wide receiver at Washington High School in Chicago and the 2005 Heisman Trophy Winner while at the University Of Southern California. He also excelled in track and field at USC, breaking the 100 meter dash world record. Moore was a first round draft choice by the Falcons and he is in his fourth season with the team. On a personal note, Moore is twenty-five years old and single.

"Now him, I would looove to meet," I said, elbowing Tacara and pointing to Calvin's photo.

Tacara's hazel eyes lit up. "Omigod. You and every other woman in Atlanta," she chuckled with a sardonic brow.

"So, do you think Steve would introduce us?" I crossed my fingers, hoping that Tacara could convince her linebacker boyfriend to set me up with his teammate.

"Shayla, I've heard that CK Moore has so many women that he doesn't know what to do with all of them. And I know that Steve is not going to introduce you to a womanizer like him. Girl, he's a hoe." Tacara looked at me evenly. "And I thought you wanted to meet a Christian guy anyway," she reminded me.

With a shrug, I turned away from my roommate and closed the program. Yes, I had said I wanted to meet a God-fearing man, but I was beginning to think my prayers for someone of spiritual valor were in vain. I'd been without a boyfriend for almost two years. Fed up with being alone, I wanted to meet a man who could drape me on his arm and turn heads in a room – and someone with a positive cash flow. *Hmmm.* I had read that Calvin Moore had recently signed a new multi-million dollar contract with the Falcons. Anyway, Tacara had encouraged me to come to the Falcons game so Steve could introduce me to someone "really nice," as she put it.

An olive skinned girl with naturally wavy hair cascading down her back and high cheek bones, Tacara always got the best boyfriends; the athletes, the doctors, the lawyers, the strong Christian men. I guess, in a way, I wanted to be like her. She had met Steve six months ago and they were already looking for engagement rings.

"Oh, baby!" Tacara screamed as Steve sacked the Eagle's quarterback. "Yes!"

"Defense! Gotta have defense! Gotta have defense!" the crowd roared in unison.

Uninterested in the game, I forced myself to chant along. The mindless stream of words came from my lips, "Defense. Gotta have defense." I stood alone, wondering when I might feel the strong arms of someone like Calvin Moore around me. *It would be nice to be in love. Candlelight. Moonlight. Kisses and Hugs.*

Tacara awakened me from my daydream. A broad smile broadened her face as she stared at the scoreboard. *The Falcons must have won.*

As the crowd dispersed, we hurried to the player's dressing area to meet Steve. Gorgeous cover-girl and video-vixen type women stood outside waiting for the players. Even those holding children by the hand looked flawless in their high-heeled Jimmy Choo shoes, Prada and Louis Vutton handbags, Channel sunglasses and bling that was blinding. Their taut arms, tiny waistlines and toned thighs spoke of hours spent with personal trainers.

Since most of the Black women were fair complexioned, my darker caramel skin stood out. I tossed my black, thick, flat-ironed hair over my shoulder, thankful I'd gone to the beauty salon prior to the game.

The thirty minute wait dragged on forever. My feet ached in my stilettos. *What was I thinking wearing heels to a sporting event?* Finally, a few football players streamed out of the dressing room, clean and dapper. Even the ones not pleasing to the eye had a debonair, powerful appeal. Then Calvin Kendall Moore strutted out of the dressing room like a gladiator with the finesse of a model. My knees all but buckled. He was more handsome in person than in the game day magazine. Chiseled cheek bones, a square jaw-line, thick eyebrows, a low, even hair cut, a buffed body, and alluring narrow and seductive eyes that immediately met mine. I smiled and looked away, feeling totally smitten.

"Lord, he is fine," I mumbled to Tacara who was engrossed in a conversation with a woman sporting a diamond ring so big, it seemed to pull her hand downward.

Tacara turned and asked, "What did you say, Shayla?"

"Oh nothing," I bit on my bottom lip. I didn't want the other girl to get a clue of my attraction to Calvin.

But as soon as they began to chat again, I glanced around. Calvin had disappeared. Just like that, I'd missed my opportunity to meet him. My heartbeat accelerated. *God, please don't let him be gone.*

I spotted him talking to an attractive woman with long, wavy hair. They were standing a few feet away from me. I didn't want to stare at them, but she was pointing her finger in Calvin's face, and I overheard their conversation.

"Don't make a scene out here, okay?" Calvin growled in a tightly controlled voice.

"You know what CK? I don't want anything else to do with you. I'm tired of your B.S. Go be with that ghetto stripper from the club," she snapped before walking off with long, definite strides.

Calvin glanced at me and smiled. "Women," he shook his head from side to side.

Not knowing how to respond, I replied, "Men." My stomach churned. Calvin gawked at me from head to toe, slowly casting his eyes along my five foot seven inch frame. His eyes stopped for a fleeting second at my breasts before he cocked his head sideways, and rested them on my buttocks. Pleased I had worn my coral-colored sundress, I pressed my shoulders back and lifted one corner of my mouth in an awkward smile.

I tried to give him my "smile-look away-smile" again flirty expression, but Calvin's lingering gaze made me blush. His eyes gripped mine to his like super glue.

Holding a Gucci duffle bag with one hand and rubbing his chest with the other, he strode over to me like a man about to claim his prize. "Are you waiting for someone?"

I wanted to say, "Yes, I'm waiting for you." But I figured that would be too forward. "No. I'm with Steve and Tacara," I said, noticing that Steve had just joined us.

"CK, what's up my man?" Steve asked as he looked at Calvin and then me with a slight frown. He placed a firm hand on my shoulder. "What's goin on?"

They shook hands and bumped each other's fist, and Steve's frown turned into a smile.

"I'm trying to meet this lovely young lady, man." Calvin stared at me with a raised eyebrow.

"Man, hell naw. You always want to meet somebody, but Shayla is a good girl. Hell to the no," Steve told him.

"Well, a good girl deserves a good man," Calvin replied. "Man, what's up wit'chew?"

Steve shook his head. "Man, naw. I don't know about this."

"Aww Steve, why don't you introduce them," Tacara interjected.

"Well it looks like they have already met. Trust me, this man ain't shy," Steve replied with slight sarcasm in his voice.

To my surprise, Calvin took my hand in his. My heart pounded.

"Don't listen to him," he said in a faint voice. "I could be your knight in shining armor."

"Man, come off it," Steve said. "You need to come with a better line than that lame crap."

Calvin paid no mind to Steve. He cupped both of his hands over mine. I melted. I looked into his sexy brown eyes. My mama had warned me never to believe in love at first sight. She tried to teach me to be practical about love, but as Calvin

Moore stood there in a fitted suit, accentuating his Adonis-like prowess, I knew mama had been wrong.

"You are gorgeous," he said. "What's your name?"

"Shayla."

"Are you married, Shayla?"

"No."

He took a step forward. "Boyfriend?"

I smiled shyly. "No."

"Well, can I be your new boyfriend?"

Steve and Tacara burst into laughter. Beginning to perspire, I averted my eyes from Calvin's. "Can we be friends first?" I finally said.

"Naw. I want to be your man. You are exquisite."

"Exquisite?" Steve interrupted. "Man, puleeze. Don't you ever get tired of yourself?"

Calvin flashed Steve a steely look. "Man, you didn't want to introduce us, so see your way out of this, aight?"

Two little boys around eight or nine years old interrupted the heated moment. Holding out a pen and paper to Calvin, one of the bright-eyed youngsters asked, "Can we have your autographs, please?" The second boy handed his paper to Steve.

Calvin slowly let go of my hand. "Aww man, you guys have bad timing," he chided. "I'm standing here talking to my new girlfriend."

The boys giggled. I grinned. I could not help being attracted to Calvin's magnetic personality.

"You are my hero," the little boy said while Calvin was signing his autograph. "I'm your biggest fan of all time."

"Well, that's all good. Just remember to always put education before sports. Okay? And do what your mama says do."

His words skittered in my heart. *A man who has a positive message for kids.* After Calvin signed a dozen or two more autographs, he politely told his fans that he wouldn't be signing anymore today. "But catch me after the next home game," he insisted.

Once again, Calvin eyes bore into mine. He took my hand in his and held it tightly. His touch was strong and warm and I didn't want to let go. The smile on his face widened. My stomach somersaulted. I tried not to expose my giddiness for Calvin by giving Steve and Tacara a wink. *They probably already know I'm head over heels for him.*

"C'mon, Shayla," Steve spoke in a father-like tone.

"I'll take you home," Calvin leaned forward and whispered in my ear.

"Maybe we can get together another time," I said hesitantly. I really wanted to go with him, but I felt it would be inappropriate to leave with someone I had just met. "Not this time," I said softly as I looked into his soothing eyes.

"Aww, c'mon," Calvin murmured with a gentle, almost pleading look.

"It's just that I didn't plan to leave with you. I can't," I said shaking my head and then looking at Steve and Tacara. I didn't want them to think of me as too easy, but I wanted Calvin to know that they were the reason I wouldn't leave with him.

Calvin slowly let go of my hand. "Okay. I guess I'll see you around."

Oh no. This can't be it. Please don't let me go. My heart sank. I stalled, wanting Calvin to say something more. *Please, ask for my number.*

Tacara winked at me. "Let's all go for a bite to eat," she suggested. "I made reservations for us at Frank Ski's restaurant and I'm sure we can add another person to our party." She glanced at Calvin. "Can you meet us there CK?"

"I'd love to, but I can't. I've got a couple of things lined up," Calvin said. His chin was high. "I'm doing this Nike commercial tomorrow and I have to meet some people at my crib for prep." Calvin turned to me. "But maybe I can see you a little later?"

"That's possible."

"Give me your number then."

"Sure," I exhaled.

After he put my number in his cell phone, he grasped my hand again and gently squeezed my fingers. "I'll call you . . . tonight."

"I'll be waiting to hear from you," I murmured.

Calvin softly stroked my cheek and backed away. *He is the one.* I watched him disappear into the crowd. *He is definitely the one for me.*

I watched Monday Night Football the following week in total frustration. Calvin scored two touchdowns and danced into the end zone, but my heart danced in misery. He had not kept his word to call. *Maybe he didn't find me so intriguing after all. Perhaps he kissed and made up with the girl I saw him arguing with.* It wouldn't have felt so bad had I not told several co-workers, my sister and my mother that Calvin Moore wanted to take me out. *How silly of me.* Embarrassed, I crawled into bed and hoped that those I had bragged to would not try to follow up with questions about my date. *What date?*

One afternoon while I was watching television, my cell phone rang, but "private" showed on the screen.

"Hello?" I answered with curiosity.

"Hello, Shayla?" a male voice asked.

I sat upright from my slouched position on the love seat. "This is Shayla." My heart began to pound.

"Hi, sexy."

"Who is this?" I asked, pretending I didn't know who he was. But I hadn't given any other man my number lately.

"It's CK."

"Oh, hi, CK." I tried to remain calm. My emotions were mixed with frustration and joy. After all, it had taken him nine days to call. "How are you?"

"I'm aight. I miss you, sexy."

"Any-way."

"Anyway what? I do miss you. When can I see you?"

"I don't know," I said. *Maybe he needs a challenge. Why should I be ready and available when he took so long to call?*

"Aight, if you don't want to see me..."

"I do want to see you," I interrupted. "It's just that I thought I'd hear from you before now." *I blew it. Why did I say that?*

"Yeah, I wanted to call you sooner, but something came up. Can you hang out with me after the game Sunday?" he asked gently.

"That might work." I sighed. At this point I was willing to accept anything.

"Did you miss me?"

"What?" I tried not to laugh.

"Dayum, girl, why are you trying to act all hard-to-get? Did you miss me?"

"Well, maybe I just need to get to know you before I start missing you. I can't miss what I've never had."

"You can have it anytime you want it," he shot back in a sexy tone.

"Calvin, I mean, really." I drew a deep breath. "I don't know."

"You don't know about what?" he asked, sounding clueless.

"I don't want to move too fast. And obviously you don't either, since you waited so long to call," I chuckled, hoping I wasn't coming across as too demanding, too soon. "But I'd like to get to know you better. And you might need to know that I'm not into casual sex."

"I haven't said anything about sexing you. I told you I want you to be my lady."

I sat back, trying to calm myself. "Calvin, I'm very attracted to you, but I'm a good girl, and I'm not sure if you're used to my kind. You seem to be a fast mover in a way. We should develop a friendship first, don't you think?"

"With all the chemistry we've got it's gonna be hard as hell for us to just be friends."

"I'm just not ready for anything physical though," I said softly, already feeling my resolve to stay celibate until marriage, *this time around,* go out the door.

"Okay, dayum. You are real uptight for some reason. I'm gonna have to calm you down. You might need the Moore effect."

"The what?"

"The CK Moore effect. The more you see me, the more you'll want me," he boasted.

"Okay," I laughed. *This is one cocky guy.* But his arrogance did not turn me off in the least.

"Could you do me a favor, sweet pea?" Calvin asked.

"What can I do for you, Calvin?" I leaned forward on my elbow.

"When you come to the game Sunday, wear your hair really curly just for me."

"Really curly?" I repeated, wondering why such a request.

"Yeah, wear it curly."

"Okay. I guess I can do that small favor. So will you leave two tickets? I'd like to bring my sister."

"That's cool. I'll leave them at the player's will-call window, but sista is gonna have to get lost after the game. I want to take you out. Just you and me."

"That's fine," I licked my dry lips.

"Aight. Lock this number in your phone and text me your last name so I can leave you and your sis some tickets. I need to roll, so meet me at the same place as before. See you after the game, okay?"

"Okay. But that number didn't come through."

"Bye, love." Calvin hung up.

"Hello?"

After hanging up the phone, all kinds of thoughts crept through my mind. *Did he mean to hang up on me?* And here I was thinking my straight hair was one of the things that had gotten his attention and now he was telling me to wear it curly. *What is that all about?* As I sat on the plush chair in the spacious two bedroom apartment that Tacara and I shared, I imagined Calvin holding me through the night. I became excited just thinking about us eventually making love. I had only been intimate with two guys in my twenty-five years. *I'm not about to let my heart rule my head. Not over a professional football player I hardly know.*

Game day finally arrived. Calvin texted two days earlier, asking for my last name to leave tickets. He ran two kick-off returns for touchdowns. Two young ladies sitting in front of me, looking to be in their mid-twenties, bent over in laughter when Calvin shook his body in rhythmic contortions after both of his touchdowns.

"I told you he was going to do that dance," one said. "He told me he was going to do it just for me."

I winced. *Just one of his fans*, I figured.

At the end of the game, my sister Sydney and I made small conversation as we waited for him. Steve had already come out of the locker room and he and Tacara zoomed off as if they had someplace to be in a hurry.

Just as I had done at the last game, I wore a sundress this time also. The hemline fell three inches above my knees. My five-inch, beige strap sandals enhanced my legs and my French pedicure. I usually didn't wear much make-up, but this time I added a little extra blush to my high cheekbones and waxed my thick eyebrows so that my brown, slanted eyes would look even more enchanting. I had added more MAC gloss to my pouty lips, and as I applied it, I thought about Calvin kissing it off. I figured kissing wasn't a sin. It just wasn't my nature to jump right in bed with a man. *I hope he doesn't expect me to.*

It took Calvin longer than the first time to come from the dressing room. *Interviews, probably.* My stomach felt queasy. I hoped he would like my curls, and I prayed he and my sister would have a good rapport.

Finally, Calvin emerged. When he looked in our direction, I waved to get his attention.

"There he is," I squealed.

"He is cute," Sydney said.

Calvin walked over to me, wearing a boyish smile. He leaned down and gave me a peck on the lips.

"Hi, Beautiful," he said looking at me without blinking.

"Hi, Calvin," I replied, feeling weak for him already.

"This has gotta be your sister?" He looked at Sydney.

"Yep. Calvin, this is Sydney. Sydney, Calvin."

They exchanged handshakes. Sydney had always been hard on me when it came to my choice of guys. None of the relationships I had previously experienced seemed to measure up to her expectations.

After we walked to the parking lot I gave my sister a quick hug. Calvin said good-bye to her. When he opened the passenger door of a dark blue Ferrari, I slid in.

"Nice car," I said.

Before closing the door, Calvin bent down and planted a wet, warm kiss on my eager lips. He stroked my hair lightly. I drifted toward him like a magnet.

He dashed to the driver's side of the car, got inside, and started the engine. The sound of jazz blaring through the speakers made me feel romantic. We drove slowly down the streets of downtown Atlanta. The night was beautiful. The temperature was about ninety degrees and quite pleasant for late September. I had no clue where we were heading as Calvin merged onto I-75 going north.

"Calvin?" I said, breaking the peaceful silence between us.

He turned the stereo volume down. "Yeah, baby?" He took my hand and kissed my knuckles softly.

"You played a great game."

"I was thinking about you the whole while," he said, and turned his head to look at me. "You're so beautiful and sexy. I love your hair like that. I can't wait to love you."

"Where are we going?" I asked. Uneasiness rose inside me. *I know he's not thinking of taking me to his place. Not tonight. He hasn't even taken me to dinner.*

Calvin leveled his piercing brown eyes on me with a charming, yet lustful smile. "We're going to Ray's," he said.

"Ray's?" I repeated. "Who is Ray?"

"So you've never been to Ray's On The River?"

"No. I don't think so. Is it a restaurant?"

Calvin brought my hand up to his lips and kissed it again. He snickered. I felt a bit naïve. I was relatively new to Atlanta. I did not frequent nice restaurants or get out much, for that matter. I spent most of my hours working as a buyer for Saks Fifth Avenue. My college degree was in marketing from West Georgia College; about sixty miles from Atlanta, but my love for clothes had led me to pursue a career in retail.

Calvin drove faster and our conversation waned a bit. A more upbeat, profanity filled Lil' Wayne CD was now playing

− a huge difference from the original jazz CD. He bobbed his head to the rhythmic beat, tapping the back of my hand with his fingers.

When we arrived at Ray's On The River we were greeted by a tall, blond hostess who congratulated Calvin on his win. She quickly seated us at a table in front of the jazz quartet over the long bank of windows overlooking the Chattahoochee River. As soon as Calvin put in his order for a bottle of Dom Perignon, the guests at the outlying tables began to pursue him for autographs. After signing a few, he returned his attention back to me.

"Let's make a toast," he said as he scooted his chair closer and picked up his glass of champagne. I picked up mine and waited for the first toast.

"Here's to our first night out together, and many more to come," We clinked glasses and took a few sips.

After dinner, my resolve to abstain from sex without having a ring on my finger dwindled as Calvin drove us to Country Club of the South, a sprawling gated subdivision on the north side of Atlanta. The homes were huge mansions, and his house seemed to be the largest one in the gated community. His European stucco home, with its four-tiered waterfall out front, rose up on a high hill like a palace. When he led me inside, my mouth fell wide open. I marveled at the contemporary décor, architectural prints, black art, circular stairway, and tumbled Italian marble floors. There was even an elevator going to the next floor.

With his hand placed softly at the base of my spine, Calvin led me to the backyard, where a huge swimming pool and a tennis court took up over an acre of land.

As I stood admiring the magnificent view of the pool, Calvin put his arms around me and whispered at the nape of my neck, "You are my starlight."

As his tongue probed my ear I told myself it was too much, too soon. But the more my mind said no, the warmer my body became.

Calvin turned me around to face him. He moved closer until our lips met. My heart began to race as he tantalized me with a deep, tasty kiss. When I realized what was happening, I pulled back. *No rang, no thang.* I closed my eyes and clenched my hand into a fist. *This is not just an average guy I'm with, Lord. It's Calvin Kendall Moore . . . my dream man.*

"What's wrong, Shayla?" Calvin wanted to know. He traced my lips with his fingers.

"I'm just scared," I said softly.

Calvin kissed the tip of my nose, then he planted several kisses as his lips moved down my neck. I felt his moist tongue against my skin. It was at that moment when my knees actually buckled.

Chapter Two

Thrill of Victory, Agony of Defeat

C alvin and I had been seeing each other on a regular basis for a little more than four months. We had experienced some very romantic moments. There had been some trying times as well. Most of our arguments stemmed from Calvin's inability to control his roving eye, and his cheating ways. If he saw a fine lady, he looked. I had also learned that a monogamous relationship was a challenge for him. But I was patient and willing to stand by him no matter what the cost. A lot of women found Calvin irresistible because he was one of the best looking and highest paid receivers in the NFL. He was making 10 million a year, plus endorsements. It was absurd for me to think that other women would not pursue him. I also realized that a man will be a man, and temptation would be hard for him to resist.

In spite of our growing pains, Calvin always managed to smooth things over. I was totally pacified whenever he would buy nice things for me . . . designer outfits and handbags, a diamond tennis bracelet from Tiffany & Co. − practically anything I asked for. He would even give me the keys to his Porsche from time to time. But there was the one thing Calvin had kept to himself. He had never admitted or confessed his love for me. Even so, I had this deep feeling that he did love me. After all, I tolerated a lot from him. Sometimes a week or two would pass without any word from Calvin. When we were together, his cell phone would vibrate at odd hours of the morning. He was also a self-centered man. But his good qualities outweighed his bad ones. I was his guest at VIP functions, he was a very passionate lover, and he made me laugh.

I found my new, upscale lifestyle one that I never wanted to give up. It was filled with glitz and glamour, and I didn't want to date an average guy again. On the flip side of the coin, I sometimes felt like I was Calvin's showpiece. He always told me what to wear and how to fix my hair. He liked it curly. He even told me I had to look the part if I wanted a role in his life. That was just fine with me.

The Super Bowl XLIVII crowd at Sun Life Stadium in Miami rocked the entire stadium like a mini earthquake. The Atlanta Falcons were down 17 to 21, and the game was winding down to the end of the fourth quarter.

"Shayla," a small voice pierced through the crowd during a time-out. The voice was that of Tacara. She looked gorgeous from head to toe. I was a little envious of her relationship with Steve, since they were already talking marriage. Tacara never tolerated bad behavior from Steve. She had grown up with seven brothers, and she had no sisters. Her brothers had schooled her about men. As for myself, I had only one sister. My father had died when I was three-years-old. Although my mother remarried, it ended in divorce after only two years. All I remember is a lot of bickering and fighting, so I had no good role models or anyone I could confide in about matters of the heart.

"Tacara," I said, as I motioned for her to come and sit in the vacant seat beside me. "I want you to meet Calvin's mother."

Carefully, Tacara made her way through the crowded seats. From the corner of my eye, I could see Calvin's mother, Norma Jean, checking Tacara out . . . looking her up and down.

"Girl, you look great," I said admiring Tacara's BCBG jacket that was stripped at the arms, giving a glimpse of her flawless skin. "I was wondering if we'd see each other in this crowd. Look at you."

Tacara's lips curved into a knowing smile. She always graciously accepted compliments. "I looked for you at half-time," she said. At that moment she caught Norma Jean's eye.

"Oh, this is Calvin's mom, Norma Jean, and her friend John," I said.

"Hello," Norma Jean said with a smirk on her face.

This was my second time being at a game with her. She was only forty-one years old and very snobbish. Calvin had been born when she was only sixteen. She and Calvin's father had never married, but according to Calvin, Norma Jean had "boyfriends," and John was the lucky one she had invited to the Super Bowl. He didn't seem the least bit interested in her. John eyed every female that he saw. He even seemed more interested in me than Norma Jean.

John leaned forward to get a better look at Tacara. "Now whose girl are you?" he asked flirtatiously. Norma Jean elbowed him.

"Steve Brown. Number 95. The Powerhouse," Tacara replied as if she had practiced the line.

A gentleman sitting in front of us turned to see who was talking. "Steve Brown is an awesome player," he quipped.

"Yep," Tacara answered, smiling from ear to ear.

"And CK Moore is too," I added, matter of factly.

I had flown in the night before the Super Bowl. For some strange reason, Calvin asked me not to come early for the pre-game parties. Tacara, on the other hand, had been in Miami to enjoy the festivities for the entire week. I wanted her to give me all the details, but I didn't want Norma Jean to hear our conversation.

While fidgeting and hoping Calvin's mom would turn her attention back to the game, thoughts of the night before the Super Bowl boggled my mind. When I checked into the Fontainebleau Miami Beach Hotel, Calvin had left two dozen roses in my room. There was also a skimpy negligee on the bed. I knew right away it would be a night to remember. An hour before his curfew, Calvin knocked at my door. We made love for the whole hour. He usually did not like to exert a lot of energy before a big game, but he told me I was irresistible. Calvin did not have a condom. I had always depended on him to have the protection lined up, but last night I gave in without any hesitation. The thing that bothered me the most was I had recently gotten off the pill. I had not told Calvin. I squirmed in my seat at the thought of possibly being pregnant, *and Calvin had better not given me some sexually transmitted disease.*

To keep myself from agonizing about last night, I turned to Tacara. "You know you have a lot to tell me," I said.

Tacara frowned. "I do?"

"C'mon Tacara, you've got to fill me in," I said in a low tone. "Have you seen Calvin with anybody else?"

"Shayla, you need to stop," Tacara said calmly. "I thought you were trying to be less suspicious and more confident and secure in this relationship."

Twiddling my thumbs I said, "Believe me, I am. But I still want to know. Have you seen him with anyone?"

Tacara looked from side to side, and then at me. "I'm not gonna lie to you."

"What?" I stared at her.

Tacara giggled. "Girl, no. I haven't seen him with anyone. That man has been busy like the rest of the players. Football is their job. I didn't even see him at any of the parties I attended."

I felt somewhat relieved. I didn't think Tacara would lie to me. She had been supportive of my relationship with Calvin, even when I was fretful. Not once had she told me to let him go, or that he was "no good" for me. Steve Brown and my sister had told me just that. Sydney had initially liked Calvin, but once she noticed my uneasiness about his elusive ways, she became suspicious of him. She started acting like a self-righteous Christian. She had strong opinions about premarital sex, and felt that my having sex with Calvin had clouded my vision. *She is such a Holy Roller.*

My attention was diverted to the game when the crowd erupted with thunderous cheers.

"Go boy!" shouted a woman sitting next to me.

The Falcons had just gotten an interception. Everyone in the stadium rose from their seats. All I could see was a red and black uniformed figure going towards the end zone. I grabbed Tacara's hand.

"Go!" Tacara yelled. "Run! Run!"

"Run!" I screamed. I let Tacara's hand go and covered my mouth when the ball carrier was stopped at the 30-yard line.

Falcons' fans jumped up and down with excitement. The gentleman who was first sitting where Tacara was now seated returned to reclaim his seat.

He grunted under his breath, so I whined, "Sir, just let her stay here for this one play. The game is almost over."

The salt and pepper haired man slid into the aisle with a grimace.

The Falcons did not score after the third down. Only five seconds were left in the game. Tacara and I held each other's hand again. A field goal would not do; the Falcons had to make a touchdown or lose. Suddenly there was an eerie quietness over the stadium. Norma Jean looked flushed. Her boyfriend was holding her hand.

The Falcons decision was to try winning the game on the fourth down. From the line of scrimmage, quarterback Benjamin Dale took the handoff. He dropped back to look for a receiver and then took off as the Tennessee Titans defensive player pursued him. Just when another big guy was within steps of tackling Benjamin, he released the ball. I held my breath as the ball spiraled in Calvin's direction. A defensive back from the Titans team was right at his side.

"Oh my God," I gasped. Calvin leaped into the air and snatched the football away from the offender and came down with both feet dragging along the back of end zone. He had made the winning touchdown. The crowd was in a pandemic state jumping up and down, screaming. Some were yelling, "We won. We won!" Balloons, tissue and confetti flew everywhere. I exhaled and let out a loud scream. Tacara and I embraced each other, rocking back and forth. Norma Jean was locked in John's arms and tears were flowing down her cheeks.

"That's my son," Norma Jean exclaimed, wiping the tears from her eyes. "That's my son."

It surprised me that she was so emotional and excited. "And that's my man," I yelped. Tacara and I let go of each other's embrace. I then gave Norma Jean a big squeeze. She let go of John and hugged me lightly. When I looked her in the eye, she turned away quickly. *I'm not going to let her attitude rain on my parade.*

After all of the excitement in the stands, I walked down to the special area for family and close friends with Norma Jean and John and about a dozen of Calvin's relatives. I had met most of them when the Falcons played a home game against the Saints, right before Christmas.

Calvin's uncle, Dante', was stone drunk. He staggered in my direction. "Did you see my boy?" he said, his breath reeking with liquor. "Did you see CK snatch that ball?" He looked me over. "Ahhh hell. Look at you lookin all Calvinized."

Norma Jean elbowed her brother. "Dante, shhh," she hissed.

"Woman, I ain't shhin nothin, I'm happy as a lamb." Dante stepped from side to side waving his arms as if he were flying.

Norma Jean gave him a rebuking look. I found his acts comical, so I laughed at him. He continued to wave his arms as he staggered in front of us. When I looked at Norma Jean again, her eyes had welled up with tears. Calvin had told me that her father had been an alcoholic and had recently died of cirrhosis of the liver. *Maybe Norma Jean is thinking about him.*

I couldn't wait to see Calvin. I knew that he would be thrilled about being chosen the Most Valuable Player of the game. While we waited for him to take his shower and do his interviews, I decided to find Tacara in the crowd. I walked around in the packed room. As I scanned the crowd, I noticed a girl who looked familiar. She was tall with long hair and dewy, bronze skin, just like the one arguing with Calvin after the game on our first meeting. The queasy feeling I always got when things were not quite right gripped my stomach. *That has to be her.* She whispered to the girl next to her. They sneered. I wanted to ask what they were laughing about, but I continued to look for Tacara. I was almost sure she was the same girl. She looked to be in her mid twenties. Her hair was straight, quite opposite to the full, fluffy look Calvin said he liked. I couldn't figure out if she were Black or Latina. Her features were keen and exotic looking. I also wondered why she was at the Super Bowl and which player she was waiting for. *Why is she in the VIP room?*

Spotting Tacara, I squeezed my way through the crowd as quickly as I could. "Tacara, girl, what's up?" I said, tugging at her arm.

"Not much," Tacara said. "Let me introduce you to Steve's parents. Mr. and Mrs. Brown, this is Calvin Moore's girlfriend, Shayla."

"Hi," Mrs. Brown said.

"Calvin really played a heck of a game," Mr. Brown commented. Steve resembled his father. Handsome and robust. They even sounded alike.

"He did," I agreed, smiling. "And Steve played well too." I tried to be as polite as possible to the Browns without seeming disengaged in the conversation. I really wanted to know what the girl meant to Calvin. *She's got to be here to see another player.* I turned back to Tacara. "I need to ask you something," I mumbled.

"What now, Shayla?' she asked in an irritated tone.

I gave Tacara a somber look. "Oh, it's like that now?" I pouted. "That's okay, forget it."

"I'm just kidding, Shayla," Tacara laughed. "What do you want to know?"

"That's okay," I said stubbornly. I didn't want her to think I was insecure.

"Girl, if you don't ask me the question I'm gonna kick your butt," Tacara said, batting her eyes.

"Yeah, right,' I snapped. "And that will be the day."

"C'mon Shayla. What's up? What's on your mind?"

"That girl over there," I said quickly, nodding my head in the direction of the entrance.

"Which girl?"

"Can you see the two girls standing by the double doors? The tall ones."

Tacara leaned forward, looking in the right direction. "I can't see who you're talking about."

"The ones talking to the security guard."

"Oh!" Tacara said, as if she recognized them.

"Who is the one with the black hooker boots on in 75 degree weather? Have you seen her before?"

Tacara, opened her mouth to speak, but hesitated. "Oh, her," she finally said.

"Tell me. What's up? Have you seen her before?"

"Yeah," Tacara looked down at the floor and then at me. "I saw her in the hotel lobby the other night, but I don't know her," she stated. "Have you seen her before?"

"So, she was at the hotel?" My heartbeat quickened. "Who was she with?"

"Shayla, what is going on?" Tacara asked again. "What's up?"

"Nothing is up. I'm just wondering if she is one of Calvin's old girlfriends. She gave me this nasty look when I walked in."

"Well, I have seen her before, but I haven't seen her with CK. And if you're suspicious then you should go straight to the source. There's CK," she pointed towards the door.

Calvin walked in the room carrying his Louis Vuitton duffel bag and sporting a flashy single-breasted, Italian-style black suit with lavender and mauve window panes and a shiny purple tie. I wondered how he managed to be the first player out of the dressing room. He was never first. I tried to be calm, but he reached out for the girl's hand. Without hesitation, she hugged Calvin. My eyes widened in disbelief.

I clutched Tacara's arm, then I gradually let go. "I'll be back," I said.

"Shayla!" I could hear Tacara calling, but I rushed off in Calvin's direction in a jealous rage.

By the time I reached Calvin, he was no longer talking with the girl. He was hugging his mom and other family members. Calvin's *admirer* and her friend were still standing a few feet behind Calvin, so I moved in closer so he would notice me. He did. He moved quickly towards me with a big grin, and before I knew it, he had taken me in his arms and lifted me off the ground. He swung me around and around. All my fears dissipated. When my feet landed on the ground, I boldly took Calvin's face in both hands and pulled him towards me. I kissed his lips. He kissed me back . . . a long, peck-style kiss.

"Mmmm," Calvin groaned as he pressed his lips against mine.

Dante' shouted, "Go on, Calvin! Score again, Mo-Fo. Keep on scoring," as he swung his body in gyrations.

I pressed my lips against Calvin's for as long as I could, but he finally pulled away.

"Look, I gotta go back inside and do some more interviews. It might take a while," Calvin looked at me and then his family. "So, if y'all want to meet me back at the hotel…"

"We ain't hearin it man," Calvin's cousin Dexter interrupted. "We wit'chew. We ain't leavin."

"Aight. Well, I need mom for a minute," Calvin said.

I held on to Calvin's hand, excited and loving all the attention we were getting. I hoped that he would ask me to come inside the press room to stand by his side.

"Mom, I want you to come with me to pose for a few pictures," Calvin said.

"Boy, I need a mirror." Norma Jean said. She patted her cropped hair in the back.

"Mom, you look fine," Calvin told her. He let go of my hand as he took Norma Jean's. "We'll be back."

My lips twitched as I gave Calvin one of those *please take me* looks, hoping that he would feel my vibe.

Calvin shot me a smile. "We'll be back," he repeated as he leaned down to give me a peck on the lips.

I was somewhat disappointed as Calvin walked away with his mom. I felt slighted, but I also felt that Calvin's open affection for me clearly meant that I was the love of his life. I immediately turned my attention back to the girl Calvin had hugged when he came out of the dressing room. I looked around to see if she was still standing nearby. I did not see her. I wondered too if she had seen Calvin kiss me. I hoped she had.

By the time Calvin finished his interviews and taking in more Super Bowl hoopla at Sun Life Stadium, two hours had gone by. The crowd began to wane, and Calvin's agent, Tommy Daniels, made arrangements to have a Hummer limousine waiting for Calvin's entourage. I felt a certain calm as I waited there in the midst of the most important people in Calvin's life. *This is not the time or the place for me to be acting insecure.* I vowed to fake confidence and forget about the girl.

Back at the Fountainebleau, the lobby was packed with people and Calvin was bombarded by fans congratulating him. I was pretty surprised that there were so many people in the lobby, since special passes were required to enter. The hotel had been closed to the general public. A post game dinner and party had already gotten underway in one of the ballrooms. Calvin wanted to make his grand entrance – by being fashionably late. He always believed the later you walk into a crowded room, the more attention you would get. So, we were never on time for anything. Calvin truly loved attention.

After taking a few photographs and chatting with friends and well-wishers, Calvin and I headed up to his suite. We left his family members to do their own thing. Calvin had told them that he would meet them at the party "In a few," he said. Although I didn't want to appear like a leach, Calvin did not seem to mind my being by his side. He introduced me to practically everyone, sometimes saying, "This is Shayla," and at other times, "This is my girl, Shayla," - which I preferred.

Once inside Calvin's spacious suite, he placed the MVP trophy on the table and pulled me close to him.

He held me in his warm embrace for a few seconds. "This is the happiest day of my life, Shay," he whispered, squeezing my buttocks.

I held him tighter. "I love you so much, Calvin."

Calvin suddenly released me from his arms, not saying a word.

"What's wrong, baby?" I asked, feeling a little puzzled.

"Nuthin," Calvin sighed. "I got to piss." He hurried to the bathroom.

I walked into the bedroom area and sat on the edge of the bed. I turned on the television. I wondered why every time I told Calvin I loved him he seemed to get distracted. He seemed uncomfortable with my saying those words. I then began to wonder why he had never said those three words to me. *Surely, he has to love me.* Just thinking that he could possibly not love me troubled me. *Maybe I should ask him.* The phone rang, and Calvin picked up quickly while still in the bathroom. I could barely hear what he was saying to the caller. He talked in a lower tone than usual, but I was able to hear him say "I put you on the list, so I'll see y'all there," before saying goodbye.

Calvin walked in the room and looked at me with a wary gaze and then he looked away. His jaw tensed when the phone rang again.

"Hot line," I chirped.

"Sho is," Calvin said as he sat on the bed, reaching across me to get the phone. "Yo," he answered. After a long hesitation Calvin burst into laughter. "What's up, my dog!" He sat on the bed beside me. "Man, you wrong for that. You know you wrong." He laughed and leaned his muscular body against me. "Yo, man, save the drama for yo baby mama," he continued to laugh fervently. "Are you coming out tonight or what?" Calvin asked. "Yeah, yeah," he got a little serious. "We are going to a little party downstairs and then we hitten' the streets, man. It's celebration time." Calvin listened for a few seconds. "Naw, man, Shayla. Her name is Shayla," he mused, turning his body to look at me. I smiled. "Yeah, man you gotta meet Shayla. She's fine as hell," he said. "And got some good stuff too."

I lightly punched Calvin on his arm, feeling a bit embarrassed.

"Aight, man . . . aight, I'll see you there," Calvin said and handed me the phone to hang it up.

"That was my boy," Calvin explained. "He went to my high school. He's a fool. Ain't changed a bit!"

"Really?" I muttered, propping my feet up on the bed.

"I had told him about you, but he forgot your name," Calvin said casting a prolonged glance at me. "Dayum, you look good." He reached over and started caressing my thighs.

Calvin leaned forward to kiss me. I teased him by moving farther and farther away the closer he came to me. I fell flat on the bed. He rolled on top of me. Our quickie, which lasted all of five minutes, was intense. Calvin was more aggressive in his love-making than usual. I moaned throughout, "I love you!" . . . "Oh, Calvin, I love you!" – hoping that he would say the same. He didn't say one word.

As Calvin and I walked into the post-game ballroom party, almost everyone seemed to stop talking and take notice of us. I had changed into a black form-fitting Prada dress that showed off my every curve. Calvin had bought it for me after one of his weeklong disappearances. The dress was a size too small and it looked as if it were painted on my body. When I told Calvin that I thought the dress was too small, he commented, "That's how it's supposed to fit." But being the fashion guru that I am, I knew very well that the dress was too tight for my rounded bottom. But if wearing my too small dress was what satisfied Calvin, then I would wear it too small. *Whatever it takes to make him happy, I'm willing to do.*

As we walked around the crowded room and were greeted by acquaintances, comrades and fans, I began to feel self-conscious about my behind and cleavage being showcased in my form-fitting dress. I got a lot of head-bobbing and raised brows from the guys. Calvin didn't notice all the attention I was drawing. He was getting his share from the females and males. After a while, I began to feel like a trophy. I felt that Calvin wanted me with him after the Super Bowl just to have a good-looking lady on his arm. But then I thought about the Black/Latina girl. *What about her?* She was beautiful and more striking than me, I figured. *So why doesn't he have her on his arm? Obviously, I am the one he wants and loves.* The thought made me smile.

After much casual chatting, Calvin and I danced to Chris Brown's "Look At Me Now." We then danced to Ludacris' "How Low Can You Go." As we moved to the beat, a Caucasian guy approached us. Calvin was in rare form dancing very sensual and stroking my behind in ways that were clearly inappropriate for public view. He ignored the guy. He had already had three Grey Goose on the rocks. I knew Calvin could handle his liquor, but I was somewhat concerned in that the night had just begun. I also thought about Dante' and how Norma Jean reacted to his intoxicated behavior.

"Calvin." the very handsome guy yelled trying to get Calvin's attention. He appeared to be in his early 20s. Calvin continued dancing, spinning his body around – doing pelvic gyrations all the way to the floor.

"How low can you go?" he chanted. I giggled and looked at the young man standing in front of me. I simply shrugged my shoulders.

"Hey, Calvin Moore!" the young man shouted.

"Calvin, this guy is trying to talk to you, babe." I stopped dancing and took hold of his arm, trying to get his attention.

Calvin finally came to a halt then gazed at the guy. "Brad Pitt!" he shouted.

I did a double take. The young man did resemble Brad Pitt, but he was much more striking, younger, and his body more buff. He definitely had movie star appeal.

"What's up?" Calvin asked as he started dancing again.

"Man, Cristi wants you at the door," the Brad Pitt look alike said, trying to speak loudly enough to be heard over the music. "She and her friend said you were supposed to put their names on the guest list."

"Oh, snap. I forgot," Calvin said, stopping in his tracks. "Baby, I'll be right back. Don't go nowhere." He turned to the guy. "Stay right here with her for a minute, man."

"Calvin!" I objected, but he was gone in a flash.

"I can't believe he just left me hanging like this," I snarled. The White guy just looked at me. "Hi, I'm Calvin's girlfriend, Shayla," I said, extending my hand.

"I'm Dan," he said, squeezing my hand tightly.

Oh my God, he is cute. Dan was about six feet tall with broad shoulders, and his eyes were hypnotizing. *So, Calvin wants to leave me with this handsome guy?*

"Let's dance until CK gets back," he suggested as he began swaying from side to side. I danced to his rhythm, swinging my hips from side to side as we locked eyes. At that moment, Dan leaned closer to me as if he were going to kiss me. *Ahhh hell. Wait a minute now.*

"Calvin Moore is the luckiest man in the world," he whispered in my ear. I blushed, but said nothing in response to his flirtatious statement. We stayed on the dance floor as the next three songs played.

"Why, Daniel!" It was the voice of a woman behind me. I turned around slowly. She was a blond with blue-eyes, just standing there with both hands on her hips as if she were standing in attention. One of the t-strap on her dress had fallen off one shoulder. Her breasts were full and were screaming, "Look at me." *Implants.* Dan immediately moved closer to her. I continued to sway to the music.

Dan gave her a kiss on the cheek. Her stance never changed. "I've been looking for you, Daniel. Where the hell have you been?" she demanded.

"I'm sorry, sweetheart," Dan seemed a little embarrassed. "Calvin Moore needed to meet a friend, so he asked me to keep his girl company until he gets back. This is Shay…"

"Shayla," I interrupted, still looking at the girl and exuding self confidence. "I'm Shayla."

"Shayla, this is my fiancée, Angie," Dan introduced.

"So, what's going on here?" Angie wanted to know as she moved closer to me. "Why can't you keep your man with you instead of dancing all raunchy with my fiancé?"

I couldn't believe what I was hearing. *She has got to be tipsy. Or crazy, one.*

"So, where is Calvin?" Angie asked, looking at me and then at Dan.

"Come on, Angie," Dan put his arm around his feisty fiancée. "Let's go."

Angie pulled away. "No. I want to know why she is dancing so close to you and not with her so called boyfriend."

Speaking as calmly as I could I said, "Look, I didn't mean to start any trouble. I am Calvin's girlfriend and —"

Angie started laughing. "You and how many others?" she shot back, still laughing.

"Excuse me?" I retaliated, feeling a twinge of anger.

"When we were at the door Cristi said she was his girl. So, how many girlfriends does Mr. MVP have?" Angie blurted sarcastically.

"Angie, that's enough!" Dan chided, tugging at her arm. "Let's go." As Dan and Angie walked away, he turned back to me and grimaced, "I'm sorry."

I was left standing there in the middle of the dance floor alone and feeling embarrassed. Jay-Z's "On to The Next One" was playing. Everyone on the dance floor was having a ball as they rocked to the pulsating beat. I began to search the crowd, trying to spot Calvin. He was nowhere in sight. At least 20 minutes had passed since Dan had interrupted our dance to tell Calvin that Cristi and her friend were waiting for him at the door. *Who is Cristi?* I began to panic. I walked towards the entrance of the ballroom, but I still did not see Calvin. Finally, I ran into Dexter, Calvin's cousin.

"Dexter!" I yelled across the room, startling a few people who were standing nearby.

Dexter turned and met me as I approached him. "Hey, girl, where's CK?" he asked.

"I was gonna ask you the same thing," I smiled, although I had become very irritated by now. "I guess I lost him," I added.

Dexter chuckled. "Well, he's probably around here somewhere. You know how everybody's on him."

"Yeah, I know. He went to let some girl named Cristi and her friend into the party. Do you know Cristi?" I asked, trying not to let Dexter know that I was anxious.

"Naw, baby girl, I don't know a Cristi, but just lay low. He ain't gone too far. With you in that black dress, he ain't gone too far at all."

I forced another smile as I walked into the lobby, still annoyed by the way Calvin had just disappeared. I decided to call his cell phone, but he did not answer. The thought of calling his room came to mind. I hurried to the lobby phone and dialed the operator.

"Room 1015, please." The operator made the connection. The phone rang six times and just as I was about to hang up, Calvin answered.

"Hello!" he shouted testily.

"Calvin? Baby, what are you doing in your room? I'm coming up there."

"No, you don't need to come up here," Calvin insisted. "I'll be right down. I had to make a call to *Sports Illustrated*. I'm gonna be on the cover."

"Really, baby?" I felt somewhat relieved, but still a little suspicious.

"Yeah. Hey, I'll be on down in a few minutes. Just meet me back at the party," Calvin insisted. "Meet me at the dessert table."

"I can be your dessert," I said sexily. "I want to come up and celebrate some more."

"We got a lot of time for that. I'll be down in a few," he repeated. "I'll see you at the dessert table." Click. Calvin hung up on me.

I had gotten used to Calvin hanging up on me by now. If I didn't say what he wanted to hear, or if I challenged him or got long-winded, he'd always abruptly end our conversation. I told him several times that I thought it was disrespectful to hang up on me before saying goodbye. But he convinced me that he didn't mean any harm by it.

I stayed near the telephone feeling a bit perplexed. I wondered why Calvin had chosen such an inopportune time to make a phone call to *Sports Illustrated. Something isn't right.* Instead of going back to the ballroom, I decided to wait for him at the elevator. He had to come to the lobby. *I'll just give him a big hug when he gets off the elevator. He'll like that.* As I strolled to the elevator, I saw my reflection in a mirror. I felt a little ashamed of myself for looking like a hoochie mama. My dress was entirely too tight. My feet were killing me from wearing the five-inch Gucci heels. *If my sister Sydney or my mom saw me now, they'd surely disown me.*

After two elevator doors had reached the main lobby floor, Calvin hadn't shown up on either. I figured he would be on the next one coming down. The third elevator reached the lobby floor and sure enough, Calvin was standing in front. His eyes almost popped out and his body stiffened when he saw me. Standing next to him was the Black/Latina girl. I looked at Calvin and then at her. The look on her face was one of satisfaction. She flashed a quick, smug grin and stepped off the elevator in front of Calvin.

"Hi," I said nervously as Calvin strutted off the elevator barely acknowledging my presence. "What is going on?" I asked as I walked beside him.

Squinting his eyes, Calvin asked, "Didn't I tell you to meet me back at the party?"

"Calvin, I wanted to surprise you."

"Surprise me hell!" he said harshly. "You can't follow instructions can you?"

"Oh, I see. So you wanted me back inside so I wouldn't see you with that slut!" I was unable to contain my anger. "So, was that Cristi?"

"You don't know nuthin about her," he said cooly, not even looking at me.

"Oh, so it *is* Cristi?" I continued questioning him.

Suddenly Calvin's steps came to a screeching halt and he stared at me. "What is your problem?"

"Calvin, why are you acting like you just caught me with someone when it is you?" I knew Calvin didn't like scenes, but I needed to know what was going on with him and Cristi.

He looked around to see if anyone was watching us. A few people close to us seemed apparently tuned in.

"Shay, I don't need this," Calvin said, now speaking more calmly. He then started moving in the direction of the ballroom. I followed him. I wondered where Cristi had gone.

"Calvin, I waited thirty minutes for you..."

"You're a thirty minute lie!" Calvin snapped through gritted teeth. "Hey, I said I don't need this. Either you are with me or you are not. She just happened to be on the elevator. I don't have time to pacify you. Either you are in or out. And if you're in, you need to stop hassling me."

For a moment I felt guilty. After all, I had not seen anything other than the two of them coming off the elevator together. *Maybe that was just a coincident.* This was Calvin's special day. He was the MVP, and I had no right to spoil things for him with all of my insecurities. I walked a few steps behind him. I wanted to make things right, but I wanted to know who this Cristi was too. *Why had she been so upset with him after the game in Atlanta before we met? Why was she at the Super Bowl –acting as if she were his special guest? Why was she on the elevator with him after he had left me for thirty minutes?* I cringed at the thought of them possibly having been together physically.

Calvin broke our silence. "So, are you in or out Shay?" he asked as we approached the crowded area by the entrance to the ballroom.

"I'm in," I assured him and put my arm through his, hesitantly, but with much pride. So once again we were surrounded by people congratulating Calvin, telling him he is "the greatest," patting him on his back and acting as if he were indeed God's gift to the Atlanta Falcons . . . and the world.

We partied until 5am, club-hopping all night long. After we left the Super Bowl party in the ballroom, we went to nightspots; Live at the Fountainebleau, then to South Beach at a spot called Proof. The Mansion was on our list of parties to cover and finally we ended up at Passion at The Hard Rock Hotel & Casino. Celebrity guests were everywhere I looked. We sat in the Upper VIP rooms and Calvin was approached from every angle, every minute - by both male and female admirers. As I sat and watched, I began to tire of trying to figure out if Calvin was more than acquaintances to some of the beautiful women who approached him. Some seemed to know him on a personal basis. At one point, Calvin reassured me. "I might talk to other women and they might approach me, but what you need to remember is that I'm with you," he stated emphatically. "I came with you. You're the only one in my limo. I'm leaving with you. So, that's all that matters."

Was it? Well, whether it was true or not, all that mattered at this point was for me to be calm and not ask more questions.

The next day Calvin left Miami to go back to Atlanta with the football team on a chartered flight. He said he needed to get back to Atlanta and meet with Sean "Diddy" Combs about being a model in a major Sean Jean clothing line ad. I felt happy for Calvin's victories, but at the same time, I still felt stressed and sort of defeated. Although my boyfriend had just become the most popular football player in the world, I had a sinking feeling. I thought about Cristi and how she showed up at practically every party we had attended last night – always meeting his eye, but never really saying anything; I thought about how Calvin's mom had been quite distant and cold towards me. But the one thing that bothered me the most was the thought that I had allowed myself to have unprotected sex with Calvin. I wondered if I was pregnant, and for a moment, I hoped that I was.

My flight back to Atlanta left Miami a few hours after Calvin's had departed. I looked out into the clouds feeling a pang of sorrow in my heart. *I wish Calvin loved me as much as I love him.* Tacara slept like a baby through the entire hour and 30 minute flight. She and Steve had enjoyed a more private night together after the Super Bowl. In fact, he had given her a four-carat marquis engagement ring from Tiffany & Co. We had talked about her surprise over breakfast, after a few of the players left for the airport. I basked in her joy. I was truly happy for Tacara, but I wondered why some women could get what they wanted and others couldn't. My birthday was three and a half months away. I'd be 26 years old. I felt an inner ticking. I wanted so desperately to be loved. I wanted to be loved by Calvin Kendall Moore. *I want to be Calvin's wife.*

Chapter Three

Tropical Delight

"Whassup, Whassup. Hey. I'm here in San Juan, Puerto Rico living the life with my chocolate baby – Shay-la. I'm bout to get my parasail on," Calvin babbled, looking at the video camera as I taped him. He had wanted to do something a little more exciting than my rainforest suggestion for the evening, so he chose parasailing. It was frightening enough flying on an airplane, so I definitely wasn't going up in a parachute, so I chose to be the video person.

"Shay, are you still filming me?" Calvin called out, flexing his muscles.

"I got you, babe. I got you."

"Yo, I'm bout to get my Parasail on," Calvin continued talking into the camera. "I'll test the water first and then I'm gonna fly up like a Dirty Bird." Calvin flapped his arms as if they were wings and wiggled his feet in a sideways dance step. I tried to follow all his movements with the camcorder.

"Go, CK. It's your birthday. Go, CK. It's your birthday," I chanted as he continued dancing.

"Naw, baby girl, it's *your* birthday, not mine," Calvin said – still looking into the camera. "I want to give a shout out to my agent, Tommy, for calling me this morning with yet *another* sweet endorsement. Smooth C done got himself a Gatorade deal." Calvin flashed a smile. "I want to give a shout out to my lollipop behind the camera for giving me some good lovin last night too. Bae, you all that - fine, beautiful, sweet, and hella sexy in that bikini. Can we record our late night show?"

"Cut," I chuckled. "Come on Calvin. This shoot is about you."

"What?" Calvin looked clueless. "Ahh. Here she goes. I think she loves me."

"Yeah, I do," I said.

"I know you do," he agreed. "How can you not love me? I'm CK Moore, baby. The more you see me…"

"The more I want you," I said in a monotone voice. I had said it so many times.

"And you know that. Just be careful out there parasailing, Big Money."

"Hey, I like that," he said. "Aight, cut." Calvin clapped his hands like he was doing the clapper light switch commercial. He came close and leaned over and kissed me on the lips. "When I get out there, I want you to start the camera rolling before I go up. And I'm gonna land in the water. You know how to zoom in on me with a close up, don't you?" Calvin asked as he turned, headed towards the Parasailing instructors.

"Yeah. I know how to work this camcorder, baby," I said nervously. Although I knew that parasailing was fairly safe, I still could imagine the worst as I watched Calvin being strapped into the harness. If he were to receive a serious injury, he would not be able to handle not playing football. It was his life. *Suppose the rope breaks?* "Oh God, please let him be okay. Please bring him down safely," I prayed aloud.

"Oh, he'll be okay," a stern voice from behind me chimed. "Isn't that Calvin Moore with the Atlanta Falcons?"

I turned slightly to my left to see who was speaking to me. It was a Black man with a smooth, dark-colored complexion – maybe in his 50s. He was looking at me over the rim of his square glasses. His eyes were a soft shade of green.

"Hi," I said. "Yep. That's him. That's Calvin CK Moore."

"He'll be okay. God will watch over him."

I looked at the man evenly – hoping he was not some lunatic cult leader trying to convert me or recruit followers. But there was something about the extremely handsome man that made me feel comfortable. He was wearing blue shorts and a tee shirt with the words, "When All Else Fails – Try God," embossed on it. I was still holding the camcorder in my hand. I felt a tad self-conscious about my skimpy one size too small bikini. All of a sudden I wanted to cover myself. I felt too exposed, yet the man didn't seem to notice my body like most of the men I know would. He looked right into my eyes.

"You remind me of my wife when she was around your age."

"Really?" I forced a smile and then looked out into the direction where Calvin was about to take off.

"Shay – start the camcorder now!" Calvin shouted.

I turned the recorder on and begin filming Calvin as he ascended into the air.

"Calvin is parasailing here on this beautiful island of San Jaun, Puerto Rico," I narrated. "He is going up . . . and up . . . and up," I was lost for words. I continued to film for what seemed like 15 minutes or more. Calvin was shouting something back to me, but I couldn't hear him. I actually felt more relaxed now that there was another spectator – Mr. Hazel Eyes. The man chuckled as the parasailing instructor pulled Calvin down into the water. He seemed to land abruptly, but he stood to his feet shouting, "Ooooh Wee!" and quickly unbuckled himself from the harness. "I feel free!" he yelled. "I just experienced the best feeling. That was better than an orgasm."

"Ooookay," I said, not expecting Calvin's to describe his parasailing experience in such comparison. The man beside me continued to chuckle. "And Calvin Moore just made a perfect landing," I said, still videotaping the event. Calvin ran toward me smiling.

"That shit felt good! Did you get me?"

"I'm still filming you," I said.

"That felt so good, man. I think I'm gonna do it again," Calvin said, now talking into the camera.

"Oh, no you're not," I protested.

"Okay, cut," Calvin said, picking up his towel to dry his sculpted body off.

I turned the camcorder off and planted a kiss on Calvin's cheek as he continued to dry himself.

"You don't know how good that felt, but I was lying when I said it was better than an orgasm," Calvin rattled on. He finally noticed the gentleman standing a few feet away.

The man looked in our direction again and approached us. "Hi, Mr. Moore. I'm Clyde Jones," he said. "We've been trying to talk some deals with your people in Atlanta for quite some time."

Calvin extended his hand and looked at him vaguely. "Clyde Jones? Now why does that name sound familiar?"

"I'm the president of Jones Incorporated, a partner with Rolls Royce. I think you spoke with my son, Clyde Jr. during Super Bowl week. You spoke to him about getting a Bentley."

"Oh, snap!" Calvin seemed to get excited upon remembering. "Yeah, I remember. I remember. It's funny I should see you in San Juan of all places."

"I know," Mr. Jones said. "My wife and I own a house near Ponce. We come here for relaxation, about four times a year."

"Cool," Calvin murmured.

"So, you've been getting quite a few deals since the Super Bowl, I see. How'd you find time to get away to come here?"

"I had to get away, man. I needed a little vaca from all the madness. But I'm lovin it," Calvin said. "I'm ready for the season to start though. It's like I've been doing all these television appearances and magazine shoots. I'm starting to feel like I'm no longer an athlete."

"Yes. Fame in football is temporary, but you seem to handle it well. You've got to work it to your advantage as long as you're the man," Mr. Jones stated. "I was watching you parasail and your lovely lady was praying for you. Do you attend church together?"

"Naw, man. I ain't been to church in I don't know how long, but I always thank the Man upstairs. I was checkin out your tee. That's cool."

"Well, perhaps you and . . ." Mr. Jones looked in my direction.

"Shayla," Calvin answered for me.

"Perhaps you and Shayla can come out to our beach house tomorrow for dinner," he said. "How long will you be in San Juan?"

"We're supposed to be going to Jamaica on a private jet the day after tomorrow," Calvin said, gleaming with pride. "But I kinda like it here. It's kinda fast-paced, but it's laid back at the same time."

"You are right. There's a lot to do in San Juan and a lot of friendly people here. Jamaica is romantic though. You love birds will enjoy it," Mr. Jones commented. He turned to me and then to Calvin. "So, if you and Shayla want to come out for dinner tomorrow evening, I can arrange for a car to pick you up. You will love the beautiful scenery on the drive out, and I'm sure my wife Claire would love to prepare a nice Latin dish for you."

"That sounds good. But we have a limo," Calvin boasted.

"Oh, so you're going all out – even on vacation?" Mr. Jones said with a laugh.

"Yeah. Hey, I just figured if I'm gonna do it, just do it big and do it with style." Calvin added.

"Like you do on the football field?"

"You got it!" Calvin said pointing his finger in Mr. Jones direction. They both grinned.

I could only imagine the male chemistry and bonding between them. I didn't know Clyde Jones, but I knew how much Calvin wanted to purchase a Bentley. He already had five cars. I truly didn't understand his obsession with high-end cars.

"So, let me give you my number." Taking a pen and piece of paper from his pocket, Mr. Jones scribbled on the paper quickly. "You'll need directions, so have the limo driver call right before you come. It's about an hour and a half drive or so, but you'll enjoy the scenery." He handed the paper to Calvin.

"Thanks. So, what time is good?" Calvin asked.

"Say about 5 o'clock tomorrow. Where are you staying?"

"We are at the Hilton," Calvin said.

"The Caribé Hilton," I added. "It's not that far from here."

"Yes. I'm familiar with all the hotels around Condado Beach," Mr. Jones smiled as he looked at me. "So, I'm gonna let you two get back to your fun, and tomorrow, we'll feast on my wife's cookin."

"I'm looking forward to it," Calvin said. "And if you need to reach me before we get there tomorrow, I'm listed under my name at the Hilton."

"Okay. I'll see you two tomorrow. But why don't I get the two of you on video together first."

I looked at Calvin and he looked a little hesitant.

"Come on. Give me the camcorder." Mr. Jones reached out and took the camcorder from me. Calvin put his arm around me, and we smiled into the camera. "Camera's rolling," Mr. Jones affirmed.

Calvin all-of-a-sudden seemed lost for words. "Uhhh," he stammered. "Uhhh, I'm lovin every minute of this Memorial Day Weekend getaway with my sweetie, Shayla. Now this is what you call a dime!"

"I am? Oh my," I giggled. Mr. Jones seemed to take in a full body shot of us. *Oh no he's not filming my half-naked self.*

"Give me a kiss," Calvin said, catching me off guard. He pulled me closer with both arms.

"Wait," I protested. "I'm too shy to kiss on camera." I put my hand over Calvin's mouth as he leaned forward.

"Girl, if you don't give me a kiss," Calvin leaned even closer.

Our lips met for about three seconds and I looked back into the camera somewhat embarrassed – not so much because of Calvin's kiss, but because of Mr. Jones filming us. After all, I didn't know this man.

"And can you zoom in on this diamond-heart necklace I got Shayla for her birthday?" Calvin touched the tip of my heart necklace.

"Oh my. You got her a diamond, heart necklace?" Mr. Jones echoed, playing right into Calvin's boasting.

"Yeah, I did. And it's two carats. That's just my beginner's gift. If she keeps acting right, she might get some more bling."

"Put a bling on it. That's what I say!" I laughed.

"Now, now, Ms. Lucas. Do I detect a little greed in your voice?" Calvin queried, looking at me and then back into the camera.

"Naw, baby. I'm only greedy for all of you!" I enthused. I kissed Calvin on the cheek. "You C.K. Moore – the man . . . *my* man."

"Tellem, baby." Calvin and I pecked each other on the lips a few times.

I asked Mr. Jones to take a few shots of us with my camera. Surprisingly, Calvin initiated a front-to-front pose and even picked me up in his arms. I pulled at my bikini bottom – hoping that my butt wasn't showing. After chatting with Calvin for a few more minutes, Mr. Jones went his way and Calvin informed me that the distinctive looking man owned and co-owned a chain of businesses, which included restaurants, a movie theatre and Rolls Royce of Atlanta. He said that Mr. Jones played for the New Orleans Saints some 25 years ago and that he had gone on to become one of the wealthiest retirees in the NFL.

"I gotta get up with him when I get back to the A. I want to get that Bentley," Calvin said.

"But you already have five cars, Calvin. What are you gonna do with yet another one?"

"Girl, please! I plan to have three more cars by this time next year."

"So, you want the Bentley . . . and what else?"

"A Lamborgini, which is my ultimate car," Calvin seemed to wander off into dream land. "A Pagani Zonda C12 . . ."

"A Punany what?" I asked. "Sounds a little freaky to me."

"No. I said a Pagani Zonda, Silly. Yeah, it's freaky all right. It's a $750,000 freak." Calvin put his hand to his chin. "And we can get a Hummer for the weekends – me, you and the kids – so we can take a family vacation and shit like that."

I was stunned. *Did I hear him say what I thought I heard him say?* I sure did. I looked at Calvin with beaming eyes.

"Well, in that case then get as many cars as you want," I exclaimed.

"In what case?"

"You know. As long as me, you and the kids can do our family vacation thing in the Hummer," I exclaimed. I wanted him to know that I was down with having as many children as he wanted to have.

"Girl, you're a trip," Calvin seemingly snapped out of his daydream. "Let's go back to the room and get some practice then."

"Sounds good to me." We strode off arm in arm.

Once we were in the limo, Calvin gave me an enticing smile. "I want you," he said – lust wooing from his eyes. He told the limo driver that he needed "total privacy." That's when he pulled me on top of him.

"Come here," he whispered.

He obviously could not wait for our practice session to begin in the room. I did not object. He tugged at my crochet bikini bottom and before I knew it, he had entered me. I felt weightless as I allowed his hands to guide me upward and back down. His lips caressed my throat. I tried to keep my moans as soft as I could, but it was nearly impossible.

"I love you," I told Calvin, when he had succumbed to his urgency. He held me tightly as I trembled in his embrace.

By this time, I felt light-headed. Calvin Moore had knocked me out cold. I had fallen deeply, helplessly in love and I knew there was no turning back.

For the rest of the evening, Calvin and I decided to do some site-seeing in Old San Juan, which was quite medieval looking, but beautiful. We strolled through the narrow, cobblestone streets – stopping occasionally to take pictures. I was in awe of some of the historical structures such as the colonial cathedrals and the El Morro Fort at the entrance of the San Juan Bay. After scouting the city with me for a couple of hours and signing a few autographs for tourists who had recognized him, Calvin let me know that he was hungry. We decided to eat at the Hard Rock Café. We had eaten enough chicken, rice and peas, which seemed to be the typical Latin dish. *I want a good old American hamburger and fries.*

Our waitress was gorgeous. Most of the women in San Juan glowed with beauty and sensuality. Although I thought Calvin would surely behave himself by not flirting with our waitress in front of me, he couldn't seem to take his eyes off her. He turned his head each time she walked by. I even showed my displeasure by lightly kicking him under the table a few times, but he still marveled at the voluptuous girl. She was wearing a box-fitted short skirt and a bustier style top that showed off her full breasts. Her long, dark hair reached her behind and she had a light brown complexion, an oval-shaped face, big, bright eyes and a mole right above her top lip. *She is so pretty. Well, isn't this just great?*

"Could you teach me some Spanish, Seniorita?" Calvin asked her as she placed our entrees on the table.

"You don't know Spanish?" she asked him, smiling. She then gazed at me. I tried not to react, but I did want to kick Calvin really hard this time.

"No. I want you to teach me," Calvin said boldly.

"Okay," I interrupted before he got too far. "That's enough!"

"Enough what, baby?" Calvin sipped on his tropical drink.

I looked at the waitress. "You can leave," I said testily. She sauntered off with an awkward smile.

"Oh, Lord," Calvin said. "Remember I'm here with you and I'm leaving with you. Why you getting all upset?"

"Cause you are disrespectful, Calvin," I tried to remain cool. "I don't care if you are leaving with me. You don't have to disrespect me."

"How am I disrespecting you? You just too jealous."

"I'm not jealous. I just don't want you flirting with her like that. If you want to learn Spanish, go buy Rosetta Stone."

Calvin leaned back in his chair and began to laugh. "You are killing me, man." He sipped on his drink again. "You are really killing me."

"So, does she remind you of Cristi Perez or someone else?" I knew I was going into dangerous territory, but the girl did have that Cristi look, being that Cristi was from the Dominican Republic and could easily be mistaken as Puerto Rican.

"What?" Calvin asked in a high toned voice.

"She reminds you of Cristi, doesn't she?" I tried not to sound annoyed.

"Now, why you want to go there?"

"I'm going there, Calvin. What is it? Do you like these exotic-looking island girls or something? Is that your type? You like that Kim Kardashian type."

"You my type."

"No. I don't think so. I've noticed that all your ex girlfriends look mixed or Latin or Middle-Eastern. I'm just saying."

"Well, why am I with you then? You're not mixed or Latin or Middle-Eastern."

"I know I'm not. I'm Black. But sometimes I get the feeling that you'd prefer that I was a couple shades lighter or had light eyes or something."

Calvin seemed to become vexed. "What is up with you?" he said. "You are really buggin."

"I'm just making an observation," I asserted.

"Well, you sound insecure as hell."

"I'm not insecure at all," I lied. "I just get tired of you disrespecting me by acting like these women are so beautiful that you have to turn your head every time one walks by…"

"Damn," he interrupted. "Look I can be with whoever I want to, but I choose to be with you."

"But everybody has a type. Just admit that you like that type."

"Hell, if you really want to know . . . good pussy is my type," he said coldly. "You really need to shut up. You sound real stupid."

His words stung like bees attacking my heart. "Well, obviously you like stupid women that you can hurt with statements like that. I don't know too many women who would let you talk to them that way or allow you to outright flirt with other women in front of them."

"Damn!" Calvin blasted, raising his hands in the air in disgust. "I can't please you. I buy you nice things, bring you to an Island for your birthday and this is the thanks I get?"

Calvin and I ate in silence for the next few minutes. When the waitress returned, I observed Calvin's reaction. He knew I was watching him, but he continued to check her out - as if he wanted to devour her.

"So, would you like dessert?" She asked, smiling at Calvin.

"No. I'm his dessert, thank you," I said sharply. Calvin leaned inward with a smug smile.

"Oh. Well, I'll be back with your check," the waitress muttered and walked away quickly.

Calvin slid his chair closer to mine. "Are you okay?" he asked.

"I'm fine," I said dryly.

Calvin stared at me for a few seconds then touched my neck and the diamond necklace around my neck. "Whose heart is this?" he asked, urging me to look in his eyes.

"You say it's yours," I said softly, feeling my heartbeat quicken.

"It *is* mine. I told you my heart belongs to you, so don't be getting jealous when other women are attracted to me," he turned my chin towards him so that our eyes met. "I love you, Shay. You're the kind of woman I could see myself marrying one day."

OH MY GOD. I almost melted. "Well, why don't you?" I asked, shocked that those words actually came out of his mouth.

Calvin leaned back abruptly as if he needed to regain his composure. "I can't marry you if you're gonna be jealous and acting like a little girl," his expression darkened. "You just need to work on some things, and who knows, maybe we can go there one day. But don't think you're gonna get there with me by being jealous and being possessive. A man hates to feel possessed and trapped – especially CK Moore."

"I wouldn't try to possess or trap you," I said softly. My heart was still hammering.

"Well, don't!" he insisted. "I am not the one. And make me one promise."

"What, Calvin?"

"That you'll never try to go through my phone again."

"Go through your phone?" I frowned. I was confused. "I haven't gone through your - "

"Promise me!" he interrupted.

"Okay. I promise." I said. I had, indeed, tried to go through his iPhone while he was asleep last night, but he had it on lockdown. And I do mean lockdown. *Dang! He wasn't asleep. He saw me.* I was speechless for a few minutes. I then caressed Calvin's knee.

"And I like you just the way you are," he said.

"I'm glad." I smiled.

My mind spun with possibilities after Calvin mentioned marriage. If he married me, I would be the happiest woman in the world. I was determined not to blow it by being jealous. And I hoped I did not appear too insecure when asking him if he were attracted to Hispanic or lighter-skinned women. I was pleased with my complexion. But when I was growing up I was often told, "You are so pretty to be dark-skinned," which seemed more like an insult to me than a compliment. The lighter-skinned, "red-boned" girls always seemed to get a little more attention than I did in college. As the years passed, it seemed darker skin was in. The girls getting hit on the most had a browner hue with sexy, hourglass figures and round behinds – and I definitely had that going for me. I knew that I was "eye candy" for Calvin, but I also knew there were better looking women everywhere. Many people actually said Calvin and I looked like brother and sister. Like him, I had dark brown skin (his a tad richer). My eyes were narrow like his, my nose - keen and cute, my lips - full, my facial structure - defined, yet soft, my cheekbones - high. I got my long, thick tresses from my dad's side of the family. His mother was Ethiopian. My mother's side of the family had Indian and African roots. But both my mother and sister had more red to their skin-tone – making them a lighter brown than me.

The next morning Calvin and I ordered room service for breakfast. We ended up sitting on the balcony, enjoying the tropical breeze. It was our last day in San Juan before heading to Jamaica. We had a lot planned for our two days in Jamaica. I told Calvin I just wanted to chill out before going to the Jones home for dinner. He decided to go to a casino while I got the works: A massage, a manicure and pedicure and a shampoo and roller set at the salon. My hairdo turned out full and curly - just the way Calvin liked. After returning to the room from a day of pampering, I put on a conservative Donna Karan denim sun dress and my low-heeled sandals. I didn't want to look too provocative around the Joneses. I could already tell that Clyde Jones was a religious man and I definitely wasn't up for a sermon from him or anyone else for that matter. I was doing the best I could spiritually – under the circumstances. The only sin I felt I actually practiced without guilt was sex. *Truly God doesn't expect me to resist a lover like Calvin, does He?* I had resisted a lot of temptations in my life, but I could not resist a man who gave me the affection that I had always fantasized about.

I had lost my virginity to a man ten years my senior when I was 16 years old. I was devastated when he decided to end the relationship after our second sexual encounter. At the time, I was volunteering as a junior counselor at the YMCA for summer camp, and the man was a counselor and a lifeguard. I was immediately attracted to his strong, athletic build, and he was obviously attracted to me. When I told him that I was only 16, he said he couldn't believe it and that he had to keep his distance from me. But he really didn't keep his distance until after he broke my heart . . . and my hymen. I cried a lot after that – suffering inwardly. He told me that if I told anyone we had sex; he would get fired and be arrested for statutory rape. I eventually told my sister, but we agreed to keep it just between us.

It took five years for me to trust a man again with my body. At 21, I had made it through four years of college, untouched by a man, although I kissed a whole lot. I met Jeffrey, my second lover at a Hawks basketball game in Atlanta. He was tall, sort of lanky – 6'6 – and a pretty boy –

curly hair, smooth light mocha skin-tone, walked like he was gliding on air. He was also a star point guard basketball player at the University of Georgia and was a year younger than me. We dated for about six months before our relationship turned physical. On my graduation night from West Georgia College, I gave in to his impatient demands for sex. He got a room at the Howard Johnson Hotel and he made love to me all night. We ended up dating for two years before he went off to Paris to play for a European basketball team. At first he kept in touch through a written letter here and there, weekly phone calls and e-mails, but the calls soon became few and far in between, and the e-mails, non-existent. We eventually drifted apart and from what I heard a few months later, Jeffrey married the coach's daughter, a white girl. He eventually got cut from the basketball team, but decided to stay in Paris.

I met Todd a couple of years later. I was truly intrigued with his disk jockey lifestyle. He pursued me from the day we met at Macy's department store, when I sold him a tie. But something just didn't seem right about Todd. At 30, he was still living at home with his mom and was often at my place morning, noon and night – even while I worked at Macy's and studied to become a buyer. Although Todd showed me a good time by taking me to the best concerts, private CD release parties and music functions, he never tried to have sex with me. He would always stop at heavy petting – kissing and touching. Todd told me he wanted to wait until marriage to consummate our relationship. I was okay with that, since I had just begun attending a Bible-based church that taught abstinence until marriage. Strangely enough, I never truly felt any passion for Todd, and obviously, he never felt passionate about me. He would tell me that it was so hard for him to resist me, yet he always seemed to resist with no problem. I eventually started to wonder why I was with him. He had asked to borrow money from me a couple of times and never paid me back. And he loved being around the artsy-type people – hairstylists, designers, singers. I broke things off with him after he locked me out of my own apartment. He told me that he forgot to leave the key in our designated place. I was told by him to hang out with some friends for a few hours until he could get back to me. I would learn, just some months ago, that Todd had been spotted at several gay night clubs in Atlanta. I wasn't surprised. I was just glad I had never had sex with him.

So, here I am, after almost two years of not being in a relationship, riding in a limo with Calvin "CK" Moore. I rubbed Calvin's knee and exhaled thinking of all of my past experiences. I felt happy that I had finally found my soul mate in him.

"What are you thinking about?" he asked looking at me and then out the window.

"Just how happy I am with you," I sighed with a smile.

As the limo rolled along the streets of San Juan, Calvin and I took in the beautiful Island – the leaning palm trees, the enchanting blue ocean, the lush tropical gardens, and the celestial coastal sites. Calvin held me close, seeming to be more relaxed than usual. After entering the gates of the Jones' villa, which was more like a world class castle, Calvin and I were speechless. The white, four story mansion was luxurious. The dramatic waterfall near the entrance flowed down to a bridge that crossed over a small body of water. On the right side of the bridge was a tropical garden with flowers and to the left were giant rocks with water cascading over them. The property looked like something out of a storybook. It was three times the size of Calvin's house. *Simply stunning.*

Calvin and I held hands as we walked towards the estate. Mr. Jones suddenly appeared from behind the white doors greeting us with a smile.

"Welcome to our home," he said. He was wearing white linen, looking very clean-cut and polished.

"This is beautiful," I said, still in awe.

"This is sick!" Calvin added under his breath. Lately he had started calling things that were beyond belief "sick."

We walked inside the magnificently landscaped mansion with Mr. Jones leading the way to even more alluring attractions. There was a glass wall that allowed us to look right into the front yard again. As I tiptoed on the marble floors I felt as though I should have worn something more elegant. I had the feeling of being in some king and queen's palace. Truly

Mr. Jones was wealthy, but this home was beyond any wealth I had imagined. Mr. Jones pointed out special highlights of the home – as though he were our tour guide. He showed us his contemporary and romantic art collections he had acquired over the years, and he told us it had taken him and his wife ten years to get the Mediterranean style home the way they wanted it to look.

"You all want to take a breather?" Mr. Jones asked as we walked through the living room and out by the infinity pool which seemed to flow into the sand and ocean. He must have sensed that his gorgeous home had definitely taken our breath away.

"Naw. We cool," Calvin said, still looking around in amazement.

Suddenly a woman that I assumed was Mr. Jones' wife appeared in the foyer. Also dressed in white, she looked quite angelic – probably in her mid 40s. Her smile was warm and inviting. She was about 5'3 inches, and her skin was pecan-colored and smoother than her husband's. Her eyes were dark and alluring. She had a square jaw-line with perky cheeks. Her dark hair was shoulder length with curls.

"Welcome," she said, approaching us with a wide smile. "Clyde told me about you two joining us today. Welcome to Ponce."

I extended my hand. "Hi, I'm Shayla."

"Hi, Shayla." Her handshake was firm. Interestingly, she held my hand longer than I expected. I felt a strange, yet soothing feeling from her touch – like I knew her.

"Your home is so beautiful." I said. "Thanks so much for having us for dinner." I slowly removed my hand.

Calvin extended his hand to the dainty woman. "Hi, I'm Calvin Moore. Nice to meet you."

She shook Calvin's hand. "Oh, I know about you Mr. Calvin Moore. We are Falcons' fans. I know all about you, CK," she chuckled.

"Claire is my wife of 34 years," Mr. Jones announced proudly.

"What?" Calvin stepped back. "She looks only 34."

"Flattery will get you nowhere, son," Claire said with a wink. "But thanks for the compliment."

After we ate Claire's cooking, which consisted of Puerto Rican stewed chicken, fried plantains, cheese-flavored rice fritters, yams, a medley of green vegetables, rum cake and a pineapple-coconut beverage, Calvin and Mr. Jones went out to play golf. The golf course was in the back of the mansion, so Claire and I sat out on the balcony watching their golf game and enjoying the breeze. The ocean, which was about 100 yards from the balcony, gave me a feeling of tranquility. I asked Claire to tell me how she and Clyde had met. I wanted to know about their courtship.

"I was 26 years old at the time we met," Claire smiled, as she reminisced. "I had finished nursing school and was working at a children's hospital in New York. Clyde had been asked to speak to the handicapped children, and I happened to be working that weekend. He came into the hospital and talked to the kids about having faith and loving God, and he told them they could overcome all obstacles in life – even with a disability. I was so touched by his speech. He was only 21 and he had such strong faith in God. He had so much wisdom for his young age."

"So, you were 26?' I asked curiously, noticing the age difference.

"Yes. Clyde is five years younger. I'm 63 now and he is 58."

"You've got to be kidding me!" I said, quite surprised she was 63 years old. She looked 45.

"Yes. I turned 63 a few days ago."

"Really? What date is your birthday?"

"May 26," she answered.

"No way!" I laughed, shaking my head from side to side. "That's my birthday!" This was getting a little eerie.

"Really?" Claire asked, not acting too surprised.
I had never met anyone with the same birthday as mine. "So, finish telling me about how you and Mr. Jones got together." I was anxious to know.

"Well, like I said, Clyde seemed very centered spiritually, and his speech actually had me in tears. Afterwards, he came up to me and asked my name. I told him, but there were so many children needing his attention. So I handed him a brochure that I had put together for the children. It had my picture and all my pertinent information on the cover. I did tell him if he were ever in New York again we'd love for him to speak to the kids again. Then I was on my merry way."

"Oh, so he didn't stay in New York?"

"No. He was just visiting from New Orleans. He had just been drafted by the Saints and was doing volunteer work for his foundation – The Clyde Jones Foundation for Underprivileged Children. He would speak to kids each time he visited a different city."

"That's nice."

"Yes, indeed. He is such a caring man," Claire said proudly. "And a few weeks later I received a letter from him."

"A letter?"

"Yes. Back in those days, men used to write letters to the women they were interested in. I know young people today have all that text-messaging stuff going on," she chided. "Clyde told me how beautiful I was and he wanted to know if he could come back to New York just to see me again."

"Wow! He was pretty straight-forward?"

"Most athletes are," she said matter-of-factly.

"So, did you call him?"

"No. I wrote him back."

"Oh?"

"I wrote and told him that I would be glad to meet again, but I also told him there was one condition."

"And what was that? May I ask?"

"I told him he'd have to speak to my students I was mentoring at a middle school in the Bronx."

"How did he respond to that?"

"He wrote me back and told me that he'd be glad to. After that, we wrote back and forth for a few months."

"So, he didn't call you?" I was ready for Claire Jones to cut to the chase and tell me the real deal.

"He called me a few times, but Clyde was young and he was used to meeting beautiful women. He was a star football player. I wanted to take it slow."

"Really?"

"Of course! Men need a challenge, you know." Claire chuckled. "I learned that very early in life, although I was still anxious to get to know him."

"So, what happened after a few months of writing letters and talking to him on the phone?"

"He flew to New York to see me."

"And?" I was getting more excited.

"We started dating, then he asked me to marry him. We got married the next year. We actually got married six months after our first date."

"Oh my! I just love happy endings," I squealed. "That is so wonderful!"

"Oh, yes. God truly brought us together. We were meant for each other."

"Well, I just turned 26, and I really want to be married and have kids." I felt comfortable opening up to Claire.

"Oh, don't rush it now. I have six children. I gave birth to four children and we adopted two. I didn't have my first until I was thirty three. You let God work His perfect timing."

"You are right," I said. Claire and I were silent for a few seconds. She looked so content – so regal. I sat there hoping my life with Calvin would turn out like Claire's with Clyde.

"You know everyone has a different path," Claire injected, almost as if she were reading my mind. "Your life will not be like mine. You have to allow Jesus to lead you up the right path for you. In time, you will get what is purposed for you."

I was a little shaken by her words, not knowing exactly how to respond. I scratched my head and shifted my body, trying to think of something to say. "Yeah, I really want to become more spiritual," I said, not knowing why that lie came out of my mouth. *Well, it's not really a lie.*

"For sure, you will become more spiritual. You don't have any other choice, do you?" Claire spoke with an eerie tone.

I looked at her and her eyes seemed to sparkle. I wanted her to teach me things that I needed to know. I sensed that she knew my pain, my anxiety and my dreams, but somehow I felt that she knew what I'd have to go through with Calvin.

"Dinner was simply delicious," I commented, feeling the need to change the subject.

"Thank you, Shayla. I love to cook. Would you like another helping?"

"Oh, no! I am stuffed. My tummy is feeling like a balloon right now."

"Well, maybe it's the little baby starting to grow inside you," Claire said looking at me with a genuine smile.

I became flushed. *What is she talking about?* "Uhhh . . . I don't think so. No babies for me until I'm married."

"That's the righteous way," Claire said. "That way, you cut down on a lot of unnecessary pain. But sometimes we have to do things our way. Just know the Lord is always there for us." Claire got up from her seat. "Let's get those young men inside. They will be out there until night falls if we don't stop them."

I got up – feeling a bit faint. After getting my bearings, Claire opened her arms and hugged me. I hugged her back – feeling my eyes tear up. I didn't understand why I wanted to cry.

"God will bless you with your husband in due time," she said as we relaxed our embrace.

I felt tears rolling down my cheeks. I couldn't help myself. When we walked back inside the mansion, Claire gave me a Kleenex to wipe my tears. She didn't say a word to me about the tears. She seemed to understand my feelings even though I didn't seem to understand myself.

On our way back to the hotel, Calvin barely spoke. When I asked him what Mr. Jones was like he just commented, "Cool." He fell asleep 10 minutes into our ride. I could only think of Claire and the impression she had left on me. I wanted to talk with her again, because she seemed so peaceful and spiritually grounded. But then I thought, *She's 63 years old. I'm only 26.* Maybe I was expecting too much, too soon for a young woman my age. In fact, I had never experienced total peace. When Calvin woke up, right before we entered the driveway to the hotel, I was still thinking about Claire Jones. Calvin stretched his arms, making a growling sound as he yawned.

"Uhhhh," he moaned.

"Calvin?"

"Yeah?"

"So, what did you think about Mr. Jones' wife, Claire?" I asked.

"Oh, she's cool," Calvin said rubbing his eyes. "Jones said that she is blessed with the gift of prophesy."

"What?" I asked in a strained voice. "The gift of what?"

"He said she can foresee things before they happen sometimes. She supposed to be prophetic. I ain't wit that shit."

I was speechless. I got out of the limo trembling and feeling a tad dizzy. I thought about the conversation I had with Claire and how she had commented about a baby growing inside of me. I grabbed Calvin's arm. My mind was running rampant with all sorts of thoughts. *When was my last period?* I had not kept up with dates.

"Baby, will you ask the driver to take me to the grocery store? I want to pick up one last souvenir for my mom," I lied.

"They have a grocery store right around the corner. I'll walk with you," he said. "I thought you had gotten everything earlier today."

"I just remembered something she specifically wants though and they don't have it at that grocery store. You just go get some rest. You've been out in the heat all day. You look drained." Calvin rarely wanted to tag along with me, so why was he volunteering to go with me now?

"Aight, well, I might go over to the casino until you get back . . . and tonight we going to Club Egyptian. I wanna check that spot out."

"Okay, baby, I'll see you in a few." I hurried to flag down the limo driver before he pulled off. "Hosea, I need you to take me somewhere."

I slid into the back seat. My heart raced as Claire's words echoed in my head, "Maybe it's that little baby starting to grow inside you." I held my head in my hands wanting her haunting words to stop. My stomach was churning. Once I got inside the grocery store I went straight to the aisle where the pregnancy tests were. I quickly chose the one that shows two negative signs if you're not pregnant or one positive sign if you are. *That seems simple enough.* I also got a bottle of Bacardi Rum and a beach towel. After returning to the hotel, I wasted no time. I went into the lobby restroom and urinated on the test stick for five seconds. I lay the test flat, nervous about the results. The directions said to wait two minutes, so I forced myself to not look at the test. I walked out of the restroom stall, washed my hands and combed my hair. That had to have been the longest two minutes of my life. Deep down I really did not want to be pregnant before marriage. I knew it would change my life, and I felt that Calvin would probably distance himself from me, thinking that I tried to trap him.

After two plus minutes of waiting, I nervously went back into the restroom to see a blue plus sign staring me in the face. I picked the test up, thinking that I was possibly imagining the blue plus sign. But when I looked closer it was very clear – just like you see on the TV commercials. I swallowed hard, feeling faint. Seconds later, I sank to the floor with knots in my stomach. A little baby was growing inside of me.

Chapter Four

Nightmare

The ride was very bumpy and I held on to Calvin's arm tightly as we rode in a small crop airplane to Montego Bay, Jamaica from San Juan. I had managed to regain my composure about the pregnancy test results. I just decided not to think about it until I got back to Atlanta. *There is no way that I can tell Calvin that I am pregnant right now.* I needed the doctor to be the one to confirm my pregnancy anyway. I didn't necessarily trust a positive blue sign on a pregnancy test. *Maybe it's not accurate.* But then Claire's words haunted me. "Maybe there's a little baby growing inside you." I had thought about calling Claire after Calvin revealed her prophetic nature. I had heard religious people talk of prophets and people who had healing powers, but I had never encountered such a person.

I felt exhausted mentally and physically after landing in Montego Bay. Calvin and I took a private car to the Half Moon Resort. He told the driver he wanted to go scuba diving and that he also wanted to swim with the dolphins. It behooved me that Calvin still had energy after a night of drinking, gambling and partying. When Calvin asked me what I wanted to do, I sighed.

"I just want to relax at the resort. I'm tired."

"Well, you can relax all you want, but I'm gonna go swimming with the dolphins. They already have it set up for me at the resort." Calvin looked at me frowning. "What's wrong with you? Why are you so tired?"

"Calvin, we've been gone for four days, and staying up til 3 in the morning. Can't I be tired?" I said defensively.

"Yeah, you are tired," Calvin commented sarcastically. I nudged Calvin's arm with my elbow.

"Ouch, Girl. You got a little violent streak in you, don't cha?"

"You know that didn't hurt."

"I'm gonna get you some Red Bull cause you can't be getting tired on me the last two days." Calvin looked at me. "You can rest when you get back to Atlanta."

"I know," I said feeling like I should at least act as vibrant as possible for the next couple of days so he wouldn't start to suspect anything.

When we got to the Half Moon Resort our Royal Villa was quite inviting and charming. White and elegantly furnished, we had our own private swimming pool, our own chef, and a personal housekeeper and butler. We were only a few feet away from the turquoise ocean – and the sound of the waves hitting the shore made me feel relaxed and revitalized. I was happy that the people in Jamaica spoke English, but I still had trouble understanding them because of their Calypso-African-English accent. I also found it interesting riding on the left side of the street as opposed to the normal American right side. The Island had many hills and lush mountains. It was much more rural than San Juan. And from the time I stepped off the plane the Jamaican men seemed enchanted with me. In fact, the stares I got from the native men made me feel like I was a "dime" for sure. *It's payback time for all the attention Calvin got in Puerto Rico. Ha.*

I watched and filmed Calvin swim with the dolphins a few hours after we got settled in at the villa. My stomach actually felt a little pudgy, so I brought along my sarong. I wondered how far along I was. I did recall getting a slight period just last month. But then I remembered that I had only flowed for two days - very lightly. *Okay I'm not going to think about this.*

"I want to rent a jeep and drive to Negril," Calvin said as we walked along the beach. I was truly enjoying the atmosphere – the tropical trees that bowed – forming unique shapes, the gentle breeze, the fresh smell and the birds chirping right where we were, but I figured it was too tranquil for Mr. Hyper Calvin.

A couple of hours later, we did indeed head to Negril in a sporty, red jeep Wrangler. *Dang, my man has got the hookup.* We had the jeep so fast that I couldn't figure out where it came from. The drive to Negril was a little over an hour from

Montego Bay. I had heard that it was the more romantic side of the Island, so I wasn't too opposed to leaving our haven for more romance. However, I was frightened as Calvin drove like a man out of control. I could have sworn that we were about to encounter head on collisions. Jamaicans did not adhere to the speed limit and often passed cars on the two-lane street like they were trying to drag race. *How could such a laid-back country have such maniac drivers?* And Calvin seemed thrilled to be driving just as dangerously. He was driving like he had stolen the jeep and was trying to get away from the cops.

"Calvin, please slow down!" I begged, as he barely missed an oncoming car.

"I know what I'm doing. Stop being so damn nervous," he barked, swirling the steering wheel of the jeep to the right quickly and going even faster. "There's this restaurant in Negril called Rick's Cafe and I'm trying to make it there before it gets dark. I want to jump off the cliff."

"Hunh?" I frowned.

"Yeah, everybody jumps off the cliff there. I can't wait!"

"Okay . . . If you say so." I didn't know what had gotten into him. He was acting like a wild child who had never been out before.

"They have really good food there too," he said.

"I thought you had never been here before?" I said suspiciously, wondering how Calvin seemed so familiar with the road and wondering how he knew all about the restaurant.

"I haven't been here before. Why do you think I've been here?"

"Cause you seem comfortable driving and you definitely know more about this place than I do."

"And?" Calvin seemed to be getting agitated.

"And I was just wondering who you came here with before me?" I said smiling and hoping that my smile would make Calvin more light-hearted about my insinuation.

"What in the hell did I tell you about questioning me?" Calvin said abrasively.

"Calvin, don't go getting excited. Calm down, sweetie," I said softly.

"Naw, forget that shit. I get so tired of your accusations…"

"Calvin, honey . . . I'm not accusing you of anything. I was just making an observation." I put my hand on his knee.

Calvin pushed my hand away. "Look, don't say nothing else to me, okay!"

"Well…"

"Shut up!" he shouted while looking at me with one of the meanest looks I've ever seen him have. "You are always observing shit. Maybe you should have been a damn scientist or something, but don't dissect me!"

I rode along in dismay and tight-lipped as Calvin drove even faster. My eyes started to well up, but I tried to hold the tears in. I stared out the window. I was truly sorry that I had suggested that Calvin had possibly been to Jamaica with someone other than me. I was even more sorry that I had gotten him so upset that he might not enjoy the rest of his evening. *I'm always making the worst comments and showing my insecurity.* Why couldn't I get it through my thick skull that men don't like being questioned?

When Calvin and I finally made it to Rick's Cafe, he was distant towards me – barely saying anything. Daring locals dove more than 50 feet into the blue sea from a rocky cliff and Calvin jumped off the cliff twice as I filmed him. He seemed pleased once he came out of the water, stating, "This is really getting my adrenaline flowing," and even casting a smile at me. But his daredevil moves were scary for me to watch. After the cliff jumping, we dined at the restaurant and watched the sunset permeate over the ocean. Our waiter had told us that Rick's Cafe was one of the best places to view the sunset. It was quite splendid. I ate jerk chicken, rice & peas, cabbage and coco bread. Calvin nibbled on curry goat, stewed peas and plantains. He seemed fidgety – looking back, as though he were looking for someone. Right in the middle of his dinner, a tall Jamaican man approached Calvin. He stood quickly.

"I'll be right back," he said and walked away with the tall man.

I began to grow weary when Calvin had not come back after 15 minutes, but I still enjoyed the music. A Raggae band was playing and the restaurant had turned into a festive night spot, where people were up dancing. Couples were sitting close to one another and making toasts. I even witnessed a marriage proposal. *Dang, I wish Calvin could have seen that. Maybe he will get motivated to do the same with me soon.* I grew even more concerned about his disappearance when 30 minutes passed, but I definitely wasn't going to go look for him like I had done at the Super Bowl party. The thought of him coming off that elevator with Cristi sent a funny feeling through my body. I had thought about contacting Cristi when I got back to Atlanta to see what the situation really was between her and Calvin. I did not feel as though Calvin had been totally honest with me – when he told me they dated his senior year in high school and throughout college, but that he hadn't been with her physically in three years. He told me she was now dating a guy in the NBA. He said he had no love for her. *Sure.* I discarded the thought to contact Cristi, realizing how insecure it would make me look. *Calvin is here with you, Shayla*, I tried to convince myself. But Calvin was not there with me. He had left me at a table – alone – on an Island where men didn't seem to care if you were with a man or not. They flirted big time.

"You look so beautiful sitting here and I bet you're as sweet as a papaya." I heard a voice in that Jamaican accent. I smiled, sensing that Calvin was disguising his voice. I looked around saying, "Calvin" as my eyes met a dreadlocked man with a wide gap in his tooth. He looked like he hadn't bathed in days.

"I can be Calvin if you like. No Problem," he said sitting down in the seat once occupied by Calvin.

"No, there is a problem." I felt uneasy. "My fiancé is a professional football player and he is very jealous, so if I were you, I'd get up."

"Oh, no problem, Mon. But why would he leave a lovely lady like you all alone? He must be missing a screw in tis head," the man said in a deep accent.

In the nick of time, Calvin appeared. His eyes, a bit red shot now, met mine and I winked at him.

"See, there he is," I pointed to Calvin.

The man turned to Calvin. "Respect." He reached out and shook Calvin's hand. "Everyting Irie, Mon." The man stood up. "But you should never leave your beautiful fiancée alone like dat on an Island like dis."

"Yeah, well, she's not my fiancée," Calvin said curtly.

I was shocked that Calvin was saying this and that his attitude still seemed bitter. I stared into his glassy eyes. He was carrying a small bag in his hand. I wondered what was in the bag, but wouldn't dare ask.

"Okay. I'll be seein you," the man said and walked away quickly, almost stumbling.

Calvin sat down and I continued to glare at him as he put three $50 bills inside the black folder with the bill inside without even looking at it.

I felt I had to say something. "Calvin, are you okay? I asked softly.

"I'm fine," Calvin answered quickly. "Let's go." He got up and I grabbed my purse and followed him. He seemed to not want to even walk with me. Every time I'd speed up to his steps he'd walk faster. Finally, I just grabbed his arm. I was surprised he didn't jerk his arm away from me. I wondered what in heaven's name had him so upset. I was beginning to wonder if he actually had come to Jamaica with someone else – prior to me. But I figured I should leave the past in the past.

The drive back to Montego Bay was frightening. Calvin was driving like a maniac again and I even screamed a few times, thinking that my life was about to end as we came head on towards two cars.

"Baby, why are you driving so fast?" I didn't want to upset Calvin, but I also didn't want to die in Jamaica.

"I want to hurry up and get back to our spot so I can smoke this good ass weed," Calvin said picking up the brown bag that he had acquired after disappearing at the restaurant. "They gave me some good, high grade gunja. I'm gon get lit!" Calvin said with a wicked smile.

"Calvin, when did you start getting high? I didn't know you got high."

"Girl, please. Don't worry. I'm gonna give you some of this shit too." Calvin put the bag between his legs. "To calm your nervous ass down."

"I don't get high," I said, quite disappointed and surprised that Calvin smoked marijuana. "I can't believe you just did a commercial before we left Atlanta with Partnership for a Drug Free America. That is not a good look. You really have a problem."

Suddenly Calvin stopped the jeep abruptly. The tires made skids sounds. I didn't see a car in front of us, causing his abrupt stop, so it scared me for him to just put on the brakes in the middle of the road. There weren't any cars on the darkened street and there wasn't even a street light in sight. When I turned to Calvin, he had this explosive look on his face.

"Calvin, what's wrong?" I asked with a tremor.

"Get out!" he said harshly.

"What?" I asked, not believing my ears.

"Get out, Shayla!" He yelled, looking quite livid. "Now don't let me have to come around and pull you out."

My pulse began to race. In all my 26 years I had never been loved so passionately by a man one day and felt like I was his worst enemy the next day. I truly didn't know what had gotten into Calvin.

"Calvin, it's dark out here. I don't know the way back to the hotel. What is going…"

Before I could finish my sentence, Calvin opened his door and got out of the jeep – making his way around to my side. I unbuckled myself – fearing what Calvin planned to do. I jumped out quickly. Calvin proceeded to get back inside the jeep. Astonishment coursed through me when he actually drove off. I stood out in the dark street with a pit in my stomach – feeling like my world had just crumbled. I wondered what on earth had caused Calvin to just snap. I feared for my safety. I didn't know what to do, which way to walk and I had no cell phone or money. I continued to stand out in the muggy dark air, motionless and confused. I began to sob. *This isn't supposed to be happening.* Of all the things that I had justified concerning Calvin's bad behavior – this was a clear sign that I was in love with a ruthless, selfish, bi-polar acting man. A man who had professed his love to me, yet who had left me out on a darkened street of an island that I knew nothing about. *What kind of monster is Calvin? Do I want this man to be my child's father?*

I began walking slowly in the direction that Calvin had driven, putting my purse strap around my body. I felt like I was hyperventilating. "Stupid Bastard!" I began to curse aloud. "I can't believe he did this to me." My stomach was tied in knots. Five minutes into my brisk walk I noticed a hotel sign - The Negril Tree House. As soon as I turned to walk closer to the hotel, lights glared in my direction from an oncoming vehicle. My nerves were truly shot. I was fretful that I could be raped or even killed as the vehicle slowed down when it got to me. I deliberately turned my head in the opposite direction to avoid contact with any strange person.

"Shayla!" I heard Calvin's voice. "Shayla get in. Come on, baby. Get in," he said in an almost sorrowful tone.

I wiped my tears and hesitantly walked towards the jeep – feeling unsure of what Calvin would do next. He pushed the door open. "Get in." I slowly stepped up and jumped inside. I closed the door cautiously as I trembled in fear. I didn't even want to look at Calvin. I stared straight ahead. But Calvin seemed to suddenly find something very humorous. He started laughing fervently and was hitting the steering wheel. Something had him in stitches. *I don't get it. What's so funny?* He continued to laugh uncontrollably. I finally turned and faced him.

"Calvin, I don't see anything funny," I said softly.

Calvin was still laughing. "Ahhh, bae, you thought I was really gonna leave you out there in the dark like that?" He looked crazy – like he was already high off something more than some weed.

"Calvin, you hurt me!" I said, wiping my tears. "Don't play with me like that."

"Ahhh, Shayla – now be real. You thought I was gonna leave you, baby?" he asked seeming to get more serious.

"I didn't know what to think. You scared me," I cried.

Calvin giggled a little then made a serious face. "I'm sorry, baby. Forgive me, aight?" Calvin touched my breast playfully.

I pushed his hand away. "Calvin, stop!" I said with force.

"Okay, Shayla, fine. You ain't no fun." A slight smile creased his face.

"No, I am not!" I felt drained.

"Well, whatever," Calvin said and put the jeep in drive.

Silence filled the air as I continued to wipe my tears and tried to get a grip. Calvin began laughing again. "Baby, why are you crying? I can't believe you thought I was gonna leave you. Girl, don't you know I love you. I would never do no shit like that."

I didn't respond to Calvin, nor did I feel moved by his words of love. I felt like he was actually quite serious when he put me out of the jeep, but that his conscious got the best of him when he drove a few miles down the road and realized what he had done. *Now, he wants to make light of it and make me feel like I was the uptight one – like always.* I didn't say another word to Calvin all the way back to the resort. I was still in shock.

When we got to the villa, I was sure that Calvin would try to make love to me, but I was wrong. He went straight for the brown paper bag. He clearly ignored me. He took out a plastic bag full of marijuana, unwrapped the plastic, and rolled the weed in some white paper. He then lit it and began to inhale. The strong smell filled the room quickly. Calvin seemed very comfortable getting high. He walked over to the iPod dock and blasted Wacka Flacka Flame "O Let's Do This," and started to rap along with the explicit version of the rap tune, saying the F word a couple of times with force. Then he rapped to the song's chorus, "Yeah, O Let's Do It, Ay, O Let's Do It, Ay, O Lets Do It. Yeah, drug dealing music, Ay, I influence, Ay, I influence." He danced, inhaled and rapped. I watched in amazement as he danced like he was putting on a show. He really had some flexible moves. After "O Let's Do This," Calvin seemed to get more excited when "Lose My Mind," with Jeezy featuring Plies played. He truly had me thinking he was about to lose all of his. He rapped to the song – knowing every word. "Why yall trippin . . . I'm just fine," Calvin rapped jerking his body forward and then back. "12:45, bout dat time . . . couldn't get it all week, time to unwind . . . drink like a tank, lose my mind." He stopped to smoke more of the joint – sucking on it like it was better than sex. When the marijuana smell got even stronger, I decided I couldn't take it anymore. I went outside to sit near the pool in the dark and let Calvin have his wild boy solo party. He didn't seem to notice or care that I had left.

I thought about calling my mom. I had promised her that I would call to update her about our trip, but I realized it was bad timing. It was 1am and she would probably sense my upset and hear the loud music in the background. I sat still for a moment, thinking about Calvin's behavior. I started to think about Claire Jones too. *Maybe I'll call her.* I believed I could trust her and maybe she could even give me some insight on my relationship with Calvin. I quickly discarded that idea too.

Calvin got high for an hour and fell asleep in his clothes. I turned the iPod off, put on Calvin's tee shirt and tried to push his body vertically across the bed. He had fallen asleep horizontally with both arms spread across the bed – leaving me little room to lie down.

"Calvin, get up and get in bed," I slightly shook Calvin, trying to wake him.

Calvin moved a little and moaned. "Uh-uh."

I tried to move his body so that I could get in bed, but I was unsuccessful. He was too heavy – like dead weight – and it was obvious that he didn't want to be bothered.

"Calvin!" I shouted, shaking his arm harder.

Calvin made a groan and swung at me, as if I had frightened him. He opened his red, dreary eyes wide. He looked at me like he didn't know who I was.

"Calvin, I'm trying to get in bed. C'mon, let me help you get in bed right," I said rubbing his head, trying to comfort him.

"Okay. I'll get up in a minute," he grunted and put his head back down. He fell right back to sleep.

"Calvin, no. Don't go back to sleep. You have to get out of these clothes and get in bed," I said shaking him.

"Cris – sti, please. Stop now," Calvin said jerking away from me, but not looking up. I stared at the back of his head for a few seconds, realizing that he had called me Cristi. I lost it. I popped him upside his head with my open hand so hard, that my hand hurt from the hit.

"Ouch! That shit hurt." Calvin raised himself up and looked at me. "What the hell is yo problem?"

"Cristi!" I barked, standing to my feet. I wanted to hit him again, but I figured I better not.

"What?" he asked, looking confused and out of it.

"Cristi Perez is my problem. You just called me Cristi!" I yelled.

"I know one mutha-fu-thang," he drawled. He was so high he couldn't even curse right. "Hit me again and Imma kick yo ass." Calvin quickly rose up, only to lie back down.

At that point I knew that he would not be moving to get in bed nor to let me beside him. I did not want to be near him. I was engulfed with so much anger that I wanted to throw cold water on him. *Or maybe I should just scald his trifling ass.*

While Calvin was in a deep sleep, I decided to see if his iPhone was unlocked. It was. I wanted to pry as much as I could, so I scrolled though the name directory first - looking for Cristi Perez's name. Not found. I then went through his pictures. My heart sank as I saw one naked or lingerie shot after another of shapely, sexy-looking women. I knew none of them – but looking at the pictures was like looking at a copy of Playboy Magazine - butt shots, boob shots, even some vagina shots. I shook my head in disbelief. I finally saw a picture of what appeared to be Cristi, which was logged under PC, her initials backward. She was holding her stomach though – like she was pregnant. My body stiffened. *What the hell?* I stared at the photo, trying to figure out if her belly was really that big or if it was the angle of the shot. I turned the phone upside down, sideways and then held it closer. *This girl is pregnant.* My hand shook and I dropped the phone. My stomach tightened as I began to cry.

Here I was worried about telling Calvin about my own pregnancy, but it was pretty clear that he had another future baby's mama, Cristi, who was sending him pictures – looking to be about three or four months along. Although Calvin had sat me down and told me a little about Cristi last month, revealing that she was Dominican and had moved to the States at 15 - attending his high school her senior year (which is when they began dating) he always referred to her as "Ghetto Fab." He said she wasn't on his level and that she and her NBA guy were both alike – "hood." *God, I hope it's his baby and not Calvin's.* Calvin had sworn up and down that he and Cristi were *just friends* now – without the intimacy. He also told me that Cristi had slept with one of his college teammates, which is what broke them up in the first place. I thought about telling Calvin I was pregnant before we left Jamaica, which would give him time to let it sink in once we returned to Atlanta. *He'll just have to figure out what he's going to do with two women being pregnant by him.* But I didn't want him to go running to Cristi after he returned from the islands. I tossed and turned on the sofa, fearing that he actually loved Cristi.

I recalled Calvin's words of love to me again. Yes, he had acted quite bizarre in the jeep by telling me to get out, and he had smoked some marijuana. But maybe I needed to be more understanding of him. He had a lot of pressure on him, being a star athlete. He was also an advertiser's dream man – having acquired Nike, Versace sunglasses, Gatorade, Sean Jean, Sprite, and a couple of other endorsement deals since the Super Bowl. *The worst thing I can do is to add more stress to Calvin's already hectic lifestyle.* Football camp was starting in mid July, and Calvin had told me that he wanted to start getting more disciplined about two months prior to camp. That meant no outside stress. It also meant getting his body in tip top shape by running six miles a day, working out with his trainer, and eating more healthy food.

I dozed off a few times during the night, still perturbed that Calvin had called me Cristi and wondering if I should tell him about my pregnancy and about the discoveries I had uncovered in his iPhone. I picked up his phone again – staring at the picture of Cristi with child and transferring her number to my phone. After putting his phone back where I found it, I cried myself to sleep. I had a nightmare that Cristi and I went into labor at the same time and were in the same hospital. When it came time for Calvin to choose who he wanted to be with in the delivery room, he chose Cristi – leaving me alone to feel the excruciating pains of labor. Finally Calvin came to my room, with Cristi and their infant. It was a boy. He stood in front of me with both arms cuddling the infant and Cristi was laughing wickedly. Calvin said, "You tried to trap me, but I have my family right here. Why are you so stupid? Wake up and smell the coffee."

In the dream I started screaming and crying and calling him obscene names and that's when I woke up – breathing hard and in tears. I was glad that it was a nightmare and not real, but it bothered me. I jumped up and went to the bathroom – seeing that Calvin had turned vertical in bed – the right way. I looked in the mirror and felt sad about my predicament – being pregnant and in love with Calvin. I returned to the bedroom and slid in bed beside him. I moved to the edge of the bed – as far away from him as I could possibly get without falling out of bed. He must have felt me get in. He rolled over towards me and embraced me – spoon style – like he had actually missed my presence. He clung to me tightly. I could feel his heartbeat against my back. He rubbed my arm tenderly. I still got shivers, even after knowing what I knew. I heard Calvin's snores a few minutes later as I lie in his arms - bewildered.

I released Calvin's hold on me a couple of hours later – hoping not to wake him. I had not slept. I put on a pair of jeans and headed out by the pool. I had to call Claire. I also knew that I needed to call my mom.

"Good morning," Mr. Jones answered vibrantly.

"Hello. Is Mrs. Jones there?" I asked nervously.

"Yes. Claire is right here. Who is calling?"

"Shayla Lucas. Hi, Mr. Jones. Calvin and I really enjoyed ourselves at your villa the other day."

"Shayla. Why, hello, young lady. Where are you calling from?"

"We are here in Montego Bay."

"And having a ball I hope?"

"Yes," I lied. "It's really nice. We have been non-stop since we got here."

"Shayla, Claire is looking at me like I better give her the phone now, so I'm gonna let you speak with her, okay?"

"Okay."

"But you take care of yourself and God bless you."

"God bless you too."

It took about a minute for Claire to finally come to the phone. As I waited, I heard Mr. Jones ask her if she wanted to take the call in the other room. Finally, Claire answered.

"Why, Shayla, I'm so pleased to hear from you. How are you, doll?" Claire sounded concerned – like she knew I was going through some turmoil.

"Oh, I'm okay. I just wanted to call you to thank you for such a lovely time in Puerto Rico and for cooking Calvin and me that delicious dinner."

"Well, you are certainly welcome, but it's quite early for you to be thinking about me. I know that you enjoyed spending time here. You didn't have to waste your cell phone minutes calling me."

"But I wanted to. I just really got a lot out of our conversation that day."

"Ahhh. That's sweet. But just remember the present moment is all you have and the future will take care of itself."

I didn't know what she was talking about, but it sounded good. I wanted so desperately to ask Claire what she knew about my future – even wanting to tell her that there was a baby growing inside me like she had said.

"Hello?" Claire said.

"Yes. I'm still here."

"Is there something you want to say to me or ask me?"

"Well, I . . . I, I." I stuttered. "Calvin told me that you were blessed with some spiritual gift and I just wanted to know your opinion about Calvin and I."

"I really don't have an opinion about you and Calvin, but I do have a word for you."

"Excuse me?" I was a little puzzled.

"I don't judge others, but I think that you're a beautiful young lady with a bright future ahead of you. But you must depend on the Lord for your happiness and not another individual, because people will disappoint you again and again," Claire said in a tone that was filled with wisdom and warmth.

"Mrs. Jones, I'm just not sure right now. Calvin says he loves me and sometimes I think he is the one. I felt that way from the first day I met him."

"Now, you don't go putting your claim on any man," she said in a scolding tone. "You let God bring the right man to you and let go of all that pain."

"So, you don't think Calvin is the right man for me?" I asked, getting weepy-eyed.

"It's not me to tell you what's right for you. But I will say this. Until you become happy with yourself, you will never be happy with any man. You've got to find inner peace and joy."

"But Calvin makes me happy. I'm just insecure at times because he gets so much attention. But I know that he loves me."

"I'm not sure if you are listening to me and you may not be ready to receive my words, so just ask the Lord to help you to make the right choices and learn to love yourself."

"Mrs. Jones…"

"Call me Claire," she interrupted.

"Claire, I really am ready to receive what you have to tell me. Is there something that I need to hear or take heed to?" I asked. "Please tell me."

"Dear, ease you mind. Your burden is much too heavy and if you're not careful you're going to weigh your emotions down. Just give your concerns to God. Let Him fight your battles. He knows what's best and He wants to take you to a higher level than where you are."

"So, you don't think Calvin and I are meant to be?" I pressed.

"I don't think you feel that you and Calvin are meant to be," she said matter-of-factly.

"Yes. I do," I said confidently, but feeling not so confident.

"Well, Calvin has to believe that you and he are meant to be," she said. "It's a two-way street. And you should want to spend your future with a man who not only loves you, but who respects you." I was silent again as Claire continued. "No man wants a doormat. We teach people how to treat us. Shayla, the Lord has someone for you who is loving, respectful and who is not caught up in his own fame, but his name is not Calvin Moore, dear."

I wanted to hang up on Claire at that moment. *Who is she to be telling me that Calvin is not the one for me?* Maybe I wasn't ready to hear Claire's words after all.

"Shayla, go ahead and enjoy your day. You are on vacation and should be having a good time," Claire said.

"Well, we are leaving going back to Atlanta first thing tomorrow."

"Well, let's definitely stay in touch," Claire said as though she was ready to get off the phone with me. "I'll definitely pray for you and I'm sure that you'll be calling me in a few years to tell me about the God-fearing man you are going to marry."

"A few years?" I definitely didn't want to hear that. "But what you don't understand is that I have already met him," I said. "I'm truly in love with Calvin."

"Well, then that's your choice. God never forces His will on us. If you insist on your way, sometimes you'll get what you want. But it surely won't be like the joy of making the right decisions with God's blessings."

It was truly time for me to get off the phone. Claire wasn't really making any sense to me. I believed that Calvin had been brought in my life by God and that I could win him over if I showed him how unconditional my love was for him, but here Claire Jones was telling me about choices and not being a doormat. Truly she must have never experienced true, unconditional love where no matter what a person did to you; you'd still be there for them. That, to me, was true Christian love. *Claire is cold in her approach towards men. That's not very Christian-like.*

"You don't understand my words now, but in time you will," Claire said. "Life experiences teach us things no person can teach us."

"No, I don't quite understand, because I thought that you are supposed to have unconditional love for others and I know that Calvin has some faults and a lot to learn, but don't you think he needs someone who will stand by his side even when he's at his worst?"

"No," Claire said quickly.

I waited for her to say something else but she didn't. I wasn't quite sure what to say. "Well, thanks again for dinner. I will definitely stay in touch with you," I said as politely as I could.

"All right, Shayla. You be good and if you ever want to talk, feel free to call me."

"I will. Thanks."

"Bye, now."

"Bye."

After hanging up, I began to cry – again. *What is going on with my emotions? Is this the emotional effect of pregnancy?* Claire had definitely not said what I wanted to hear and I wasn't sure if calling her had caused me to be in more inward turmoil than I was already in. I picked up the phone to call my mom, wiping the tears from my eyes. I cleared my throat when I got her voicemail. *Thank God she didn't answer.* "Hi, Mommy. Where are you this early in the morning? Well, Calvin and I are in Jamaica and I just wanted to let you know that my flight gets in around one tomorrow. I'll call you then," I tried to sound chipper in the mix of my sorrow. "And no, he didn't propose to me yet, but I'll have to show you the beautiful heart necklace he bought me. And some other things. He's definitely the one, Mommy. Well, tell Sydney I said hello, and I'll talk to y'all tomorrow. Love you. Bye." I hung up.

I breathed a sigh of relief that I didn't have to speak those words to Connie with her feedback. She was super inquisitive and I was sure that she would sense my unsettled emotions.

When I walked back inside, Calvin had gotten out of bed. I heard the shower running.

"Shay, is that you?" he asked.

"Yeah, it's me."

"Where have you been, girl? I thought you had left me," Calvin said.

"I thought about it. But I figured I might as well stay one more day with you," I said with little emotion.

"Come in here," Calvin said.

"For what?"

"I got to show you something."

I slowly walked into the bathroom.

"Take off those clothes and get in here with me."

"Cal – vin. You know I'm upset with you."

"For what?" he frowned. "Oh, I know you aren't still trippin cause you got out of the jeep? I was just playing with you." Calvin stepped out of the shower naked and on hard. "Come here – take this off," he begin peeling my clothes off. I felt like the first time I fell for him – weak in the knees - but with a twinge of bitterness. I wanted to resist. I really did, but it wasn't happening. He circled the outline of my mouth and pulled me closer. My lips parted in anticipation for his passionate kiss. His hands grasped my buttocks and he pushed against me, leading me into the shower. The water hit our bodies as we continued to kiss. "Let me put this towel down, baby" Calvin said as he put two towels flat on the shower floor. He then picked me up in his arms and told me to grab him around his neck. I wrapped my legs around him and gasped as the memories of his behavior from the previous night were overshadowed by the pleasurable anticipation of him delighting me. I wanted him so fiercely.

"I love you," he said in a throaty voice. He then filled me with his passion. I arched my back as the pleasure became unbearable. *Claire didn't know a damn thing.*

The remainder of the day went well for Calvin and me. We drove to Ocho Rios, on the opposite side of Jamaica, where we climbed Dunn's River Falls and shopped at some of the duty free shops. We also watched some of the cruise ships dock. Calvin was affectionate – holding my hand and not even swirling his head to look at some of the striking women we passed. He seemed more into me. I felt queasy a whole lot, but I told Calvin that I suffered from motion sickness at times. When twilight approached, Calvin and I were very exhausted, but we still went to Jimmy Buffet's Margaritteville and Coral Cliff Gaming Lounge on Montego Bay's hip strip, once we returned from Ocho Rios. After we danced for almost two hours straight, Calvin asked me what I wanted to drink.

"Oh, just get me some cranberry juice," I said, remembering my pregnant state.

"Cranberry juice? Now I know you gotta come better than that. I'll get you a sex on the beach," he said looking at me mischievously. He brushed his hand up my thigh – near the split of my dress.

"We can do that later." I removed Calvin's hand and cupped it in mine. "Just order me a cranberry juice and orange juice mix, baby. I need something refreshing."

"Okay. If you say so," Calvin said and proceeded to get our drinks.

"Calvin," I said as he started to walk away.

"Yeah. " He turned to face me.

"Don't stay gone long, baby" I said sweetly.

Calvin smiled. "I won't. I promise."

I felt comforted by Calvin's attitude. Our last day on vacation together had turned out better than I imagined. Cristi's expanded stomach came to mind a few times throughout the day, but I couldn't let what I had seen on his cell phone spoil my trip. I knew I'd have to find out more once I got back to Atlanta though. *But she is not with him. I am.* Calvin certainly had his ways, but nobody was perfect. I decided to at least take a little of Claire's advice – to ease my troubled mind. I had a feeling that everything between Calvin and I would work out just fine.

Chapter Five

Come Hell or High Water

ore than five weeks had passed since our island getaway and I still had not told Calvin that I was carrying his child. My OBGYN confirmed that I was, indeed, pregnant. I was 13 weeks along now – and my stomach was poking out a little. I could not bring myself to tell Calvin the news yet, because I wanted to sit down and explain things to him, but he had only spent two days with me since our return from the islands. He had acquired two new lucrative endorsements, Gatorade and Subway, and was in and out of town – doing television commercials, magazine shoots, working out with his trainer – becoming ever so popular. He had been classified by a reporter as the "Golden Boy of the NFL," and many articles that were written about him also described him as the football player with "movie star" appeal. He was even asked to make a cameo in a Tyler Perry movie.

Although I had planned to tell Calvin of my state the last time we were together (three weeks ago at his house), his mother showed up unexpectedly – making it impossible for me to break such news. The next day I pulled up Mediatakeout gossip site and was shaken (but not surprised) that a report had come out with Calvin dancing with several women at an ESPY Awards after party. When I scrolled through some of the comments, one of the readers commented, "Yeah, wish I could have a baby by him and be a millionaire. I heard that one of his girlfriends, Cristi, is preggers and he has another one on the way by a girl in Miami. Those are some lucky hoes." On top the post hurting me, it made me sick. I vomited immediately after reading it and decided to call Calvin.

"So, it's really true!" I screamed.

"What's really true, Shay?"

"So, you have a baby on the way by Cristi Perez and some chick in Miami too?"

"What?" Calvin said. "Girl, I don't have time for this. Who said that?"

"I read it on Mediatakout!" I shouted. "I just forwarded it to you."

"Now, I know good and damn well you not believing no Mediatakeout. What did I tell you about reading those gossip sites?" he said calmly. "Shay, I'm gonna have to talk to you later. I'm in a meeting. Don't believe that bull."

"But I need to know about Cristi," I said. "Is she pregnant?"

"Hell, I don't know," he said. "And if she is, it ain't mine. Shay, I gotta go. Imma call you later okay. Please stop believing everything you read. I'm in a meeting. Bye."

Had Calvin not told me he was in a meeting or hung up on me I would have told him I was pregnant, but I always seemed to have bad timing with him. I really felt that telling him in person was the best thing, but after our conversation about the Mediatakeout posting, his distance became even more apparent. I was the initiator at most times, moping and asking to see him. He would tell me that we would get together as soon as his schedule let up. It got so bad that I started asking him, "Do you love me?" when I would finally reach him on the phone. He would respond, "You know I do." One time after I demanded, "Well, tell me you love me then!" Calvin roared into the phone, "Girl, I'm on my grind trying to make some things happen. Love is the last thing on my mind!" Appalled and hurt, I hung up on him. He did not call back.

With Calvin missing in action for two weeks now and my stomach growing bigger, I was worried. I began calling him constantly, but he would ignore my calls – sending me right to his voice mail. Not a soul knew of my pregnancy because I did well at camouflaging with fashionable loose-fitting designer tops and baby doll dresses – which were quite trendy. My boss Deidra had wanted me to travel to Milan, Italy for a week to view several fashion shows and select merchandise for the fall collection of Savvy wear at Saks, but I lied and told her that my passport had just expired. Although going to Milan had been one of my lifetime dreams, I was afraid to travel out of the country pregnant. Deidra just gave me this stiff smile and told me that another opportunity would come along for me after my passport was renewed. But an inner voice told me that she didn't believe me at all.

Speaking of inner voices, I could not escape Claire Jones' voice no matter how hard I tried. Each time I'd pray to God – asking Him to allow Calvin to marry me, Claire's words "His name is not Calvin Moore, Dear," rippled in my mind. I was distraught. *Well, if Calvin isn't going to be my husband, then who is?* I certainly didn't want to raise a child without being married – like Calvin's mother had. I also knew the void Sydney and I had felt after our father died. There were too many unwed mothers out there. I did not want to be another statistic. *I want a love-filled future with my child . . . and Calvin.*

As I entered my apartment after work, I noticed Tacara's luggage by the couch. She had been traveling quite frequently and was planning a Valentine's wedding the following year. Our communication and girl talk had dwindled somewhat since Tacara was rarely around. I even begin to be envious of her – mainly because of her marriage plans. Wedding magazines were scattered throughout our apartment.

Tacara must have heard me enter the apartment. "Hey, Girl!" she exclaimed – walking into the living room still in her flight attendant uniform.

"Well, hello, Stranger. I thought you had moved out on me," I said.

There was something different about Tacara, but I couldn't pin point what it was. She seemed to have a glow.

"Sit down!" Tacara ordered, her cheeks appearing red and her flawless smile wide.

"What is it?" I queried, feeling that it must be something really exciting for her to tell me to sit down.

"Steve asked me to marry him," she said exuberantly.

"Again?" I said calmly – putting my purse on the swivel bar stool and proceeding to the kitchen. I had a craving for some Frosted Flakes, although it was past 9pm.

"He wants to get married next week before football camp starts," she shrieked. "I'm gonna do it."

"But what about all of your wedding plans for February?" I asked, wondering if she was also pregnant.

"Shay, I don't know. But something hit us last night."

"Last night?" I questioned, feeling a pang of jealousy.

"Yeah. Last night he was in New York with me on my layover. And we just wondered why we had to wait to get married in February when we want to be married now. Girl, I think we are just gonna go ahead and do it early."

"But what's the rush? Are you pregnant?" I said.

"Shayla, please. Of course not. We're just ready to spend the rest of our lives together as husband and wife, that's all. And I called my minister and he said he could marry us next Saturday," Tacara said, running her fingers through her long tresses.

"But that's stupid," I blurted out, pouring milk into the cereal bowl.

"What?" Tacara frowned.

"If you're not pregnant, I don't see what difference . . . let me see, August, September, October, November, December, January, February," I counted on my fingers. "I don't see what difference seven months is gonna make."

Tacara was still frowning at me. "You know, Shayla, I thought you were gonna be happy for me. Why are you so against this marriage?" She walked into the spacious kitchen looking at me evenly. I tried not to look up as I crunched on my cereal.

"I'm not against the marriage at all!" I objected in between bites, half looking at Tacara. "But how you gonna come home telling me all of a sudden that you are getting married next week when you haven't even given me any notice to find another roommate? I can't afford this place alone!" I said, feeling as though I should sit down and finish eating. My voice and body were beginning to shake.

"Oh, as far as the apartment, Steve said that he would pay my portion of the rent for two more months. You know our lease was ending at the end of September anyway, right?"

"I can't believe you!" I said, shaking my head.

"You can't believe what, Shayla – that I have found someone who loves me so much that he wants to spend the rest of his life with me?" Tacara asked.

For a moment I could not speak, and then I lost control. I threw what was left of the cereal and milk on the floor – almost by accident. I stood to my feet. Tacara seemed startled by my actions. She took a step back.

"I can't believe how selfish you are and how you think the whole world revolves around you!" I yelled, glaring at Tacara with tears in my eyes.

She stood in front of me mute with her mouth wide open. I managed to walk past her and went into my bedroom, where I buried my head into my pillow and sobbed. I felt like I was becoming an emotional basket-case and it was all because my relationship with Calvin seemed to be unraveling. And now the only true friend I had in Atlanta was leaving me to marry a man who adored her and who practically put her on a pedestal. I groped the pillow tightly as thoughts of spending the rest of my life as a single mom made me quiver. I then heard a knock at my door. *Surely Tacara isn't trying to talk to me after I went off on her.*

"Yeah?" I murmured, wiping my tears with the pillow.

"Shayla, I need to talk to you now!" Tacara said firmly.

"What is it?" I said as I sat up. "There is nothing to talk about."

Tacara opened the door to my room. I could tell by her red cheekbones that she was quite upset.

"I don't appreciate you going off like you did when I have been nothing but a true friend to you," she said as her voice cracked. "What is wrong with you?"

"I'm pregnant!" I cried.

"What?"

"I'm pregnant," I threw the pillow on the floor and lifted my top up to allow Tacara to see my bulging stomach. "And Calvin doesn't even know. I don't know what to do."

"Oh, Shayla," Tacara whined as she walked in and sat on the bed beside me. "Shayla," she said, extending her arms. I fell into Tacara's small frame feeling like a wreck as tears drenched my face and her uniform dress. Oddly, it was the first time I had felt some relief in a long time. Tacara gently patted my back, like she was a loving mother. "It's gonna be okay," she assured me.

"No, it's not," I said, pulling away. "It's not gonna be okay, because from what I hear, Cristi is pregnant by Calvin too."

"Oh no," Tacara responded softly. "You're kidding?"

"I wish I was kidding. I've really gotten myself into a mess, and Calvin is getting ready to start playing ball again. He just doesn't need this stress," I cried.

"Shayla, what?" Tacara said. "You have to tell him. How far along are you?"

"I'm 13 weeks."

"Well, Calvin is responsible for this too. Forget his not needing any stress!"

"But he's gonna hate me."

"He is not. And he will get over it, Shayla. You've got to tell him!"

"Tacara, he hasn't even called me in more than a week and every time I try to talk to him he's rushing off the phone - having to do this or that." I broke down again.

"Shayla, don't let him diss you. He is so full of himself. You are way too nice to him."

"But he might really diss me after I tell him I'm pregnant."

"You know what, Shayla? Sometimes you amaze me. I don't believe you are actually worried about Calvin's reaction. If he disses you, then you don't need him anyway."

"Oh God, I just don't know," I said leaning back on the headboard. I was surprised when Tacara lifted my shirt to look at my belly.

"You don't look three months," she observed. "But you are used to having a flat stomach, so I can definitely tell you are pregnant. Oh, Shayla. Have you told your mom? Who have you told?"

"You are the first person I've told. I've been absolutely crazy, and Calvin has been doing all these commercials and just swamped with engagements. He has not paid me a bit of attention since our trip together," I said sadly.

"Well, Calvin needs to get back to reality. Shayla, I really try to be non-judgmental about your relationship with him, but why do you treat him like his shit don't stank? I mean, he does whatever he wants and calls you – whenever – and you're always so available and so forgiving. Why do you let him treat you like that?"

"I don't know," I shrugged. Tacara was, indeed, beginning to sound judgmental. I looked down. I definitely didn't need to be badgered when I felt so pathetic.

"I'm sorry," Tacara said touching my hand.

"That's okay," I said. "Calvin says I'm insecure and have to work on myself, so I guess that's what I need to do."

"Oh my God, forget Calvin!" Tacara shouted. "Don't let him brainwash you, Shayla. He is just trying to make you feel like something is wrong with you so he can control you!"

"But he's right."

"What?" Tacara said with a pinched mouth.

"I mean, I do feel insecure. And maybe if I were more confident I wouldn't be in this predicament," I touched my stomach. "I would have stayed on the pill."

There was a silence that filled the room. When I looked at Tacara I noticed that her big eyes had a certain sadness in them.

"But you didn't stay on the pill," she said softly. "And now you must face the music and allow Calvin to take part of this responsibility."

"Oh, Tacara, you have other things to think about – like a wedding next week, so please don't allow me to burden you with my troubles," I said sincerely.

"I'm not sure whether we will marry next week or not. He just suggested it. But you are right, I have put too much time into planning a big wedding to just settle for a small one next week."

"I'm sorry I said what I said. I just lost it. I don't know what got into me."

"That's okay. I understand now." Tacara smiled.

"If you and Steve want to get married tomorrow, I'll be there because I know that you two love each other a lot. I wish Calvin treated me like Steve treats you."

"Well, Steve is not perfect, Shayla. But I don't allow Steve to treat me with disrespect. I had to demand respect from day one," she said.

"Yeah, I know. And I'm just not good at things like that – like not tolerating shit from a man. I guess I like being treated like shit somehow," I said wearily.

"So, when was the last time you talked to Calvin?" Tacara asked.

"Like I said, last week. I've been calling him and leaving messages, but he won't call back. He's really gonna disappear when I tell him I'm pregnant."

"Shayla, please tell him." Tacara picked up my phone and handed it to me. "Here."

"But I can't."

"Girl, just tell him that it's important that the two of you talk in person. Just tell him before football camp starts. Tell him!"

"But I'm scared," I said holding the phone as if it were some foreign object.

"Shayla, I promise this will relieve a lot of stress for you. Calvin needs to know."

"Okay. But I know he's not gonna answer. I tried calling him all day at work," I began to push the buttons to Calvin's number on my phone.

"If you get his voice mail, just leave him a message and tell him that you really have to talk to him and that it's urgent. He'll call back."

"I don't know," I said. "You don't know Calvin."

"Hello!" He answered. I was very surprised and felt like hanging up, but I didn't.

"Hello?" he said again.

"Calvin?" I said softly.

"Hey, what's up?" he said hurriedly. "I'm sitting here talking to some of my boys. I just got back in town, so let me call you back."

"Calvin, No! I need to talk to you. It's important." I said sternly.

"What's up?" Calvin sounded a tad concerned.

"I need to talk to you in person."

"No. Tell me now. What's up?" he demanded.

"I can't tell you now, but... "

"Look, Shayla," he interrupted. "I don't have time for your games."

"I'm not playing any games. We really need to talk, baby."

"Well, you sound sick and stressed. Are you feeling okay?" he asked gently.

"No. I'm not feeling all that great..."

"Well, do me a favor," he interrupted.

"What?"

"Take two aspirin and call me in the morning," Calvin said and hung up. I looked at Tacara, pretending Calvin was still on the other end as I listened to silence and then a dial tone.

"Okay, Calvin. I'll see you in a little while," I said, speaking into the receiver, not wanting Tacara to know that Calvin had hung up on me. "Okay, bye."

All the while, Tacara was shaking her head. I put the phone down feeling more frustrated and rejected.

"Why couldn't he have come over here?" Tacara asked. "It's too late for you to be driving way out there."

"No. I'm going," I said standing to my feet, feeling mad as hell at Calvin.

"Shayla, I was hoping he would come to you. You have spoiled that man rotten."

"It doesn't matter," I mumbled.

"But I'm worried about you. Maybe you need a good night's rest."

"Damn, Tacara!" I snapped. "You told me I should tell him and now you say wait til tomorrow? I'm going to tell his black ass tonight. I'm tired of this shit!"

Tacara looked at me in silence as I combed my hair and cried. After deciding to just pull my hair back into a ponytail, I grabbed my purse and my keys and left the room. Tacara followed behind me.

"Do you want me to go?" she asked.

When I got to the kitchen I noticed the mess that I had left on the floor. I put my purse on the bar stool and grabbed a few paper towels. I didn't want to leave the evidence that I was going crazy behind.

"Shayla, I can go with you," Tacara continued. "I just feel uncomfortable about you confronting Calvin tonight."

"What do you mean, confront him?" I looked at Tacara. "He knows I'm coming."

"Well, stay cool," she said. "You are really upset, Shayla. Maybe you need to sleep on it a night."

"T, do you know how many nights I've slept on this?" I said looking at Tacara quizzically. "I knew I was pregnant when I was in Puerto Rico. I'm tired of sleeping on it."

"Oh," Tacara said. Her voice gave a hint of approval.

I got up from cleaning my mess up and grabbed my things again. Tacara's petite body was blocking my way. "Just be calm," she said, finally moving her arm away from the bar table so that I could get by. "Try not to lose your cool if he starts trippin. Just come home, because he might act stupid now," she warned.

"I don't care how he re-acts," I said trotting towards the front door – still fuming from Calvin's rudeness. "I'm just gonna tell him."

"Shay, be careful."

I turned around to look at Tacara as I swung the door open. "Stop saying that," I said. "I'll talk to you later." I reached out and Tacara walked towards me and embraced me.

"Call me tonight," she demanded.

"What?" I said halfway out the door.

"Even if you decide to spend the night let me know."

"I'm not spending the night with Calvin," I said.

"Well, if you change your mind, call me so I won't worry."

"Okay. Girl, I've got to go!" I said turning my back to Tacara and walking away.

"See ya." Tacara said.

When I got inside my car, a 2008 C250 Mercedes that I was leasing, I blared Drake "Over" as loud as I could. I gripped the steering wheel and begin to cry. I wiped my tears trying to figure out how I could convince the security guard at the entrance of Calvin's sub-division to let me in without him calling to get Calvin's approval. The tight security was one thing I hated about Country Club. Even if I wanted to surprise Calvin, or just drive by his house to check on him, I couldn't.

And then the solution to my problem popped in my head. I drove 15 minutes more, switching from Drake to Alicia Key's "Try Sleeping with a Broken Heart" and sang along. But the song started making me feel sentimental and I realized how much I really loved Calvin. I reminisced about the times Calvin had made love to me in San Juan in the limo, on the balcony, and in Jamaica in the shower. I thought about his magnetic smile, his personality, the gifts he had bestowed upon me and the couple of times he had told me he loved me. I wanted the intimacy back so desperately. *I have to have it back.*

When I got to the security gate at Calvin's sub-division I felt faint. *How am I gonna pull this one off?* The security guard, Jonathan, was familiar with me. He looked at me with a slight frown, like he was surprised to see me.

"Hi," I said nervously.

"You need me to call Calvin Moore?" He asked, still frowning.

"No. Actually I'm going over to another friend's house." I tried to keep a straight face so that Jonathan wouldn't suspect anything. "Leslie Pennington. Tell her that Shayla Lucas is here to see her."

Jonathan stared at me for a few seconds then dialed a number. I was about to pee on myself. I was anxious – wondering if Leslie, a dentist who lived two doors down from Calvin and who was very fond of me, would allow me to come through the gates. "Oh God," I moaned.

"Okay," Jonathan said with a smile. "She said to let you in."

I breathed a sigh of relief and gave Jonathan a slight smile. I wondered if Leslie really thought I was coming to visit her at 10:30 at night. Calvin had introduced me to her a couple of months after we started dating. I had gone to her office to get my teeth whitened once since then and had made acquaintance with her when she invited Calvin and me over for dinner after a game. She was 45, single and gorgeous. She dated younger guys, but I never had any reason to believe that she and Calvin had anything more than a platonic friendship. At present, she was seeing one of his teammates, a guy 15 years her junior, but said she didn't want to marry again. She had recently divorced a gynecologist who had left her with the Country Club estate. Leslie told me she was just having fun. At times I'd get suspicious of her and Calvin, since he seemed to have a soft spot for her. I just noticed that his pupils would dilate when he'd look at her and when he spoke of her his voice would change – getting gentler. I guess I was overly observant though.

With rampant thoughts going through my head, I drove up to Calvin's driveway. I noticed a black convertible 328 BMW that I assumed was one of Calvin's "boys" cars – as he called his friends. I turned off the ignition, jumping out of the car. I knew I looked pretty bad, since I had cried so much, but I didn't care too much about my appearance. I rang Calvin's doorbell and waited anxiously for him to come to the door. After ringing the doorbell four times, the door was finally swung open and I was greeted by a face I had never seen before. My stomach seemed to plummet to the ground and I stiffened as the beautiful woman in front of me returned the same stiff look. Her skin tone was light brown and her hair was below shoulder length and looked wet. It had honey brown highlights. Her oval shaped face was pretty and her skin smooth – her eyebrows perfectly arched. Her eyelashes looked false, but the closer I stared into her eyes the more I realized that her long eye lashes were natural. We were about the same height. She was dressed in loungewear – a loose fitting top that was so sheer I could see her nipples through it.

"I'm here to see Calvin," I finally said, coming out of my shock.

"And you are?" she asked, blocking the doorway, like she lived there.

"I'm his girlfriend, Shayla!" I snapped. "Excuse me . . . and who are you?"

"Well, maybe you should speak with C.K. about that. Was he expecting you?" she asked with a smug expression.

At that point I stormed through the door – brushing against her, since she was blocking the entrance. She finally stepped back and I continued to walk inside the house and into the kitchen. I had never answered Calvin's door for him before, and I wondered who this bold woman was – seeming to act as though she belonged in my man's house.

Just as I got to the hallway leading to the circular stairs I heard Calvin shout, "Who is that, baby?" and he appeared with a towel around his waist. His body was damp like he had just gotten out of the shower. When his eyes met mine, his body stiffened. He looked as though he had seen a ghost.

"What are you doing here?" he snapped with clenched jaws.

"Calvin, it's imperative that we talk," I said as calmly as I could, my eyelids burning from trying to keep the tears back.

"Naw," Calvin said getting to the bottom of the stairs. "It's imperative that you get out of my house."

Calvin grabbed my arm. I trembled in disbelief as he pushed me back towards the den area – clutching my arm tightly.
"Let me go!" I said, jerking away from him. "I'm pregnant, Calvin," I shouted. "I came to tell you that I'm over three months preg..."

Before I could finish what I was saying, Calvin took my arm again – this time griping it so forcefully and pushing me backward towards the door that I lost my balance in my resistance. I fell to the floor.

"C.K!" the girl gasped as she looked on.

I kicked at Calvin. "You bastard!"

"Shayla, get out!" he yelled with hostile eyes, stepping back as I pulled myself up from the floor. I wanted to scratch his eyes out, but I knew that he was already provoked and that I was putting myself in harm's way by provoking him more. I shot him an evil look.

"You lay another hand on me, I'll kill you!" I said flatly, but charged.

Calvin's eyes widened. He looked shocked and somewhat intimidated.

"I'm so tired of you treating me like shit!" I yelled, unable to tame my emotions any longer. "If you didn't want me in your life then all you had to do was tell me, but you were the one to take me on vacation – telling me that you loved me and that your heart belonged to me! And yes, Calvin, I am pregnant by you, but I'm not gonna beg you to be with me. I'm having this child without you." I then jerked the heart necklace off my neck, breaking the chain, surprising even myself. "And you can have this necklace back!" I threw the necklace at Calvin. He caught it. "You don't even have a heart," I said with squinted eyes. I then looked at the young woman, who seemed scared out of her wits. "He's all yours," I said and calmly walked through the kitchen, the living room and out of Calvin's house.

As I cranked the car and put it in reverse, I clutched the steering wheel and drove as fast as I could out of Calvin's community. I was unable to see the roads clearly due to my tears. I started to curse, but stopped because everything in front of me looked blurry. On top of my tears hindering my vision, the sky seemed to open up with rain and lightening. It was coming down hard. I wiped my eyes with my right hand and looked back up to see a truck coming head on towards me. My heart raced uncontrollably as I realized that I was in the wrong lane. I swirled the steering wheel as fast as I could to the right - trying to avoid the truck. The driver's horn made me panic even more.

Before I could gain control of my car, I screamed in shock as I lost total control and went into an embankment - hitting something very hard. At the impact of whatever I hit, the airbag in my car jolted me – hitting my face and my upper body with force. The front glass shattered, hitting me in my face. I could not move. It seemed as though the car was at a strange angle – maybe sideways or upside down. I felt an excruciating pain in the pit of my stomach. I felt rain coming in on me as well. It was coming hard, high and quick – into my car.

Oh, God. Please let my baby be okay, I prayed inwardly, getting the strength to put my hand on my knee – which seemed like it had been crushed. Tremors surged through my entire body. *Something terrible has happened.* I just knew it. My pelvic area and stomach throbbed. When I moved my hand from my knee up my thigh I felt something thicker than water, soaking my linen dress - blood. I swallowed hard – not able to breathe normally, and then I blacked out – unconscious.

Chapter Six

Intervention

When I regained consciousness and opened my eyes, the fuzzy vision of a large, open room that I was unfamiliar with frightened me. My entire body ached and I gasped for breath since my airway was somewhat blocked by the tubes in my nose and mouth. I clasped the bed rails with my hands, letting out a painful moan, remembering the events that had taken place. I felt disoriented, confused and anxious. I wondered how serious my injuries were. It was obvious that my right leg was weighed down by something, because I could not move it. I felt a pain shoot up my knee. I felt wounded and impaired, but most of all I feared that I had lost my baby. I let out another moan – this time, a loud one.

Within seconds a blond-haired lady in a nurse's uniform appeared. Tacara was behind her. I tried to speak, but found it difficult. My lip seemed heavy.

"My ba-by," I finally muttered as I looked at Tacara's tear-drenched face. The nurse walked over to me, checking my vital signs, blocking my view of Tacara.

"Just relax," the woman said, putting a light to my eye. "You are going to be just fine."

"Wha . . . What about my baby?" I murmured, wanting to jerk the tubes out of my nose.

"Don't try to talk," the nurse said. "Just get some rest and the doctor will be in here shortly," she assured soothingly.

"Is my baby okay? Please tell me," I said feeling my lip split when I stretched my mouth. I put my hand up to my mouth, feeling blood.

The nurse grabbed my hand and gently pushed it down. She then dabbed the corner of my mouth with a cloth that she got from the table beside the bed.

"You burst your lip. So try not to open your mouth too wide when you talk," she said, continuing to gently dab the corner of my mouth. "As you know, the first trimester of any pregnancy is crucial and the trauma of your accident caused you to miscarry," she said as her eyes met mine with sorrow in them.

"No!" I cried, turning my head away from the nurse. "No!"

"Oh, Shayla, I'm sorry," Tacara said as she walked over to my bed and gripped my trembling hand. I kept my head turned to the side as tears flowed down my cheeks. My heart felt like it had ruptured. *How could I have been so callous in my driving? Why couldn't I have died along with my baby?* I began to think about Calvin and how he literally tried to push me out of his house. I couldn't hold back my grief any longer.

"I wish I had died," I sobbed. "I don't want to live."

"Shayla, don't," Tacara said, starting to cry herself. "Please don't."

"Your heartache is understandable," the nurse intervened. "But you have a lot to be thankful for and to live for. From what I understand, the front end of your car was totaled. You are blessed to be alive with only a few injuries."

"I don't care!" I cried. "I want my baby!" The inward pain was intense. I didn't understand what I had done to deserve such a curse. Having a baby meant more to me than I realized. I actually felt a double loss, since it was apparent that Calvin had moved on to yet another woman.

"Can you take these tubes out of my nose?" I asked, wiping my tears and feeling nauseous. I felt a strange cramp in my stomach. I leaned over the bed rail and vomited on the floor before the nurse could get anything for me. Both she and Tacara held on to me as I continued to throw up. I felt weak. Afterwards, Tacara held my head as the nurse cleaned around my mouth with a wet cloth. I felt faint, incoherent. I then heard a man's voice.

"How is Ms. Lucas?" he said in a deep throaty voice. For a moment I wanted it to be Calvin, but I realized the tall man who stood before me was a doctor – a black man who had on glasses and who was wearing a white jacket.

"She just vomited. We may need to give her a sedative," the nurse said.

"Noo!" I moaned, feeling another spasm in my stomach. "I don't want a sedative. I want my baby." I bawled, taking my hand and pulling the tubes out of my nose. The doctor approached me. All I could remember next was seeing him put something through the IV and feeling myself go into an unsettling sleep.

I heard the voice of my mother talking to someone as I awakened from my sleep. I tried to lie there and just listen – not wanting anyone to know I was awake. I then heard my sister Sydney's voice, then Tacara's.

"I feel part responsible for this," Tacara said

"Tacara, you know it's not your fault," Sydney said. "Shayla is stubborn. If you tell her not to do something she'll do it anyway."

"But that's the thing," Tacara said. "I told her she should tell Calvin and I knew I should have gone with her. I should have driven her because she was way too upset. I thought Calvin had told her that she could come over, but he claims that she just showed up at his house – unannounced."

I continued to listen to them talk about me as if I were in a coma or something.

"I wish she had left Calvin alone a long time ago," Sydney added. "He's nothing but a low-life dog. And he better not bring his black ass here. I'm liable to lose my Christianity."

"Shhhh, Sydney!" Connie scolded. "This is not the time for that."

"I know," Sydney said. "But that boy makes me lose all my religion. And when I talked to him he had the nerve to say he loves Shay. I told him that he didn't love anybody but himself."

I was very surprised that Sydney had talked with Calvin and that he had confessed his love for me to her. My adrenaline was truly escalating as I continued to lie there with closed eyes – not quite wanting to intervene. I wanted to hear what else they had to say.

"Her losing that baby was a blessing in disguise," Sydney said in a monotone voice.

At that moment I opened my eyes and turned towards them.

"How can you say that?" I said, trying not to cry but being unsuccessful as my eyes watered.

All three of them looked stunned. Connie moved closer to me, grabbing my hand.

"Oh, baby," she said. "How are you feeling?"

"I just lost my baby," I said warily. "And obviously Sydney doesn't have a clue of how that feels." I stared at Sydney.

"I'm sorry, Shayla, I..."

"What?" I interrupted. "You are self-righteous and insensitive? Is that what you were gonna say? How could you say it was a blessing that my baby died?" I was furious.

"I didn't mean it that way." Sydney said softly, moving closer to my bed.

"Yes, you meant it that way." I pushed the button beside me, requesting the nurse. "I want my privacy please." I jerked my other hand away from Connie's.

"Shay, baby, we love you." Connie said gently.

"Please get out!" I yelled. "I want to be alone."

Suddenly Connie started crying. "But Shay, baby, you are scaring us. We don't want to leave you alone."

Tacara and Sydney were holding hands. They were all looking at me like I was some crazy woman who was about to snap.

"Am, I okay?" I asked in a dry tone.

Connie wiped her tears. "You're gonna be fine. You tore a ligament in your knee, but other than that, you only have a few bruises. But you're okay, thank God."

"Well, why do they have this IV in my arm?" I questioned, looking at the dripping fluid that was going into my veins.

"Because you lost a lot of blood," Connie explained. "Honey, I didn't know you were expec-ting," her voice broke as she begin to cry again.

"Well, so much for that, you know?" I said trying to appear tough. "But I really want some time alone, so if y'all could leave me alone I'd appreciate it."

"Baby, are you sure?" Connie asked, putting her hand on my head and rubbing my forehead gently.

"I'm sure, Mommy." I said, taking her hand away from my head. "I just need some time alone to think."

Connie hesitated for a few seconds while she continued to stare at me. "So, you want us to come back in an hour or so?"

"Yeah, an hour would be good," I murmured. "Can you get me a mirror?" I wanted to see my face. I knew that my lip felt heavy, but my entire face felt somewhat numb. Connie gave me a sullen look. When I looked at Tacara and Sydney they were still holding on to each other. They looked flushed.

"Can somebody please get me a mirror," I snapped, wondering why they were hesitating.

Connie grabbed my hand. "Baby, you have some scars. The window shattered and cut you. But you're going to be fine."

"Please get me a mirror," I insisted.

When I looked into Connie's compact mirror, I almost fainted. My face was a hideous site. It looked disfigured. My bottom lip was swollen twice its normal size and a patch covered my right cheek.

"What is this?" I asked, touching the patch and getting full with tears again.

"You had to have stitches, but the doctor said the scar will eventually fade," Connie said.

"The scar?" I repeated. "I'm gonna have a scar?" I threw the mirror on the floor.

"Oh, Shayla, you'll be okay. You will be just fine," Connie assured. Tacara bent down and picked up the mirror and handed it to Connie. She grabbed my other hand.

"I can't believe this," I cried. "I've lost my baby and now I'm gonna have a scar on my face for the rest of my life."

"Shayla, your face is gonna be fine," Sydney snapped. "Just be grateful that you are living and that you only have minor injuries."

"Oh, you shut up!" I shouted. "Do you think losing a baby and losing half your face is minor? Please get her out of here!"

"C'mon now, Shayla. She's just trying to soothe you," Conniie said.

"Soothe me? Well, I don't need her kind of soothing. I want to be alone," I rang the nurse's button again. "Please leave me alone, now. Please."

"Is everything okay?" A nurse asked as she entered my room with two dozen red roses and two balloons. One of the balloons read "Get Well Soon" and the other read "I Love You."

"Somebody sent these beautiful roses for Ms. Shayla Lucas," she said smiling. "Is she up yet?"

I looked at the gorgeous arrangement of roses half suspiciously as the nurse put them on the stand beside me.

"Oh, how pretty," Connie said.

It hit me that the roses had to be from Calvin. After all, *who else would send an "I Love You" balloon to me? And who else knows of my accident so soon – only one day after it happened?* I was filled with conflicting emotions. Emotions that I had indeed felt before . . . emotions that were torn. *He loves me, he loves me not* kind of emotions.

"Would you like to read the card before I examine you?" the nurse asked, still smiling.

"Nope. I'll read it later," I responded without emotion. "My visitors were just leaving so that I can have some private time to myself."

After my mom, Sydney and Tacara left the room and the nurse examined me, assuring me that my scar would indeed eventually fade, I turned to the beautiful roses that had been sent by Calvin. The small note card read. "Sorry for the misunderstanding. I love you still. C.K."

Misunderstanding? What misunderstanding? I wondered what information Calvin had been given, and what was it to misunderstand about him being with another woman and pushing me out of his house. I felt angered. I threw the card on the floor and cried until it hurt too much to cry anymore.

On the third day of my stay in the hospital I had knee surgery to mend the torn cartilage in my knee. Prior to my operation I got another bouquet of flowers from Calvin, along with a huge "I Love You" teddy bear. A few hours after I awoke from surgery, I was perplexed that I had not received a phone call from Calvin. As a matter of fact, I wondered why I was getting no calls at all – although I had dozens of cards from friends and family. My boss had even stopped by to visit me. *But why hasn't Calvin come to see me?*

Connie was staring at me as I dozed on and off. "How do you feel, pumpkin?" she asked. I could tell that she was very exhausted. Her eyes looked weary – with bags underneath them. She was wearing very little makeup.

"I'm okay," I said, still feeling sedated. "Did anybody call?"

"Your calls are being monitored by the hospital desk clerk. She is taking messages for you." Connie looked at me cautiously. "We didn't want any disturbances before your surgery. But I'll have them allow incoming calls in here as soon as you are better."

"But where is my cell phone?" I asked. "Who has my cell?"

"Sydney has it." Connie said. "It's been off though. She wouldn't dare…"

"Did Calvin call the hospital?" I interrupted.

My mom looked at me and frowned. "Yes, he did. We asked him not to disturb you though," she said softly.

"But I need to talk to him," I said. "He's got to know that I didn't mean to kill our baby."

"Oh, Shayla," Connie said as tears plunged forth from her weary eyes. "You didn't kill your baby. Now, you just relax."

"Is she awake yet?" Sydney said walking inside the room. She strutted with a pep to her step. Her long hair bounced as she walked towards my bed. People always said that Sydney and I looked a lot alike. We both had delicate, oval-shaped faces and we had never gotten up the nerve to cut our long tresses. Sydney was a shade lighter than me – a pecan colored tone. Her 5 foot 5 inch frame was complimented by a curvaceous body, but not quite as curvy as mine. Her legs were muscular and athletic though. Mine were not as muscular.

Sydney ran track from the time she was in high school until her senior year in college. She had continued to be a runner – sometimes running 3-5 miles a day.

Sydney and I locked gazes for a few seconds before either of us spoke.

"So, how are you feeling?" Sydney asked, putting her purse in the chair beside the bed.

"Oh, Sydney, I'm doing great. I just lost my baby, I can't walk and I have a scar going down the side of my face," I said sarcastically. "I'm doing just great."

"Well, Praise the Lord!" Sydney said with a chuckle. "At least you have your sense of humor."

"Where is my cell phone and why did you and Mommy tell Calvin not to disturb me?" I asked, looking at Sydney and then back at my mom.

There was a long pause. At first I didn't think they would answer me.

"Hello?" I said.

Sydney picked up her purse and dug into it - pulling out my cell phone. "I turned it off," she said. "And as you know, I don't know your code, so I'm sure your voice mail is full. But Calvin is the reason you are here in the first place." Sydney handed the phone to me. "We think you need to leave him alone."

"We think?" I said feeling frazzled. I turned on the phone, waiting for it to get reception, but I couldn't get a signal. There was no service.

"You get no signal in this room. I've tried it with my phone already," Sydney confirmed.

"So, what did you tell Calvin," I asked – putting the phone down, hoping I would eventually get a signal.

"Shay, please don't worry yourself about him. We want you to get well so you can…"

"Mommy, don't," I interrupted. "I want to know what Calvin was told."

"First of all, we didn't tell C.K. anything – just not to come by here again," Sydney said. "Tacara was the one who spoke to C.K. about your accident and he told her that you came barging into his house unannounced." Sydney looked at me evenly. "He told her that you were ranting on and on about how you are pregnant and that he asked you to leave because he had company."

I swallowed. I couldn't believe Calvin had actually admitted that he had another woman over.

"He came up here acting all concerned before your knee surgery – but we told him to leave and to give you some time to get emotionally stable again," Sydney said.

"Emotionally stable?" I repeated. "Do y'all think I'm crazy or something?"

Sydney turned her head away from me, looking straight ahead. She did not answer me.

"No, Shayla, we don't think you're crazy," Connie said. "We just don't want you letting a man cause you to kill yourself. Baby, there are other men out there and I told you not to try to trap Calvin," she said sorrowfully.

"You know what?" I said feeling like they were ganging up on me. "I wasn't trying to trap Calvin. He knows that. He was just as responsible for me being pregnant as I was if that's what you're talking about." I began to sob. "I know Calvin loves me. And if he makes me happy, why can't you be happy for me?"

"But he doesn't make you happy, Shayla," Sydney said. "He makes you miserable. He dates multiple women, and a lawyer friend of mine told me that some girl is suing him for child support. And plus, Cristi Perez goes to the same Dominican hair salon I go to, and she found out that I was your sister and made it a point to let me know that she is pregnant by Calvin."

I felt as though someone had thrown fuel on my already fiery soul. My stomach felt weak. *How could Sydney be telling me this?*

"Not now," Connie said, glaring at Sydney. "This is not the time."

"But she thinks Calvin loves her and love doesn't do what he is doing to you, Shay," Sydney said, her voice becoming shaky. "If he loves you he would respect you and he wouldn't have thrown you out of his house like the guy did in that Tyler Perry movie."

"He did not throw me out! And what does a Tyler Perry movie have to do with anything?" I yelled, feeling debased by Sydney's words. "You weren't there. You don't know what happened. You are just uptight and judgmental cause you haven't had sex in six years!"

"Hey, hey, hey," Connie said. "Shayla, you are getting way too upset. We just love you and want the best for you."

"Well, if Calvin doesn't love me, then why was he here at the hospital and why has he sent me all these flowers?" I pointed to the assortment of roses. "Maybe he doesn't love me in the way you think he should, but I know he loves me, and I want this phone connected – because I don't appreciate y'all holding my calls from me."

"We only wanted you to get better first," Connie said softly.

"And we wanted you to speak to a counselor," Sydney added.

"A counselor?" I looked at Sydney, wondering if I had heard her right. "You are the one that needs counseling. I need you two to leave, please. I need some time alone."

"But honey, we…"

"Look," I interrupted Connie before she could finish. "Please respect my wish. I want to spend 30 minutes alone. Can you at least do that?" I asked in a strained voice.

"Okay, baby," Connie bent down and kissed my forehead. "We love you though."

"Yeah," I muttered.

"C'mon Sydney, let's go get a bite to eat," Connie said.

"Okay," Sydney said, standing to her feet and looking at me. "Do you need anything?"

"Right now all I need is for you to leave," I said.

After they left the room I sunk further into the bed covers. I wanted to scream.

On the fourth day of my hospital stay at Piedmont Hospital, the doctor said I could go home the following day and Calvin finally got through to me on the phone. He had sent another two dozen white roses that morning.

"Shayla?" he said after I answered the phone in my room.

"Yes?"

"This C.K."

"Hi," I said dryly.

"Damn, it's good to hear your voice," he said. "I love you."

I paused for a few seconds as Connie stared at me, seeming to know that it was Calvin on the line.

"Shay?" Calvin said.

"Yeah?"

"You hear me?"

"Yeah, I hear you . . . I hear you. I just have somebody looking down my throat," I said, smiling at Connie and feeling more alive now that I was talking to Calvin. Connie frowned, but she seemed to get the hint. She slowly got up and headed towards the bathroom.

"You sound so good. You don't know how worried I been about you." Calvin said. "I am so sorry about what happened, baby."

"Are you?" I asked softly.

"I am, baby. I feel like it's my fault. I didn't know you were pregnant though."

"Well, it's not your fault," I said as a sense of peace came over me. "I should not have come over to your house uninvited. But I didn't know you had another girlfriend."

"Another girlfriend?" he repeated.

"Yeah, I wish you had told me that you didn't want me anymore."

"Shay, I do want you," he said sincerely. "That girl was just a friend. She's not even speaking to me anymore."

"And are you upset about that?"

"Hell, no. Shayla, remember what I told you when we first got up with each other?" Calvin asked. "You are the one for me. I had told her about you, so I don't know why she was answering my door and acting like she didn't know you're my girl. I love you, Shay."

"I don't know if you do or not," I said, wanting to hear his words of love again. "I don't think you love me at all."

Connie walked back into the room hearing my last words. She looked at me nervously.

"I'll just have to show you how much I love you then," Calvin shot back quickly.

"I guess," I said feeling uncomfortable by Connie's presence and the way she was looking at me.

"So, how are you, baby?" Calvin asked. "You better?"

"Oh, I'm okay. I have a huge scar going down my cheek and I'm gonna have to be on crutches for about six weeks, but I'm okay."

"Well, when you getting out?"

"The doctor said tomorrow."

"Can I come get you?"

I paused for a few seconds. "I don't know. My mom is here and I'm supposed to go back to Macon with her until I can get around on my own again."

"Well, you don't have to go to Macon. I can take care of you."

"What?" I said. "Boy, you've got football. How are you gonna take care of me and be in training camp too?"

"But you can stay here at the house. I'll hire a nurse to take care of you."

I laughed, which was the first time I had actually laughed in a while. Connie stood over me. A fake smile creased her face.

"Well?" Calvin said.

I sighed. "I'll think about it," I said. "But I'm going home for a day or two first anyway – before we leave for Macon."

"So, can I come get you tomorrow?"

"Okay," I said in a faint voice. "But we really need to get some things straight. Can you call me back a little later?"

"Aight, love" he said. "I'll call you around nine tonight. Your cell phone on?"

"Naw, I'm in a dead zone in this hospital. Just call the room."

"Well, I can't wait to see you, Shay. You accept my apology?" I had never heard Calvin sound so sweet.

I giggled again. "Just call me later, okay," I said.

"Okay. Shay, I'm so glad nothing bad happened to you. I don't know what I would do without you."

"Uh-huh," I muttered. His words were a balm to my soul.

"Bye, baby," Calvin said.

"Bye."

After I hung up, Connie seemed to force another smile, but I knew she was curious about my conversation. I didn't owe her any explanation, but I felt somewhat obligated to tell her something.

"Calvin wants to pick me up from the hospital tomorrow and take me back to my place," I said looking away from Connie to avoid her eyes.

"Well, if that's what you want, Shayla." Connie sounded disappointed.

"Mommy, Calvin had nothing to do with the accident," I finally faced her. "It was raining and I was speeding... and that's why I lost control of my car – not because of Calvin."

"But you had gotten into a fight with him, Shayla. He had another woman at his home," Connie said, as if I needed to be reminded.

"I know, Mommy. Don't remind me," I sighed. "But all couples argue. That girl is not in the picture. She was just a friend anyway. She knew about me. You have to understand that Calvin makes millions a year and women are gonna chase him. I'm not saying he's perfect, but was my daddy?"

"Don't you dare compare him to your dad," Connie snapped. "He is dead and gone!"

I never understood why Connie's emotions always seemed to stir at the mention of Joshua Lucas, my father. We rarely talked about him, and I knew little about him – only that he was a very handsome and debonair man who had swept my mom off her feet the first day she met him. I had seen a few pictures of him, but I didn't remember him at all, since I was three when he passed away. My mother had told me that he was in the Army and that they met at a military ball. I also knew that he was from North Carolina, but strangely, my mother never made an effort to stay in contact with his family after his death. His death was untimely and unexpected. Connie said he had been having severe headaches and died of a fatal brain hemorrhage. He was only 26 when he died. My mom married David Brown five years after his death, so memories of my dad and his life became a mystery to both me and Sydney.

"Mommy, why are you so sensitive about daddy?" I asked Connie. "You get so uptight when I mention him." I was truly concerned about Connie's reaction, but treading lightly.

"Your dad was a good man," Connie said, nodding, but looking down. "He died much too young."

"Mommy, what is it?" I pressed. "Why can't you talk about my dad without almost falling to pieces? Is there something you haven't told us?"

Connie looked in turmoil as she glared at me. "Tell you something like?"

"I don't know." I shrugged. "But I wish you'd stop getting all torn apart at the mention of him. Why are you still mourning his death?

"I can mourn how ever long I choose to mourn," Connie said. "You just make sure you love the right man – the one who loves you – so you won't be in grief your whole life."

I paused for a few seconds, trying to comprehend what Connie was saying, but I didn't get it. "Mommy, that's okay. I just want Calvin to pick me up tomorrow when I check out." I pulled my hair to the side. "And I would really appreciate your support. I mean, it's already obvious that Sydney is perfect. I have my flaws though, and maybe loving Calvin Moore is one of my biggest ones, but it hurts me more when I don't have my family's support."

"Sydney is not perfect. She just wants what's best for you and so do I," Connie said.

"Okay. Well, thanks for wanting what's best for Shayla, but Shayla can make her own decisions. Shayla is an adult."

"Yeah, I guess you're right about that," Connie said with a sad tone.

On the fifth day of my hospital stay I felt excited about getting released, but I was even more excited about seeing Calvin. He had called the previous night, just as he said he would and confirmed that he would pick me up and take me back to my place, since I wouldn't be staying at his house. My plan was to bring up Cristi Perez being pregnant and the way he had dissed me at his home, but I decided to wait on the talk. I really didn't feel I needed to go to Macon with my mom in a couple of days and thought I might be making a mistake by not taking Calvin up on his offer to stay at his house. But I knew I'd cause a raucous with my family if I did decided to stay with him. Plus, Connie had cared for me so much while I was in the hospital. *I don't want to hurt her.*

After returning from my apartment, Connie helped me put on a comfortable, light-weight white sundress that I had instructed her to get from my closet. The swelling in my face had gone down somewhat, but the scar was still covered by a huge bandage. The doctor advised me not to wear make up for a while. I had no bounce in my hair, but I still decided to wear it down. Connie bumped the ends of my hair so the ends didn't look so frizzy. I truly needed a trim.

When Calvin walked through my hospital door, my heart pounced with excitement. Chills swept over my body. I was totally taken by his presence – once again. He was carrying a bundle of balloons in one hand and a wrapped gift in the other.

"They nearly mobbed me in the lobby," he said with a sheepish gaze.

When his eyes met mine I smiled. I felt awkward that both Sydney and Connie were in the room, but still pleased about Calvin's presence. He spoke to Connie and Sydney and then walked towards me, where he put the balloons on the table that was already full of flowers and balloons from him.

"Somebody must really love you," he said, having to move some of the flowers for the new balloons to fit on the table. He then swirled around, with all our eyes on him, and bent down and kissed me on my forehead. I moved over slightly, to allow him to sit beside me on the bed. He embraced me. He hugged me with a firmness I was not used to. Tears welled up in my eyes as I held him tightly. He then let go to look into my eyes. He touched my face lightly.

"I am so sorry," he said with a tremor in his voice.

"I think I'm getting sick," Sydney interjected as she stood to her feet.

Calvin placed the gift in my hands. "This is for you," he said. I decided to ignore Sydney.

"Calvin," I said, looking at the perfectly wrapped gift. "You know you didn't have to buy me anything."

"I wish you hadn't lost the baby," he said in a throaty voice. He actually looked anguished – as though he had been enduring my pain. His eyes were sunken and filled with sadness.

Calvin turned around to face Connie. Sydney had already left the room.

"Mrs. Lucas, if you need anything while Shay is in Macon, please don't hesitate to let me know. Shay is my everything," he said as he grasped my hand.

Connie gave Calvin a "Yeah, right" kind of look. She then spoke. "Well, I'm sure Shayla will be just fine with me. I'm her mother. She is *my* everything – so you remember that."

"Well, if y'all need some extra cash or anything, I can take care of it," Calvin said.

"Thanks for the offer, but we don't need your money," Connie said in a harsh tone.

"Mommy, come on. He's just offering his help," I said.

"Sure he's offering his help!" Connie said. "Because he thinks money and gifts can buy you." Connie glared at Calvin. "But what it boils down to is that if you can't respect my daughter, then your money doesn't mean a damn thing."

"Oh, my God, Mommy!" I said, shocked at Connie's attitude and her words.

"You are so right, Mrs. Lucas. You are so right," Calvin said as Connie stood to her feet.

Connie looked at Calvin with vengeance in her eyes. "I'm going to find Sydney," she said. She then looked at me with a softer look. "Do you want me to take any of this stuff with me?"

"No. That's okay," I said, hurt that Connie was being so cruel to Calvin.

"I can make a few trips back up to get all of Shayla's items," Calvin said looking at me and then back at Connie.

"Well, call us later," Connie said to me dryly.

"Okay. I will," I said.

Connie walked out of the room slowly, without saying goodbye to Calvin. I cupped his hand with both of mine.

"I'm sorry," I said. "They are really trippin because…"

"I know. I know," Calvin interrupted. "You don't even have to explain. I'm hated. I know."

"Well, they don't hate you," I said. "They are just protective of me."

"Let's just forget about them for right now," Calvin said. "Why don't you open your gift?"

I looked at the beautifully wrapped gift and smiled. As I began to strip the paper off the box, I felt jitters. I had always been into gifts and surprises and Calvin knew it. He knew the right things to buy me and to say to me to make me believe that he loved me. I opened the box and felt something hard wrapped in tissue paper – like a book. As I pushed the tissue paper aside, I was quite puzzled to find a big, white Holy Bible inside.

"Oh my," I stammered. "So, I guess I need Jesus."

"It's genuine leather," Calvin said. "Take it out."

I took the heavy American Standard Bible out, feeling chills.

"Calvin, it's so beautiful. How did you know I needed a Bible?" I asked, looking into his eyes. I was still confused.

"I just wanted to give you something that would be with you forever," he said, touching the Bible. "No matter what, you can't get mad at me and throw this at me. Read what I wrote inside."

I looked at Calvin speechless for a few seconds, not sure of how I should feel or react. When I opened the Bible there inside, taped to the first page was my heart-shaped diamond necklace, plus another diamond-studded heart added to the chain. Underneath the necklace was Calvin's handwriting. I read it silently:

Dear Shayla,

> *This Bible is my gift to you to remind you of my deep-felt love for you. This necklace is a token straight from my heart. It's your heart and mine. Please wear it and always know that no matter what we go through, my love for you is undying.*
>
> > *Remember, My heart belongs to You!*
> > *C.K. Moore*

"Oh, that's so sweet," I said as tears flooded my cheeks. "I love you."

Calvin took my hand in his and kissed it. He then took the tape off the double heart necklace and proceeded to put it around my neck.

"Now I'm gonna tell you one more time, Shay," Calvin said as he stood to fasten the necklace. "My heart is with you." When he sat beside me again he kissed me gently on the lips, several times. We embraced.

"My heart is with you too," I cried. "Always."

Obviously some fans got wind that Calvin was at the hospital. When he rolled me to the lobby in a wheelchair, hoards of people swarmed around us, taking pictures and asking for his autograph. Calvin picked me up in his arms and carried me to the limo, which caused even more photographers to zoom their lens in on us. There were so many flashes coming from cameras that I could hardly see. Calvin seemed to enjoy the attention as he put my crutches in after me.

When I got inside the limo I was surprised even more to see rose petals all over the limo floor and on the seats and "I Love You" helium balloons floating to the top of the limo. While Calvin went back upstairs to get the rest of my things from the room, I sat in the limo feeling overwhelmed with feelings of both joy and pain. Joy that Calvin had truly showered me with outer things that expressed his love for me, but pain from the reality that I had lost our baby and that I really didn't know if Calvin's expressions of love would be here today, but gone tomorrow.

Chapter Seven

Tis the Season

I had made it through rehabilitation and my body was back to normal, although the scar on my cheek had not faded like the nurse and doctor promised that it would. At most times I'd wear my hair over the scar. It wasn't that it was a hideous site, but it was definitely noticeable. It was an indication to others that I had been cut and a reminder to me that I had lost my baby. It was also a reminder of Calvin's unfaithfulness. And to add insult to injury, Cristi Perez had indeed had Calvin's son. She named him Calvin Moore Jr. *Damn her*. I had moved back into my apartment after staying with Connie for eight weeks to regroup physically and emotionally when I received a personal call from Cristi telling me that she had given birth to Calvin's child. I was shocked, to say the least. I thought back on the call that put a dagger in my heart.

"This is Cristi Perez," she said after I answered the phone. "Is this Shayla?"

I could have sworn that my breathing stopped as I sat on my bed slowly. I had only been back in Atlanta for two days and had even forfeited going to Calvin's football games to take care of myself – get my own act together, stop worrying about him, and try to get my mind, body and emotions in order – as Connie and Sydney and Tacara and even my own boss had advised me to do. I had been given a two-month leave of absence from Saks and spent most of my days in Macon reading self-help books, working out and looking at Reality TV. And Calvin seemed different. He called nightly – with our conversations sometimes lasting two hours. He sent flowers, cards, and money. I was convinced that my time away from him – working on my own growth – had motivated him to pursue me more. He seemed to finally realize how special I was. He seemed to appreciate and respect me more, so two days after I returned to Atlanta why did Cristi Perez have to throw salt on everything?

"This is Shayla," I answered after a long pause – not quite sure what she'd say.

"Shayla, I know that we have never met personally, but you know who I am," she said boldly. "And I know who you are," she added in a nicer tone.

"Get to the point," I said directly.

"The point is that Calvin and I just had a beautiful baby son last week and I would appreciate it if you would not call him in the middle of the night – disturbing us – like you did last night."

"Excuse me?" I said dumbfounded.

"I didn't stutter," Cristi said. "You awakened both Calvin and I and the baby when you called him at 2am and I'd appreciate it if you would respect the fact that we have a son together now and we are trying to work out our relationship."

I opened my mouth, but nothing came out. I felt like hanging up, but I didn't. Instead, I started laughing into the phone. I surprised even myself.

"And what's so funny?" Cristi asked curtly.

"You!" I continued to laugh. "Calvin had said that you are ghetto, but I didn't know you were stupid too."

"I beg your pardon?" Cristi said.

"I don't think I stuttered," I said coldly. "You're stupid." I really wanted to curse her out, but I tried to remain calm. I had indeed called Calvin at 2am the previous night – just to tell him that I loved him, but he didn't answer. He had called me at 10pm.

"No, honey. You're the one that's ghetto and stupid. Trying to kill yourself over a man. Yeah, I know all about your little car accident – trying to gain sympathy from Calvin. But guess what? He still came running back to me. You don't mean nothing to him."

My heart fell. Cristi's words stung big time. *Did Calvin really tell her that I tried to kill myself?* Feeling the sting of tears, I went to push end on my cell phone, but when I heard a baby start crying, I decided to just listen. The infant's cries grew louder and louder. I could do nothing but hold the phone and imagine Calvin's child in her arms. The cries from the baby's voice had me in a tormented trance. I felt paralyzed.

"Shayla, listen," Cristi said in a soft tone. "I know you probably love C.K. just as much as I do, but we have a baby now. His name is Calvin Jr. We call him Little C . . . and C.K. was with me when I gave birth. He's the spitting image of him," she said and sighed. "Hello? Are you still here?

"Yeah," I gutted out.

"Well, I don't know what C.K. has told you about me, but we've been together on and off for 10 years. I've been through a lot with him. He said you knew about me from the start. But I gave him space because he needed to see that I'm the one for him, and he has," she said and paused. "All I'm asking is that you please back off now, so that we can work our issues out. That's all I'm asking."

The baby continued to cry and my toughness faded to weakness. I didn't know what to say. Cristi was making me feel like I was Calvin's jump-off, and that she had been his main girl all along.

"I know you've been away for a few months and C.K. told me that he didn't plan to see you anymore, but that you tried to drive off a cliff," she said. "Just be strong. There are other men out there – and even in the NFL. Now that the baby is here you need to respect us."

"You are such a bitch!" I blasted. I didn't mean to call her a name, but she was bringing out the worst in me. "And a lying conniving one at that. Ain't nobody tried to kill themselves over Calvin!" I then heard the baby's cries grow even louder.

"Shhh, C.K. Jr. It's okay. It's okay," she said, obviously knowing that calling the baby C.K. Jr. would make me even more upset. I could envision her holding Calvin's son as the baby screamed a long, tormenting cry. I swallowed hard, realizing that if I said anything else to Cristi that I'd burst into sobs. *I can't let her hear me break down.* So, I did what maybe I should have done the minute she confronted me. I hung up.

It took me the entire day to get my bearings. I thought I was actually having a nervous breakdown. I wasn't even able to stand up straight. I was glad that Tacara was away on a trip and I had the apartment to myself. I called Calvin every 15 minutes, leaving frantic messages and putting 911 in his phone. . . but he didn't call back all day. I was crumbling.

Finally, after a full day of anguish, Calvin called around midnight. I had calmed my emotions just a tad by reading the 23 Psalms in the Bible that Calvin had given me. *Did he really think I tried to kill myself? Is this the reason he gave me this Bible?*

When I answered the phone, I was greeted by Calvin's unfazed attitude.

"Yeah, what's up?" he said dryly.

"Calvin, I've called and texted you all day," I said frantically.

"Yeah, I told you not to do that shit. I didn't have my phone with me today," he said in a calm tone.

"So, you didn't get my messages? I left several messages for you."

"How many messages did you leave?" he asked as though he was clueless.

"Several!" I said. "So you don't know that your wife called telling me not to call you at 2 in the morning because I was disturbing your new baby, Calvin Jr?" I put emphasis on the name.

"She ain't my wife," he said, still calmer than I expected him to be.

"But she is the mother of your son, right?" I questioned, feeling agitated.

"Right," Calvin said emotionless.

"And you were with her last night at 2 in the morning, right?"

"Look. I am not about to hold this phone and be questioned by you," he said. "I've been dealing with a situation with my coach all day and this is the last thing I need."

"But did you tell Cristi that I tried to kill myself?" I yelled.

"Kill yourself?" he said in a strained tone. "What are you talking about?"

"Calvin, that's what Cristi told me. She said that you said I tried to drive my car off a cliff."

"What the . . . " Calvin snickered. "Girl, don't believe nothin she say. But like I said, I got this big crisis I'm dealing with. I can't handle no bull shit about Cristi tonight, Shay. I got some problems I need to deal with."

"What's wrong?" I asked, knowing that I shouldn't let Calvin change subjects on me, but feeling that I had to in order to avoid a dial tone.

"Nothin," Calvin murmured. "It's just some shit I don't even want to talk about right now. Who is there with you?" he asked.

"Nobody," I said, wiping a tear from my eye and wondering why he was asking. "Tacara went on a trip and won't be back until Thursday."

"Well, can I come over?" Calvin asked.

"What?" I said. I was surprised Calvin wanted to see me.

"I'm depressed and I need to be with you," he said.

My heart melted. It didn't take much. *I know it, I'm a fool, but everybody plays the fool sometimes.*

"Calvin, I just feel so hurt," I said. "When Cristi called today telling me about your son, it really took me for a loop. And then she said that you told her I tried to kill myself and that you no longer wanted to see me and that you two were working things out. I just felt so…"

"Hey, hey, hey," Calvin interrupted loudly. "Can I come over or not?"

"Yeah, you can come over," I said softly.

"Aight, see you in 30 minutes. I just want to love you, okay?" Calvin said in a sexy tone.

"Okay."

When Calvin walked through my apartment door he grabbed my face with both of his hands and kissed me hungrily – darting his tongue in and out of my mouth. I could smell and taste alcohol on his breath and mouth. He sucked on my neck and stripped my satin negligee off so fast that I heard it tear. My heart raced with desire, lust and love. I felt so wanted by Calvin, and his passion for me turned me on. Calvin quickly shed from his blue jeans and then from his underwear and tee-shirt. When he glided himself inside me – rocking me and holding me and telling me how good I felt, I reached my peak quickly.

"I love you, Calvin. Oh, baby, I love you!" I said in short soft breaths as he growled against my skin.

"Is this pussy mine forever, Shayla?" Calvin panted while rocking me harder.

"It's yours forever, baby," I said. "It's yours forever."

"You gonna love me forever?" he asked as he moved his hips with more force.

"I'll love you forever," I repeated.

"And you're gonna do whatever I say?" he said, still pouncing on me.

"Whatever you say, baby," I said, feeling exhausted and exhilarated.

"You gonna do whatever I tell you to do!" Calvin said, cupping my cheek. "Say it."

"I'm gonna do whatever you tell me to do, baby. Whatever," I hollered.

Calvin continued his gyrations for a few more minutes and we skyrocketed simultaneously. It was the second time for me.

"Yes . . . yeah," Calvin moaned.

"Yes. Oh yes," I said as Calvin's sweat dripped on me.

After it was all over and done, we laid on the living room floor holding each other. I felt rejuvenated, renewed, healed. Thoughts of Cristi and her baby went to the back of my mind as I rubbed Calvin's stomach – dreaming of someday becoming his one and only . . . his wife.

Two months had passed since that night, and once again, I knew I had let passion overrule. I didn't know what it was, but each time Calvin made love to me I seemed more bound to him – emotionally and physically. Perhaps repeating Calvin's words during our lovemaking was having more of an effect on me than I thought it would. Perhaps I was actually being hypnotized by Calvin each time we had sex, because I'd lose all logic and reasoning afterwards. I'd forget what I was mad at Calvin about. I felt like he had a spell on me. I felt whipped by his sex. All I knew was that it was seven days before Christmas and Calvin had better be thinking about whipping out a ring. He had been having a great season, and the Falcons were headed to the playoffs again. But Calvin's behavior was becoming ever so strange. I never knew when he would be the most loving man or when he'd snap or ignore me. He was, indeed, the most unpredictable man I had ever met. Of course I wasn't the happiest woman with him, but without him I was miserable. *This has to be love.*

Sydney had honked her horn several times and I grabbed my purse and turned on the alarm before leaving my apartment. We were headed to Phipps Plaza mall to get Connie's Christmas gift. Even though I did not want to be bothered with Sydney's attitude, I had to do what I had to do.

When I got inside Sydney's Camry, I adjusted the seat and leaned back.

"Hey," she said.

"What's up?" I said turning to Sydney. She looked quite spiffy in a black leather jacket, skinny jeans and a black felt hat with a light grey trim. Her skin was flawless. She looked more vibrant and starry-eyed than usual. Sydney had a certain glow.

"So, what are you all glistening about?" I asked, turning down the volume to Mary, Mary on her car stereo.

"Don't do that," she said. "I really like this song." Sydney turned the song back up - singing along with Mary, Mary. "You don't know how much I pray, don't know how much I gave, don't know how much I changed, I'm just tryna explain. It's the God in me," she sang.

I just listened, preferring to be listening to something else, but I didn't want to disrespect Sydney by turning the volume down again. She seemed so into the song, raising her hand - like she was getting happy. After the song went off, I turned the station to V-103. Robyn Thicke was on singing "Sex Therapy." Immediately Sydney turned the volume down.

"Syd-neeey!" I said teasingly. "I really like that song."

"You need help," Sydney said turning the car stereo completely off.

"Well, pray for me Sydney, okay, cause I do need help," I said with sarcasm. "And with you being so perfect, I'm sure God would listen to you."

"I didn't say I was perfect!" Sydney shot back.

"But Sydney you know you've told me once and you've told me a thousand times that actions speak louder than words," I said. "You don't have to say you're perfect. You just are."

"Shayla, what is it with us? Can't we just get along?" Sydney said as she looked at me and then back at the street.

"We are just different. I mean, I try to get along with you, but…"

"It's Satan," Sydney cut in.

"Satan?" I said.

"Yes. The devil doesn't want us to get along. He tries to put a wedge between close relationships, but it's Christmas and I really do think we should put our differences aside and try to get along."

"Aight then," I said, not wanting to argue with her. "From this point on we are gonna make an extra effort to get along."

"In Jesus' name, it is done," Sydney said and gave me a wink.

I smiled and shook my head.

We walked through the crowded mall - going into Nordstrom, Barneys, and Saks - trying to find Connie a wool coat, but Sydney and I could not agree on anything, since our tastes were completely different. She liked the more conservative, tailor made coats while I liked the more trendy styles. Finally, Sydney and I decided on a brown, wool two-piece suit with a coat dress jacket and an A-line skirt. We went in half on the $700 suit, which I was able to get a 40% discount at Saks. I also got Connie a nice wool hat to enhance the suit.

While Connie's gifts were being wrapped, Sydney and I decided to go inside the Versace store. I had not bought Calvin's gift yet, and I knew he was Versace crazed, since he had gotten the endorsement to model Versace sunglasses. Right as we were about to enter the store, I heard a woman call my name.

"Shayla, is that you?" the voice called out.

I looked from one side and then to my other side, unable to detect where the voice was coming from.

"I'm behind you," the woman said.

When I looked around, my eyes lit up. It was Claire Jones.

"Hiiii," I said looking at Claire, who looked quite enchanting.

"My son joked that he was going to leave me to go catch up with you two gorgeous young ladies. And when I looked around I recognized you," Claire said.

When I cast my eyes on the man standing beside Claire Jones, my mouth flew open. He was handsome, indeed. He looked to be about 6 feet 4 inches, with a brown complexion and beautiful hazel eyes, like his dad's. He shifted his feet – seeming a little nervous as he gazed at both Sydney and me, and then back at me with a longer gaze. For some reason, my pulse was racing. I didn't know if it was because I had come into proximity with Claire Jones, the prophet, or if her son had me all jittery. I wondered if this was the son who had talked with Calvin about some business deals over the phone a few months ago.

"It's so good to see you, Claire," I said as I reached out to hug her lightly. Claire's hug was firm. Once we let go of each other I thought I should make an introduction. "This is my sister, Sydney. Sydney, this is Claire Jones. Calvin and I met her in Puerto Rico."

"Hi. It's nice to meet you," Sydney extended her hand, shaking Claire's first then her son's. I could tell that Sydney was thinking the same thing I was thinking about Clalire's son. *Damn, this boy is fine!* Well, not the *damn* part.

"This is my son, Diego!" Claire said smiling. "He lives in London and is home for the holidays."

"Ohhh," Sydney said gleefully. "Have you acquired that nice, European accent yet?" she said in an almost sexy tone.

Look at Sydney trying to flirt. I looked Diego over slyly. He looked to be about my age, maybe a few years younger, He was dapper. From head to toe he was well groomed, sporting a leather coat, blue jeans and a sporty grey, Kangol cap.

"I'm trying not to acquire that European accent, but I don't know. I've been over there for almost two years now," Diego said. He actually did have a slight British accent. His voice was deep, yet gentle. I felt drawn to him.

"So, what are you doing in London?" Sydney inquired. *I can't believe her. She is actually trying to make a move on this man.*

"I'm a management and financial consultant for Rolls Royce Motor Cars of London," he said. "Basically, I sit in meetings with managers and shareholders all day."

My curiosity was piqued. When I looked up coyly at him, our eyes locked. I looked down quickly, not understanding why my heart was still galloping. He continued to stare at me.

"Well, that sounds interesting," Sydney said. "Do you like it there?"

"Yes, I love it there. There are a lot of opportunities and a lot to do," he said. "Where are you ladies from?"

"Macon, Georgia," I said, not wanting Sydney to monopolize the conversation.

"We are original Georgia Peaches," Sydney said in yet another sexy tone.

"Georgia Peaches, indeed," Diego said in a low, sexy tone. But he looked right at me.

"Well, I want him to come back home," Claire said. "I miss him."

"Ahhhh, Mama, you know I can't move back right now," he said grabbing Cliare and squeezing her shoulders. "But I will visit as much as I can. I promise."

We all stood there in silence for a few seconds and then I felt compelled to say something.

"So, what do you predict, Prophet Claire?" I said, looking at Claire nervously. "Will your son return to the States or not?" Immediately I felt embarrassed.

Claire smiled, but Diego looked at me with a frown followed by slight a smile.

"Oh, I don't make predictions," Claire said emphatically.

"I know. I know," I said, trying to play off my blunder. "How is Mr. Jones?" I knew I needed to change the subject.

"Oh, dad is fine," Diego said. "He acts younger than me sometimes."

"And how old is that, Diego?" Sydney asked.

She is really tripping. What is going on with this saint?

"I'm an old man," Diego said glancing at Sydney and then at me.

"Yeah, right," Sydney said. "You look around 21 or 22."

"Why, thanks." Diego said with a smile. "I'm 30 though."

"30?" Sydney said as though she didn't believe him. "You've got to be kidding me."

I looked at Sydney and grunted. She was being much too verbal for me.

"You look great for your age," I said, not wanting Sydney to get more attention from him than me. "It must be those dimples."

"Oh, no," Claire said and chuckled. "Don't swell his head. Remember I've got to live with him until the New Year."

Overcome with a strange feeling of wanting to know more about Diego and a feeling that I shouldn't want to know more about Diego, I chose to end the conversation.

"Well, it was good to run into you, Claire," I said. "I've been thinking about you."

"Well, good," Claire said. "You look absolutely beautiful and I've been thinking about you too . . . and praying for you."

Here we go. Everybody wants to pray for me. I wondered if Claire knew that I had lost my baby a few months ago. I wondered if she knew all the pain I had endured. I wanted to pull her aside and ask her what she knew about my life, but I knew I couldn't. So I leaned over and hugged Claire again.

"Thank you," I said. "And have a great Christmas and New Year."

"You do the same, "Claire said. "Do you still have my number?"

"Yes, I do," I said. "You gave me your Atlanta number and the number in Puerto Rico."

"Well, give me a call sometime," Claire said sweetly. "Don't be a stranger."

"Yeah, don't be a stranger," Diego said as he gleamed at me with dreamy eyes.

"Okay," I said blushing. "It was nice to meet you, Diego."

"And it was a pleasure meeting you two beautiful ladies," Diego said. "Hopefully if you're not a stranger we'll meet again."

I looked at Sydney and she was smiling with wide eyes.

"Merry Christmas," I said.

"Merry Christmas," Diego said as he extended his hand. His handshake was firm and his hands were warm. I felt flustered with emotions I wasn't supposed to be feeling. He slowly let my hand go. He then reached over to shake Sydney's hand. I noticed that their handshake wasn't prolonged like ours was.

"Merry Christmas," Diego said again.

"Merry Christmas," Sydney said excitedly.

"Bye," I waved, as Sydney and I turned to go inside the Versace store.

When we walked halfway into the store I could not hold my emotions in any longer.

"Was Diego fine or what!?" I said turning to look at Sydney.

"Yes, he was!" Sydney said enthusiastically. "Fine, indeed. And he liked you."

"What?" I said, still feeling the thuds of my heart.

"He liked you, girl. You better not be a stranger," she quipped.

"Girl, I'm in love," I said guiding my thoughts back to Calvin Moore - *my everything*. "Diego seemed kinda interested in you to me."

"Girl, please. Naw. He liked you, trust me," Sydney looked at me. "Plus, I'm in love too," she added.

I looked at Sydney cautiously, surprised by her words once again.

"So, *you're* in love?" I asked.

"Yep. My time has come," Sydney said in a matter of fact way.

"So, you are really in love with Aaron?" I asked. Sydney had been seeing him for eight months and they had been spending a lot of time together, for sure. *But love?*

"We are in love," Sydney said in a squeaky tone." She was behaving so peculiar to me.

"So, is he the one?" I pried. "Has he convinced you to give up your virginal ways?" I needed to know if my older sister was having sex. I tried to look at the men's shirts and act like I wasn't really interested in her answer . . . but I was.

"Now you know I'm not a 29-year-old virgin. But in case you're wondering if Aaron and I have had sex, the answer is no," she said in a slightly snappy tone. "I'm a born again virgin."

"Well, how do you know he's the one if y'all haven't consummated the relationship?" I asked with a chuckle. "Giiirl, don't buy no shoes without trying them on first. They might not fit!"

Sydney chuckled. "You can't compare trying on shoes with sex," she said. "Aaron and I are on the same page though. We are waiting til marriage, thank you."

"Marriage?" I said looking at Sydney levelly. "So, he's talking marriage?"

"Well, like you said I always say, actions speak louder than words," she said with a smirk. "But yes, we are talking about marriage."

Damn, my holy roller sister is gonna beat me to the altar. I began to hurriedly look through the men's clothing feeling a twinge of jealousy. *Does everybody have to bypass me? When is Calvin gonna step up?*

"Let's go," I said, feeling disgusted. "I don't see anything in here."

I was truly exhausted after leaving the mall. While Sydney sang along with the Mary, Mary songs I sat back in the car seat feeling a bit depressed. Calvin had an away game this weekend in Green Bay, so I felt so lonely. He didn't call much on his road trips, and when I would hear from him he'd chat with me for about five minutes. I knew that football was taking all of his time though, and he told me that his goal was to become a two-time Super Bowl MVP. He told me that I needed to give him his space at times, but that I would be rewarded. *Maybe my reward will be a diamond, engagement ring this Christmas. Oh, how I hope so.*

On Christmas Eve, Connie drove up to Atlanta from Macon. Sydney was hosting our annual Christmas Eve dinner party at her house. Since I was a little girl, I always remembered exchanging gifts on Christmas Eve with my family. I was really excited this Christmas because Calvin was coming over to spend time with me and my family. My mother had also invited her brother, Martin, who had flown in from Dallas, Texas and he had told her that he was bringing his new wife, Quanda, a woman 25 years his junior. Sydney had invited Aaron, and Aaron had invited his mom, Deborah.

The snow had not come in as predicted, but the weather had become more frigid, with temperatures dropping in the teens. When Aaron lit the fireplace, Sydney's ranch-style home looked so cozy and festive. She had a seven foot live tree with red bows and candy canes on it. Gifts were stacked high underneath. The smell of Christmas was definitely in the air. Sydney and I had done well on our pact to get along. I had even gone back to the mall with her to help her choose Aaron's gift.

Sydney had gathered everyone around the tree to sing Christmas carols and I was beginning to get somewhat perturbed. Calvin had not shown up yet. I had spoken with him earlier during the day and he promised me that he would be at our dinner party, no matter what. But it was 8 pm, and I told Calvin that dinner was being served at 7 pm. We had eaten ham, turkey & dressing, collard greens, black-eyed peas, and candied yams. I was stuffed. "Where are you, Calvin?" I thought to myself as Sydney led us in singing "Silent Night." Aaron had his arm around her – acting like he was all in love. Martin's wife was acting fidgety, twiddling her thumbs. She was only 21 years old, but really cute. Connie looked so happy to have her family all together for Christmas. She had gotten her hair cut into a stylish cut that made her look 10 years younger. Aaron's mother could really sing. She sang louder than anyone else. You could tell that she sang in the choir at church.

"Okay, okay," Sydney said after we finished singing "Silent Night." She looked at everyone. "Do y'all want to sing another song or start opening gifts?"

"Let's sing Jingle Bells," I said, still perplexed that Calvin hadn't shown up and trying to buy him more time before everyone started opening gifts.

"Jingle Bells?" Sydney repeated.

"Yeah, you know that song . . . Jingle Bells, Jingle Bells, Jingle all the way," I started singing. Everybody joined in. Afterwards, Sydney seemed a bit anxious.

"Okay, okay, okay," she interjected. "I think we should go ahead and open the gifts," she looked at me. "Unless you want to wait longer for Calvin to get here."

All eyes were on me. "Well, I, I, I," I stuttered. "He was supposed to be here. Let me go call him. Could you all excuse me for a minute?"

I left the living room and went into the kitchen and dialed Calvin's number. No answer. His voice mail didn't even pick up. I called again. Still, no answer. My stomach was beginning to feel upset and my hand shook nervously. "Oh, God," I said softly. "Please let him be on his way." I wanted to cry, but I knew I couldn't get wimpy and teary-eyed on Christmas Eve in front of my family. I tried to stall to avoid facing everyone in the living room. I walked around the kitchen – wondering if I should call Calvin's mom. And then I got the weirdest idea. I decided to call Claire Jones instead. *Perhaps she has some words of encouragement for me.*

"Hello?" a man's voice answered.

"Hi, this is Shayla Lucas," I said as my voice trembled. "Is Claire Jones there?"

"Shayla Lucas? Hi, Shayla," the man said. "This is Diego."

"Oh, hi," I said feeling a slight rush. I really didn't want to talk with him though.

"So, are you having a nice Christmas Eve?" Diego asked.

"Oh, yes, it's nice. What about you?"

"I am. Hey, why don't you come out here? We are all sitting around watching a movie and drinking some eggnog. I'm sure Claire would love to see you," Diego said cheerfully. "And I would too," he added in a lower tone.

A shiver went down my spine. Diego sounded so good, but all I could think about was Calvin. *Why can't he be Calvin?*

"Oh, that's nice of you to ask, but my family and I are over to my sister's. We just had dinner and now we're about to open gifts. But maybe I'll stop by and say hi to you all before the New Year."

"Please do!" Diego said with emotion.

Wow. This man really likes me. This fine, beautiful man really likes me. But he is not Calvin. A corporate guy over a millionaire football star? I don't think so.

"Well, I'll go get Claire for you," he said.

"Oh, that's okay. She's probably busy," I said. "I'll call her back." For whatever reason, I didn't want to talk with Claire now. I definitely didn't want her telling Diego that I was going through hell being Calvin's girlfriend.

"Oh, she'd be upset with me if I didn't let her speak with you. Hold on a minute, okay?"

"Okay."

"And Merry Christmas."

"Merry Christmas to you too," I said.

It seemed to take Claire forever to come to the phone. I kept looking out the kitchen window to see if Calvin had arrived. I saw a few cars pass by Sydney's house, but none of them were Calvin's.

"Shayla?" Claire's voice sang into the phone.

"Claire, how are you?" I said.

"I'm just fine. My son told me that he invited you over, but you won't come," she said sounding disappointed.

"Oh, I'm spending the evening with my family," I paused. "And Calvin. I don't know what could have happened to him though. He's late – again." I started laughing a little, hoping that Claire wouldn't sense my worry.

"And how is Mr. Calvin Moore?" she asked. "We watched his game last week. He is really doing well. I'm assuming all is well with him?"

"Oh, he's fine. And we're fine. It's just hard for us to spend quality time together when he's always on the road and doing this or that, but I'm not complaining. I'm sure there have been many times when Mr. Jones was missing in action and you had to handle feeling lonely in his absence too."

Silence. Claire didn't respond.

"But I was just calling to say it was so nice seeing you again, and I'd love to meet with you for lunch one day – just to talk," I said. "Can we do that?"

"Oh, Shayla, that would be great. In fact, you should come by and join us on the 28th. We're having a brunch here at the house. All six of my children will be here."

"And what time is that?" I asked, peering out the kitchen window again.

"It's at noon. Please promise me you'll come by."

"Okay. I'll call a day before so I can get your address," I said totally oblivious to what I was really promising her.

"Shayla!" Connie said, walking into the kitchen, surprising me. "Are you coming back in here so we can start opening gifts? Is that Calvin?"

"Mommy, I'll be in there in about five minutes," I said. "You scared me."

Connie rolled her eyes at me and walked away. Once again, I peered out the window and to my surprise and delight there was a car in the driveway. It looked like one of Calvin's high end cars.

"Claire," I said with excitement. "I've got to be going. Calvin is here. He just drove up."

"Oh, good," she said. "But I want to see you in a few days, young lady, and then we can schedule lunch and catch up."

"I'm looking forward to it," I said.

"And remember, God loves you," she said.

"Thanks," I said. "See you soon."

When I hung up the phone and opened the door, before he could even ring the doorbell, I felt overwhelmed with joy as I saw him walking towards me. *I knew Calvin wouldn't stand me up on Christmas Eve – not in front of my family.* But when I looked closer, I realized it wasn't Calvin. My joy was stolen quickly when I realized it was Sydney's ex boyfriend from college, Curtis. I was wracked with disappointment as Curtis strolled to the door smiling – with a gift in his hand.

"Hey, Shayla. I haven't seen you in a while," he said in a perky voice.

Since my feelings were truly hurt, I didn't say anything.

"What's wrong?" he asked, as he stopped in front of the door.

"Hold on a minute," I said in a sour tone and proceeded to get Sydney. Sydney was already on her way to the door. She was shaking her head.

"Did he finally get here?" she asked.

"No. It's Curtis Frazier," I said.

"Who?" Sydney said in astonishment. "Oh no." Sydeny seemed to tense up.

When Sydney went to the door I stayed in the kitchen listening to their conversation. She told him that she had a boyfriend who was there with her and she told Curtis that he needed to leave. He said, "But I love you, Sydney. You can't just forget about what we shared." After whispering words that I couldn't quite make out, Sydney slammed the door in his face without taking his gift. *What is this all about?* I heard Curtis crank up his car and drive off.

"The party is this way, Shayla," she said pointing near the living room. "We are waiting on you."

I didn't appreciate her bossing me, but I strolled in front of her to the living room, confused about Calvin and curious about Sydney's confrontation with Curtis.

"Now, let's open gifts," Sydney said as though she were the head woman in charge.

There was no order to the gift opening. I tried to fake my excitement as I opened a gift from Martin and Quanda, which was a black sweater that I knew I'd never wear.

"Oh, this is cute," I lied.

When Aaron stood up, all of a sudden, and turned the stereo down and instructed everyone to give him their full attention, I knew something was up. Sydney had already opened his gift to her, a beautiful pair of diamond earrings, so I wondered what he was going to say.

"First of all, I'm so happy to be spending this Christmas Eve with the woman I love, Sydney Lucas and her family."

"Ahhh," Connie said.

I glanced at Sydney and she was smiling with a proud look on her face.

"Thank you, baby," she said.

"Well, I have known Sydney for eight months to this day and baby," he said, turning to Sydney. "Each day I spend with you I feel like I'm the most blessed man in the world. I mean, you, Sydney Lucas are the sunshine of my life . . . the apple of my eye."

"Go head, boy!" Martin shouted.

"You are the key to my happiness. And that's why I want to ask you – in front of your family and all these witnesses – one question." Aaron fumbled through his pocket and pulled out a small grey box.

Everyone gasped. Sydney's eyes widened as she put her hand over her mouth. Aaron dropped to one knee and opened the box, where a beautiful diamond ring, seeming to be at least two carats, was exposed. My mouth swung open in awe.

"Sydney Lucas, I love you. Will you marry me?" Aaron said, enunciating his every word.

"Yes! Yes! Yes!" Sydney jumped up shouting. She jumped right into Aaron's arms, almost knocking him over.

The sounds of sniffles filled the room.

"Hallelujah," Connie cried.

As Aaron slid the diamond on Sydney's finger, my heart felt crushed. I couldn't understand my feelings. I wanted to be happy for Sydney and tell her that she deserved the love she was getting, but I began to cry. Sydney turned around to see me crying. She outstretched her arms to me and we locked in each other's arms. We were both in tears.

"I want you to be my maid of honor," she said. "I love you, Shayla."

"I am so happy for you," I cried, trying to stop thinking about myself and bask in my sister's joy. But the tears from my eyes flowed. I couldn't stop them. Even after the excitement about the proposal had calmed down a bit, I was still crying. *Damn.*

Interestingly, everyone seemed to believe me when I told them that Calvin's mother had gotten ill and that he had to take her to the hospital. I told them that I was in the kitchen talking on the phone with him earlier. At 1am I put my gifts and Calvin's gift from me, an Apple iMac I had saved up for and used some of his money to purchase too, in the trunk of my car. I went back inside to hug everyone and tell them that I'd see them tomorrow sometime. They had started watching some home videos.

"Are you all right?" Connie asked with a concerned look.

"I'm fine," I said. "I'm just so happy for Syd," I lied.

Driving back to my apartment from Sydney's was an effort. I held the steering wheel tightly, not wanting to allow my upset to cause me to be distracted and have another accident. I didn't understand Calvin's lack of respect for my feelings. It was a familiar feeling, but I knew I had to make it home safely. My head hurt. I thought about all the things that had happened that day . . . talking with Diego and feeling his excitement for me, talking with Claire and accepting her invitation to come over to her home, Sydney's unexpected engagement, Curtis showing up to see Sydney and her slamming the door in his face, and most of all I thought about Calvin standing me up. I wondered how Calvin could be such a low life and how could God, who Claire claimed loved me, allow me to feel so miserable – so unworthy of love.

Chapter Eight

Arrested Development

"Love endures long and is patient and kind; love never is envious nor boils over with jealousy, is not boastful or vainglorious, does not display itself haughtily. It is not conceited (arrogant and inflated with pride); it is not rude (unmannerly) and does not act unbecoming. Love (God's love in us) does not insist on its own rights or its own way, for it is not self seeking . . . "

I was reading the Bible that Calvin had given me - 1 Corinthians 13- hoping I'd get a better understanding of this thing called love. Two extra strength Tylenols just wasn't doing the job for my headache. I had cried until 5am, unable to sleep, calling Calvin's cell phone and home number. After I got exhausted from trying to hunt him down I started reading the Bible. *Haven't I been all of these things to Calvin that love was supposed to be?* I had been patient, kind and long-suffering. Oh, I had suffered long and hard for love, so why was I home alone on Christmas morning after being stood up by the man who supposedly loved me too? *What is this thing called love and why am I so unsuccessful at achieving it?*

All I wanted was a man to be with – someone to complete my life . . . someone to be my knight in shining armor. Sydney had found her knight, Tacara had found hers, so what was it about me that repelled love? *What trick is it that I'm unaware of?*

I tossed and turned in my bed trying to put my finger on the problem. And then a pensive thought came to my mind. "You don't love yourself!" I was startled at the thought, which seemed more like a voice. *Yes, I do. I take care of myself. I work out, I eat right, I upkeep my hair, nails, and skin. I buy myself the finest clothes. I do all these things to attract Calvin and he still . . . .* I stopped in my thoughts. *For Calvin?* Well, everybody has to have something or someone to give them an incentive to be a better person, and Calvin was mine. Plus, even before Calvin came into my life I pampered myself so that I could attract the right man. And then another thought popped into my mind (another voice). "You're too nice, Sucker. You're a weakling." *Hey, hold up, thoughts. You can't bombard my mind like this.* Isn't "nice" what Love is all about? I just read "Love is kind" in the Bible and I felt I was all those things – except not boiled over with jealousy. I was green with envy because someone, *some female, I'm sure*, was getting the attention from Calvin that I so yearned for. I was jealous because Calvin's NFL popularity had taken him to heights that made him unavailable for me. *I'm jealous as hell.*

I glanced back at the chapter on love in the Bible. I skipped to verse 8 – "Love never fails." I read it again and again and then I closed the Bible and sunk in my bed covers. *So, why is love failing me?* I closed my eyes tightly, and prayed out loud, "God, why is love failing me? Please show me." At that moment, a more soothing thought entered my mind – Diego Jones. I thought about how cordial he was and how he had invited me over last night. I thought about how our gazes locked when we met each other last week. And then I thought about Calvin Kendall Moore. *I wished I had not lost our baby.* I had been back on the pill, *but maybe I should get off again . . . by mistake.* The oldest trick in the book seemed to still be working for many. Calvin had to know that pregnancy was a big possibility since he refused to use protection. *He really does want me to have his baby. I was supposed to be having his child, and not Cristi Perez.* And then a horrible thought came to my mind. "He is with her and they are making another baby right now." I sat up straight in my bed. "Noooo!" I cried. Eventually I fell asleep.

The phone rang a few hours later, startling me. *Oh, please be Calvin.* I picked up the phone after the second ring- not even seeing whose name came up on my caller ID.

"Hello?" I answered anxiously.

"Merry Christmas, girl!" Tacara shrieked. "Are you still asleep?"

I sank back in my bed, feeling disappointed. I looked at the clock, realizing I had slept longer than I thought. It was 10:30 am.

"Yeah, I stayed out late last night. Merry Christmas," I said dryly.

"Is CK there with you?"

"No. Why?"

"Oh, I just asked. What do y'all have up for today?"

"I don't know yet," I said, searching for words. "Calvin's mom got sick and I thought you were him calling. He had to take her to the emergency room last night." I closed my eyes and cringed. I had lied once again, but how could I tell Tacara that Calvin had stood me up – again. Sometimes lying is so much easier.

"So, is she gonna be all right? What's wrong with her?" Tacara probed.

"Oh, I don't know. He said something about her having stomach pains. Where are you – at Steve's?"

"Yeah. Guess what he got me for Christmas?" Tacara said gleefully.

"Whaat?" I murmered.

"A 328 convertible BMW, baby!" Tacara said with laughter.

"A BMW?"

"Yes, girl, I was so surprised. When I opened the gift he gave me this morning it was this BMW key on a BMW key chain. So, I'm thinking that the key was to his car, right... and that what he had for me was inside his car or something. I was clueless. So, I said, 'Baby, is my gift in your car or what?' And he told me to go look in the garage!" Tacara exclaimed excitedly. I wanted her to hurry and finish her story. "So, I went out to the garage, and girl, I almost fell out when I saw that red convertible bimmer with a big bow on the front with Merry Christmas Tacara on it. I just about fainted!"

"So, you didn't have no kinda clue at all?" I said suspiciously and unexcited. I was tired of these damn surprises, where everybody else was getting what they wanted, except me.

"Shayla, I didn't have a clue. We went out to dinner last night and then to a movie, and when we got back I guess it was about . . . ahh . . . what time did we get back last night, baby?"

"Around 11 or so," I heard Steve say, sounding like he was sitting right beside her.

"Yeah, about 11:30," Tacara continued. "And I was dead tired, so I went to bed and I remember him telling me that his brother was coming by to pick up the toys he had left over here for his kids – and I didn't think anything of it. But girl, they had it all planned out. Rick came to pick up the toys all right, but he brought the car too! Steve had let him keep it over at his house for a couple of days."

"So, is it brand new?" I asked, feeling jealous pangs.

"Yep . . . brand spanking new. What are you doing? I was gonna come by and pick you up for a ride in it and you can have brunch with us too."

"I haven't even gotten up yet," I said quietly. "And plus. I need to call to see how Calvin's mom is. When do you go back out on a trip?"

"Girl, I have to leave at 5pm. It's a 3-day trip. I am so tired of working on holidays," Tacara said somberly.

"I thought you were thinking about quitting," I said.

"I am, but I'm trying to hang in here until a couple of weeks before the wedding. After that, I'm walking," she said. "I can't deal with flying too much longer, although Steve is trying to convince me to stay on to keep the flying perks. But I try to explain to him that I have to quit if he wants me home with him every night, so he wants me home every night."

"Yeah," I muttered. *Rub it in why don't you!* "So, what do you plan to do after you quit?"

"Have some babies, girl!" Tacara laughed. "I'm 27 and I want to have two kids before I'm thirty. I don't want to be an old mom," Tacara giggled. "Stop, Steve."

I then heard the two of them laugh fervently.

"What's up?" I asked, highly agitated.

"He's putting the pillow up my shirt. Steve, stop, boy!" Tacara said.

"Well, I'm gonna let y'all go," I said. "I need to get up out of this bed."

"Yes, you do, Shayla!"

Just when Tacara said that, the other line beeped. It was Connie.

"Hold on a sec," I said to Tacara. "Hello?" I answered.

"What are you doing, Shaaaay?" Connie said with a drawl.

"I'm on the other line," I said. "I'll call you right back."

"Well, Merry Christmas!" Connie said in a strained tone.

"Yeah, Merry Christmas," I repeated in a monotone voice. "Mommy let me call you back after I get off the phone."

"Well, you don't have to sound so happy to hear from me!" she said sounding offended.

From Connie's tone I realized that I really did have an attitude, and I tried to adjust it quickly.

"I'm sorry, Mommy. I'm just getting up though and this is Tacara on the other line telling me about this new BMW Steve bought her for Christmas."

"My, my," Connie responded. "That's nice."

"Yeah, so I'll call you back, okay," I said quickly.

"Okay."

"Bye," I said and clicked back over to the other line. "Hello, Tacara?"

"Yeah?"

"Listen. I need to check on Calvin's mom. Are you coming over here before you go out on your trip?"

"Well, I hadn't planned to unless you were gonna go for a ride with me and to have brunch, but . . ."

"If I don't see it before you leave, I'm sure I'll have many chances to ride in it when you get back," I interrupted. "So, I'll just see you when you get back. I need to go to the bathroom. I can't hold it any longer."

"Okay. Well, call me and leave me a message about CK's mom. I'll be back the day after tomorrow and I'm off New Year's Eve, so maybe we can all do something."

"Okay, bye and Merry Christmas," I said wistfully.

"Bye, Shayla. Have a great Christmas, okay?" Tacara said in an almost sorrowful tone.

For the next half hour I dialed Calvin's cell phone and his home number, but both voice mails were full, so I couldn't leave a message. *How odd.* After Connie called again, detecting that something was bothering me, I told her that I had terrible stomach cramps and could not move from the bed. And that is where I lie crying for the remainder of the day – wrapped in my sheets, unable to eat, unable to comprehend why Calvin had disappointed me on Christmas.

Around 4pm Sydney called inviting me to have dinner at her place, but I told her the same lie I had told my mom. "My cramps are real bad today, so I'm just gonna stay in bed until I feel better." Interestingly, Sydney did not pry or say that she hoped I felt better. She didn't ask about Calvin's mom or anything. She just responded, "Well, if you change your mind, we are serving dinner at 6, and going to see a movie at 8."

"Okay," I said, wondering why Sydney chose not to even acknowledge my predicament. But it was starting to dawn on me that maybe my family really didn't believe me at all. Lately they were behaving very strange in regards to Calvin. They rarely commented about anything I'd say about him, and seemed to take a very non-emotional and detached stance. Maybe they had jointly decided to ease up on me about leaving Calvin. But the more I lie in bed crying, I wondered if I should, indeed, release Calvin and start a new life. The hurt I was feeling was emotionally draining. I felt like my life was going down hill.

After reading 1 Corinthians again, I tried Calvin's number once more. Afterward, I vowed to never dial his number again. *If he cared anything about me, like he said he does, he would be with me on Christmas.* I grabbed the remote control and turned the television on – becoming more angered as I thought about Calvin. I flipped through the channels, but decided to turn to ESPN to see what was going on in the sports world. When I saw Calvin's image my heart beat quickened and I felt a tightness in my chest as though I was having a heart attack. "Oh my God," I gasped as I fumbled with the remote control – trying to turn up the volume. Calvin's face was plastered on the television screen. All I could hear from the report was "arrested" and "DUI." As soon as I turned up the volume loud enough to hear the sports announcer, he switched to another news story. I put my hand to my heart feeling thuds pound against my chest. I picked up the phone and frantically dialed Tommy's number. I figured the first person Calvin would call would probably be his agent, who he said always had his back. Any time anything would go wrong, Calvin would always seek Tommy's advice before anyone else's. Even when he'd experience personal upsets, Tommy seemed to be the one he'd confide in.

"Hello -o?" A woman answered.

"Hello," I quivered. "Hello?" I realized that my call had been intercepted by whomever had called me.

"Shay-la," Sydney said. "What is going on with CK?"

"I don't know. I'm trying to find out," I said hurriedly. "Did you see the report on ESPN?"

"No. I saw it on the local news. There was a news flash that Calvin had been arrested in the early hours of the morning for reckless driving and driving under the influence," Sydney said.

"What else did they say?" I said feeling my heart pound even faster.

"Well, that was about it. They said they'd report more on it at 6," Sydney said with a pause. "Is he okay?"

"Don't ask me any questions because I don't know," I snapped. "I'm trying to find out what's going on now," I said in a calmer voice. "So, let me call you right back."

"Okay."

"Bye," I said hanging up. Before I could dial out, the phone rang. "Dammit!" I cursed. It was Tacara.

"Yes!" I barked into the phone, unable to calm myself.

"Shayla!" Tacara said breathlessly.

"Yeah?"

"On my way to work I heard on the radio that CK had been arrested last night!"

"What did they say he was arrested for?" I asked, hoping that Tacara had more information and feeling more comfortable talking with her than Sydney.

"They said something about possession of marijuana. You haven't talked to him?"

"What?" I said. "Possession of marijuana? I thought it was DUI or reckless driving?"

"Well, they said that too," Tacara sighed. "I think they said he was out on bail, so I guess you haven't talked to him?"

"No, I haven't." I admitted. "I just can't believe this shit. I knew something was wrong. I knew he wouldn't just stand me up last night for no reason."

"Well, I think they said that he was arrested at three in the morning. So, you weren't the woman in the car with him?" Tacara said softly and hesitantly.

"What woman?" I asked feeling a sharp pain in my abdomen.

"Oh, well it must have been his mother. "You said he had to take her to the hospital?" Tacara said in a questioning tone.

For the next few seconds I seemed to drift off in my thoughts. *Woman in the car* was all I could think about. *Who was the woman in Calvin's car? Was she also arrested? What were they doing out at 3am?* The questions bombarded my mind as if there was someone else actually right there – asking me to fill in the blanks.

"Shayla, are you still there?" Tacara asked.

"Oh, yeah. I'm here," I said. "I just need to reach Calvin."

"Well, go ahead and try to reach him and I'll call you when I get on my layover – later tonight."

"Okay," I said, feeling like a darker cloud had been cast over me.

"Bye, Shayla. Love you," Tacara said.

"Bye, Love you too," I said and hung up.

I tried not to jump to any conclusions, but I felt embarrassed that the news reports were reporting that Calvin had been arrested and on top of that, a woman was in the car with him. How was I going to explain this one to my family – to anyone, for that matter?

I dialed Tommy's number, feeling relieved when a man's voice answered.

"Hello?" the man said anxiously.

"Tommy?"

"No. Tommy's not here."

"Do you know where I can reach him? I really need to speak with him," I pleaded.

"Who is this?" the man asked.

"This is Calvin Moore's girlfriend. I know that he's been arrested and…"

"Oh, hi Cristi. This is Michael. Are you okay?"

Feeling as if someone had ripped my heart out, I was speechless. I wondered how much more I would have to take on Christmas Day.

"This is not Cristi," I finally whispered. "This is Shayla Lucas."

"Oh, that's right, Shayla. I meant Shayla. How are you? This is Tommy's brother, Michael."

The damage had been done. He had called me Cristi and no matter how quick he tried to smooth things out, he had revealed to me what I most feared – that Cristi Perez not only had Calvin's baby, but she was considered his girlfriend, his significant other – and not me. I felt foolish.

"I've been trying to reach Calvin and I figured Tommy was somewhere with him," I said feeling even more foolish. "I really don't know what's going on."

"Hold on. Tommy just came in," Michael said.

He must have put the phone on mute, because there was a silence that followed. I began to feel more frantic as I waited more than five minutes for Tommy to come to the phone. I flipped though the channels again. Just when Tommy said hello a report came on Channel 5 about Calvin's arrest. I heard Tommy say hello a few times, but I was so into the news report that I couldn't respond to Tommy. The reporter said: "Atlanta Falcons wide-receiver and Super Bowl MVP Calvin Moore spent Christmas Eve in jail after being arrested for reckless driving, DUI, and the possession of marijuana. Police say that Moore was driving 100 miles in a 60 mile per hour zone and when they stopped him, found him highly intoxicated. Police also found two bags of marijuana under Moore's seat. Moore, who was released this morning on $50,000 bail, says that he was just trying to make it home before Santa Claus arrived down his chimney," the reporter chuckled. "We'll have more on this story at the top of the hour."

There was a picture of Calvin in his football uniform on the side of the screen, but I didn't hear the reporter mention anything about a female being in the car. *Maybe Tacara had her information wrong.*

"Hello?!" Tommy said again into the phone.

"Tommy. Oh, I'm sorry. I was just listening to this news report about Calvin. This is Shayla. Where is he? I've been trying to call him all day!" I said trembling.

"Hi, Shayla. Everything is fine. Calvin is at home, but there is an army of news reporters outside his subdivision and everybody is calling him, so he had to shut down the phones. Those damn reporters act like he has committed a murder or something." Tommy sounded rather calm. "Are you okay, dear? You haven't gotten any calls from reporters, have you?"

"Tommy, I'm fine and nobody has called me – not even Calvin," I said trying not to break down. "I had to find out about this through ESPN!"

"Yeah, well Calvin didn't even call his mother, so don't feel bad. I bailed him out this morning, and he's just been trying to get some rest – which is hard to do with those nosy ass reporters and photographers hounding him. But I'm sure he'll call you soon."

"So, who was the woman in the car with him?" I asked, feeling that I had to know the whole story or I'd explode.

"Now, now, Shayla. Don't jump to any conclusions. I'm sure that CK will explain it all to you when he is more coherent."

"So, there was a woman in the car with him? Don't lie for him, Tommy."

"Shayla, I'm not lying for Calvin, but even if I did tell you the brutal truth, what difference would it make? You'd still be right there," Tommy shot back with a sound of sarcasm in his voice.

"What do you mean?" I queried, feeling surprised that Tommy had made such a statement. He always seemed so supportive of Calvin and me, and had even told me to hang in there when I complained to him once about Calvin's lack of attention towards me.

"I'm sure Calvin will be calling you soon, Shayla. Just relax. He's got to deal with this charge now, and we can't let his endorsements be affected by this," he said like he was scolding me. "As a matter of fact, I need to make a few calls now. When I talk to CK I'll tell him to call you."

"Okay," I said softly.

At the top of the hour, when the evening news came on, I sat in front of the television feeling fueled by anger, yet confusion. If Calvin had indeed been arrested at 3 am, that still did not explain why he had not shown up for the Christmas Eve gathering I had invited him to at Sydney's. I wondered what on earth he had been doing, and most of all, *who was the woman in his car?*

The news about Calvin was the second story the newscaster reported. She said the same thing I had heard earlier – that he had been driving under the influence and taken in for having marijuana in his Lamborgini, but this time there was video footage that went along with the report. The video showed Calvin being handcuffed and entering the back of a police car. The reporter then continued her report: "Moore, who could also face charges for endangering the life of another, was accompanied by a female companion whose identity remains unknown at this time. The woman insisted or not being videotaped and covered her face with a scarf throughout police questioning. She was found innocent of any wrongdoing and was let go after Moore's arrest. In the meantime, Moore was released this morning on $50,000 bail."

The video footage then showed Calvin leaving jail with Tommy and two other men by his side. One of the men I recognized as Calvin's attorney, Scott Wright, but the other, I didn't recognize. There were hordes of photographers and news reporters all around Calvin. He looked exhausted and embarrassed. When reporters shot questions at him he hung his head low and didn't say a word, which was very unlike Calvin. I speculated that he had been advised to keep quiet.

I bawled in disgust. I then took at hot shower and tried to get the water as hot as I could without scalding myself. I felt like dirt was all over me. I scrubbed my body hard with the hand towel, feeling as though I was so filthy, that it would take at least a half hour to get rid of all the uncleanliness. "Please, cleanse me, God," I cried. After being in the shower for more than thirty minutes I wrapped myself in a towel. I actually felt like a new person. The scar on my face even seemed a little less obvious, as I examined it in the mirror. A certain peace came over me that I could not explain. In my strange metamorphic experience, I was guided to light the Christmas tree – along with a few candles in the living room.

As I sat in front of the bright tree, I imagined myself free. Free from all the pain I had been through, free from worry. Free from my addiction to a man who was not good for my soul. I closed my eyes – accepting that my relationship with Calvin was not healthy. I was so in love with Calvin that I had let having him, possessing him, become my addiction – but over and over, his love had eluded me. *I have got to let go and let God.*

After praying to God to the best of my ability to cleanse me and help me to let go of Calvin, I put on a velour Juicy Couture sweat suit. It was winter green and made me feel good. I made up my face as if I were going out to a festive party – using more eye makeup than my usual daytime makeup. I tried to tone down the bags underneath my eyes with powder. I combed my hair up and pulled it to the side, letting the curls fall over my scar. I then put on my Christmas ornament earrings. "I am free, indeed," I said softly to myself in the mirror after putting on my lip gloss.

The phone rang and rang, but I had no desire to answer when I saw Calvin's name come across the phone screen. "Kiss my ass!" I said out loud, refusing to answer the phone. After 15 minutes, Calvin still continued to call. *What does he have to say?* I decided to pick up the phone out of frustration.

"Yes!?" I shouted.

"Yo! Why didn't you answer the phone," Calvin said. "What were you doing?"

The nerve! "Calvin, I've been worried sick about you. Is everything okay?" I asked, feeling indifferent.

"Yeah, everything is aight. At least it will be," he said calmly. I was waiting on Calvin to say more, but he didn't.

"So, what happened last night, Calvin?" I asked trying to exude the same calmness in my tone that Calvin had in his, but finding it difficult. "I heard about you being arrested on ESPN just a couple of hours ago. What happened?"

"That MF Dante' got me drunk last night before I could get to you, and then that drunk ass and his boys pulled me out to Magic City," Calvin explained.

"Magic City?" I questioned, my calmness leaving. "The strip club? So, that's where you were?"

"Yeah, Dante is dating this girl who dances there, and his ass got so messed up, that I had to take her home," Calvin said. "Never shoulda agreed to it," he added.

If there was such a thing as a bad vibe, I was surely feeling one now. I felt that Calvin was straight out lying about Dante's girlfriend. Red flags were everywhere in my mind.

"So, was the unidentified woman in the car with you the woman who dances at Magic City?" I asked, feeling humiliated.

"She is Dante's girl, Regina, and I was just trying to do that ass hole uncle of mine a favor by taking her home when I should not have been driving myself," Calvin said, still in a calm tone.

"Oh, the Good Samaritan, CK Moore. You are such a loser!" I said in disgust.

"What?" Calvin said. "I ain't no damn loser. Shii'it, all I do is win."

"Please," I said, trying not to cry again. "No, you are a loser, Calvin. You're a liar and a loser!"

"You know what, Shay . . . I thought you really believed in me. I didn't even have to call you and . . ."

"You didn't have to call me?" I lamented. "Calvin you stood me up to go to Magic City and then got arrested with a stripper in your car! How do you think that makes me feel?"

"You know what? I feel a dial tone coming on. I don't have time for this shit!" Calvin said.

"No, Calvin, I know you don't have time for this shit, as you have proved over and over again. But you have time to be out in the streets with drunks, strippers and hoes. I am so tired of you humiliating me and dissing me. And you know what, Calvin?"

There was a long pause and then Calvin answered, "What?"

"I feel a dial tone coming on!" I said and hung up. I cried in anguish, but this time my cry was different. I had never talked to Calvin with such force before, except for the time he tried to shove me out of his house. But never had I felt such power – such anger. I didn't even care if Calvin called me back or not.

When the phone started to ring again, after only a couple of minutes, I knew it was Calvin, so I didn't bother to look at the phone. It was unlike me to ignore him, but I wasn't going to pick up the phone if it killed me. I decided to listen to his message a few minutes later.

"Shayla, I love you. Why are you trippin when I need you? I don't understand why you're doing me like this. Why are you turning your back on me now – of all times? I need you. Call me back."

It was actually kind of satisfying hearing Calvin's pleas for me. I sensed a desperation in his voice, like I had never heard before. But I wasn't about to call him back. Whatever it was inside me, giving me strength, I don't know, but I felt no temptation whatsoever and I wasn't moved by his words of love either.

Since my eye make up had been ruined by my tears, I walked in the bathroom and patted my eyes with a Kleenex. I pulled out Kleenex after Kleenex, wiping the tears as they flowed. Deep inside, I knew that Calvin was with the woman from Magic City by his own choice. I had already heard through several sources that Calvin frequented strip clubs. Calvin had admitted to going "once every blue moon" when I questioned him about it. He told me that all men go to strip clubs from time to time and he also said that many men take their women with them. I found the thought of going to see another woman shake her naked ass in front of my man disgusting and demeaning.

The phone rang again and startled me a bit. Again, I let it ring until my answering service picked up. When I listened to the message, Calvin sounded angry.

"Shayla, if you don't talk to me right now this relationship is over! I mean it, cause I don't have time for this shit. You claim you love me, and I love you, baby, so please call me back. If you don't call me back in five minutes, it's over between us. I'm serious. I got to keep it moving. I got a lot to deal with and I don't need a fair-weathered woman in my life whose just gonna be in it for the good times and gifts. So, if you don't call me within five minutes, don't call me again! It's over."

I trembled, but I didn't let his words move me. I still felt that same peace I had felt when I asked God to set me free. It didn't really bother me that Calvin was threatening to be done with me. I washed my face and started over with my makeup – toning it down a little and not using any eyeliner this time. This wasn't the time to be highlighting my eyes. I also pulled my hair back down. I wasn't quite ready to pull it up yet, being that the scar was still quite visible.

Calvin called a couple of more times, but he did not leave a message. I managed to gain my composure enough and call Sydney's house to let her know that I was coming over. I'm sure she was surprised when she asked me about Calvin and I responded, "I don't want to talk about him right now." She went silent on me for a few seconds. She then said, "Everything will be okay."

When I arrived at Sydney's house everyone stared at me with suspicious eyes. I knew that my crying had caused my eyes to be puffy, but I wasn't crying anymore and I wanted to forget the pain I had experienced over the last 24 hours. I managed to eat a little and even laugh at my young twin cousins, Tad and Tia, who were showing everyone how to Dougie, a dance I wasn't familiar with, although I had heard the "Teach Me How To Dougie" tune on the radio. Although I rarely got to see the twins, when I did see them I always got a kick out of them because they were such vibrant teenagers. Tad looked a lot like his father, Martin, tall and striking. At 14 years old I was sure he was getting lots of attention from the girls at school. Tia was pretty and shapely for her age. Her eyes slanted like Sydney and mine and her hair was thick and long too. It was interesting seeing Tad and Tia dance with Martin's 21-year-old girlfriend. She was more their age than Martin's and knew how to Dougie too. I wondered how she felt dating a man old enough to be her father. She seemed comfortable with it though.

Instead of gong to see a movie, we just sat around and talked, danced and laughed. I temporarily forgot about my pain. But I started to feel sad again as it grew later in the night. When I insisted on turning on the 11 oclock news a silence fell over the room. The second story was about Calvin. I inhaled as the reporter told the same story. But this time, she added something new. "Channel 2 learned that the woman companion riding with Calvin Moore is a stripper at a popular Atlanta night spot. She was questioned by police at the time of Moore's arrest, but released. Charges of endangering the life of another are pending."

My heart sank. Although Calvin had already told me that the woman in the car was a stripper, hearing it on the news made me feel like a bolt of lightning had struck me twice. There was no explaining I could do. And as hard as I tried to keep my cool, tears started to fall again, which caused everyone to glare at me in concern. Connie sat beside me and embraced me.

"Shay, baby, it's okay. It's okay," she said, rubbing my hair.

The room became so quiet that the sound of my controlled cry was all that was heard. I wasn't sure who it was, but someone handed me a box of Kleenex. Nobody said a word, except for Connie, who encouraged me to "Go ahead and cry."

I finally managed to stop crying. As if the news report or my tears never happened, everyone started talking again and telling lame jokes. Before I knew it, I was laughing at some of the jokes. I felt embraced by a love that calmed me – the love of my family and the love of God. My family had clearly chosen not to judge me at my most vulnerable moment. And by that, I was soothed.

Chapter Nine

Ahhh Sookie Sookie, Now!

"10, 9, 8, 7, 6, 5, 4, 3, 2, 1 . . . Happy New Year!" I shouted to the top of my lungs and raised my champagne glass high, as I watched the Times Square crowd in New York go wild. I couldn't believe that I was actually celebrating New Year's Eve alone – watching Dick Clark's New Year's Rock & Eve hosted by Ryan Seacrest. I had worked all day long at Saks and had hurried home after work to take down my Christmas tree and holiday decoration before the New Year rolled in. Connie had always stressed the importance of taking down Christmas decoration before the New Year as a way of releasing the old and bringing in the new. Her mother, Granny Tula, had brainwashed her to believe that if you left your Christmas tree up into the New Year, you'd have the same problems from the previous year. Call me superstitious, but I definitely wanted to rid myself of all of the calamities I had experienced in 2011. I was ready for a fresh start.

I had made it through the week by going home with Connie to Macon for four days after Christmas. Although I felt as though I was running away from my problems, I also knew that running away was what I needed to do for my sanity. I had contemplated leaving Atlanta without letting a soul know where I was, but I ended up leaving an outgoing message on my home voice mail, informing callers that I had gone to Macon for a few days and would return on December 30th. Although I knew that I didn't have to be accountable about my whereabouts, in a sense I felt that disappearing would be something Calvin would do, and I didn't want to be like him. He had left two messages on my cell phone the day after Christmas and one on my home number, telling me that he loved me and needed me. He said he wanted to prove to me how much her cared. I was not quite sure what he meant by proving how much he cared, but neither was I tempted to find out. I realized that Calvin was causing me too much inner pain, and I wondered if there was something wrong with me for allowing such treatment. Deep down, I felt sorry for Calvin though. It was like he was a lost child who had been given an entire toy store, but he didn't know what to do with all the toys since there were so many. He'd play with one toy for a while and then he'd get bored and end up going from toy to toy, never really being satisfied. In a way I felt like I was one of Calvin's toys. But now, I was getting tired of being toyed with. *I deserve better treatment and respect from a man.*

While sitting on my sofa, sipping my Moët & Chandon champagne, I wondered how I could help Calvin realize that he had a problem. I figured he would be calling again, although I had been home for two days now and hadn't gotten another message from him. The news about his arrest seemed to have intensified. He had pleaded guilty to the charges against him and was to be sentenced on January 10th. In the meantime, the NFL had suspended him for two games without pay and fined him an additional $20,000. "The Calvin Moore Arrest" was the main story news reporters highlighted – especially all the sports channels. Being that Calvin was the Atlanta Falcon's hottest commodity, for the league to slap him with a two-game suspension at playoff time was a real big deal. Fortunately, the news about the lady in the car with him, the stripper, had died down, although the gossip sites went wild – saying that he had gotten her pregnant. I blocked that out of my mind though. The charge of endangering the life of another was dropped, so Calvin was faced with charges of DUI, reckless driving and possession of marijuana. One of Calvin's sponsors, Drug Free America Foundation, had dropped him two days later, but amazingly, none of his other six sponsors had pulled the plug . . . . *at least not as of yet.*

I wondered what Calvin was doing on New Year's Eve. Since the week had obviously been a bad one for him, I assumed that he would be laying low and trying not to be in the public eye. *Here I am, already consumed with thoughts of Calvin during the first few minutes of 2012. Well, I can't just forget him that easily.* And then the phone rang and I dropped my champagne glass reaching for the phone. My blurred vision prevented me from seeing the name on the caller ID.

"Happy New Year!" I said, feeling quite tipsy.

"Please make mine happy." It was Calvin. As much as I was still upset with him for making a fool of himself and embarrassing me, I felt a warm feeling and I knew that I couldn't avoid talking to him this time.

"Calvin?" I said softly, trying to pretend that I didn't quite catch his voice.

"Baby, I just want to prove to you how much I love you," Calvin said in a sexy tone. "Shayla, I miss you. Why have you left me hanging like this, baby?"

I didn't know what to say. My heart was racing like the many times before when Calvin was in his seductive mode. But I knew all too well that a fast-beating heart could lead me back in the throes of passion and then back in the throes of heartache. *This time has to be different. I can not get caught up in him emotionally and physically. I have got to do this for my own sake.*

"Shayla?" Calvin said.

"Yeah, I'm here." I said unemotionally.

"I'm on my way to get you."

"What?" I asked, feeling like I had already lost the battle to stay strong.

"I need to talk to you, baby, in person. I'm on my way to get you."

"Coming to get me for what?" I asked, feeling confused, but curious.

"Just be ready . . . and pack your bags for a couple of days," Calvin said. "Warm weather stuff."

"Calvin, I can't go anywhere. I have to work the day after tomorrow, and . . ."

"Shayla, just be ready. I'll be there in an hour. Just be ready," Calvin said softly, but sternly.

"Calvin, I can't. I . . ."

"Shayla, be ready," he said again, solidly. "I have something I want to show you. Now, just trust me on this and stop being stubborn."

"Calvin, I'm so scared. I just . . ."

"Shay, there is nothing for you to be scared of. I love you, and finally I'm ready to prove it to you," Calvin said.

"What do you mean you're ready to prove it?" I asked, wondering what he had up his sleeve.

"Shayla, do you love me?"

"Yeah."

"Do you believe God put us together for a reason?"

"Well, yeah, I did. But . . ."

"But nothing. Just be ready in an hour because I need to see you. I really need to see you," Calvin said desperately.

I was speechless again, but someone was calling on the other line. The number showed up as private. I clicked over without responding to Calvin's plea.

"Hello? Happy New Year" I said softly.

"Happy New Year! Is this Shayla?" A distinguished male's voice came over the line.

"Yes, it is," I said, curious about who was calling.

"Hi. This is Diego Jones . . . Claire Jones' son."

"Oh, hiii," I sang as I felt a slight hot flash.

"I know that you are surprised to be hearing from me. My mother was so kind to give me your number. I just wanted to wish you a Happy New Year," he said.

"Why, thanks!" I quipped, feeling a little nervous.

"And I was also calling to see if we could get together tomorrow for lunch or dinner," Diego said smoothly.

"Oh really? Tomorrow?" I asked, not knowing how to respond.

There was then a click on the other line, indicating that Calvin had hung up.

"Oh, did I interrupt you? I'm sorry. I didn't ask if you were busy," Diego said.

"Oh, no. I'm not busy."

"Well, I just thought it would be nice to see you again before I head back to London."

"When are you leaving?"

"The day after tomorrow. And I apologize for asking you out at the last minute, but I called a few days ago and got the message that you were out of town . . . in Macon for a few days?"

"Yeah, I went back home with my mom. Sorry I missed your mom's brunch."

"Oh, that's okay. Did you have a nice time?"

"Well, it was more relaxing than anything else."

There was a long pause and then he spoke.

"So, what do you say? I was thinking that we could go out to dinner tomorrow evening around 6, just to chat and get to know each other a little better."

"Oh, okay. That sounds nice," I mumbled half-heartedly.

"Are you sure?" Diego asked.

"Yeah, I'm sure," I hesitated. "I just can't believe it's a New Year."

Diego chuckled. I giggled too, feeling that he somehow understood my discomfort, but flattery.

"Well, I can pick you up tomorrow around 5:30 if that's okay with you?" Diego said cautiously.

"That's fine with me," I said quickly. "I just need to give you the directions to my place."

"I'm ready," Diego said. "I can put it in my GPS."

"I live near Phipps Plaza, where you first met me," I sighed and gave him my address slowly.

"Got it!" Diego said.

"There's a security gate, but you can just ring me under my last name, and I'll let you in."

"Well, that sounds simple enough."

"It's pretty simple."

"So, I'll see you tomorrow," Diego said. "Apartment 610 at 5:30."

"I'm looking forward to it," I said trying to sound relaxed but feeling like I was going to pee on myself.

"Bye, Shayla."

"Bye."

After hanging up the phone, I got a tingly feeling that started in my legs. I sat still for a moment, trying to figure out my next move. I felt confused. I knew that I loved Calvin with all my heart and had never so much as thought about going out with another man since we started dating. I was faithful, loyal and had inwardly and outwardly pledged my heart and body to only him, so why had I all of a sudden accepted a date with the debonair Diego Jones? *Oh Shit.* I picked up my champagne glass off the floor and stood to my feet. *I have to do something.* Calvin had hung up while I was talking to Diego. I knew he would be coming over. He had stated so clearly that he was on his way to get me and I knew he hadn't changed his mind just because I had put him on hold.

After putting the champagne glass in the sink and the fourth of a bottle of champagne that was left back in the refrigerator, I stumbled to my bedroom. *What am I gonna put on?* I was definitely more tipsy than I needed to be. I felt disoriented. I pulled out the leopard print cat suit that I had ordered from Victoria Secret's catalog. *This will definitely give Calvin a rush.* But after thinking about all that had happened, I realized that I didn't need to get Calvin all sexually enticed and hungry for me. *I have to say no. Just say no. Damn, I shouldn't have drunk that champagne.* I put the leopard print getup back in the closet and pulled out some black jeans and a soft, red silk blouse that Calvin had bought me last Christmas. Red was his favorite color and it looked good against my almost chocolate skin tone.

My home phone rang. I walked over to the bed stand and saw that it was Connie.

"Yeah, Mom."

"Happy New Year, Shay, baby!" Connie squealed.

"Hey, Mommy. Happy New Year," I said, feeling a tad dizzy. I sat down.

"So, you decided to stay in after all, huh?" Connie asked gleefully.

"Yep. Is church over that quick?"

"Quick?" Connie said. "We were in there since 9 o'clock."

"Oh," I muttered.

"So, are you planning to go over to your sister's for dinner tomorrow and eat some of those collard greens so you can be blessed with money?"

"Actually, no, Mommy," I said. "You and your superstitions!"

"Why not, baby? They are gonna be expecting you."

"Well, I'll just call and tell them that I have a dinner date," I said cockily.

"A dinner date?" Connie repeated. "Not with Calvin Moore, I hope."

"No . . . with this new man named Diego Jones!" I said feeling and little excited saying his name, but still feeling my head spin a bit from all the champagne I had drank. "But Mommy, I've got to talk to you about it later. I've got to take care of something."

There was a long pause before Connie spoke. I think she was expecting me to say something else.

"Mommy, I'll talk to you tomorrow. I love you!" I said in a hyper tone.

"Uh-huh. We will have to talk tomorrow, Ms. Dinner Date!"

I chuckled, but I knew that if I didn't hurry up and get off the phone I wouldn't be dressed appropriately when Calvin arrived. I had on a white, satiny lounge outfit with sheer arms. It made me feel virginal, but I was sure that it would make Calvin feel like having sex. *I have to hurry up and change.*

"Okay, Mommy. Happy New Year!" I said and hung up.

The phone rang again, but I let my voice mail pick up this time. If I kept talking on the phone, I'd never get dressed. It was only Tacara ranting about how Steve had surprised her with a Prada bag with $1,000 in it for a New Year's gift. *Who cares?* I loved Tacara with all my heart, but lately she had been bragging a whole lot.

The doorbell rang at 1:30am. Calvin knew my security code to get past the metal gates and he always rang the doorbell and then knocked in his normal way - 2 knocks, and then a pause followed by four rhythmic knocks. I was nervous as hell walking to the door. I kept thinking that Calvin would convince me to either go with him or have sex with him and I didn't want to do either.

When I opened the door, Calvin jumped towards me and grabbed me before I had a chance to look at him good. He held me tightly, so I lay my head against his chest – feeling his rapid heart beat from underneath his body-fitting sweater. He smelled so good, so clean, and his arms around me made me want to forget all the vows I had made to myself. *But this time I'm going to be strong.* I pulled away from Calvin, gaining my strength back.

"What's wrong?" Calvin asked, closing the door. He was still as handsome as he was the first day I met him. He was more handsome. He was sporting his diamond-studded silver chain with the number 85, his jersey number. He had on a black turtle neck and some blue jeans. Before I could respond to Calvin's question, he grabbed my face with his hands and kissed me passionately. I kissed him back, but I knew that I had to stop his seduction.

After he moved his hand from my face to my buttocks, I pulled away. "Calvin, no," I said. "I don't want to do this."

Calvin looked at me hungrily, but he seemed to want to respect my wishes.

"I didn't come over here to make love to you," he said looking me over. "Although I want to. You look so good," he said softly. He embraced me again, tightly.

I tried to push him away, but I felt myself getting weaker and weaker. Calvin wasn't letting up in his grip.

"I'm so sorry, baby. I love you. I am so sorry," he whispered.

I finally managed to pull away again. "What are you sorry for?" I asked, looking him straight in his eyes. "Why are you sorry?"

"I'm sorry for hurting you," he said boyishly.

I could tell that Calvin really didn't like me putting him on the spot. He seemed uneasy.

"And how did you hurt me?" I said.

Calvin snickered. "Oh, you forgot?" he said. "Good." He looked down at my feet. "Why don't you have your shoes on? C'mon. Let's go get your shoes and your stuff. The limo driver is waiting." Calvin lightly guided my arm and I walked with him into the living room.

"Calvin, I am not going with you," I said softly, but sternly.

"Ahhh, Shayla. C'mon now. Don't mess this up. Don't do this." He turned me around to face him. "Don't you love me?"

"Yes, I do, but . . ."

Before I could finish my sentence Calvin started kissing me again, first on my lips and then on my neck. I was really getting aroused, but I pulled away and stepped back a few feet.

"Calvin, don't make this hard for me. I have made up my mind and I don't want to have sex with you and I'm not going anywhere with you. Whatever you have to say to me you need to say it now," I said.

Calvin looked at me for a few seconds with his "I got her" smirk. I knew him so well.

"And this is not funny, Calvin. I'm tired of you playing with me like I'm a toy. This is no laughing matter," I said.

"Who's laughing?" Calvin asked as he broke into a crooked smile.

"Well, you looked like you wanted to laugh and for some reason you don't take me serious. But I am serious when I say that I'm not having sex with you and I'm not letting you take me off somewhere to confuse me. So, whatever it is that you need to say, you need to say it now," I said quickly and sat down on the sofa.

"You been drinking?" Calvin said, looking at me with a raised brow.

"Just a tad, but I know exactly what I'm saying and what I'm doing. I'm not gonna get with you tonight, Calvin. Things are different now. I'm not gonna give in to you." I started flipping through the channels. I knew I couldn't fall back into the same hole by succumbing to Calvin.

Surprisingly, Calvin stood in front of the television, blocking my view. He looked so good that it hurt, but I knew that it would hurt more if I allowed my emotions to get the best of me.

"Turn off the TV," he said in a strong voice.

"What?" I said looking at Calvin. "I will not."

"Turn off the TV and listen to what I have to say to you," he said gently.

When he moved from in front of the television I clicked it off. He sat down beside me. I held my hands together, feeling unguarded and vulnerable.

"Shay, I feel lost without you in my life and I am sorry for not being there for you," he said.

"Uh-huh, and when did you realize this?" I said folding my arms trying to be tough. *Damn, I feel weak.*

"Baby, look at me," Calvin muttered grabbing my chin and turning my head to face him.

Oh God. I'm losing it. Why did I let him come in? Why did I even answer the phone? I'm losing it. As Calvin stared into my eyes with sad eyes I felt like he needed me. I wanted to embrace him. Tears begin to trickle down my cheeks and Calvin wiped them. I felt sentimental, but this wasn't the time. *No, heart, you will not rule me.* At that moment, I hit Calvin, hard, against his arm with my opened hand.

"You hurt me!" I lamented. I then hit him again and again in his chest, but with my fist this time. Calvin blocked my licks with his arms. I don't know where the streak of violence was coming from, but I stood up and continued to hit Calvin over the head, on the arm – anywhere I could.

"You bastard! You hurt and embarrassed me," I cried. Calvin took many of my blows, but he also dodged a few of them.

Finally, after I grew tired of hitting him, I sat on the opposite end of the sofa and held my head in my hands and sobbed. Calvin was quite for a few minutes. And then I felt his hands taking my hands away from my face. He pressed his opened mouth against mine.

"I love you," he chanted over and over as he kissed me. He then pushed my hair back with both of his hands and stared into my eyes. "Shayla, I love you and I will never hurt you again. I want to marry you."

"What?" I managed to say as I stared back into Calvin's eyes.

"I want to marry you, Shayla. I don't want to live without you," he said emotionally. His eyes were beginning to tear up.

I pushed Calvin away from me. "Now see, you are trippin," I said as my adrenaline flowed more. "You don't know what you are saying."

"Marry me, Shayla," Calvin said clearly and unwaveringly. "I want you to be my wife."

I looked at Calvin suspiciously, but I didn't detect any deceit. I could tell that he had not been drinking or smoking, which was probably due to his suspension. And then it dawned on me . . . *Calvin is just desperate because of his arrest and his suspension. He'll say anything to get me back on his side.* As usual, he was full of talk.

"Calvin, talk is cheap," I said as I exhaled nervously.

When I looked back up, Calvin was on one knee and fumbling through his pocket. *Oh, God. He has a ring. He has a ring.*

"Well, let me show you then," he said as he pulled out the biggest diamond ring I had seen in a while. My head was spinning. I tried to get up and run from him, out of disbelief, but when I stood up, the room seemed to go around in circles. I fell to the floor.

When I awoke from fainting Calvin had me in his arms on the floor. He had a cold towel to my forehead. I looked up at him and he was smiling.

"Well, I took you fainting to mean that you will marry me?" Calvin said softly. He then lifted my hand and kissed it. "And I put a ring on it, dammit. Do you like it?"

I slowly looked at the ring. It was absolutely stunning. I couldn't believe it was actually on my finger. The platinum princess-cut diamond had to be at least six carats. It had baguettes surrounding it. To say that I was in shock was an understatement. Calvin took my hand and kissed it again.

"So, you like it, babe?" he asked with dreamy eyes.

"Cal-vin," I finally said. "It is sooo beautiful."

"So, will you marry me?" he asked as he put his fingers through mine.

"Calvin, I love you. Yes, I will marry you," I said as I guided Calvin's head down so that we could kiss.

After our uninhibited love making, I lay in Calvin's arms as his fiancé and the happiest woman in the world. Although Calvin went to sleep on my bed quickly after our intimacy, I couldn't sleep at all. I was still in a state of shock that Calvin had actually proposed to me and had given me a huge ring. I was anxious for the sun to come up and for Calvin to wake up so that we could discuss our wedding plans. I thought about turning on my computer and changing my status to "engaged" on Facebook, and sharing the news with my thousands of followers on Twitter and Instagram, but then I remembered Diego Jones. *I have to call him at the first opportunity I get to tell him that I am engaged now, and that I won't be able to go out to dinner with him.* My stomach was churning. I really didn't want to hurt Diego's feelings. *And what about Claire? What will she think of me?* The last time I spoke with her was on Christmas Eve. I had not even called to let her know that I wasn't able to make it to her brunch. But she had to have heard about Calvin's arrest on the news. I wondered what she had said to Diego when he asked her for my number. *Or maybe he didn't ask for it at all. Perhaps Claire voluntarily gave it to him. Maybe she sensed my loneliness.*

But I wasn't feeling lonely anymore. I was feeling loved. At the same time, I was scared. *What will people think?* After all of the crying I had done in front of everybody on Christmas Day I knew my family would definitely have their reservations. *But who cares what people think?* After all, I was marrying Calvin Kendall Moore, the man of my dreams. Nothing else really mattered at all. I would be Shayla Moore. *Shayla Moore, Shayla Moore.* "Shayla Moore," I whispered with a smile.

I finally dozed off. Calvin and I slept until 10 the next morning. He had told the limo driver to leave the previous night and asked him to pick him back up at 11am. I cooked Calvin pancakes, eggs and turkey bacon and allowed him to explain everything about his arrest. I listened intently as Calvin told me every detail of what happened that night on his way to taking Regina home from Magic City. He tried his best to convince me that she was, indeed, Dante's friend and he apologized over and over for causing me such pain and embarrassment. When I anxiously asked him about setting a wedding date, his response was "We'll set the date as soon as this court stuff is over with. I promise." He said that he wanted to get his slate clean first. I figured I couldn't ask for anything more, since the charges against him and the publicity had been quite overwhelming. I told him I would stick by him.

Although Calvin wanted me to spend the entire day with him by packing a few things and going back to his house and then by taking a three day vacation to Destin, Florida, I told him that I could not go. I explained to him how I had asked my boss for extra days off when I had the accident and then again right after Christmas and that I really wanted to keep my job. I had sensed that Deidra was really getting concerned about my reliability. She even asked me if I was sure I was able to attend a major fashion conference that all Saks buyers were required to attend on spring fashions. The doubt in her voice kind of put me on alert that I really did need to put more into my job.

After Calvin left I tried calling Diego to cancel plans with him, but Mr. Jones informed me that he was not at home and that he probably wouldn't be talking to Diego until tomorrow. I told Mr. Jones that Diego and I had made plans for the evening, but that an emergency had come up and that I would not be able to see him before he left going back to London. There was a long pause before Mr. Jones said anything and then he said, "Well, the best laid plans sometimes go awry." I truly didn't know what to come back with after that. I wondered what he was trying to say. *Is he planning on finding Diego and telling him that I can't go out with him or is he just planning on being philosophical? Damn, the Joneses.* They always had a way of making you really think about things.

"Well, do you think you'll be able to get in touch with him somehow?" I said, feeling guilty. "Do you have his cell number?"

"No, baby. See, you don't understand." Jones said. "Diego went out of town and he cut his cell phone off because he's leaving the country tomorrow. I'm sure that whatever plans he made with you, he's going to keep them, no matter what."

"So, there is no way you can call him?" I said, perspiring. "I didn't know he was going out of town."

"Well, he made plans with you later, so I'm sure he'll be back by then," Jones said.

I wondered why Mr. Jones was making this so hard? *Surely he can get in touch with Diego if he really wanted to.* I wanted to hang up on him, but I didn't.

"Okay. Well, if you happen to talk to him, please have him call me," I said, feeling very irritated.

"Okay, now. You have a blessed New Year!" he said jovially.

"Bye," I said.

I wracked my brain for 30 minutes after hanging up from Mr. Jones, trying to figure out how I was going to get out of the date with Diego. I had promised Calvin that I would come by his house around 6 to spend the night. I planned to give him his iMac then. And then the most polite and sensible solution came to my mind. *I'll just tell Diego face-to-face, when he gets here. I'll tell him that after we hung up from talking last night, I got engaged!* I looked at the big rock on my finger and smiled.

When Tacara got home she was more than surprised when I showed her my ring. In fact, I thought she was going to faint herself. "Oh, Shayla," she said as she seemed to marvel at the beauty of my ring. "Shayla, when did this happen?"

"Oh, God, Tacara. Can you believe it? I am so happy. You're the first person I've told."

"So, tell me what happened." Tacara said with excitement as she stepped back and grabbed my hand – looking at the ring again. "Oh My God."

"Tacara it happened so fast," I said softly. "Calvin came over last night and the next thing I knew, he was proposing to me. Girl, I literally fainted!"

"No way!"

"Yep. I fainted when he pulled the ring out, although I was a bit tipsy," I chuckled. "When I came back to, the ring was on my finger. I can't believe this. Girl, I am still in shock."

"Shay-laaaa," Tacara gasped, still seeming to be in awe. "This looks like it's eight carats."

"Really? You think it's eight?"

"For sure. Look at this huge diamond in the middle. Hell, that's 6 carats right there. And then you got all these other ones on the side. Got to be more careful!"

Tacara and I both laughed. "It's hard to let it sink in, but I'm engaged, girl. And we're gonna set the date for sometime next year. We are gonna set a date sometime after this trial stuff is over with."

"So, how do you feel about that?" Tacara asked.

"You know, girl, I knew all along that Calvin loved me and maybe it just took something crazy like this arrest for him to realize how much he loved me and how he didn't want to lose me. I'm just glad the boy came to his senses, because I was seriously at the point of throwing in the towel."

"Well, sometimes it does take giving up someone to gain them back," Tacara said philosophically. "I'm glad he woke up too. So, are you getting ready to go out with him? You look nice," Tacara said, looking me over. I had on a winter white turtle neck sweater, a gold skirt and some suede boots. It was 5:00 pm and I was planning to hurry to Calvin's house as soon as Diego left. I had called Calvin and told him to expect me between 6:30 and 7, instead of 6.

"T, girl, you are not gonna believe this," I said.

"What?" she said curiously.

"I have a date with someone else," I said smiling a bit.

"You what?"

"Girl, I met Claire Jones' son – remember me talking about her?"

"Yeah. The lady you met in Puerto Rico who already knew you were pregnant before you knew?"

"Yes. Well, I met her son at the mall recently. He called before Calvin came over and proposed last night inviting me to have dinner with him today. I tried to cancel things this morning, but when I called to tell him his dad told me that he had gone out of town for the day and would not cancel plans with me no matter what. He said Diego had disconnected his phone because he's heading back to Europe tomorrow."

"So, you still have a date with him?" Tacara asked, looking confused.

"Tacara, he'll be over here in less than 30 minutes." I looked at my watch. "And I have to break the news to him in person, that I'm engaged now."

"Shayla! Oh, you're gonna hurt that boy's feelings on the first day of the year!" Tacara said in exasperation.

"I know. I know. It makes no sense. This first day of 2012 has been one of the best days of my life so far, but also the most confusing. Diego is sooo nice and Lord is he fine!"

"Is he now?" Tacara said mischievously. "Well, hey. You're not married *yet*."

I rolled my eyes at Tacara. "Girl, don't go there, okay. Plus, he lives in London. He's going back tomorrow."

"Oh. Well, that settles that," Tacara said smiling.

"It was already settled," I said quickly. "I'm marrying Calvin."

"Miracles do happen!" Tacara said.

"Ta-ca-raa!" I whined.

"I mean, good things do happen. I'm just happy for you."

"Well, I'm happy too."

Diego was ringing my doorbell at 5:30 on the dot. I had it all planned out. I would let him in, and then quickly tell him about my engagement. I would then offer him some wine or Eggnog before he went on his merry way. I had rehearsed how I would break the news to him. I'd say, "Diego, before you get settled, I have to tell you something." I would then proceed to tell him that I had a surprise visit from my boyfriend last night, right after he and I had talked, and that my boyfriend, Calvin Moore, had surprised me by asking me to be his wife and that I had accepted. *It's that simple.* I nervously swung the door open.

The smile on Diego Jones' face was warm and infectious. His light, hypnotic eyes pierced into mine and sent some type of wave up my body. He must have thought I was crazy to be standing there in the doorway just staring at him, but my words froze in my throat. He frowned a little. I still couldn't talk. I knew that Diego was a good looking man, but I obviously had forgotten how good looking, tall, and sexy he was. He also had the deepest dimples. He was wearing a beige mid-length wool coat and some brown corduroy pants. His hair was cut low. He had a bouquet of flowers in his hand. I noticed tulips and daffodils, my favorite flowers.

"Are you okay?" he asked. He seemed truly concerned about my momentary paralysis. I tried to snap out of it.

"Diego," I said softly. "You didn't have to bring me anything." I couldn't believe I was so nervous.

"Oh, it's my pleasure. I thought you might like these for the New Year," he said looking at me. "You look gorgeous. Wow."

After taking the colorful flowers from him and smelling them, I didn't know what to say or do next. "They smell good," I said looking up at Diego, who seemed to be smitten with me. He was still smiling.

"So, are you ready to go or do you need to go get your coat? It's pretty frigid out there."

"Oh, I'm sorry, Diego. Please come in," I said stepping aside. "Excuse me for being so out of it. I just wasn't expecting . . ." I stopped myself. I couldn't tell him that I wasn't expecting him to look so handsome and make my heart beat with intensity. I bit my lip. "Come on in and I'll put these in a vase."

Diego walked slowly behind me. I could feel his presence and I got a whiff the chocolate scent of his cologne.

"You can have a seat and I'll be right back," I said coyly.

I strolled to my bedroom and looked in my bathroom cabinet for the vase that I had stowed there after Calvin had given me roses before. My heart was still in the speed zone. I poured water into the vase and slowly put the flowers inside. I then glanced at my ring. It glowed, even in minimal light. Without thinking about what I was doing, I slowly pulled the perfectly fitted ring off my finger and put it in my jewelry box. *I can't tell Diego that I am engaged right now. I just can't.* I picked the vase of flowers back up and put them on my nightstand. After grabbing my coat, I walked back in the living room. Diego was sitting comfortably on the couch with a look of anticipation and expectancy in his eyes.

"So," I said softly. "What do you have an appetite for?"

Chapter Ten

Oh, What a Day!

The ride to Cheesecake Factory was about a seven minute drive from my apartment, but it seemed to take forever for us to get to the Buckhead restaurant. I tried to remain relaxed and poised as I sat quietly in the Lexus that Diego was driving. He had Anthony Hamilton playing on the stereo. I held my hands together firmly, feeling somewhat uncomfortable to be going out to dinner with someone other than Calvin. And to add to my discomfort, I felt guilty. *How could I say 'yes' to marrying the man of my dreams and then deliberately take off my engagement ring and go out with another man in the same day?* Of course Diego was a good looking, intelligent man, but there was something more about him than met the eye. I felt like I had met him before. I was very drawn to him.

When we got to the restaurant, Diego ordered jambalaya and I ordered a salmon filet entrée.

"I'm not a drinker, but if you'd like some wine or champagne, I'll order some," Diego said.

"Oh, no. I don't drink either," I lied with a nervous smile.

Diego looked irresistible as he sat in the booth right across from me. He had taken off his coat, revealing his wide, toned shoulders. I tried to keep my eyes from meeting his. After all, it was his eyes that seemed to put me in a trance. But I could not avoid looking at Diego directly when he started the conversation up again.

"I'm really glad we're getting this chance to get to know one another a little better before I leave," he said leaning forward, as if he wanted my full attention.

I sipped my tea nervously, feeling a bit lost for words. "I know. So when do you think you'll be back again?"

"Oh, that depends," he said. He shifted back in the seat. "I'd probably be back sooner and more often if I had something to come back for."

Diego's insinuation sent shivers up me. I smiled shyly and took another sip of my tea.

When our entrees finally arrived, Diego said a short grace and we both began to eat very properly and slowly, like we were trying to savor each bite, each moment. Our conversation went from us talking about our favorite foods (we were both seafood lovers), to our favorite hobbies, to where we saw ourselves in ten years. Diego said he would probably return to the U.S. in five years. He said he loved living in London, but that he'd rather "settle down" and "raise kids" in the States.

"So, how many kids do you plan to have?" I asked boldly.

"Well, since I won't be the one having them I'm going to check with Mrs. Jones to see if we can handle four or five."

"Mrs. Jones?" I said, knowing that Diego Jones wasn't already married, but wanting him to clarify himself still.

"Well, Mrs. Jones-to-be, whomever she might be," he said smiling. "I'm surprised you're not married yet."

I felt uncomfortable with the direction the conversation was headed. I picked up my tea again. "I'm just 26," I said nervously. "People are getting married later these days."

"So, have you ever been engaged?" Diego asked quizzically.

My arm shook as I tried to sip more of my tea, but to my own surprise and embarrassment, I spilled the tea onto my chin and sweater. I felt clumsy and unsophisticated, but more than that, I felt trapped by Diego's loaded question. As I reached for a napkin, under my glass of water, the entire glass of water rolled over – spilling on to the table in my direction.

"Uh-oh," Diego said. He tried to help me by wiping the water up with his linen and asking the waitress if we could get a few more linen, but the water had already started to spill into my lap. I quickly scooted out of my seat and stood to my feet, dodging most of it. *What a klutz.* After wiping off my sweater as much as I could with the linens, I told Diego that I'd be right back.

Once I got inside the bathroom I looked myself over and adjusted my sweater a bit so the stain wouldn't show. I looked a frantic mess. *I should have never come out with Diego. I need to get myself out of this date as soon as possible.* I knew I couldn't handle his questions nor could I handle being near him. I was too attracted to him, and it was very obvious that he was more than attracted to me.

"Oh, God. I can't take this," I said under my breath as I put lipstick carefully on my lips. While I was looking in the mirror, someone else came into the bathroom. At first I wasn't going to look up to even acknowledge the woman, but I looked in the mirror and saw a refection of a woman who looked just like Cristi Perez. I continued to stare at her through the mirror, dabbing the corner of my lip with my finger. She glanced at me and continued to walk past me. *It is Cristi Perez!* I noticed that same confident, but willowy walk the day I saw her coming off the elevator with Calvin, almost a year ago. I stood stiff, still looking at her through the mirror – hoping she wouldn't notice me. She had her hair in a ponytail. And then, as if something hit her, she swirled around to look at me before entering the bathroom stall. I looked down and opened my purse to put the lipstick back in it.

"Excuse me," she said.

I pretended as if I didn't hear her. I had experienced enough drama in one day and didn't want a confrontation with Cristi to be the grand finale. I ignored her and walked towards the door.

"Excuse me, Shayla," she said.

I turned around slowly, not knowing how to react. I squinted my eyes, as though I didn't know who she was.

"So, you don't know who I am?" Cristi said, blinking her eyes.

"You look familiar," I said as I stood shuddering. "Should I know you?"

"Oh, come on, Shayla. This is me, Cristi Perez. CK's baby mama," she said confidently as she started walking towards me. "I know I've put on a few pounds from the baby, but I don't look *that* different. Isn't this a coincident for us to be at the same restaurant on New Year's Day? I'm glad I ran into you."

"And why is that?" I asked. A woman came in the bathroom, so I had to move closer to Cristi to let the lady past me.

"Well, first of all I was curious to know if you are still seeing CK, because I'm not," she said.

"Let's just put it like this, I am *engaged* to Calvin, okay," I said arrogantly. "And I really don't need any kind of confrontation with his *baby's mama* because . . ."

"Wait. Hold up. Hold up," Cristi said as she raised her hand to stop me from continuing. "You are what?"

"You heard me right," I said stonily. "Calvin and I are engaged!"

"So, where is your ring?" Cristi asked, looking me over. Her eyes had a hint of laughter. "Show me the ring since you're all engaged, because I just finished talking to him."

I realized that I didn't have the proof with me and that I had left the ring in my jewelry box at home. *How am I supposed to tell Cristi that?* She wouldn't believe me. I also realized that the man waiting on me at the table was not Calvin, but Diego Jones. *What on earth have I gotten myself into?* I searched for words to respond to Cristi.

"You know, for you to be such an attractive woman, you don't have a bit of class," I said and swung the bathroom door open. "I don't have time for this," I stammered and walked away from Cristi.

"You need to wake up and stop fantasizing!" I heard Cristi say as I walked as fast as I could back to the table where Diego was sitting with a puzzled, impatient look on his face.

"Diego," I said feeling like I was almost out of breath. "Diego, we have to go. Can you take me back to my apartment now? Something crazy has happened."

"Now?" Diego questioned. His face tightened, but he still looked poised.

"Diego, I am so sorry," I said. "Where is our waitress?" I looked around for her.

"Is everything okay?" Diego asked. "You look like you just saw a ghost."

"No, everything is not okay. I'm going to find our waitress, and I'll pay for our dinner this time. I have to get back to my place as soon as I can." I grabbed my coat and put it on quickly.

"Well, there's no need for you to find the waitress or to pay for dinner because I've already got it covered," he said as he stood. "I took care of it while you were in the ladies room."

"Oh, good," I said. "Let's go please. I'll explain things to you in the car."

Diego still had a bewildered frown on his face, but he put his coat on hastily. I felt like such a fool, but I didn't want Cristi running back telling Calvin that I was out with another man. And on top of that, I did not have on the ring he had given me. It was obvious that Cristi didn't believe Calvin had given me a ring anyway.

As I walked in front of Diego to the valet area, I could feel someone looking at us. I challenged myself not to look back. When Diego gave the valet guy the ticket, he told us that it would take four or five minutes. I felt frazzled.

"Excuse me, sir, but we can walk to our car. Just tell us where it is," I demanded. Diego looked at me as though I had lost my mind.

"Oh, that's okay, ma'am. We'll bring the car to you," the valet driver said.

"No!" I said with a raised tone. "Just tell us where the car is and we will walk."

The valet driver looked at me curiously and then at Diego.

"She's the boss," Diego replied blandly.

The car was in the back of the restaurant, which put us out of the visibility of those dining inside the restaurant. I sighed as Diego opened the car door for me.

"I'm sorry," I said, feeling a bit unsteady as I got inside the car.

Diego didn't say anything. He just glared at me with wary speculation and closed the door. I was shivering. I had really messed up this time, I figured.

When Diego got inside the car, I was surprised when he looked me squarely in the eyes. "You want to tell me what this is all about or would you rather talk about it later?"

I felt uncomfortable with the stern, but gentle way he was looking at me. It almost seemed like he already knew that I was trying run from someone.

"I'm sorry," I said looking away. "I ran into someone who I didn't want to see."

Diego cranked the car, which made me feel better. I knew I was wrong for rushing him, but I didn't know what else to do.

"I feel so silly, but there was this person in there that I really had to get away from," I said softly.

Diego drove out of the restaurant parking lot and up Peachtree Rd. I didn't speak again until we got to the red light at Piedmont.

"Are you upset with me?" I asked.

Diego looked at me with intense eyes, and just when I thought he was going to say something he leaned over and kissed me. My heart raced as he planted a soft peck on my lips. As if my mouth was waiting for his, I kissed him back - unexpectedly and naturally. My stomach was filled with butterflies as we kissed. *This has to be against the law.* I was truly enjoying Diego's soft, full lips as both our lips parted slightly – and the moistness of our tongues collided. The driver behind us began to blow his horn, as our lips parted.

"Oh, the light changed," Diego said carefully. He made the turn as if nothing happened between us.

I felt like I was melting. *This isn't supposed to be happening.* I was not supposed to be feeling all mushy for a man that was not Calvin Moore. I inhaled and exhaled, as I twiddled my thumbs. And to make me even more flustered, Diego reached over and grabbed my hand, squeezing it gently as he drove in silence.

"I guess you're not upset with me," I managed to say softly, feeling as though I had to say something to break the silence and the intensity of the moment.

Diego gazed at me and smiled. He didn't respond in words, but he squeezed my hand tighter. I didn't quite understand the way I was feeling or the way my body was reacting to Diego Jones. Goose bumps tingled against my skin. I also felt safe to be in his presence. I felt protected and like he understood me, although we barely knew each other.

When we finally arrived at the entrance of my apartment complex Diego let go of my hand to put in my code. I cupped my hands together, hoping that Diego would not reach for my hand again. *I have to tell him I'm engaged. I need to nip this in the bud right now before I allow things to go further.* I tried to reason with myself, but I still felt a strange attraction towards Diego that would not let me break his heart.

Once Diego got to my apartment building, he turned the car off, which made me a little nervous. *Surely he is not expecting me to invite him back in, is he?*

"I'll walk you to your door," he said softly, as though he wanted to make his intentions clear.

Suddenly I didn't want him to leave. I didn't want our date to end. I wanted to talk with Diego more. I needed the warmth and acceptance he was giving me.

"So, what time does your flight leave tomorrow?" I asked, feeling that this could not just be the end of it for us. I even begin to feel a little sad that he had to leave.

"Around five in the morning. And I haven't even packed yet," Diego said.

I started to feel like Diego was trying to end our date. *Perhaps there was something that had clicked in his head warning him about me.* I didn't really know, but he seemed reticent all of a sudden, as if something had changed.

"Well, I really enjoyed going out with you, and maybe when you come back in town we can do it again," I said. I couldn't really read him. *What is he thinking?*

"I would really like that," he said as he leaned closer to me.

Diego didn't have to lean much, because I leaned toward him and placed my lips against his. This action was very uncharacteristic of me, and quite confusing, but I wanted to kiss him again. We kissed each other first with soft pecks and then Diego put his hand at the back of my head and guided me closer, allowing our kisses to grow deeper and more passionate. He was definitely a great kisser, and I felt as though an electrical wave was going through my body. When I turned my head, causing our kiss to be interrupted, Diego kissed my cheek and rubbed my hair gently.

Diego's eyes met mine finally and we looked into each other's eyes like we were both mesmerized. He continued to stroke my head and hair with his strong hand.

"I'll call you from London," he said and placed a soft peck on my lips.

I didn't know how to respond. *Am I supposed to ask for his number? Am I supposed to say 'okay' and kiss him again? Am I supposed to tell him about my engagement?* My emotions stirred as I chose not to say anything – but to just stare into Diego's eyes.

I forced myself to gently pull away from him, allowing distance. I didn't want him to get the wrong impression of me by thinking that I wanted him in a lustful way or had fallen for him on such a short date. I convinced myself again, to cut my emotions off and not allow Diego to see or taste anymore of my vulnerability.

"Well, I better get upstairs. But thanks again for everything, Diego. I apologize again for the scene at the restaurant," I said in a professional tone.

"That's okay," Diego said with a chuckle. He opened his car door and got out. I then opened my door and proceeded to get out of the car as well. When Diego came to my side of the car he had a frown on his face.

"With me, chivalry is not dead, so you can stay put the next time," he said, reaching for my hand.

"Okay, I responded, as I stepped aside and let Diego close the car door. He was, indeed, a gentleman.

We walked hand-in-hand to my apartment. His hand was warm and comforting. I still felt tense, but I also felt like my date with Diego had been a great ego booster. *What a way to start off the New Year.* At my apartment door I faced Diego and he embraced me and kissed my forehead.

"So, I'll be in touch," he said softly, but convincingly.

I didn't want him to go, but I knew I shouldn't suggest that he come inside. I was curious to know when he'd be in touch again, but I stared up at him and smiled. *Get a grip, Shayla.* "Have a safe trip back," I said in almost a whisper. *Damn, I wish I could invite him in.*

I was hoping Diego would kiss me again, but instead, he kissed two of his own fingers and touched my lips softly with them.

"Good night," he whispered.

"Good night," I echoed.

After letting myself into my apartment, I backed up against the closed door and closed my eyes. I put my hand on my heart, realizing that I was highly excited.

"Oh, God," I said breathing rapidly.

The apartment was dark, so I figured Tacara had left. I stepped cautiously into the living room and turned on the lamp. I practically fell on the love seat, still feeling flustered. I felt I needed to calm down before I did anything else. *Oh, what a day, what a day!* I had gotten engaged, made love to my fiancé, gone to dinner with Diego Jones, saw and got into a confrontation with the mother of my fiancé's child, and kissed Diego Jones like he was my fiancé. *What on earth am I ever going to do?* I had to call Calvin. *I need to let him know that I saw Cristi before she calls him.*

When I dialed Calvin's number, my palms were sweating. I didn't know what I was going to say, but I was going to make up something. I prayed that I would get his voice mail. After all, Calvin had not been answering his phone since the arrest.

"Hello?" he answered on the first ring.

I closed my eyes and gritted my teeth. "Calvin?" I said softly, after hesitating.

"Shayla, what is going on?" he asked in an annoyed tone.

I immediately feared the worst. *Not only had Cristi called him, but she told him that I was out with another man,*

"Nothing is going on," I said.

"You were supposed to be over here, Shay," Calvin said. He sounded like he was scolding me. "What is taking you so long? You bet' not be getting cold feet, girl."

I exhaled. *Maybe Cristi hadn't called him after all.* He sounded too playful. I was still antsy though. I didn't even feel like going over to Calvin's house tonight. I needed some time to myself to think. I needed to get my equilibrium back. But I feared that not going to his place would be a big mistake.

"You just make sure *you* don't get cold feet," I said. "I got tied up talking to Tacara and then we went to get a bite to eat at Cheesecake Factory . . . with her brother." I lied. "I was going to call you to let you know that I would be late, but the time got away from me." After a long pause, I figured it might be best to tell him I saw Cristi. "So, you haven't talked to Cristi Perez? She didn't call to tell you that she saw me tonight?"

"Naw, I ain't talked to her, but she did call here a little while ago leaving some crazy message. I didn't even listen to all of it. She lies too much."

"What did she say?" I said not understanding Calvin's calm attitude. "I'm just curious."

"She said that you told her that we engaged. After that, I just erased the message, babe." he said. "Hey, I don't want to talk about Cristi. All I want to know is why you aren't over here! You didn't get my message?" Calvin sounded like me when I'd question him.

"What message?" I still thought about what Cristi had said in her message to him, but I figured I should just let it go.

"I left you a message, Shayla – about an hour ago. What is up with you? I'm gonna have my driver come get you because you are trippin now that you got the ring."

"What?" I said and faked a laugh.

"Yeah, my boys warned me that once I gave you the ring that you would start buggin out and I be damned if they weren't right. You having second thoughts about being my wife, Shay?"

Calvin had struck a nerve. "Calvin, it's not that I'm having second thoughts. It's just that I don't know how serious you are. I have been through a lot of disappointments over the last few months. I just hope you're serious about marrying me."

"Girl, do you think I'd buy you a $850,000 ring and not be serious about you?" Calvin shot back. "Maybe I should have held off . . ."

"No . . . no," I said thinking about the cost of the ring. It was so like Calvin to tell me how much he had paid for it. "I'd just rather be married. I don't want to be drawn back into this relationship if you are not ready to be totally committed."

"Do you want to know how committed I am, Shayla?"

"Yeah, how committed are you?" I asked, ready to challenge him.

"I'm so committed that I will marry you next week!"

"Next week?" I repeated.

"Okay. If next week is not good enough for you, I'll marry you to-mor-row!" Calvin said with emphasis. "I'm not kidding. We can get our blood tests and go to the Justice of the Peace or if you want, we can do it in Vegas. Shii'it, that's what's up. In fact, let's do it. Can you be packed in a few hours?"

I was speechless. In over a year of being with Calvin I had never known him to be so willing to marry me. I also never detected such certainty in his voice when it came to our relationship. I felt like fainting again, but instead, I stood up straight and walked into my bedroom where I slowly sat on my bed.

"Calvin, what is going on with you?" I asked suspiciously.

"Why does anything have to be going on with me?"

"I mean, what is really going on? What is the underlying reason that you are so willing to marry me? I don't get it."

"Well, get this... I want to marry you because I love you and want to spend the rest of my life with you. And this is the first time since we have been together that I have had some kind of free time where I can really think about things. And since I'm out for two games, I figure we can go ahead and make this thing legal. I've loved you all along, Shayla."

"Well, I want to ask you something," I said. "I need something from you."

"What? Damn, you already got that big ass ring!" Calvin responded in a strained tone.

"I'd like for you to call my mother and apologize to her and to my sister for putting me in such an embarrassing situation." I said. I knew that my family would be more supportive of my decision to marry Calvin if he made some kind of atonement. Calvin hesitated though.

"Yeah, whatever you want," he finally said, dryly.

"Calvin, I mean seriously. My family is very important to me and it's important for me to have their blessings."

"Well, if we gonna elope, you might not have their blessings," Calvin said.

"No, my family is always forgiving, but they've seen me almost have a nervous breakdown because of you. So, you just need to smooth things out a little," I tried to convince Calvin.

"Well, I'm not marrying your family. I'm marrying you, but I'll call them both . . . your mom and Sydney and I'll apologize to them when you get over here."

"No, I don't have to be over there for you do to it. I'll text you their numbers after we hang up."

"Shayla, why are you making things hard for me? My name is gonna be mud to them either way."

"Calvin, I want to be your wife, but all I'm asking is that you apologize to my family . . . and you need to even apologize to the public."

"What?" Calvin asked in a strained tone.

"Calvin, the reporters are saying all these negative things about you and the Internet is full of dirt that I choose not to believe. I was thinking that you need to apologize to the people who think of you as a role model. I know only one sponsor has dropped you, but if the Falcons win without you in the playoffs over the next two games, you are gong to be looked at as a liability, not an asset. Before we go to Vegas, you need to hold a press conference and ask your coaches, teammates, sponsors and fans to forgive you."

"First of all, I ain't no damn liability and the Falcons know that," Calvin said. "I can't believe this. I mean, I'm supposed to hold a press conference telling people I was wrong for having a few drinks too many?" he asked.

"And don't forget about the marijuana possession," I reminded him.

"Shit!" Calvin barked. "When did you become the expert consultant? My lawyer was telling me to hold a press conference too, but I thought that shit would make me look worse."

"No, actually, it will make people more forgiving of your mistakes," I said. "And I'll help you write the speech. And if you want to go to Vegas after that and get married, I'll marry you," I said softly.

"Well, are you coming over or not, girl?" Calvin asked.

"Are you going to call Connie and Sydney to apologize?"

"Yes, Yes. Yes!" Calvin said impatiently. "And I'll talk to my lawyer again about this press conference shit. This shit better not backfire."

"Trust me," I reassured Calvin. "It will only make things better."

"Well, get over here," Calvin demanded.

"I'll see you in about an hour," I said.

"Bye."

"Bye."

I drove to Calvin's speeding. Putting the $850,000 ring back on my finger wasn't hard for me to do at all. On my drive to see him, Connie called informing me that Calvin had indeed called her to apologize. I still didn't tell her about my ring though. I wanted to show it to her in person since she seemed quite un-impressed with Calvin's apology. She said that she didn't trust "the bastard" and suggested that he must have been high. The last thing I wanted to do was to get into a confrontation with her about my fiancé.

Thoughts of Diego Jones still penetrated my mind, but I knew I couldn't carry a torch for him. We had gotten together for a date and allowed ourselves to go a little further than we should have. We had chemistry, but I also had chemistry with the man I loved. *Surely Diego has to know about Calvin and isn't expecting anything more from me.* After all, he lived in

London, England. I didn't have time to carry on a long-distance romance with a man in another country – especially when I could marry Calvin Moore.

Calvin literally swept me off my feet when he opened his door for me. It reminded me of his Super Bowl win and the excitement from his MVP award last year. He acted as though he was so happy to see me.

"I'll do a press conference next week," he said as he put me down. "If you'll marry me the day after the press conference, I'll do it."

I looked into Calvin's eyes and saw a vulnerability I had never seen before. I knew he meant what he was saying.

"I'll marry you," I said, as Calvin drew me closer.

He kissed me and we embraced. And for the first time, I felt like I was Calvin's MVP . . . his Most Valuable Prize.

Chapter Eleven

Touchdown

*C*alvin and I were planning to elope in two days. I had kept our secret from everybody, but I was ready to shout it to the world as soon as we became husband and wife. A week had passed since New Year's Day and since Calvin shocked me by asking me to be his wife. I had bought the most elegant, strapless, white Vera Wang lace and beaded wedding dress. Calvin had allowed me to put $5,000 on his American Express card for the feminine, mermaid gown, although it was actually $10,000. I was grateful for my buyer's discount. I was all packed and ready to get on the plane to Vegas as soon as Calvin's press conference was over today. Calvin did not want to attract too much media attention, so he planned to take the last flight out of Atlanta to Las Vegas and meet me there a few hours later. I figured I could use the few hours alone in Vegas to prepare myself and make our hotel suite romantic. We had made reservations at The Bellagio Las Vegas. Luckily, we even got the honeymoon suite.

Calvin and I had been inseparable since New Year's night. In fact, things had gone so well for us that I had to stop at intervals during the day and pinch myself to make sure I wasn't dreaming. I had stayed at Calvin's every night and started to slowly take my belongings to his house. I even helped him write an apology speech, with the help of one of his attorneys. It was a speech we thought would put Calvin back in good standings with the Falcons and his fans. Although things between Calvin and I seemed too good to be true, it was a little bittersweet for me when Calvin presented me with a pre-nuptial agreement. It was five pages long. Calvin and his lawyer had obviously concocted it one day while I was at work. They convinced me that it was a necessary business agreement and a prerequisite to a healthy marriage. *Really?* Basically, Calvin's attorney, Cliff, was the only person we let in on our wedding plans. He did all the talking for Calvin about the prenup. It stated that Calvin's estate and assets were his because he had acquired them before our relationship began. In the unlikely event of a divorce, Calvin would keep his property. In the event of Calvin's death, I would acquire his property. Basically, the prenup seemed to have more financial statements in it than I could comprehend. In a nutshell Cliff explained, as soothingly as possible, that the prenup protected Calvin's fortunes. In the event that I had Calvin's children, there would be more in it for me though – according to what I read. *I better hurry up and kick a couple out.* At first I felt a little hesitant to sign on the dotted line, especially since nobody from my end had seen the agreement, except for me. But I quickly realized that marrying Calvin Moore was what I wanted more than anything in the world, prenuptial agreement or not.

I missed Diego Jones' calls twice. He called a day after he left Atlanta, informing me that he had made it back to London and asking me to call him collect at his home number between a certain time – after he got off. The second time he called, yesterday, he sounded a little disappointed that I had not called him back. He also left his cell number. He said, "Hello, Shayla. I hope that you got the message I left a few days ago. Maybe you've been rather busy. But I would love to talk with you, so call me collect or on my cell," he said as he repeated his number twice. "I look forward to hearing from you. Oh, I know there's a seven hour time difference, but I don't mind you calling any time of the day or night. I just want to hear your sweet voice."

"Ahhh," I said, after listening to his message. I wasn't planning on calling Diego though. I figured he'd find out about my marriage to Calvin sooner or later . . . and probably via ESPN or another news outlet. *Plus, Claire will tell him.* I felt guilty to be dissing Diego Jones, but we barely knew each other. And for all I knew, he could have a special woman in London. I was sure he had no problems getting any woman he wanted. *But I'm almost Mrs. Moore.* I forced myself to relinquish whatever feelings I had developed for Diego. I didn't know the purpose of our meeting, but I decided not to even nurture any kind of friendship with him.

"Shayla, where are you?" Calvin asked as he grabbed me around the waist and pulled me closer to him. "You are somewhere far off, baby. What are you thinking about?"

Calvin and I were in a room inside the CNN Center before his press conference. I was, indeed, jittery about sitting in front of more than 30 television reporters and photographers, but my mind had slipped off a moment to thoughts of Diego. I truly found it an effort to not think about him. I didn't know why I was thinking about Diego and how he'd feel about me ignoring his calls, when I needed to be thinking about Calvin's press conference and our wedding. Calvin and I were to walk into a room full of reporters and here I was wondering if Diego would call again.

I kissed Calvin on the cheek and sighed. "I'm just thinking about getting this press conference over with so I can be your lawfully wedded wife," I said seductively.

Calvin gave me a cool look. He looked at his watch. "Damn, why don't they hurry up and come get us!" he groaned. I felt impatient too. Cliff and Tommy were supposed to lead us into the press room ten minutes ago, but we had not seen them in over 30 minutes. I massaged Calvin's shoulder to calm him. He was tense and seemed very melancholy. He sat on the edge of the table and folded his arms.

"It's going to be just fine, baby," I assured him as I continued to massage his shoulder.

Finally, Cliff walked into the room smiling, which I thought was a good sign. Cliff had a strange look about him, always stoic, but he seemed very sincere and smart.

"What's up, man?" Calvin said as he stood to his feet.

"They're ready for you CK, and I think they are going to be more than receptive. But I must warn you," Cliff said with a cautious tone.

"What?" Calvin asked anxiously.

"There must be over a hundred reporters and TV crews in that room, but just go in there and do your best, man. Don't let them intimidate you," Cliff said as he reached for Calvin and gave him a quick, manly embrace.

"Man. Thank you, man. Let's go do this, man," Calvin said with a nervous smile. "Let's do this."

When Calvin and I walked into the room full of reporters and camera people who were both sitting and standing, I felt unguarded, although Calvin held my hand tightly. There were so many flashes from cameras that I could barely see straight. There had to be more than 100 people in the room. Calvin and I walked over to a long table where his other attorney, a white guy named Jack Jacobs and his agent were standing. I was instructed to sit in the seat provided for me, next to Calvin, but for some reason I wasn't sure if I was supposed to sit while Calvin made his apology speech or just stand by his side until he sat down. In fact, I wasn't even sure if Calvin was going to sit down or why he needed to.

Calvin walked up to the podium, still holding my hand and seeming to pose for the photographers. I stood beside him with a clueless smile.

"Hey, what's up, man?" Calvin said to a reporter he seemed to know. "What's up?" Calvin continued as he scanned his audience, seeming excited about the people he noticed. I knew none of them and seriously felt like I was having a hot flash. I felt faint. *Now now!* Fainting would not be the thing to do at this highly visible time. *Not in front of all of these live cameras.*

"And you all may be seated," Calvin said as he looked at me, Tommy and his two attorneys. I felt relieved when Calvin asked us to sit down, but the crowd of reporters seemed to chuckle at Calvin's posture, his statement or something he had done. Calvin had this big smile on his face. I didn't understand his elated spirit, which had occurred suddenly. But I sat down and crossed my legs. I then purposely held my hands together on the table, allowing my eight carat ring to be noticed. Yes, I had gone to a jeweler who told me that the ring was more carats than I had originally thought. I looked out into the audience of reporters and saw a couple of people on the front row whisper something to each other about me. I smiled coyly and turned my attention to Calvin. He was standing there in silence. He was just allowing photographers to snap photos of him, like he had done something honorable. I wanted so badly to pinch his leg and tell him to go ahead with his speech, but there was no way I could do it discreetly.

Finally, Calvin spoke: "Ladies and gentlemen of the press," he said with much enthusiasm. "As an NFL player and a wide receiver for the Atlanta Falcons it is my duty to uphold moral conduct on and off the football field. If I can be a Super Bowl Most Valuable Player and receive numerous accolades and effectively perform duties and challenges as a football player, surely I can effectively adhere to the laws which govern our society. Less than three weeks ago, I was arrested for possession of marijuana and for Driving Under the Influence of alcohol. At the time of my arrest I was influenced negatively on the night of what was supposed to be a special Christmas Eve for me and my loved ones . . . and my negligence got me in trouble. There is no excuse for my behavior," Calvin said in a dreary voice change. He dropped his head, finally looking at his notes. He exhaled and leaned closer to the microphone. He then looked back up. "I would like to publicly and sincerely apologize for embarrassing my teammates, my coaches, my family, my fans, my agent, my attorneys, and my fiancée," Calvin said with emphasis and turned towards me. I smiled at Calvin, feeling much calmer. Cameras flashed more. "And most of all, I embarrassed myself," Calvin continued. "The NFL has taken disciplinary action by suspending me for two games, and I have made a decision, which I'm announcing for the first time today, to complete 100 hours of community service and to give my full participation to a drug and alcohol program. Of course the judicial system will decide the rest of my punishment, but I am truly dedicated to upholding the positive image of athletes and I want to emphasize to young kids the importance of saying no to drugs and not giving in to peer pressure, no matter what," Calvin said with intensity. "Although I have had stories written about me by some of you skilled journalists and bloggers as being the hottest commodity in the NFL, I feel that my behavior on Christmas Eve truly diminished your respect for me. Of course my words will not be the determining factor that will gain your respect back, but I do ask for your support and that you won't let this one time out of character behavior on my part be turned into an attack on other innocent athletes. I am responsible for my behavior and I'm willing to pay the penalty for my indiscretion and lack of wisdom. Thank you very much for coming out today, and I'm sure that we will meet again – but under different circumstances. I am sure. Thank you."

Surprisingly, some of the media started applauding, so I joined in on the applause. Calvin looked so relieved and like a burden had been lifted off him. I definitely felt like one had been lifted off me.

"So, do you think the Falcons will make it to the Super Bowl without your efforts?" one of the reporters shouted after the applause died down.

"I'm truly confident in my team, and I think the Falcons can win the next playoff game by executing their efforts to the fullest. I'm a big part of the team, but I'm not the entire team. We pride ourselves in teamwork," Calvin answered. I was surprised he was so articulate and professional. He was doing so well.

"What will the drug and alcohol program consist of and when will you begin treatment?" another reporter asked.

"Well, I'm not sure if I would call it treatment," Calvin chuckled. "I'm not a drug addict or an alcoholic, although I do empathize with those who experience substance abuse issues. I just got caught up in a situation that night, which I truly misjudged. But to answer your question, I'm not sure what the specifics of the program are, but I do plan to begin counseling sessions – after we win the Super Bowl again," Calvin said confidently.

Someone in the audience shouted, "Yeah!" to Calvin's prediction. Many of the reporters were smiling. Cliff had advised Calvin to answer no more than five questions from reporters. So far, he had answered two. *Three more to go.* I was ready for the press conference to end.

"Mr. Moore," an attractive lady stood and got everybody's attention. "When you say that you got caught up in a situation that night, does that mean that you were transporting the marijuana for someone else or maybe participating in some form of racketeering with your friends?"

My heart felt like it sank to my stomach. Of all the questions we had gone over with Calvin, this one was totally unexpected. Calvin leaned closer to the microphone as the room grew very quiet. I looked at the reporter, who was still standing. She had her arms folded, like she knew she had something on him by her demeaning question. Perhaps she just wanted to be noticed. She was wearing a red, two piece suit that was very form-fitting and she really didn't look like a reporter at all. Her weave was full and down her back. Her makeup was heavy. But she was attractive, to say the least. Calvin's representatives were very selective on who could and could not receive credentials to the press conference, so obviously she had to be a reporter for someone.

Finally, after a long pause and some whispers in the room, Calvin answered. "I'm a professional football player. In fact, I have a five-year 50 million dollar contract, not to mention the lucrative endorsements," Calvin boasted.

Oh my God, what is he doing? He is losing it. I looked down, embarrassed for Calvin.

He continued. "I have a big mansion in an upscale neighborhood, I own six luxury vehicles. I have a family who loves me, a son who is named after me and a fiancée who has stuck by me," Calvin said turning to me again. I didn't know where he was going with this. *The real Calvin was coming out. Oh no.*

Calvin continued: "But aside from all of that, I have my reputation. I don't go to church much, but I know the good book says 'what shall it profit a man if he gains the whole world, but loses his soul.' So, the answer to your question is no. My soul is more important than stooping to such lowly, unethical acts."

Calvin's response had truly surprised me even more than the question had. He seemed to have surprised his media audience, who sat quietly, like they were mesmerized by him. I, for one, didn't expect Calvin to be quoting the Bible. I didn't even know what verse he had quoted, but it sounded real good.

"Calvin, when do you plan to marry your beautiful fiancée?" one of the male reporters shouted form the back of the room.

"Whenever she'll have me," Calvin quickly responded and winked at me. I smiled shyly. *Oooh. I am loving this.* I knew that everybody I knew and their mama had to be watching the press conference on television. I figured all of Calvin's groupies were also watching and were green with envy. I imagined Cristi Perez at home glued to her television set, crying. *Eat your heart out.* And then the thought of Diego Jones came to my mind. *I hope he's not watching.* I imagined him putting his two fingers on my lips as he departed after our dinner date. I thought about the way I had taken off my engagement ring for him so that he wouldn't know that I was engaged. *Shake him off, Shayla. Just shake him off.*

Calvin was doing so well that I wondered why I had ever doubted his intelligence. When we were together Calvin had always talked slang and conversed like he had been around the boys a little too long, but here he was in a room full of seasoned reporters answering tough questions intelligently that we had not even gone over with him.

"So, what is your fiancée's full name?" one of the men on the front row asked.

"Shayla. S-h-a-y-l-a," Calvin spelled my name out without giving my last name.

At that time, Tommy stood to his feet. "One more question," he said. "He can only take one more question."

Suddenly, ten questions or more came at Calvin at once. Calvin just looked out into the audience and lifted his hands, as if he were directing a choir.

"Say, what?" he said with a frown. The reporters seemed to find humor in his expression. Calvin chuckled too.

"I would like to know what you plan to tell all the various women who have been in pursuit of you and pursued by you, nevertheless, now that you are getting married?" the female in the red suit asked. Immediately I felt like she was after something more than a news story.

"I guess they'll figure it out," Calvin said non-challantly. "I'm off the market now. Right, babe?" he looked at me.

"Right," I blushed.

Again, the response humored the audience. I laughed a fake laugh too, but I wondered who this woman was. *What is her agenda?*

"Okay, ladies and gentleman. Thank you for your time. Those are all the questions he'll be answering today," Tommy said walking toward the podium. Calvin stood to the side, gazing at me. I smiled, feeling more relieved. Of course more reporters shouted questions, but they seemed to be football related questions. Tommy took over at that point.

"We thank you for coming out, and if there are any further interview requests please e-mail them in my care. I'll get back with you or have someone else get back with you as soon as possible," Tommy said.

"Can we take a photo of CK and his fiancée in front of the podium?" one of the photographers asked.

Tommy shook his head "no," but Calvin interjected. "We can do that, man. That'll be cool."

Tommy whispered something to Calvin that I couldn't hear, but afterwards, Calvin reached for my hand.

"Okay. Just a few shots of Calvin and his fiancée, but you're gonna have to be quick," Tommy said.

Before I knew it, Calvin led me in front of the podium. I felt nervous all over again as the cameras flashed. Calvin put his arm around me as we smiled for the cameras. He then grabbed my left hand and deliberately held it out so that the ring could be seen and photographed. "Wow," a few people gasped.

"How much?" a reporter had the audacity to ask.

With that question, Tommy seemed to get pretty agitated. "Okay, that's all," he interrupted, rudely stepping in front of Calvin and me. He then turned around to face us. "Let's go," he said in a stern tone. He whisked Calvin and me off the platform and back into the room where we had waited before the press conference.

"Yes, man! Yes!" Calvin shouted. "It's over with."

"Shhh," Tommy cautioned. "You're too loud, man. They can hear you."

"Man, I'm just happy this shit is over," Calvin said with excitement, but in a lower tone. He turned to me. "You look so good, baby." I had on a winter off white, tailored sleeveless dress by Donna Karan under a cropped jacket. It was very form-fitting on me, but classy. I had my hair bone straight, for a change. "Thanks for being there for me," Calvin said and embraced me.

I eyed Tommy as I hugged Calvin noticing that Tommy still had a look of concern on his face. He shook his head as if he were disgusted about something.

"Is everything okay, Tommy?" I asked after Calvin released me from his embrace.

"Ahh, Tommy's unemotional," Calvin said. "He ain't got no emotions." But something seemed definitely wrong with Tommy.

"Baby, who was that reporter in the red?" I asked, turning to Calvin.

"I don't know," Calvin said. "Forget about her. You always get those reporters who ask stupid ass questions. I know her kind."

"But why was she so quick to pass judgment on you? Have you met her before?" I continued to probe, looking at Tommy for answers too.

"Shayla, what is it with you?" Calvin asked and gently brushed my hair out of my face with his fingers. "I don't know the woman and have never seen her in my life. Chill, okay?"

I did feel like I was being a bit too inquisitive. After all, Calvin had just given a convincing apology speech and I was about to become his wife. I felt like hugging him.

"I love you, baby," I said excitedly as I embraced Calvin tightly.

"Damn," Calvin murmered. "I love you too."

"So, what's this I hear about the two of you sneaking out to Vegas to get married?" Tommy interjected with a stern gaze at Calvin, then at me.

I wondered who had told him about our plans. Cliff had promised that he wouldn't tell a soul.

"I don't think it's a good idea," Tommy said.

"Man, did Cliff tell you? That . . ."

"No. Cliff did not tell me a thing."

"Well, who told you then?" Calvin asked. "He is the only person I told."

"Are you sure?" Tommy asked. "But that's beside the point. I think it's a bad move to go to Vegas and get married when you've been suspended. They are gonna think you're not serious about your football career."

"Man, who is they? Plus, they know how serious I am about the game. Shii'it, I didn't suspend myself. And making Shayla my wifey don't have a thing to do with me being suspended or with football period. Man, I don't know what's up with you, but I told you a while back the Shay is the one," Calvin said.

"Well, I'm not saying that she isn't the one," Tommy said.

"Well, what are you saying, Tommy?" I asked, feeling that I needed to see my way into the conversation.

"What I'm saying is that if you're gonna do something, do it right. Why sneak and give the press even more fuel to this fire?"

"Man, that was the purpose of having Shayla with me today. The fire has been put out and the world now knows that she is my woman, so we can get married whenever we want to. We don't need to tell nobody our plans," Calvin argued. I was glad Calvin was strong-willed about marrying me.

"Well, what's the rush?" Tommy questioned.

"The rush?" Calvin repeated.

"Yes. That's what I said. What's the rush?" he said and turned to me. "Are you pregnant again?"

"I'm not pregnant," I said strongly. Tommy was really beginning to anger me.

"Man, what is up? Why are you questioning us, Tommy?" Calvin asked as he grasped my hand with both of his. I guess he sensed that Tommy's "Are you pregnant again?"question had hurt me. I didn't understand why Tommy was making such a big deal about us eloping. *People do it all the time.* I felt like he had no right to question Calvin about his personal life. After all, he was Calvin's agent, not his shrink.

"I'm just forewarning you, man. I think you're making another stupid decision!" Tommy barked and turned around and stormed out of the room.

I was definitely caught off guard by Tommy's reaction. I had never seen him become so angry before – especially over

Calvin's personal life. I stood silent, looking at the door, expecting Tommy to come back in, but he didn't.

"Why is he so dead set against us getting married?" I asked Calvin, quite puzzled.

"I don't know, but I'm getting tired of Tommy's ass anyway. I might be getting me another agent because he acts like a damn kid sometimes," Calvin said calmly.

"Was it something I did? I mean, I feel like he really dislikes me all of a sudden." I said.

"Shayla, promise me something," Calvin said.

"Okay"

"Promise me that you won't worry about the small stuff," he said. "Don't sweat the small stuff, okay?"

"Well, I just feel like Tommy . . ."

"Forget Tommy. Don't sweat the small stuff, okay, Shayla?"

"Okay, baby," I agreed. "I'm so proud of you. You were awesome in there," I said and pecked Calvin on the lips.

"So, you have your stuff all packed in the limo and you're ready to go to Vegas?" he asked, pulling me closer.

"I am too ready. I just hope you don't back out on me."

"Girl, please. I'm gonna be there. I'm ready to get married. You just don't back out on me!"

"You don't have to worry about that CK Moore," I said and leaned towards Calvin.

Right when our lips met, Tommy walked back into the room. "Okay, kids. The party is over," he said sarcastically. "The driver is waiting."

"Cool," Calvin said. "So, you ain't said didley about my performance out there, Money Man. How do you think I came across to the press?"

"It was a performance, indeed, but like everything else with you, CK, I think you've got them fooled," Tommy said. I didn't know if he were serious or joking.

Calvin and I walked out of the room with him, but I felt tension in the air. I didn't quite understand Tommy's cutting remarks at all. *Maybe he is just jealous.* After all, none of his relationships seemed to last past three months. Calvin and I followed close behind Tommy through the corridor and then down a stairway to avoid being seen by the crowd. A few photographers were still standing outside waiting to take our picture before we got into the limo. Calvin waved to them and gently guided me into the limo where the television was on and his press conference was airing again on ESPN. I turned the volume up. We caught the latter end of the news report, where Calvin was quoting the Bible.

"I didn't even know you knew the Bible like that," I said to Calvin.

"There are a lot of good things you don't know about me," Calvin responded, emphasizing the *good*.

By the time we arrived to the airport, Calvin's press conference had played several times on ESPN news. We caught a glimpse of it on CNN too. The sportscaster on ESPN seemed to make a wise crack about Calvin's apology, stating that Calvin might be going into the ministry before the season is over. Calvin just laughed at the sportscaster's remark.

"Well, I guess this is it, until I see you in a few hours, in Vegas," I said to Calvin as the driver pulled my luggage out. My flight was departing at 5:30 pm, but Calvin would be flying to Vegas on the 9:50 pm flight, which would actually get him there around 11:15 pm Vegas time.

Calvin kissed me. "I love you, Mrs. Shayla Moore," he said after our long kiss.

It was all so overwhelming to me. I couldn't remember being so happy in a long time. Tears started to well up in my eyes.

"Now, don't go boohooing on me," Calvin said "Call me time you land, aight?"

"Okay," I said softly.

Calvin squeezed my hand as I stepped out of the limo. When he finally let go of my hand, I blew him a kiss. He gestured with his hand that he had caught the kiss and he put it next to his heart.

"Touchdown," he said.

I turned around to check my baggage at the curbside, feeling deep within that this time things were really going to work out for Calvin and I. I silently thanked God for the change that He had made in Calvin. *Touchdown indeed.*

Chapter Twelve

What Goes on in Vegas, Stays in Vegas

W hen I walked inside the elaborate suite at the Bellagio in Vegas I had planned to rest my weary bones immediately, but I stood in the middle of the suite in amazement. Obviously Calvin had informed someone at the hotel that we were getting married and had paid them big bucks to decorate the suite to romantic perfection. Upon entering the suite, there was a rainbow arch of white balloons. Everywhere I looked there were red and white rose petals. I got a rush as I walked through the dining room and then to the master suite to see roses throughout each room. The master bedroom was immaculate, with a marble fireplace and a Jacuzzi with lilac candles surrounding it. The ambiance made me feel like I was a princess. I walked into the bathroom that had silver faucets that were shaped like swans. I walked back into the living room, where there was a white baby grand piano with more rose petals on top.

"I can't believe this!" I said, trembling. I was truly overcome with joy.

I had called Calvin's cell phone time I landed, as he asked me to. I knew he wouldn't be answering though, since his flight was leaving at the time that I landed. It felt great to know that Calvin was sincere in his promise to marry me. God had turned things around for us and I was forever grateful. But there was still one thing that I felt I needed to do. *I have to call Diego Jones and tell him about my marriage plans.* I figured he deserved to hear it from me and not on ESPN, Claire, or read it online. Although we had not actually dated, I felt that if the shoe were on the other foot I'd like to be extended the respect of a phone call from someone I had just kissed romantically.

After saying a prayer and being in awe of the lovely suite, I took a warm bubble bath and slipped into my off-white, satin night gown. I had bought very romantic white and off-white lingerie outfits that I would wear for Calvin. I felt romantic.

But I needed to call Diego. I picked up my cell phone to dial his number. It was 8:30 pm Vegas time. I knew I needed to put polite closure to what Diego and I had briefly shared. After finding his number, I pushed send.

"Hello?" he answered after the third ring.

I wanted to push "end." I was speechless. Diego sounded warm and chipper and here I was calling him to tell him that I was about to marry Calvin.

"Hello?" he said after a few more seconds.

"Diego?" I finally said softly.

"Yes? This is Diego."

"Diego, hi. This is Shayla Lucas."

"Shayla. How are you?" he said excitedly.

"I'm okay," I said shivering.

"Is everything okay? What time is it there?"

"Oh, I'm in Vegas. It's just a little past 8:30 here in Vegas," I said as I began to agonize about whether I really wanted to tell him or not. I went speechless again and he didn't immediately fill in the silence. I didn't know how to say what I had to tell him. I still wanted to push end on my cell phone, but it was too late now.

"What's going on in Vegas?" he finally asked.

"I'm getting married," I blurted out.

"Seriously?" he said in a high pitch tone that I couldn't really tell if it was a question or not.

"Yep. My life has really done an about face over the last couple of weeks, and more specifically my boyfriend has done an about face. Calvin and I are marrying tomorrow and I just wanted to be the one to tell you," I said as my heart raced.

"Well, congratulations, Shayla! That is all right... that is all right," he said enthusiastically.

I felt a little soothed by his words, but confused. Diego didn't seem to be bothered at all by the news of me marrying Calvin. I didn't know what to think.

"Well, do I have your blessings?" I asked with a tremor in my voice. I knew it was a silly question.

"Of course you do. I hope the two of you are very happy," he said, sounding genuinely sincere.

"Why thanks," I said and let out a fake giggle. "You know, you're the first person I've told."

"Really? I feel honored," Diego said quickly.

I didn't know if Diego was trying to be sarcastic or if he was just being extra nice, but I felt a little rejected. I guess I wanted him to protest and tell me that he had really wanted to get to know me better.

"Well, Diego, I wish you the best, and I'm sorry we didn't meet at another time," I said in a sad voice.

"Well, timing is everything, but as long as you're happy, that's all that matters."

"I'm happy."

"Good."

"So, take care, okay?"

"Okay, you too."

"Bye, Diego."

"Bye."

After I hung up, my eyes welled up but I held the tears back by blinking. I couldn't understand my emotions, but I felt like I had just broken up with someone that I had experienced a longterm relationship with. And then my phone rang. I jumped, thinking that it was Diego calling me back. The number said private.

"Hello?" I answered softly.

"Shayla, what up, baby?" Calvin's voice came across the other end of the phone.

"Calvin, where are you?" I said as I clutched the phone, feeling that something was wrong.

"I got good news and bad news," Calvin said calmly.

"Calvin, you're supposed to be on the plane. Where are you?" I asked frantically, fearing the worst.

"I'm not on the plane, Shayla. I'm still here in Atlanta, but just listen . . ."

"But Calvin you are supposed to be here. We are supposed to get married, Calvin. What is going on!?" I said, getting more frantic.

"Shayla, I am gonna marry you, but it's just not gonna be over the next few days."

"What?" I shouted. "I can't believe you are saying this, Calvin. Please get on the next plane and come. You promised me, Calvin. You promised me!" I pleaded as my heart sank.

"Shay, I got reinstated to the Falcons. They want me to play in the next game. That press conference did more good than we thought, baby. But I'm still gonna marry you. I promise."

"Calvin, I don't believe you!" I said furiously.

"You don't believe me?" Calvin said. "Well, just turn on the news, Shay. They reinstated me to the team, you understand? I am playing in the next game and I have a meeting and 9 o'clock in the morning. I found out right when I was about to board the plane."

"But Calvin, you promised me that you would be here and that you would marry me," I cried.

"Dammit, I am gonna marry you, but I was reinstated to the damn team. They reversed the suspension. Do you understand the words that are coming out of my mouth!?" he shouted.

"No, I don't understand, Calvin," I said harshly. "You made a promise and you are gonna get on the next flight to Vegas. The team will just have to see you the day after we get married." I was starting to lose control.

"Shayla, I'm gonna hang up and let you calm down, okay?"

"You better not hang up this damn phone!"

"Look Shay, I have a game to play Sunday. I don't need this shit!"

"You bastard!" I screamed, as anger seeped through my pores. "I'm here in Vegas waiting on your black ass and . . ."

At that point Calvin hung up.

"Calvin?" I said, knowing that he had already hung up. I was overcome with disappointment and rage. I started whaling. I called Calvin back, but got his voice mail. After frantically calling back-to-back four times and getting his voice mail, my own phone rang, startling me again. It was Calvin calling back.

"You're coming?" I asked anxiously.

"Shay, I can't come, but I want to, baby. I really want to," Calvin said.

"I can't believe you are doing this to me, Calvin," I cried, wanting him to feel my hurt and disappointment. "I just can't believe you would do this."

"I know it hurts. I feel like crying too, but my coaches met with the commissioner after the press conference and just as I was getting ready to board the flight I got this call from my coach telling me that I was no longer suspended and that I needed to report for a meeting in the morning. If you don't believe me, just turn on ESPN. It's already on there. They reversed my two game suspension."

I cried into the phone as Calvin became silent listening to me sob. "I believe you," I finally said. "I just feel so stupid. I thought you really wanted to marry me."

"I don't know why you feel stupid, baby. We haven't told nobody," Calvin said.

I let out another sob, remembering that I had just called Diego.

"Shayla, why don't you come home on the first flight out tomorrow? Come be with me."

"So, can we get married in Atlanta?" I asked desperately. I felt the tides were turning against me quickly. I felt a horrible pang. I needed some type of verbal commitment from him at least.

"Shayla, just come home and we'll talk about it."

"You don't want to marry me anymore now that you're back playing ball," I cried.

"Yes, I do! Stop saying that," Calvin said. "I'm gonna marry you. Do you think I would have given you that ring and had that room laid out like that if I hadn't planned to be out there with you, making you my wife?"

I couldn't speak because I was so full of tears and pain. I felt that if Calvin didn't come to Vegas to marry me tomorrow that he would never marry me. Just the thought made me feel hopeless. I cried more.

"Shayla, be strong now," Calvin said, sounding concerned. "Just come back in the morning. I'll call my travel agent after we get off the phone and book your flight."

"I'm not coming back!" I said in a tearful voice.

"What?"

"I just want to stay here. You can come out here tomorrow after practice," I said. "Please, Calvin."

"Shay, listen," Calvin said calmly. "I'm still at the airport. I'm calling you from the Crown Room and I need to go, aight. But I'll call you back in about an hour, okay?"

I could not say anything or I felt like I would sob again.

"Okay, Shay?" Calvin said.

"Okay," I whispered feeling so drained that I wanted to give up.

Calvin did not call back until three hours later and he still told me that he could not come to Vegas to marry me tomorrow. He said, "I promise we'll make plans to marry some other time." After crying even more, I became all cried out and fell off to sleep around 4 am Vegas time. I told Calvin that I wanted to stay in Vegas another day. I also gave him an ultimatum. I told him, "If you can't marry me within the next two weeks then I want out of this relationship." I knew that it was a pretty bold and emotional ultimatum, but obviously Calvin took me serious. He said, "Okay, baby. I will find some way between practice and games to do that."

I still had the feeling that Calvin wasn't going to keep his word and that he was making the promise just to soothe me. There was something in his voice that made me doubtful. He sounded like he didn't really need me anymore. *Why does he need me? He has football again.*

I woke up around 10 am the next day. I put on a red cardigan sweater that draped, metallic leggings, and suede booties. As exhausted and puffy-eyed as I was, I decided to go shopping. I shopped at Fashion Show Mall until my feet hurt and my arms were full. The purchase of one outfit, shoe or accessory after another gave me a temporary high. Vegas had some really savvy boutiques. I was so overcome with despair from Calvin standing me up that I charged close to $9,000 on his American Express card. I bought a Gucci bag and Gucci sunglasses totaling $1,000, a Versace patent-leather trim jersey dress for $1,200, three pairs of Jimmy Choo shoes for $2,000, a Dolce & Gabanna silver anchor necklace for $250, two Chanel dresses for $1,500, a Prada jacket for $1,500 and various shirts, pants and skirts from Zara and Nordstrom for $2,000. The night before I left for Vegas Calvin had told me to hold on to the American Express card in case of emergency. He had gotten American Express to add my name to the card, but the bill went directly to him. I didn't feel guilty at all about charging the items to Calvin's card. I felt like I was feeling an emergency all right . . . an emergency case of heartache. *The only way I can feel better is to shop until I drop and eat fattening foods.* But since I didn't want to gain weight, shopping seemed to be the best alternative.

When I got back to the room at the hotel, I fell on the bed, exhausted. I had turned my cell phone off the entire day, so after resting for about 15 minutes I decided to turn it back on. "You have eight new messages," the recorded voice said, making me curious and anxious about the number of messages I had received. I had been gone from the room for about six hours. *What could have transpired during that time?*

The first three messages were from my mom, Tacara and my boss, but the next message was from Calvin. "Shay, hey bae, it's CK. I just got out of practice and was just thinking about you. Call me when you get back to the room, aight, bye."

The fifth message was Calvin. "Damn, baby. You must be really enjoying yourself. Why you got your cell phone off? I been calling you for an hour. I also called you in your room. I miss you. Call me. Bye."

The sixth message was Calvin. "Shayla, I don't know what's going on with you, but I'm worried about you, baby. You don't need to be out there in the streets in Vegas. It's dangerous. Call me time you get in. And I want you to know that I'm gonna make you my wife as soon as I can. I love you. Bye."

The seventh message was Calvin. "Shayla, this is ridiculous. What kind of games you trying to play? You are scaring me, girl. If you don't call me back within the next 30 minutes I'm gonna have somebody go look for you. Now I know you're not still holding a grudge because I got reinstated to the team and couldn't come out there. I told you I would make it up to you. Damn!" he said and hung up. For the first time since my hurt about being stood up, I laughed at the way Calvin's voice changed the more he called, revealing his irritation.

And of course the eighth message was Calvin. "You know what, Shayla. I need you to get back here because you don't know how to act when things don't go your way. You're acting real childish. I've done everything I can for you to make you happy and this is the damn thanks I get?" Calvin hung up.

I laughed out loud about Calvin's numerous calls, feeling that he had to be concerned about me to leave so many back-to-back messages. But what did I need to thank him for? *Standing me up? He has lost his mind.* Calvin had also left several text messages. After reading the texts, I sat on the bed and stared into space. It was heartwarming to know that he was unsettled about my short disappearance, but the pain was still there about him not being in Vegas to marry me.

The phone rang in the room. I was tempted to let it keep ringing to see what kind of message Calvin would leave next, but I couldn't resist picking up the phone.

"Hello?" I said softly.

"Shayla, damn!" Calvin said in a raised tone.

"Damn, what?"

"Where in the hell you been?"

"Calvin, I'm in Vegas. If you remember, I came out here to marry you, but you didn't show up . . . so I went shopping. Is that okay with you?"

"You went shopping?" he asked suspiciously.

"Yes, Calvin. Shopping."

"So, it took you all day to shop?"

"Yeah, it could have taken me longer, but my arms got too full. I had to have some of the stuff shipped back to the hotel," I said. "So, how was your day?"

"You know what, Shay. I don't know what kind of games you playing, but you need to get on the next flight back here."

"So I can do what? Come home and wait on you to marry me?"

"Naw, see, you are putting pressure on me now and I don't like that," Calvin said.

"I'm not pressuring you, Calvin. I mean if you don't want to marry me, I'm sure you don't mind me staying out in Vegas for ... another week, maybe?"

"What are you gonna do in Vegas for a week, Shay?

"Oh, so much. Shop some more, go to the spa, maybe do a little gambling. They have some shows here I want to see too. I can find a lot to do here." I was trying my best to get to Calvin.

"As long as you don't do all that shit on my dime, cool. You go ahead and stay right there in Vegas, Shayla. I'll talk to you later," Calvin said dryly.

"Okay," I said, knowing that I was risking not hearing back from him again that day, but willing to take the risk anyway. After I said, "Okay," Calvin held the phone for a few seconds without saying a word and then he hung up.

I stretched out on the bed, not sure what to do next. I knew Calvin would be more than upset once he found out about my purchases. *Oh well. He reneged on his promise to marry me in Vegas,* I reasoned. I knew that I was being stubborn and even irrational when it came to the charging all that I had charged on his credit card, but I had wanted to come back from Vegas as Mrs. Shayla Moore. The only thing I had gained was $9,000 worth of clothes and accessories that I really didn't need.

Three hours passed and Calvin did not call me back. After ordering room service I turned on the television where I flipped through the channels until I found ESPN. I sat on the bed drinking the Moët that I got from the mini bar straight out of the bottle. I contemplated whether I wanted to stay another night in Vegas or head back to Atlanta on the all-nighter flight, which left in two hours. Right when I made up my mind to stay another day, a news report about Calvin came on.

"Calvin Moore was back at practice this morning after the NFL and the Atlanta Falcons reduced his two-game suspension to team counseling, in a bizarre twist to this saga," the newscaster reported as footage of Calvin was being shown of him at practice. "Charges of DUI and possessing marijuana are still pending, but Moore's press conference on Monday convinced the NFL to reconsider their two-game suspension of Moore and allow him to play in the final playoff games and through the Super Bowl, if the Falcons win the next two games. We caught up with Moore after practice for a few minutes and asked him what he thought about the NFL's quick decision to reinstate him."

The camera zoomed in on Calvin as he was leaving practice. I sat straight up in bed, half excited, half nervous as Calvin began to speak.

"A guardian angel must have been watching over me. I'm glad the NFL reversed my suspension. I'm ready to win the next two games so we can go to the Super Bowl again and be back-to-back world champions. I'm not a perfect man, but at the press conference I wanted everyone to know that I will try my hardest to be the best person I can be on and off the filed. I'm glad the NFL reconsidered things and made the right decision." Calvin smiled. "Oh, and I would also like to say hello to my fiancée, Shayla, who has stuck by me throughout this entire ordeal and who continues to be a source of inspiration to me with her love and understanding."

I got such a rush that I ran to the TV and kissed it. I was so surprised and excited. I had wanted Calvin to reel me back in, and he had definitely done that. I sat on the edge of the bed, feeling overwhelmed. The newscaster was already reporting on some other story, but I was so caught off guard by Calvin's announcement that I couldn't quite move yet. I then suddenly started packing my bags. *I have to go home.* I figured if I were fast enough, I could get on the 11:30 pm Delta flight back to Atlanta. *I need to go home to my man.* I packed frantically. I had so many bags that I had to request a box. I would just ship the extra items.

Once I arrived at the airport and got through security, I called Calvin. He answered after the first ring.

"Hello?" he answered wearily.

"I'm flying standby, but I think I'm gonna make it on," I said.

"Where are you?" he asked. I could tell that I had awakened him.

"I'm still in Vegas, but I'm getting ready to get on the next flight to Atlanta. I saw you on ESPN," I said softly. "I love you, Calvin. Thank you."

"Oh, so now you believe me?" Calvin said. "Uh-huh."

"I believed you all along. I just love you so much and I had gotten my hopes up real high about us getting married. I was hurt."

"Shayla, there is one thing you need to understand about me," Calvin said.

"What?" I asked.

"I'm gonna marry you and I have never asked a woman to marry me before, so just don't doubt me again, okay?"

"Okay," I said.

"So, what time does your flight get in?"

"Early . . . like 6 o'clock am in the morning or something like that. I better go, baby. They just called my name."

"So, are you coming straight over here when you get in?"

"I don't know. I guess if you want me to," I said.

"Hell, yeah I want you to. Just come straight over and give me some of that good lovin before I have to be at practice."

"Now, now, baby. Since they reinstated you, I don't want you to overexert yourself in the wrong way. Maybe we should abstain for a while."

"Shii'it. You better get your ass over here time you land. I'll have a car waiting for you and I'll be under these covers waiting."

"I love you, Calvin."

"Love you too, babe."

"Bye."

"Bye, Love."

I rushed to board the plane and right when I sat in my first class seat at 6A, a flight attendant approached me. She had a caramel complexion and was quite attractive. She smiled, seeming extremely bubbly. I looked up at her.

"You want anything to drink?" she asked, smiling.

"No, thank you," I said wondering why she was looking at me so intently.

"You are even prettier in person," she said in a low tone. "I saw you on TV the other day with Calvin Moore."

"Oh. Why, thanks," I said, feeling like I was a celebrity.

"I'm Lea," the flight attendant said, extending her hand.

"I'm Shayla," I said as I shook her hand. Her grip was quite strong.

"I went to high school with Calvin," she said.

Oh no. I feared that my pleasant feelings would soon turn sour again. *Not tonight. I am not in the mood.*

"Really?" I said feeling intimidated all of a sudden. I feared that Lea would say something I didn't want to hear. I wondered if she had dated Calvin. I gazed up at her, unsure of how she wanted me to respond. I felt uncomfortable with her hovering over me.

"So, did you date him? I asked boldly, but politely.

Lea let out a hearty laugh. I watched her closely as she covered her mouth with her hand to hide her loud squeal. She knelt down by my seat on one of her knees. She then looked around cautiously to see who was watching, and she turned back to me with a big grin on her face.

"No, I never dated Calvin," she said. "He was too goofy for me back then, but money can change things and people," she smiled.

Calvin, goofy? She must have the wrong Calvin Moore. *Not my Calvin Moore- goofy. Not Smooth C.* And then I remembered he supposedly met Cristi Perez in high school.

"So, did he date a lot of girls in high school?" I asked anxiously.

"No. Not at all. All Calvin thought about was sports, especially football. In fact, he only dated one girl, and that was his senior year."

"Was her name . . ."

"Cristina Perez," Lea interrupted. "She had moved from the islands and she was Miss. Homecoming. I think they started dating after homecoming. He presented her with the team ball, but none of the girls liked her. She was this bi-lingual girl who just came to our school and took the title of Miss. Homecoming from all these girls who had been at our school for years. She came to Washington High her senior year. She was wild. She changed Calvin."

Suddenly Lea got up, but I wasn't ready for her to go. I wanted to hear more. Lea seemed to sense my anxiousness.

"I'll be back after we finish the service and we can chat," she said.

"I'd like that," I smiled.

It seemed to take forever for the snack service to end once we got in the air. I had planned to sleep so that I could be well-rested for Calvin, but I couldn't close my eyes. Lea was quite striking. She had a short, brown, curly hair and her smile was tooth-paste commercial beautiful. She walked with the grace of a ballerina.

Finally, she came and sat by me in the vacant seat beside me. We were on the last row, so I guess it was okay for her to take a passenger seat.

"Will Calvin be picking you up at the airport? I haven't seen him since high school," Lea said as she removed her flight attendant wings.

"No. He's sending a limo for me," I said.

"Oh. Well, that's nice. So, what were you doing in Vegas?"

Okay, honey, you are getting a little too nosy, I thought. I hesitated to answer her as I looked at the huge diamond ring on her finger that was about the same size as mine.

"Well, Calvin and I were going to hang out, but ..." I stopped in my tracks, feeling that I was sharing too much information.

"Were you two gonna get married?" she asked excitedly.

"No," I said wistfully. I still wasn't completely comfortable with Lea. "No. We were just gonna kick it and see some family of mine."

"Oh, that's nice, but I bet you could have gotten him to the altar out there," she said as her eyes lit up as she stared at my ring. "Oh, my goodness. Your ring is beautiful!" She then grabbed my hand, holding it in hers. "How many carats is this, six?"

"No, eight," I said, discreetly pulling my hand away.

"Oh, I'm sorry," Lea said, noticing my reticence. "I know you're like, 'Who does this woman think she is?' I just feel like I know you since I knew Calvin so well."

"So, you were in the same class as him?" I asked trying to get her to cut to the chase and get to the stuff I really wanted to know.

"Same class?" she said. "Calvin lived right below me in the same rat infested apartment for eight years. We are from the hood. I saw him grow up from this little, quite battered child to this senior football player who had all the colleges interested in him and the most beautiful girl at Washington High wanting to be with him."

"Wait," I said. Lea was really beginning to irritate me with her subtle, yet overt insinuations. "What are you talking about 'battered child?' Where did you get that from?"

"Oh, so you didn't know?"

"Know what?"

"I really shouldn't be telling you this . . ."

"No, tell me. I need to know what you're talking about. Don't leave me hanging now."

"Shhh," she said putting her finger to her lips. "I'm not supposed to be sitting here."

"Well, you can get up after you tell me about Calvin being battered. Who battered him?"

"Please tone down your voice," she said. "A lot of people sleep on these all-nighter flights."

I was getting pissed at Lea, but I wanted to know what she was talking about.

She shifted in the seat, leaning close to me. "Well, you know Calvin's dad was an alcoholic, right?" she asked.

"Yeah. He died of cancer or something, right?"

Lea looked down at the floor as if I had gotten the wrong info. "Well, Calvin wasn't really close to his father. He hardly knew him," she said emphatically. "I'm surprised he hasn't told you this. Oh my goodness, I feel so bad for telling you this."

I rolled my eyes to the ceiling and looked at Lea, trying my best to be patient with her and not tell her to get up and leave.

"Calvin's real dad was a pro football player. But the man that raised Calvin is in jail – his step dad by default."

"What?"

"Yeah, it's a sad story, but Calvin's Mom's boyfriend, the man in jail, used to beat and torture Calvin because he found out that Calvin wasn't his biological son. He was so mean. It was unreal. I used to hear Calvin crying all the time. He even ran away a few times. Everybody on the block was scared of his so called dad. Calvin tried to do everything to please him. But at most times, he'd just play sports and go into a shell. He never socialized much until his senior year, after he met Cristina. She brought him out. Henry wouldn't let him do anything."

"So, why is Henry in jail?" I asked, never having heard Calvin mention a Henry before or even that his mother's boyfriend raised him.

"Girl, he got convicted of stalking then kidnapping some woman. My mom told me that. It just happened a few years ago. Calvin's mom left Henry right after Calvin went to college on a scholarship to play ball. She was never married to Calvin's biological father. They just had a fling, so Calvin didn't really know his real dad. Henry was in his mom's life before she became pregnant, so naturally, he thought Calvin was his child. Calvin's mom was afraid to leave him. He used to beat her too. She and my mom were really close."

I looked down, trying to hide my shock. I felt that Lea's story had some validity though.

"So, what about Cristi?" I asked.

"Oh, she was a wild thang. I'm almost sure that she was Calvin's first love and the first girl he ever had sex with. She wouldn't let that boy breathe. When I saw you on TV with Calvin during his press conference yesterday you don't know how glad I was that it was not Cristina Perez. She had gold-digger written all over her even in high school. Supposedly, she came over with her family, but was dating some minor league baseball player from the islands at the time. I think she truly fell in love with Calvin, but from what I heard, she would go off to see her minor league guy a lot too. He's still playing baseball, from what I hear."

"Oh, okay." I said, as I thought about Calvin being abused as a child.

"Did Cristina have a baby by Calvin?" she asked

I cringed at the reality that Cristi had indeed had Calvin's son.

"That's what I hear," I said emotionless.

"Listen," Lea said softly. "I need to get back up and work. Just do me a favor and never mention to Calvin that I had this conversation with you. I just felt comfortable opening up to you because sometimes it's easier to figure out a person if you know their past scars and history," she said somberly. "Calvin didn't have the best childhood, and I'm sure that he is probably seeking now what he didn't get back then. You know, love, admiration, attention. Just hang in there with him. Because most men who don't get the attention they needed as children look for it through any and everybody when they grow up."

Lea squeezed my hand and stood up. "Just hang in there," she repeated and walked away.

I was quite numb from her revelation about Calvin's childhood. I wanted to ask her more questions, including for proof that she really grew up with Calvin. I also wanted to know who had given her the enchanting diamond ring. I closed my eyes and imagined Calvin as a little boy and teenager, shunned and tortured by his mother's boyfriend. *How could Norma Jean allow this? What kind of mother would allow a man that's not her child's father to beat and abuse him?* I got full thinking about it. In a sense I felt like Calvin was a lot like me. We both never knew our real fathers. Just like I sought validation through his love, he sought validation from others constantly. He was searching for the attention he had missed while growing up. For Calvin the attention now came through football and people who put him on a pedestal.

I couldn't wait to get to Calvin's house so that I could wrap my arms around him and give him my unconditional love.

Chapter Thirteen

Soul Ties

Two weeks had passed since my return from Vegas and I couldn't quite believe what was happening to me on this 24th day of January. Deidra had just handed me a letter of resignation to sign, and she had given me no prior warning that my job was on the line. I sat in her office, furious that she had such little consideration for me and my welfare. I understood that she was my boss, but I thought she was my friend as well. After all, she had visited me in the hospital after I lost the baby and had always told me to call her if I needed anything.

"But, Deidra," I protested. "What if I don't want to sign this letter of resignation? I don't want to resign." I looked at her in confusion.

"Shayla, you've only been to work three times since the New Year and we need someone more responsible. I've tried to be understanding, but we've found somebody else to replace you," Deidra said matter-of-factly.

"Deidra, I don't understand why you couldn't tell me that my job was on the line," I said, with a look of disappointment.

"I have told you several times," Deidra said quickly. "You just didn't listen. But to make this easier for both of us, you can go ahead and sign the letter of resignation and clean out your desk by the end of the day. And I'll be willing to give you a decent recommendation despite your lack of responsibility and despite your poor reliability record."

"I'm not signing this Deidra, because you didn't give me any fair warning." I pushed the letter of resignation towards her on her desk.

"Well, then you are fired, and that won't be a very good thing in your pursuit of another job in this industry, will it?" Deidra asked adamantly. "And maybe you don't need a job right now, Shayla," she said snatching up the resignation letter.

"Maybe you just need to take some personal time off for yourself, so you can concentrate on Calvin and being with him, because every time I turn around you're asking for time off to go to his games, be at his press conference and to heal the emotional and physical wounds that he causes . . ."

"Excuse me?" I interjected, highly offended by Deidra's words.

"You heard me right," Deidra said, not backing down. "You have put Calvin Moore before your job and even before yourself, Shayla. And your personal life is your personal life, but when it comes to Saks Fifth Avenue, we need someone with more dedication and work ethic. Now, are you going to sign this or not?" Deidra held up the form letter.

I was shaken by Deidra's abruptness, but I knew she was right about me putting Calvin before my job. Since Calvin and I had gotten engaged, I had called in every week. I had only been to work twice since I had returned from Vegas. I had attended both of Calvin's playoff games, one in Denver and the other in Baltimore, in which the Falcons had won and were headed back to the Super Bowl, indeed. But Deidra had no right to say that I was putting Calvin before myself and rehash old hurts. I felt she wasn't empathetic at all. *Maybe she is just envious.* Saks was her life and she had put her all into her job ever since her divorce a year ago.

I took the letter from Deidra and gave her a pensive look. I then slammed the paper on her desk and picked up one of her pens and signed my name to the resignation letter. I handed the letter back to her.

"You know, jealousy gets you nowhere," I said with calm bitterness.

"Jealousy?" Deidra said and laughed. "Oh come on, Shayla. You know I'm not jealous of you."

"Oh, you are jealous," I said. "You're a hater. I have someone who loves me and all you have is this job, which can't hold you at night."

"Look. Just leave, Shayla, because you're going to need more than some man who holds you at night."

"You don't know what I'm gonna need," I snapped.

"You're right. I don't know," Deidra said and stood to her feet. "Please leave." She pointed to the door.

After giving Deidra a piercing look, I walked towards the door, opened it, and slammed it behind me as hard as I could. I went straight into the buyer's office and cleaned out my desk frenziedly. Three other buyers were in the office, but no one said a word to me as I threw my things into Saks shopping bags. They must have already known that I was being asked to resign. I felt hurt, but I wasn't about to let them see me cry.

After packing my things, I rushed out to my car and drove home quickly. I lived only a short distance from Saks and I knew that my apartment would be a safe haven for me to ball my eyes out. Upon entering my apartment, I heard my home phone ringing.

"Shit," I murmured, not wanting to talk to anyone – not even Calvin. He was once again enmeshed in football and the upcoming Super Bowl. We had just argued the previous night about our wedding plans. He didn't want to set a date. Calvin had told me that he needed time and didn't give me any additional explanation. After I returned from Vegas and we had a passionate morning of lovemaking, I thought Calvin was becoming more vulnerable. I even felt that I had an edge by knowing about his past hurts and pains from childhood. But just as I was beginning to see the more loving, concerned, vulnerable side of him, he seemed to change overnight. Calvin scored four touchdowns, helping the Falcons secure a Super Bowl rebirth, and once again, I felt like I came last in his life. I knew I came after football, his numerous endorsements, and his son, who Calvin suddenly started talking about more. He called him "Little C." I became truly threatened knowing that Crisiti had been Calvin's first love. Each time I mentioned marriage, Calvin seemed to grow quiet and distant. Finally, last night, during our conversation, Calvin blurted out, "I just need more time, Shayla!" in a tone that revealed his impatience with me. My response was, "Okay. Calvin. You take more time," and I hung up on him for a change. I felt that Calvin was somehow falling out of love with me and I was definitely confused when it seemed that everything was going so well for us when he was suspended from the team. *Things will be better once the season is over.*

"Hello?" I answered, after throwing some of my Saks bags on the living room floor.

"Shayla, it's me,' Sydney said. Her voice sounded distraught and her breaths were fast.

"Sydney, what's wrong?" I asked, fearing something had to be wrong for her to sound so out of breath.

"It's Curtis."

"Curtis?" I echoed in confusion.

"Yeah. He has been constantly showing up at my place uninvited – like he did on Christmas Eve, and I just need to come over there and stay," Sydney took a breath. "Can I spend the night over there tonight?"

I was definitely caught off guard by Sydney's question. She had never asked to stay overnight with me. For a brief second I imagined that she and Aaron had broken up. *But why is she talking about Curtis?*

After a little hesitation I answered Sydney. "It's no problem. You can stay over here, but I'm supposed to leave the day after tomorrow for the Super Bowl."

"Oh, so you're going early this time?" Sydney asked, seeming to have calmed down a bit.

Although her question seemed innocent, it still brought back memories of last year's Super Bowl and how Calvin had invited me to come to Miami only a day before the actual game. I cringed, thinking that Calvin's son with Cristi might have been conceived then. I wanted to hurry and finish the strange conversation I was having with Sydney, so that I could call Calvin in New York, which was the host city for the Super Bowl in five days. I wanted to tell him that I no longer had a job.

"Is everything okay with you?" Sydney asked, not giving me time to answer her question.

"Not really," I said somberly. "I'm having a pity party right now, so don't get offended if I'm not very talkative when you get here."

"Well, they say misery loves company," Sydney responded in an understanding tone. I definitely wondered what had Sydney saying she was miserable. She was definitely not her self-righteous self.

"So, when are you coming over?" I asked.

"As soon as possible," Sydney said.

"Okay. Well, I'll see you in a few," I said, feeling a little soothed that I would have company, especially since Sydney was being more real with me.

"Bye."

"Bye."

After dialing Calvin's cell phone and not getting an answer. I dialed his hotel room in New Jersey. I figured that he would probably not be in his room, but to my surprise, he answered.

"Hi, Calvin," I said dryly. "I'm surprised you're in your room."

"Yeah, I was just getting ready to leave. The limo is waiting for me downstairs," he said quickly.

"Don't act distant, baby. I have some bad news," I said, feeling annoyed by Calvin's rushed tone.

"What's wrong?"

"Deidra fired me!"

"What?"

"Well, she actually asked me to resign... and I had to because she was gonna fire me if I didn't. I can't believe she was so mean to me. I feel so betrayed."

"Well, why did you get fired?" Calvin asked.

"She had the nerve to say that I was irresponsible and that I put you before my job."

"She was trippin," Calvin said, seeming slightly disturbed about me losing my job.

"And now I have to dish out almost $2,000 a month for this apartment after Tacara gets married next month. Baby, how about us getting married this spring? What do you think about that?"

Calvin was silent for a few seconds, which made me anxious. I braced myself for his words of rejection. *Why did I even mention marriage?*

"Don't worry about it," he finally said softly.

"Don't worry about what?" I asked curiously.

"About losing your job. You don't need that job anyway."

"I don't?"

"Naw. Once you become my wife, I'd rather you not work anyway, and for now, you can just move in with me."

"I can?" I said, feeling comforted, but confused.

"Yeah, baby. When one door closes, another one opens. We'll be married soon, so after the Super Bowl I'll have some of my boys move your stuff into my place," he said.

"So, you're saying that you want us to live together before marriage?" I asked, still feeling a sense of joy, but disappointed that he did not say anything when I mentioned the spring wedding I had in mind.

"Shay, I want to be with you all the time, okay?" he said, reassuring me. "But I just don't want us to up and do it. I want us to send out invitations and shit like that. We can do it this summer or sometime around then."

My heart pounded quicker from excitement. "Well, what about May 26?" I said, feeling more hopeful.

"May 26? I thought I said this summer, Shayla. More like August."

"But May 26 is my birthday and it's the Saturday before Memorial Day. Everybody will be off that weekend, and what better day to spend my 27th birthday than marrying the man I love?" I said softly.

"Aight, Shayla, damn." Calvin was obviously folding under my pressure.

"You are the man of my dreams, baby," I said elated.

"Yeah, yeah, yeah. But I'm late, Shayla. I've got to go."

"So, May 26 it is?" I asked, needing confirmation from Calvin.

"May 26, Shayla. Damn! And just pack your shit, but don't be bringing a whole lot of unnecessary stuff into my house."

"Okay," I responded, not quite understanding what Calvin meant. But I was too excited to think about it.

"So, I'll call you later."

"Okay, baby. You don't know how much I love you," I said.

"Aight, girl. I'll talk to you."

"Bye, baby," I said.

"Bye."

I jumped so high that I could have sworn my head hit the ceiling fan. Calvin and I had actually set a wedding date, and although it was still four plus months away, I would actually be busy planning so much that I was sure time would fly by. I couldn't wait to tell somebody. Unlike the Vegas plans, I didn't have to keep the May wedding plans a secret. I squealed in joy, and then as if someone had slapped me, I snapped out of my elation. *Calvin has disappointed me before.* My feelings about our relationship were like a pendulum, swinging back and forth. Today I might be joyous, but tomorrow I didn't know how I'd feel. It was all dependent upon Calvin's interaction with me. "Tomorrow I'll be joyous too!" I said aloud. I decided right then, that there was no way, no how I was going to continue the spiraling emotions. I determined that I would be as cheerful, as loving, as attractive, and as understanding as possible when I was in Calvin's presence. I resolved to make myself so lovable that Calvin would not be able to resist marrying me.

After Sydney showed up, I shared the news with her that Calvin and I would be getting married on my birthday. I had already shown her my ring on a previous occasion. She appeared in awe of the ring, but did not say a thing about Calvin and I being engaged. This time Sydney couldn't ignore my words nor hide her feelings. At first her eyes lit up and a stunned smile came across her face. But I immediately felt like this wasn't the time to revel in the excitement of my wedding date with Sydney. Something was wrong with my sister. I was truly concerned.

"That's good," Sydney said with a worried look. "So, you're gonna be celebrating a birthday and a wedding anniversary every year."

I looked at Sydney with apprehension, as she walked into the living room and practically fell on the sofa. Although she never wore much makeup, today she was wearing none at all. Her long hair was lifeless and she didn't even have on a coat. It was 32 degrees outside.

"Sydney, where is your coat?" I inquired.

"Oh, shoot," she said, gazing down at herself. "I just ran out of the house into the garage without thinking about a coat."

"What is wrong, Syd?" I asked my sister, who I had disliked for her goody-two-shoe ways, but loved for her strength, which seemed lacking today.

"I don't even want to talk about it," she said, averting her eyes from me.

As happy as I was about my wedding plans, I felt a twinge of hurt because of Sydney's downtrodden spirit. "Is it Aaron?" I pried. "Are y'all still all right?"

"For now, we are officially broken up," Sydney said. I could tell that she was holding back tears.

"What happened? And why were you so frantic when you called me?"

"Oh, Shayla," Sydney said, reaching out to me, which caught me by total surprise. I embraced her as she sobbed. I didn't know how to sooth my older sister. She had always seemed so strong and resilient, and now I was in this uncomfortable position of being her shoulder to cry on.

"It's okay," I said for lack of knowing what else to say.

"I've really messed up," Sydney said as she pulled away from our embrace. "Aaron will never want to marry me, and God will never forgive me."

"I thought God was a merciful God, willing to forgive anything?" I said consolingly.

"But not when you've lived a lie," Sydney said as she closed her eyes. "God is not mocked," she said hauntingly.

My eyes grew moist as I watched Sydney burst into tears once again. I wished so much that she would just tell me what had happened. *Perhaps she doesn't trust me enough.*

"Sydney, you can trust me," I said grabbing her hand.

"But you're not gonna respect me anymore," Sydney cried. "I've been living a lie."

"But, Syd you are my sister. I will always love and respect you. I always will." I squeezed her hand.

Sydney pulled her hand away from me slowly and covered her face with her hands. She reminded me of myself when I had been heartbroken and in agony over Calvin. Maybe she was more like me than I realized.

"Well,' Sydney began softly. "Aaron found out that Curtis and I had been sleeping together."

I stared at Sydney with a stunned look. I was lost for words.

"I have been having a sexual relationship with Curtis on and off for over a year now," she revealed as she cried. "I don't know why I didn't think that it would catch up with me or that Aaron wouldn't find out. I don't even like Curtis that much as a person. I can't stand him!" she lamented.

I continued to stare at Sydney. Her words seemed unbelievable. After all, she and Curtis had broken up many years ago and she had professed that she had been celibate for over three years.

"Aaron is such a good man," Sydney continued. "We decided we weren't gonna have sex until we got married and I told Curtis about us and the decision we had made. But almost every time Curtis and I got together we ended up getting physical. I told him it had to stop. I told him that I was in love with Aaron and had given my life to the Lord, but he always pressured me for sex, and I somehow always gave in." Sydney burst into a sob.

"Take your time...take your time," I said soothingly.

Although Sydney seemed overcome with torment, she started laughing. "You sound like one of the deacons at my church," she said. But quickly she began to cry again. "I can't believe what has happened. Curtis has been harassing me, popping up out of the blue, calling me at odd hours . . .and yesterday he told Aaron about us having sex."

"Oh, no," I gasped.

"He somehow found out where Aaron works and he waited on him after work and told him everything!" Sydney said, clearly heartbroken. "He told him that I was a whore and that we had been sleeping together way before I got engaged to him. And even once after he gave me the ring," Sydney cried. "And when Aaron approached me about it, I told him the truth. I had to tell him the truth. I'm don't trust Curtis. He is dangerous."

"What the hell is wrong with him? How did all this happen?"

"I don't know, but Curtis is obsessed with me. And I think just because we were having sex he thought I was gonna break up with Aaron and be with him. And I know I was wrong. I know I had no business sleeping with him. I don't know what I was thinking, because after he came over on Christmas, when you answered the door, I met with him the very next week and told him that that was our last time doing it."

I still looked at Sydney with my mouth half open. "But Sydney, why were you having sex with Curtis? There must be something that made you keep giving yourself to him like that," I said, quite confused about Sydney's dilemma.

"The thing that kept me giving myself to him was a soul tie, I guess."

"A what?" I frowned. Now Sydney had me really confused.

"Well," Sydney paused as she cleared her throat. "Sex is so powerful. And I think because Curtis was familiar with me and I was used to him in that way, we never broke up physically. It was like a bad habit we developed... like a drug. But only it was a negative soul tie."

I looked at Sydney, still clueless about what she was talking about.

"So, are you saying that he is your soul mate? I don't understand what you're saying."

"No, he is not my soul mate at all," Sydney said with force. "He is an obsessive and controlling lunatic who I allowed to rule me physically. And this is the final result of my weakness... my sin. I hate him, he hates me and Aaron hates both of us. It's the thing that happens when sex is not contained. People get hurt."

"So, did Aaron say that he no longer wants to marry you?" I asked cautiously.

"Oh, he hates me," Sydney's tears began to stream again. "All along he thought I was being loyal to him and I was living a lie. He told me that he never wants to see me or talk to me again."

"Well, if he loves you, maybe he'll change his mind," I was still trying to console Sydney. "Look how many times I've forgiven Calvin. And I know Aaron loves you."

"No, see you don't understand," Sydney said. "He was serious. He has never said anything he didn't mean. I just messed up. He has hung up on me each time I've called and I just have to face the fact that I blew it."

"So, what does Curtis have to say to you now?" I asked.

"He has been calling and calling and when I called you today he had just left my house. I didn't let him in. I told him when he called last night that I never wanted to talk to him again," Sydeny said.

"Sydney, you might have to take a restraining order out on that crazy boy. He sounds like a fool."

"I know. I know." Sydney looked at me squarely. "Do you mind if I stay here for a few days – until I can get the restraining order?"

"Of course you can," I said as my heart ached for her. "In fact, why don't you come to New York with me for the Super Bowl?" The idea just popped in my mind.

"What? Girl, no. I can't do that."

"Why not, Syd? Calvin already has me a suite and he would pay your airfare, I'm sure. Please come with me."

"I'm not gonna intrude on you and Calvin."

"Girl, you would not be intruding. Trust me. There are so many festivities that go on. There's even this event called the Super Bowl Gospel Celebration and your favorite group, Mary, Mary will be performing." I knew this would be enticing to Sydney.

"Really?"

"Yes. And Calvin is real busy most of the time, so I need somebody to hang out with. We could go to a Broadway show and get our hair did," I said with a chuckle. "And we could just live it up for a few days. When I got back from Vegas, I returned some things that I had splurged on at

Calvin's expense, so he promised that he'd make it up to me after I agreed to take most of the things back."

"Vegas?" Sydney said. "When did you go there?"

"Oh, last year," I said, realizing that nobody knew about my Vegas trip to marry Calvin. "I just want you to come to New York. Please come, Syd."

"Well," Sydney said with an apprehensive look.

"Well, the answer is yes!" I said. "Give me some good news. I just lost my job today."

"Huh?" Sydney grunted.

"Yep. Deidra Washington made me resign because she said I was ir-re-sponsible. But you know what? I'm not gonna have a pity party after all." I grabbed Sydney's hand and smiled. "We are going to the Big Apple!"

A sad smile formed on Sydney's face and she squeezed my hand.

"Okay," she said softly. "But what happened? Why did you get fired? Are you okay?"

"Honey, I'm fine." I wanted to share with Sydney that I'd be moving in with Calvin, but I thought it might not be the best time.

"Could you forgive me?" Sydney asked.

"Forgive you for what?"

"For lying to you about being celibate and acting like such a saint when I was sinking in sin," she said with a tremulous voice.

"Sydney, I still love you. I still respect you," I paused. "I'm still a little confused about Curtis and that soul tie thing, but you don't have anything to ask my forgiveness for. I'm sure that your intentions were right and you are only human." Sure, Sydney had lied, but as my blood sister, I felt like our souls would be tied for life. But for her to be talking about having a soul tie with a man she disliked was beyond me.

"Yeah, but sometimes I know I can be overwhelming," Sydney retracted her hand and wiped the tears that had started falling down her cheeks again. "It's just that I want to be a vehicle for God and I am failing. And I'm sorry for judging Calvin too. I've been mad at him because of your emotional distress over him. But maybe I do need to take the plank out of my own eye," she said. "When I go to New York I'll apologize to him too and give my blessing to your relationship."

I looked at Sydney feeling pleased that she would try to accept Calvin and that she was sharing her pain with me.

"So, will you be my maid-of-honor?" I asked.

"What a dumb question," she said with sad eyes. "Of course I will."

Sydney and I embraced again and afterward I invited her to sit in my bedroom with me while I packed for New York. She suggested warm, casual outfits for the trip. I chose sexy, form-fitting outfits. We laughed at the difference in our taste in clothes. Before long, Sydney was trying on some of my daring outfits to see how they fit her. Her body was shapely and toned, but she didn't seem comfortable with thigh high mini skirts and tight clothing. She liked more tailored outfits that didn't accentuate her figure, but in the summer she always wore beautiful, flair sundresses, that showed off her shapely legs.

"So, how long are you going to keep those dead flowers Calvin gave you?" Sydney asked, looking at the bundle of withered flowers on my night stand.

I flinched at Sydney's observation. My heart leaped as I thought about the last time I saw Diego Jones. I reminisced about the warmth of his kiss and agonized about our last conversation.

"Those flowers were given to me by Diego. Diego Jones," I said softly, feeling overcome by a strange feeling.

"Diego Jones," Sydney repeated as if she were trying to remember who he was. "Isn't that the guy…isn't that the guy we met at the mall with his mother?"

"Yeah," I said quietly.

"Well, tell me more, Shayla! Tell me more!"

"There's really nothing to tell," I said, getting annoyed at Sydney's interest. "He is back in London and he was happy that Calvin and I are planning to get married. He congratulated me."

Sydney frowned. I hoped she sensed that I did not want to talk about Diego. I looked down so that Sydney wouldn't detect my emotions.

"Wait. I'm confused. So, he gave you the flowers to congratulate you for getting married to Calvin?"

"No, Sydney. No," I said impatiently. "He gave me those flowers the first day of the New Year. He stopped by before he left for London and he just brought them with him. It was just a simple gesture. That's all." I wanted Sydney to drop the subject.

"Oh, what a gentleman. Girl, he was so handsome. And there was something about his spirit that I picked up on. If you don't stay in touch with him, I will," Sydney said as her eyes met mine.

I rose to my feet abruptly. "So, you're over Aaron already and want to move on with Diego? Don't push it okay!"

"Oh, girl. I was just kidding. My goodness!"

"Well, Diego and I are not gonna be staying in touch, but neither are you and Diego," I said firmly.

"Okay, okay. Calm down," Sydney said. "Sit down, Mamacita. It's all good."

I felt embarrassed for allowing my emotions to surface regarding Diego. I couldn't understand why the mention of him made me tremble. Instead of sitting down I walked to the bathroom to hide from Sydney what she had more than like already seen. Diego Jones had left some kind of impact on me.

Two days later, Sydney and I arrived in New York. Calvin had a limo driver pick us up at the airport and the driver took us to the Manhattan Hilton. Although the players were staying in New Jersey, where the New Meadowlands Stadium was located, many of the Super Bowl partygoers were staying in New York City. As soon as Calvin was free from practice and appearances, he called to see if Sydney and I had arrived. His voice sounded warm and excited. I didn't know if he was excited about me or about playing in another Super Bowl, but I remembered my vow to put on my best face and attitude for Calvin, no matter what.

On our first night in New York, Calvin took us to a private reception at Jay-Z's The 40/40 Club. Surprisingly, Calvin clung to me like glue, never giving me the impression that he needed his space. Sydney mingled and laughed with the various people Calvin and I introduced her to. Some even approached her, but I could still tell that she was agonizing about Aaron. The next day, after going to the NFL Experience, which offered interactive experiences and entertainment activities and a NFL Player's Wives Association event, Sydney and I met Tacara and attended the Super Bowl Gospel Celebration. The gospel sounds filled the auditorium and Sydney seemed right at home, raising and waving her hand to Donnie McClurkin, BeBe and CeCe Winans, Kirk Franklin, Israel and her favorite duo, Mary, Mary. A few times when I looked at Sydney, she was crying, especially while signing along with Donnie McClurkin's "We Fall Down," but her tears seemed to suddenly be overtaken by a peace that eventually brought a smile to her face.

On Saturday, Sydney and I went shopping at Bloomingdales and other shops on Madison Avenue and 5th Avenue. Calvin had given me a card with $1,000 in it. His note read, "This is a little something for you and Sydney to splurge with while you're in NYC . . . Enjoy!" I was so elated after leaving Calvin's room, where I had spent the night with him the previous night and allowed Sydney to have the room in New York to herself. Calvin had a 10 pm curfew and no one was supposed to have overnight guests in their rooms, but Calvin was a rule breaker, for sure. He insisted that I stay over with him, saying that my good loving would give him luck to win another Super Bowl.

When someone knocked at Calvin's door early the next morning, he assumed it was one of his coaches and jumped up and told me to go hide in the bathtub with the curtains pulled. I did just that. Fortunately, it was only one of Calvin's teammates, Michael Meeks. They laughed hysterically as Calvin pulled back the shower curtain to find me hiding with my knees buckled beneath me.

Calvin's entire demeanor during Super Bowl week was jovial and transparent. He seemed proud to introduce me as his fiancée and treated Sydney like she was a part of his family. Sydney apologized to Calvin for being so hard on him and his response to her was, "It's all good. I'm working on being a better man." He seemed to love that he had won one of my family members over. *Now if I can just get my mother to accept him!*

To my surprise, I did not run into Cristi Perez the entire time I was in New York and New Jersey. I was even surprised that Calvin's mother was pleasant to me and Sydney when we met with her for lunch the Saturday before the big game. She marveled at my ring, and when I told her that Calvin and I had set a date for May 26, she said, "That's nice," and asked me to call her if I needed any help in planning the wedding. I was truly blown away. I figured it must be the new boyfriend who escorted her to the Super Bowl. He was tall, dark and handsome. He also looked to be about 15 years younger than Norma Jean. *You go, girl.*

The night before the Super Bowl, Tacara, Sydney and Lisa, another player's girlfriend, and I opted not to get out in the cold weather. We had eaten at B. Smith's and decided to pop popcorn and sit around and watch a couple of movies. When I fell asleep later that night I had a strange dream about Diego and Calvin. Calvin and Diego were arguing over me and Calvin flaunted his money, telling Diego that he had all the material things I needed and that I would never leave him. Diego told Calvin that money could not buy me happiness and that he would give me lifetime love, security, happiness and also be faithful to me. In the dream I was torn about who I should choose, but before I could decide, Calvin pushed Diego over a dock and he sank into some deep water. In the dream I screamed, "Diego! Diego!" I then woke up, startled form my dream. I realized I had awakened Sydney with my tossing and turning. She sat up, looking startled as well.

"Diego?" she questioned. Her eyes were piercing into mine. "You just yelled out Diego."

I turned in the opposite direction of Sydney and closed my eyes. I tried to block out the gut-wrenching dream. I could not understand why, after such a fulfilling week where Calvin had put on his best behavior, Diego Jones was still in my dreams.

Chapter Fourteen

Burying the Trash

*A*lmost a month had passed since the Falcons won the Super Bowl for a second year straight. Calvin's prediction to be a two-time champion as well as a two-time MVP had come true. In a way, it was like a repeat of last year's overwhelming win, but this time, Calvin scored five touchdowns. His notoriety skyrocketed even more after the Super Bowl win. But the biggest difference between last year's Super Bowl and this year's was that I was Calvin Moore's fiancée. I had grown accustomed to all the hype and drama surrounding his fame. I was used to being written about and being photographed for several Internet sites and magazines, alongside Calvin, as his fiancée. Sometimes photographers would even shoot me when I was out somewhere alone or with family and friends. Most of the stories about me were friendly, saying that I had a sense of style and that I was "beautiful," but there were a few that called me a "fool in waiting" and several blogs tracked Calvin's cheating ways with rumors of him having more baby-mamas besides Cristi.

I wondered about all the rumors, especially when Calvin would sneak into another room to take a call at times when we'd be together, but I sucked in all the rumors after Calvin moved me into his home a couple of weeks after the Super Bowl. When I told Connie, she cried over the phone. "Oh, baby. He'll never marry you now," she said. "Why would he buy the cow when he can get the milk free?" Even when I told my mom that Calvin and I had set a May 26 wedding date she still wasn't happy.

"Calvin doesn't even drink milk, Mommy. And he doesn't need a cow. He needs a woman like me. You should not worry. We are going to be married in a few months," I tried to reassure her.

Sydney kept her lips zipped when I revealed that I was living with Calvin until we got married. I could not detect any disapproval in her voice, but I knew that she wasn't her normal self lately. She had shared with me that she and Aaron had indeed talked a few times but that he still did not want to marry her or even date her anymore. She took out a restraining order against Curtis and he had not harassed her since. Sydney had become quite melancholy, but she continued to go to church, sometimes two or three times a week, and she continued to wear her engagement ring. She said to take it off would be to lose faith. I felt sorry for her. It seemed as though she could not accept the fact that Aaron no longer wanted her. Once they started having conversations though, she believed he might change his mind. She said that she had repented and asked Aaron's forgiveness and was just putting it all in the Lord's hands. *How do you just put things in the Lord's hands?* I couldn't understand how she just planned to let the Lord take care of all of her problems.

Three weeks of living with Calvin had not been everything I had expected. Besides the disappointment of him being in and out of town a lot, when Calvin was at home he often went out with the boys and stayed out until the wee hours of the morning. He still didn't want to talk about our wedding plans and said that May was "too soon." His lovemaking had even grown quite bizarre. We had only made love twice since I moved in and those two times were like "wham, bam, thank you, ma'am," - very quick, and with little passion. I tried to seduce and excite Calvin with sometimes sleazy lingerie, but he always complained of being tired. Sure, my mom had said a man doesn't buy the cow when he can get the milk free, but it seemed as though my milk was turning sour to Calvin. *Does he even want me anymore?*

Today, I had decided to prompt Calvin into a light conversation about his fading desire for me physically. I had spent the night with Tacara, along with four other of her bridesmaids the previous night at the Ritz Carlton after an exciting, but tamed bachelorette party for her. We tried to find out where Steve was having his bachelor party, so that we could crash it, but we were unsuccessful in our efforts. Calvin had come in town yesterday morning from a video shoot in L.A. and he persuaded me to hang out with Tacara overnight.

He said he would "probably" drop by Steve's bachelor party, but gave no clue to where it was being held. He said that he was really tired and could just use a night to himself to rest. I thought it strange that he wanted a night to himself when we had not spent any quality time together lately, nor had we made love in over a week. But I remembered my vow to not question him and to be as loving and understanding as possible. *At least until we are married.* But today, I had to see why he was no longer aroused by me. I couldn't take his subtle distance anymore.

When I walked into the house, Calvin was sitting on the sofa in the den eating a sandwich. He looked rugged and manly, wearing a Nike tee shirt that he had torn off at the sleeves, revealing his muscular triceps. He was only wearing some Sean Jean underwear underneath. He didn't seem to notice when I came inside the house, but I knew that he had heard all the sounds from his alarm system – notifying him that someone had entered.

"Calvin?" I said, annoyed that he wasn't acknowledging my presence.

Calvin looked around at me. "Hey, baby," he grunted and turned back to the television. He was watching ESPN. I walked over to Calvin and sat beside him. I began massaging his broad shoulders. He seemed tense.

"Calvin, what's wrong?" I asked as I slowly turned his head to face me.

Calvin frowned and turned his head away, seeming uncomfortable with my approach. "Ain't nothin wrong. I'm just tired."

"Well, are you tired of me?" I asked softly.

"Naw," Calvin said unemotionally and scratched his head. He then put his arm around me and I leaned my head on his shoulder. "I'm not tired of you," he said reassuringly.

I felt content just to be close to Calvin, but I wanted so much to find out why he had grown so emotionally and physically distant. I pulled my head up and looked at him, which forced him to face me again.

"Do you still love me?" I asked. "Do you still find me sexy?"

As if he need not answer me, Calvin pulled my sweater up, pulled my bra straps down and started sucking on my nipple. He sucked it with such intensity that it hurt. I pulled away and shed the rest of my clothes for him. I still wanted him badly. But Calvin was not gentle at all. He didn't even kiss me while he pounced on me. After it was all over with, about five minutes at most, I wanted to cry. Calvin's lovemaking was forceful and passionless. I felt cheap. I put my pants back on quickly, overcome with hurt. I wanted to let Calvin know that he had not satisfied me, but he already seemed like his mind was somewhere else. He had not taken a thing off during our lovemaking, not even his underwear all the way. He already had the remote control in his hands and was flipping through the channels like nothing had happened. *Damn you, Calvin.* I really wanted it say it, but I didn't want him to change his mind about going to Steve and Tacara's wedding. I jumped up, trying to hide my displeasure.

"Where are you going?" Calvin asked without looking at me.

"I need to get some rest and then get my things together so I can go back to the church," I said trying to hide my hurt.

"So, what time does that wedding start?"

"Six, but the wedding party has to be there at 3:30."

"Oh," Calvin grunted.

I walked up the spiral stairs into Calvin's bedroom. *Our bedroom.* The bed was made perfectly and looked as though Calvin had not even slept in it. I was really glad that Calvin had a spacious bedroom. It was almost the size of my old apartment. He had me put most of my things in one of the other seven bedrooms in the house, but his bedroom was sleek and inviting, with a fireplace and a separate area that looked like a den. Fortunately, Calvin had allowed me to add a few of my personal touches to the already romantic décor. I had been interested in interior design in college and had a keen eye for decorating. Connie had encouraged me to go into interior design, but I never found the time between my different retail jobs. *Perhaps I can learn more about interior design now that I am unemployed.* I definitely had not missed my job at all. *Maybe I'll get pregnant again as soon as Calvin and I are married and I won't have to work at all. Maybe I should start trying now.* I was still on the pill, but I wanted to have Calvin's child as soon as possible. The thought of losing our child made me emotional. My eyes grew moist as I walked into the bathroom and examined myself in the mirror.

The scar on my face still protruded slightly. It was about two inches long, going right down my left cheek. I had been wearing my hair on that side of my face at most times, but today, Tacara wanted all the bridesmaids to wear their hair up. All of the concealing makeup I used seemed to accentuate the scar even more. Interestingly, when a co-worker, Enrique saw my scar at Saks, he told me that it made me look mysterious and sultry. He said that it would always make people have a since of wonder about me. I didn't know if he was just saying those words to make me feel good, but I hadn't gotten the courage to wear my hair off my face since the accident.

After going back into the bedroom and thinking about the quick and unemotional lovemaking that Calvin and I had just had, I slipped out of my shoes, which I had actually kept on while we had sex. When I bent down to move my ankle boots I noticed something on the floor, right under the bed. It was pink. I reached for it and found in my hands an odd pair of silk panties. My heart raced. I nervously examined the panties and knew immediately that they were not mine. I didn't have a pink pair of size 5 panties that had a slit in the crouch. For a moment, I was confused. Then I lost it. I ran down the stairs with the panties in my hand. When I walked in front of Calvin, he looked at me with a pinched look. I threw the panties at him. He ducked, seeming to not know what I had thrown at him.

"What the?" Calvin said, letting the panties fall to the floor.

I bent down and picked the panties back up and dangled them in his face. "Maybe when you invite one of your sluts over, you should have her take her panties home with her!" I said pensively.

"What the hell are you talking about?" Calvin asked with a clueless look. "Get that shit out of my face." He swung at the panties.

"Calvin, who did you screw last night while I was gone, hunh?" I asked, throwing the panties at him, which landed in his lap.

"Girl, you have lost your mind!" Calvin said and brushed the panties from his lap onto the floor.

"Oh, so I guess you have a temporary case of amnesia? Whose panties are those, Calvin?" I demanded with a raised voice.

"Shayla, I don't know who the hell you think you are talking to like that, but the only panties they could be are yours!"

"Oh, Calvin, please!" I said, determined not to let him convince me that the panties were mine. "You lie so good that I think you are starting to believe your own lies. Don't you think I know my own panties?"

"Well, obviously you don't, because the only drawers those could be are yours. Now pick your drawers up off the floor and get out of my face," he said in a cocky tone.

"Calvin, you must take me for a fool."

"Shay, leave me alone now. I'm tired and I don't have time for this panty shit. They are your panties, okay. Your damn panties. Now pick them up and get out of my face."

Confusion flickered through my mind as I looked at Calvin with anger. *Could the panties really be mine? HELL NO; they are not mine.*

"I'm not picking shit up," I said and turned away from Calvin. I knew that trying to get the truth out of him was a waste of my time. I ran up the stairs and into the bedroom where I paced the floor, trying my best to hold the tears back. The panties were evidence that Calvin had indeed had some other woman over. I just felt it. And obviously he didn't know that she left the panties on his floor. *She probably did it deliberately. He probably had sex with her and has been sleeping with her pretty regularly, which explains his lack of passion for me.* I pulled the comforter back and then the sheets, looking for more evidence that Calvin had had her in our bed. I didn't know if I should change the sheets or not, although they looked spotless. *So, that's why he was pushing me to spend the night with Tacara!* I never imagined that he just wanted me to be gone so he could whore around. I didn't know what to do. It wasn't like I could just leave and go to my apartment. In a way, I felt like I was already married to Calvin. I was cooking for him, washing his clothes, and giving my body to him, yet I didn't have his full commitment. I didn't have that piece of paper that made our relationship a legal bond.

Tacara had cautioned me about living with Calvin. She suggested that I keep my own place and ask Calvin to pay the rent until I found a new job. She also suggested that I find a roommate. She felt like I should always have somewhere to go if he started taking me for granted.

Although I tormented over the possibility of Calvin sleeping with another woman, I decided that there was no way I could prove that he had been unfaithful the previous night, so I put it to the back of my mind – at least temporarily. I was so exhausted that I fell right to sleep after laying my head on the fluffy pillow. After waking up, two hours later, I started getting ready for Tacara's wedding. I had not heard anything from Calvin, so I wondered if he was still downstairs watching television or if he had left the house. My question was quickly answered when he walked into the bedroom, sweaty. He had just worked out and was still breathing hard. I didn't know what to say to him, so I turned my back to him.

"You're gonna be late, aren't you?" Calvin said, pinching my buttocks.

When I turned around, Calvin was looking at me sexily. He put his arm around my waist. *Oh no he doesn't want to have sex with me now?!* I moved forward a few feet. Calvin moved forward with my every step. He began to kiss me on my neck. He pulled me closer to his wet, musty body, but I pushed him away.

"Stop. I've got to get ready," I said softly.

Calvin didn't pay me any mind. "Come here, sexy," he said, pulling me close to him again.

"Calvin, you stink," I said, trying to push him away.

Calvin kissed me passionately on my lips while opening the satin night top I had put on before falling asleep. I wanted to shove him, but his gentle kisses were something I had not experienced in a while. I melted when Calvin laid me on the bed and circled my navel with his tongue. My resistance was over at that point.

Although I was 30 minutes late getting to the church, Calvin's lovemaking had definitely made me feel better. He had been quite intense and affectionate. It reminded me of how it used to be for us when we first fell in love. *There is no way he could have been with someone else last night,* I reasoned. I still felt uncomfortable about finding the panties, but after seeing that Calvin had thrown them in the trash, *and he better had,* I figured that making a fuss about them would not solve anything. *Sometimes you just have to leave the trash in the trash can. I am Calvin's fiancée.* And based on the way he had just pleased me, I knew that his love for me was still strong.

Tacara looked beautiful in her flair, princess-like wedding gown with its ten foot train. There must have been 800 guests in attendance. Steve seemed enamored by Tacara as they repeated their vows. I was one of eight bridesmaids, and Tacara's best friend, Erica, had flown in from Washington, D.C. the previous night. She had only said one or two words to me at the bachelorette party, although I tried to make conversation with her. She looked a lot like Tacara in as much as they both had light eyes and fair skin, but Erica's snobbish attitude made her quite unattractive. I figured she was jealous of my friendship with Tacara.

Right after the wedding, everyone in the wedding party was asked to remain in the sanctuary to take pictures. My feet hurt badly and I was ready to come out of the bottom portion of my dress. Tacara had chosen the most unique bridesmaids dresses for us. They had a detachable portion right below the knee, and Tacara had requested that we wear our dresses long at the wedding, but to detach them for the reception. She was also going to change into another dress that was quite form-fitting for the reception. I had spotted Calvin during the wedding, but I didn't know if he had left for the reception or not. As the groomsmen and groom took their pictures I casually looked around the church, wondering if Calvin had left without me. I had already told him that I wanted him to escort me to the reception.

"Hey, Girl!" I heard Sydney's voice. "Who are you looking for? Me?"

"Sydney. You look so nice," I said, checking out my sister who was sporting a sultry silver dress with sheer arms. "Have you seen Calvin?"

"Yep."

"You have?"

"He is out there in the lobby and wanted me to tell you that he will meet you at the reception."

"Meet me at the reception? I told him I wanted him to take me! Tacara had a limo pick me up. He knows I didn't drive."

"Well, I'm just relaying the message," Sydney said. "I think he ran into a few players."

"I see him," I said, spotting Calvin peeping into the church doors. I motioned for him to come down to the front of the church.

When Calvin came to the front pew to meet me, I noticed that practically the entire wedding party and the remaining guests in the church turned their attention to Calvin and me as we embraced.

"Baby, I'm riding to the reception with you." I said.

Calvin slowly released me from his hug. "But how long is it gonna take before y'all finish taking pictures?" Calvin asked looking around at the wedding party. Before I could answer, I noticed Calvin's eyes linger on Erica, who was standing in a seductive stance with one hand on her hip and her feet apart. She was also looking at Calvin and smiled at him sexily. I felt a rush of hostility, so I boldly, but gently grabbed Calvin's face with my index finger and thumb and guided it back to me.

"What?" he said.

"I'm talking to you," I said softly. I then gave Erica a cutting look before turning back to Calvin. "So, are you going to take me to the reception?"

"Yeah," Calvin said and turned again to look at Erica. "Who is that? Is that Tacara's sister?"

I tried to hold my peace. "No. Tacara doesn't have any sisters. That's her best friend from high school," I said as calmly as I could. When I looked at Erica again she slowly turned her back to us, seeming to know that she was being talked about. I didn't quite like her turning her back either. She was definitely stacked from the back.

"Do you all mind if I leave my car here and tag along with you to the reception?" Sydney interrupted. She must have known that things were getting tense.

"Sure, you can," Calvin said quickly, giving Sydney a smile.

Damn. I had wanted to ride to the reception with Calvin alone so that we could capture everyone's attention when we walked inside the crowded reception and get photographed by all the photographers who would be waiting outside. But, I was sure everyone would still take notice, even if Calvin were escorting two women. It was difficult for Calvin not to be noticed and made a fuss over, no matter where he went.

When the bridesmaids were asked to come to the altar to pose with Tacara, I deliberately gave Erica a blank stare as to say, *Don't even think about flirting with my man.* Erica looked at me with confidence. She didn't seem moved by my threatening look. She looked in the opposite direction. When I got to my place for the group photo I looked around to see her and Calvin smiling at each other. Finally, Calvin looked at me. I frowned at him, hoping he would pick up on my displeasure, but he just smiled and turned his head back in Erica's direction. *I can't believe this. I'm really gonna have to get him straight.* All of the other bridesmaids seemed to notice that he wasn't looking at me, but at Erica. I wanted to scream right there in church.

After the photo session was finally over, I immediately walked up to Calvin. He was standing talking to a teammate who was also a groomsman, but their conversation seemed to be ending. Sydney was sitting on the bench on the first pew talking to Tacara's mother. I put my arm through Calvin's arm, feeling the need to put more clarity to being his fiancée. He looked at me as though I had interrupted his conversation.

"What's up?" he asked curiously.

"Nothing. Oh, I didn't mean to barge in," I said looking at his teammate.

Calvin and Guy both looked at me like I had indeed interrupted something, but I wasn't leaving. I clung onto Calvin's arm and hoped that Guy would get the hint that I needed some alone time with Calvin.

"So, man, I'll see you at the reception," his teammate said. I was glad he got the hint.

"Aight, I'll talk to you," Calvin said. Guy walked away.

"What is it?" Calvin said, frowning at me.

"I was just hoping you weren't planning to flirt with Tacara's maid of honor the entire night," I said directly.

Calvin stared into my eyes for a few seconds. He then slowly took my arm out of his. "Shay, I'll meet you at the reception, okay."

"No, Calvin. We need to go together."

"What you need to do is stop being so jealous," Calvin shot back. "Now don't make a scene. I'll see you at the reception. You can ride with the wedding party like everybody else!" Calvin said before wistfully turning around and walking towards the door.

"Calvin," I said in a faint voice. "Calvin!" I repeated a little louder, but he kept on walking. After realizing that he wasn't going to turn around and come back, I started walking towards him, but I felt someone grab my arm to stop me. It was Sydney.

"Let him go," she said in a commanding tone.

Sydney's words stiffened me. I knew that I would look stupid chasing behind Calvin in church. As humiliated as I felt, I didn't want to embarrass myself more, so I played Calvin's abrupt move off by sliding into the pew beside Sydney and Tacara's mother. I looked around the church to see who had seen Calvin leave. As I expected, Erica was staring straight at me. *Ugh!*

"Shayla, chill out," Sydney said. "You are letting them see you sweat. It doesn't look good."

"But . . ."

"But nothing," Sydney interrupted. "Calm down, okay? Just ride with the wedding party. I'll drive my own car and meet you there."

"Okay," I said as I forced a smile.

Tacara's wedding reception was elaborate and ritzy. I had begrudgingly ridden in one of the limos with some of the other bridesmaids and groomsmen. I was still disgusted at Calvin, although I decided to heed to Sydney's advice. Each time I looked at Erica a surge of emotions came over me, making me feel intimidated by her. I knew she was Calvin's type ...beautiful, exotic-looking, long hair, fair skin. I looked around the room for Calvin, but did not see him. After the bride and groom danced their first dance, others joined them. I wanted to dance with Calvin, but I still did not see him, so when Michael, a groomsman that I had walked down the aisle with and the backup quarterback for the Falcons, asked me to dance, I decided to accept his invitation. Michael was about 6'3 and a pretty boy. He looked like he could be from Hawaii or Samalia – favoring Dwayne "The Rock" Johnson. During the wedding rehearsal and rehearsal dinner he nicknamed me "Mrs. CK," but he also flirted with me a little too, by raising his eyebrow at me. His glanced lingered in my direction many times.

After we danced, I drank three glasses of champagne back-to-back, feeling the effect of the alcohol quickly. Not only did I feel tipsy, but my head began to pound. *I'm really not a drinker.* I walked around, still not seeing Calvin, but someone grabbed my arm. When I looked around it was Tacara.

"Tacara!" I said, realizing that I had gone the entire night without congratulating her. I surely couldn't tell her that her maid of honor was causing some problems, so I just followed behind her when she told me that she was getting ready to throw the bouquet.

Tacara must have intentionally thrown the bouquet to me, because without even trying to catch it, the bouquet landed right in my hands and the women around me squealed with excitement. "You're next!" one said. I just stood there in the middle of the floor, dumfounded as Tacara approached me with a smile and opened arms.

"This is my old roommate. She is engaged to marry Calvin Moore!" she told everyone and hugged me.

I flashed a fake smile for the photographers. "Where is Calvin?" Tacara asked. "He needs to be in this one."

"He's probably slipped away somewhere with Erica," I said for only Tacara's ears, realizing that Erica was nowhere in site either.

Tacara's eyes grew wide, but she did not respond. *What am I doing? I can't ruin her wedding day with my jealousy.* But I wanted to tell Tacara that her BFF was coming on a little too strong in her gestures towards Calvin. *Or is it Calvin that's coming on to her?*

Tacara pulled away from me. "Okay, now it's time for my husband to throw the garter. Where is my husband?" Tacara asked, looking around.

"I'm right here, baby. I'll never leave your side," Steve turned around and kissed Tacara on the lips. "Where is the garter?"

"It's on my thigh. You'll have to remove it," Tacara said sexily.

Photographers and guests gathered around Steve and Tacara as Steve cautiously raised Tacara's wedding dress and begin playing with the garter around her lower thigh. Everyone laughed heartily as Steve made a funny expression, showing how much he was in awe of Tacara. He slowly took the garter off Tacara and she blushed like a school girl.

"Gather up all the single men," he shouted before kissing Tacara again on the lips. "Whoever catches this will be the second luckiest man in the world. Of course, I'm the first!" The group of women scattered as the men came in closer to catch the garter. I too, backed away to allow the guys to participate in the garter catching. Sydney stood beside me. "Okay, single men, it's time to see who's gonna be the next groom," the DJ announced over the PA. "All single men come forward now. All single men."

There were about 30 guys waiting to catch the garter. I looked around and saw Calvin walking swiftly to where the other single guys were standing. *There he is.* I sighed. With Calvin being the best wide receiver in the league, I was confident he would catch it.

"Here we go," I mumbled as I watched the garter belt being thrown into the air. I grabbed Sydney's arm and squeezed it tightly, like I was watching a football game and the pass was going in Calvin's direction. "Ehhh," I squealed.

"Ouch, girl!" Sydney said, pulling her arm away.

It happened so fast. The garter went up and in the direction of Calvin, but the back up quarterback, Michael, had caught it with little effort. I saw him raise his hand up proudly, with the garter in it. Since I had caught the bouquet, Michael and I were asked to take a photo together. "And don't I have to put the garter on her thigh?" Michael asked, excitedly.

I slowly walked over to him and he hugged me. "So, let's get this picture in," he said.

Photographers took our picture as we posed together, but one of the photographers asked me to sit where Tacara had sat to allow Michael to put the garter on my thigh. "That would be a great picture," he said. It seemed unnecessary and inappropriate, but I obliged. I sat in the chair and Michael playfully put the garter around my thigh and then took it off, as people laughed. I looked up to see Calvin glaring at me with a solemn stare. Erica was standing beside him, checking me out. She then looked back at Calvin, as if she disapproved. I did not feel good about seeing them standing so close to each other, so I grabbed Michael by the neck and kissed him on the cheek.

"Wow!" he said.

I then grabbed the microphone from the DJ's hand. "It's fitting that I caught the bouquet because I am marrying Super Bowl MVP Calvin Moore," I gushed in the mike. My words were a little slurred because of the champagne. There were some claps in the crowded room. I then looked at Michael. "But Michael, since you caught the garter, I guess that means if Calvin Moore messes up, I might have to marry you!" Everyone roared with laugher. When I looked at Calvin though, he had a blank expression. I saw some of his teammates prod him to join me by the chair. He walked over hesitantly, and once he got near me, I grabbed him around his waist and photographers snapped shots of us. But I could tell that Calvin wasn't feeling the attention. I tried to pull him close, but he lightly nudged his elbow into me. I didn't want to upstage Tacara, so I slowly started walking out of the center of the ballroom, holding Calvin's hand as camera flashes continued to flash.

Maybe I hadn't upstaged Tacara at all. Suddenly, Tacara lifted an umbrella and began dancing with it. Many guests joined in, as white umbrellas were passed around the room. Tacara had told me about the umbrella tradition called "second line" that was passed down from her grandmother from New Orleans, but I had never heard of it or seen it before. The ballroom full of people were dancing around with umbrellas as the sound of a trombone amplified through the speakers. *Is this Mardi Gras, or what?* When someone tried to hand Calvin and me umbrellas he said, "No, thanks." I also decided not to join in on line dance.

"This is so stupid," I said to Calvin.

"Let's go!" Calvin said as he gripped my arm tightly, guiding me off the dance floor. I tried to pull my arm away from Calvin's tight grip, but he wouldn't let go. He seemed angry. I forced a smile, since some were still taking pictures of us.

"Calvin you are gripping my arm too tight," I said, finally jerking my arm away from him.

Calvin narrowed his already narrow eyes and seized my arm again tightly. "We need to have a little talk!" he said in a militant tone. "Let's go outside."

"Calvin!" I murmured as I walked with him reluctantly.

Once we got through the crowd and to a side door that led outside to the terrace, I didn't know what to expect from Calvin. It was like he had changed into a different person. Once we walked outside, he let go of my arm and faced me.

"Why are you trying to play me?" he said angrily.

"What are you talking about?"

"Don't give me that shit!" Calvin barked. "So, you gonna marry Michael if I don't marry you, hunh?"

"What?" I said. "Calvin, I was just kidding. What are you talking about?"

"Wha, Wha, What are you talking about?" Calvin repeated with an even angrier look.

For a few seconds I just looked at Calvin in shock. *Had I made him jealous, for a change, by teasingly threatening to marry his teammate if he messed up?* The longer I didn't speak, the more animalistic Calvin's eyes became though.

"Calvin. I love you," I said in a sweet voice. "Why are you looking at me like that?"

"Because you played me, Shayla," he said cuttingly.

"Baby, I wasn't trying to play you. I was just kidding around up there. Michael knows that you are the one. Everybody knows that."

"Well, why were you letting the boy feel all up your thigh, hunh? What the hell was up with that?" he said, looking at me like I was dirt.

"That's just a part of the ceremony when someone catches the bouquet and the other person catches the garter . . ."

Suddenly Calvin yanked my arm bringing me closer to him. He looked at me with a wild look and then abruptly pushed me away, causing me to stumble a few feet.

"Give me this shit!" he said, taking the bouquet from my hand. He then threw it over the banister and I watched it tumble to the ground.

"Calvin," I said trembling. "I'm sorry."

"I'm leaving," he said. "You can get your sister to bring you to the house or for that matter, go with Michael. But before you come back to my house you better know who you are dealing with because I don't play that shit!"

"I'm going home with you. I love you, Calvin."

Calvin moved closer to me and I tried to stand still without flinching. "Let me tell you something. You ain't nothing but a gold-diggen, unemployed slut with low self-esteem like the rest of these hoes I've had to deal with. Now, if you think I'm gonna be played by you too, then you can just pack your shit tonight and leave."

I could not stop hot tears from flowing rapidly down my face as I looked into Calvin's darting eyes. I felt crushed and Calvin's words had pierced me, but I also felt a strange sensation to hug him. I knew that women had indeed thrown themselves at him only because he was a millionaire athlete, but I truly cared for him. A chill went up my spine as I remembered the conversation I had with the flight attendant who told me about Calvin's childhood. As he stared at me with a threatening look, I saw a little abused boy who needed love desperately.

"Let's go home," I said softly as I raised my hand and touched Calvin's face gently.

Calvin yanked my hand away from his face and turned around abruptly. I walked fast to catch up with him and I slid my arm through his as we walked through the doors leading back inside the lobby. Calvin walked swiftly and I tried to keep up with his every step, ignoring people who were standing in the lobby – some still snapping photos of us. By the time we got to Calvin's car, which was parked right in front of the Ritz Carlton, my eyes were dry, but I felt as though my spirit was crying. I could also tell that Calvin wasn't happy. He was a multi-millionaire, he was the best in his game, he had beautiful women flocking to him. *But Calvin is not happy.* I knew he didn't mean the things he had said to me on the terrace. I figured he was just showing me a side of him that feared abandonment.

After I let myself in the car, I put my hand on Calvin's knee. "I'll never leave you, Calvin. I will never be with another man. I love you too much," I said.

Calvin didn't respond. He put his brand new Maybach in reverse with force and then in drive and sped down Peachtree Road.

Chapter Fifteen

Baby's Breath

I tossed and turned all night, unable to sleep. Calvin had not said one word to me since leaving the wedding reception and neither had he come to bed. I walked downstairs at 3 am to find him asleep on the sofa, but when I asked him to come to bed he growled something I couldn't understand and turned his back to me. I had never seen him so distant, so it worried me. Sure, Calvin sometimes had a Dr. Jekyll, Mr. Hyde personality, but I was in love with him. I had also grown accustomed to the glamour of his lifestyle – the fancy cars, limos, diamonds and the paparazzi taking our picture everywhere we went. There were definitely a lot of pains to being his girl, one being the other women, but the perks far outweighed the pains. *I'm not about to give him up.*

Calvin's words of me being an unemployed gold-digger who had low self-esteem had stung, but I knew he was only saying those things in retaliation to feeling like I had disrespected him. His words actually made me want to prove to him that I was not like any of the women he had dealt with before – and especially not Cristi. *I have to get a job.* I closed my eyes tightly, trying to force myself to sleep, but the more I tried, the more my mind raced from one rampant thought to another. It behooved me that Calvin's bad boy ways, and even the way he had yanked my arm had turned me on. *Is something wrong with me?* I wondered if it were normal for good girls like me to like bad boys. I tossed even more, thinking that I might indeed be attracted to abusive men and that I might just be with Calvin because he was a professional baller. I tormented until 5am, and then the house phone rang. Alarmed, I sat up in the bed and quickly grabbed the phone, which was on the nightstand.

"Hello?" I answered anxiously.

"I need to speak to Calvin.... It's my baby. It's my baby. Oh God, it's my baby," a woman's voice cried over the other end of the phone.

"Who is this?"

"Cristi. Please put Calvin on the phone now. It's Little C," Cristi's voice was desperate. I feared that something horrible had happened.

"Is he okay?" I asked, truly concerned.

"Nooo! He is not okay. He is not okay. Please put CK on the phone you stupid bitch," Cristi demanded while wailing.

As much as I didn't like the name she called me, Cristi sounded in total despair and panic.

"Okay. He is downstairs," I said, jumping up quickly.

"Hurry up! Please...please," Cristi cried.

I pushed the intercom button on the wall before going downstairs.

"Calvin!" I shouted into the intercom. "Calvin, it's Cristi on the phone. It's Calvin Jr. Pick up the phone!"

I could hear Cristi's sobs as I held the phone. "Oh, God please let him be all right. Please," Cristi cried.

"Cristi, I'm gonna go downstairs to wake him up, but don't hang up, okay?" I said, heading down the stairs.

"Okay. Hurry up, please. The paramedics are working on my baby and I don't know what's wrong with him," Cristi said in short, gaspy breaths.

"Okay. I'm almost there," I said as I ran as fast as I could down the remaining stairs, shaking like a leaf.

"Calvin! Calvin!" I said as I approached the den. "It's Cristi on the phone. Something is wrong with Little C."

As though a bolt of lightening had hit him, Calvin sat straight up on the sofa. His eyes were big and fear seemed to come over him.

"Calvin, baby. Take the phone. It's Calvin Jr. Cristi is on the phone. She said the paramedics are there," I said in despair as I handed the phone to Calvin.

"Cristi, what's wrong?" Calvin shouted into the phone. I kneeled to the floor beside Calvin and embraced his legs, fearing the worst, but praying for the best.

Oh, Dear God, please be with that child. Please, I prayed inwardly. I could hear Cristi's frantic voice coming through the phone.

"So, is he all right?" Calvin shouted in a strained voice. "Is my son all right?"

I began to cry seeing that Calvin was getting emotional. "Calvin, is everything okay?" I asked as I gripped Calvin's leg tighter.

"So, why did he stop breathing?" Calvin shouted. "Is he breathing now?"

"Oh, God," I cried. I raised myself off the floor and sat on the sofa beside Calvin.

"I'll meet you at the hospital. I'm turning my cell phone on. Call you when I get in the car," Calvin said and threw the phone to the floor violently.

"Calvin, is he okay?" I asked in tears. "Please tell me he's breathing." Calvin stood to his feet and grabbed his cell phone, turning it on. He said nothing to me. "He is breathing, isn't he?" I asked.

"Yes, he's breathing now," Calvin said, seeming disoriented, looking around the room. "I can't believe this." Calvin picked up the pants he had worn to the wedding off the floor and put them on clumsily.

"Oh, Calvin, don't worry. It's gonna be okay," I said as I stood and hugged him, trying to comfort him. "I'll go with you to the hospital."

"Move!" Calvin said as he pushed me away abruptly. "I don't want you to go."

"But Calvin, I care about Calvin Jr. too. I want to go with you," I whined.

"I don't want you to go!"

"But, Calvin . . ."

"No!" he shouted in a tone that was so loud it made me jump. "He's not your son!"

I looked at Calvin, still shaking and hurt by his words, but I knew that I would have to be strong. It was clear that Calvin's spirit was broken and my pushing him to let me go to the hospital with him would only make him more upset.

"Okay. Calvin. Well, please call me as soon as you find out how he's doing, because no, he is not my son, but he is a part of you and I love you," I said emotionally.

Calvin didn't respond. He still looked dazed. "Where's my damn shirt?" he grunted.

"Baby, don't wear the shirt you wore to the wedding. Let me go get you another shirt."

Before I could turn to go upstairs, Calvin spotted his shirt on the floor and picked it up. He put it on without buttoning it and slipped on the black shoes he had worn last night without putting on socks. He then grabbed his key off the table and stormed out the kitchen door.

I was not sure what to do. I was afraid Calvin would drive like a maniac. A part of me wanted to follow him, but I knew I couldn't get my clothes on quick enough nor would I be able to keep up with Calvin's speed. My heart ached for Calvin Jr. Since I had moved in with Calvin, Cristi had been no real issue or threat, but Calvin had started talking about Little Calvin Jr. more and more, which made me aware that he did spend time with his son. I realized that he had to see Cristi if he saw Calvin Jr., but it didn't worry me. He had several pictures of Calvin Jr., who was a cute, healthy looking baby with silky black hair and a beautiful light brown complexion. From his pictures, he looked a lot like Cristi, but he had Calvin's square jaw line and narrow eyes. Calvin had revealed to me that Calvin Jr. had been born a month early, which made me wonder if his slightly premature birth had anything to do with what he had experienced tonight. He was only five months. I could only imagine Cristi's despair if she discovered that her son was not breathing.

For the next three hours, after taking a shower and getting dressed, I sat on the sofa hoping I would hear from Calvin and calling him a few times, but I had not heard from him nor would he answer his cell phone. I even tried to call every hospital in Atlanta and the outskirts of Atlanta, but no hospital had records of admitting a Calvin Moore Jr. The sun was already peering through the curtains and I had not slept at all. It was going on 9 am. Calvin had left one of his phones on the floor by the sofa, so I picked it up and turned it on. The blackberry rang time I turned it on.

"Hello?" I answered. "Calvin?

"No, I'm calling for CK. Is he there?" a woman said.

"No. Who is this? This is Shayla, CK's fiancée."

After a long silence the woman grunted and then spoke. "This is Champagne."

"Champagne?"

"Yeah. That's what CK calls me. Could you tell him to call me when you speak with him, please?"

"Champagne is obviously your stripper name and not the name your mama gave you. Champagne, did you know that CK is engaged to me and we will be marrying in a couple of months?"

"Well, that's not what he told me," Champagne quickly said.

"So, exactly what did he tell you and why are you calling him?" I said, starting to get irritated.

"He told me he loves me and that we are gonna get married," Champagne replied.

"Oh, is that right?"

"Yes, it is. And I am seven months pregnant," she added. "And CK is the father."

A chill shot up my spine. "You know what? I don't have time to sit here talking to some ignorant, ghetto slut who calls herself Champagne. Don't call Calvin again. Find yourself another daddy for you baby!" I hollered and hung up on Champagne.

I burned with anger as I ran upstairs and paced the floor, which was becoming more of my norm since I had moved in with Calvin. *Could Calvin really have another woman pregnant?* I started thinking about the panties on the floor. *They weren't mine.* I then remembered Calvin opening a letter from Miami-Dade's Family Court that Calvin destroyed in the paper shredder as soon as he opened it and read it. I thought that was strange. The Internet blogs said that he had two or three babies by two or three different baby's mamas. I needed to accept that Calvin had not been faithful to me. He never practiced safe sex with me. *It's a wonder I haven't contracted a disease from him.* That was Calvin's saving grace. The fact that every time I went to the gynecologist I received a clean bill of health or only had a yeast infection or a non sexually-related bacterial infection here and there made me cling to the fantasy that if Calvin was cheating, he used protection. *But could I just be lucky?* With the high rate of HIV and AIDS by young African-American women, I knew I couldn't keep playing with fire by sleeping with Calvin unprotected, especially after getting signs all the time that he was sleeping around. I felt like such a weakling, but I didn't know what else to do. I didn't like what was becoming of my life and my morals. Here I was, almost 27, attractive and well-educated, but I didn't have a job and was living with and planning to marry a man who constantly cheated on me and who had fathered at least one child while we were dating. *Maybe my self-esteem is lacking. I don't know who I am anymore.* Part of me yearned to be loved by a man who could respect me and cherish me, like I thought Diego Jones would be able to, but another part of me wanted to be with a man who could give me the excitement of an unpredictable, fame-induced lifestyle.

After much torment for a while, I thought about calling Diego just to say hi, but I rejected the thought - again. I then lay my head on the bed in the bedroom and closed my eyes. I couldn't fight off the sleepy, exhausted feeling that seemed to overtake my body. I felt listless.

When my cell phone rang, awakening me I recalled the events of the previous night and rushed to answer the phone, hoping it was Calvin, but it was Sydney.

"Hello?" I answered.

"Hey. What's up? Where did you and Calvin disappear to last night?"

"Oh, God, Sydney. It is 12 noon and Calvin hasn't called yet. I am so worried about his son."

"What's wrong?"

"Last night Cristi called saying that the baby had stopped breathing."

"What?"

"And Calvin left to go to the hospital over six hours ago and I haven't heard from him since. I know I should have gone with him, but he wouldn't let me," I said.

"What hospital did he go to?" Sydney asked in a calm yet concerned tone.

"I don't know," I said as I began to cry. "He didn't tell me and I've tried calling about 10 hospitals, but none of them have admitted a Calvin Moore Jr. I don't know what to do."

"Well, stay calm. I'm sure you'll hear from him soon."

"I hope so, because this waiting around is driving me crazy. I'm surprised you're not in church."

"Well," Sydney hissed and then paused. "Aaron and I went to the early service."

"Aaron?" I asked. She hadn't said anything about Aaron last night.

"Yes. We are back together." Sydney said. "He's here with me now. I was calling to see if you and CK wanted to meet us for brunch."

"Oh, really? You two are back together?" I said. I was a bit surprised at her revelation.

"Yes. God is good all the time," Sydney said. "He heard my cry."

"Well, tell me what happened? How did you two just get back together after all that drama?" I said. I didn't want to remind my sister that she had slept with another guy repeatedly, and then again while engaged to Aaron, but I felt like them getting back together so soon was crazy.

"Oh, we've just been going to church together. We both re-dedicated our lives to the Lord too," Sydney said. "Jesus honors those who honor Him."

"That's so good," I said as jovially as I could. I truly wanted to be happy for Sydney, but it seemed as though every time something good would happen in her life, my life would be in more turmoil.

"Well, call me back when Calvin calls and don't worry," Sydney said. "I'm going to be praying for Calvin Jr. and Calvin Sr."

"Okay," I said, feeling that maybe Sydney's prayers might work better than mine.

After I hung up from Sydney's call, I felt despondent and alienated. I twisted my hair around my finger wondering if my life would ever be right or if trouble and confusion would follow me indefinitely. Each time I had been happy with Calvin something seemed to happen to make me dismal. I didn't understand why joy seemed so fleeting and why my love life had to have some much drama.

When 6 pm rolled around and Calvin still had not called, I began to really worry. I had busied myself during the day by cooking teriyaki chicken, brown rice, broccoli and corn on the cob. I also cooked Calvin's favorite sweet dish, a red velvet cake, which my mom had given me the recipe to many years ago. The thought of my mom made me realize that I had not spoken to her in over a week. She truly disapproved of my living arrangement with Calvin and when I told her that I had lost my job she told me she didn't raise me to be dependent upon a man. I was so tired of her unwarranted advice. I contemplated whether I should call her. *No. I love her. But I don't want her scolding me.*

Finally, at 8:30 pm I heard the garage door open. I ran to the door to meet Calvin. He looked exhausted. I was a little surprised he had on something entirely different than what he had on when he left for the hospital. He had on a black sweat shirt and some jeans.

"Is Calvin Jr. okay?" I asked anxiously. "Please tell me he's okay."

"Hopefully he will be," Calvin answered in a despondent tone.

"Oh, Calvin, baby," I said embracing him tightly. "I have been so worried. I love you so much."

"Get off me," Calvin said coldly.

I pulled away and looked at him sadly. "Calvin, please don't be mean. You're scaring me."

Calvin just stared at me intently.

"What's wrong?" I asked. Calvin didn't answer. He walked right past me into the kitchen and then into the family room where he fell on the La-Z-boy recliner like he was depleted of energy.

"So, what is wrong with him, Calvin? Is Calvin Jr. going to be okay?" I asked, sitting on the sofa opposite him, trying my best to tread lightly.

Calvin didn't answer again. He looked down at the floor. And then without warning, Calvin started crying. I was so caught off guard by his cries that I sat looking at him for a few seconds, not knowing what to do. He rocked back and forth in the chair. He seemed to be in deep emotional and physical pain. I finally rushed to console him. I sat on the arm of the recliner, bringing Calvin's face to my chest. He continued to moan, a controlled cry as I held him. I was quite confused over Calvin's outburst, but he was also embracing me, which made me feel comfortable.

"It'll be okay, baby. I promise everything will be okay," I cried.

"But how do you know?" Calvin shouted as he pulled away from me. His eyes were filled with tears. He glared at me as though he really needed me to tell him why his child would be okay.

"Because…because," I stammered. "Because Calvin Jr. is an innocent baby and God is going to take care of him. I just know it," I said grabbing Calvin's head and pulling him closer to me again.

"But he is so little," Calvin cried. "And they put him in this incubator. He is too young to be going through this."

"So, what did they say is wrong, baby?" I asked trying to still be as comforting as possible.

"They don't know," Calvin said. "He is having problems with his lungs, with his breathing… and they don't know why."

As much as I wanted to give Calvin answers, I couldn't. I kissed him softly several times on his forehead.

Within the hour, Calvin had taken a shower, eaten my cooking and then he left again for the hospital. Although he told me that Calvin Jr. had been admitted to Elgleston Children's Hospital, he urged me not to come by the hospital and not to call to check on him. "I'll call you," he reiterated.

I knew that I couldn't convince Calvin to let me go with him, so I agreed to his requests and told him that I would continue to pray for Calvin Jr. He kissed me lightly on the lips before leaving, which made me feel like he trusted me.

I did not hear from Calvin again until 6am the next morning. He called saying that he had crashed at the hospital and that Calvin Jr. was still in an incubator to assure that he would get adequate oxygen. When I asked him if the doctors had diagnosed his son's condition, he said that the doctor speculated he had some type of respiratory disease, but that he would more than likely grow out of it. Calvin also said that Calvin Jr. would have to undergo several tests over the next couple of days, but that he was expected to "pull through."

"I pray so, baby. I really pray so," I said feeling relief. "I want to be there for you through this," I added.

"I know you do... and you have been," Calvin said calmly.

"But I want to be there with you now. Please let me come be with you," I sighed.

"No, Shayla," Calvin said firmly. "I'll be home in a couple of hours. Just be *there* for me."

"Okay, baby," I said sullenly. "But I want you to know that I love you more than anything and anybody. You are my life."

There was a long silence.

"Did you hear me, baby?" I asked Calvin.

"Yeah, I heard you."

"I'm serious. I love you more than anything in this world and I want to be in your life forever. I will love you unconditionally, no matter what."

"Thank you," Calvin replied without emotion.

For the next few days I only saw Calvin for an hour or two throughout the day when he'd come home to shower and return a few phone calls. Calvin told me that Calvin Jr. had been diagnosed with a condition called Croup Virus, which usually occurs in children older than Calvin Jr. but the disease causes an unusual cough and trouble breathing. He said that his son had a severe case of it, and that his lungs had been compromised. Calvin also told me that he was concerned about the way Cristi was caring for Calvin Jr. He said that she would take his son into hair and nail salons, and would let any and everybody hold the baby. I speculated that Cristi Perez was unemployed like me and that Calvin was indeed taking care of her too. I did not want to be like Cristi, so I vowed to get myself a decent job. In fact, I had answered an ad in the newspaper for a fashion show coordinator at AmericasMart Atlanta, a large wholesale mall for buyers. The job requirements read they were looking for someone with years of retail experience, management skills and a love for women's fashions. *That seems like the ideal position for me.* When I called and spoke with a woman conducting interviews via phone, she seemed impressed with me enough to ask me to come in for an in-person interview. I knew that I had to regain control of my life and not let Calvin be my main focus. *Getting a job in my field will give me a sense of my own identity.*

On the day of my interview, I got dressed in a grey, Ann Taylor texture print wrap dress with a V-neckline and crossover bodice. At first I had thought about wearing a suit, but I felt the stylish wrap dress showed more of my personality. I put on my black sheer panty hose and some black pumps. When I pulled my hair all up I still felt self-conscious about the scar, so I allowed a few curls to fall loosely on my face. Still not pleased with my hair, I let it all fall down and just settled for my usual look.

Calvin was downstairs and it was the first time he had been home for more than three hours since Calvin Jr. had been hospitalized. He had informed me that his son was released from the hospital the day before and that the doctor had given him a good prognosis. I was glad that everything was back to normal. I had missed Calvin's company for more than a week and was planning a very romantic night for us.

When I walked downstairs, Calvin whistled at me. "Damn, you look good," he said as he stopped eating the pancakes I had cooked him and just stared at me.

I giggled; feeling like my business look must have been quite sexy too. I strutted across the kitchen floor, shaking my hips from side to side and swaying like I was a model. I even did a side turn, like the runway models do and ended with my hands on my hips.

"So, what do you think?" I asked, as Calvin looked at me lustfully.

"I think I want some," he said, standing to his feet and walking towards me.

I laughed at Calvin's comment. I wanted him too. We hadn't made love since Tacara's wedding day, 10 days ago, but I knew that I would be late for my interview if I didn't hurry.

"No, baby," I giggled as Calvin grabbed me around my waist. "You'll have to wait until tonight. I have a special evening planned for us. You know I can't be late for my interview." I pecked Calvin lightly on the lips. But he urged my body closer.

"You feel so good," he said in a sexy murmur as he started kissing me on the lips.

"Calvin, I've got to go for my interview," I said. "I need a job."

"No you don't," Calvin said, still planting kisses on me. "Give me some, Shay."

When Calvin's lips pressed against mine, I felt a sense of urgency. I didn't want to fight the feeling any longer. *AmercasMart can wait.* I wanted to give myself to Calvin right there in the kitchen. *He deserves some good lovin.* Right when Calvin was unwrapping my wrap dress, the doorbell rang.

"Who could that be?" I asked as Calvin continued to undress me. "Calvin, somebody is at the door. Go get it." I pushed away slowly and tied my dress back.

Calvin didn't seem to care that someone was continuously ringing the doorbell. He moved closer to me and undid my belt again. The doorbell chime went off six more times back-to-back.

"Calvin!" I said, pulling away from him. "I'm answering the door, okay. Just hold tight. Were you expecting somebody?" I asked, walking towards the front door.

"Yeah, but they weren't supposed to come this early," Calvin said, seeming not to mind that I was walking ahead of him to answer the door. He put his arms around my waist as I tied my dress, once again.

"Who wasn't supposed to come this early?" I asked, as the doorbell continued to chime.

"I was going to tell you when you got back," he said.

"Tell me what?" I asked, feeling somewhat confused that the person would not let up off the doorbell. Before Calvin could answer my question, I had reached the front door. Calvin was still holding me.

"Who is it?" I yelled, as I tiptoed to look through the peephole.

"It's me!" a woman answered.

At first my vision of the woman was blurry, but the longer I glared through the peephole the face became clearer. It was Cristi Perez and her baby. I continued to look through the peephole, quite stunned to see her. My first thought was that something was wrong with the baby, especially since she had rung the doorbell at least ten times, but before I could open the door, Calvin grabbed me by my shoulders and gently moved me from the front of the door. When he opened it, Cristi stood smiling with Calvin Jr. in her arms with three oversize suitcases on the ground beside her, and two Louis Vutton duffle bags.

"You were supposed to come later on," Calvin growled as he reached out for his son.

"No. I told you I was coming this morning," Cristi snapped. "Don't be grabbing for Jr.," she hissed. "You need to be grabbing some of my heavy ass bags."

Calvin ignored her and began kissing his son after taking him in his arms. "Hey, Big Boy," he chirped. "Is daddy's boy feeling better?"

Cristi's eyes met mine and she seemed to be sizing me up. She then flounced inside the living room and comfortably placed herself on Calvin's white sofa. He never allowed anyone to just casually sit on that couch. I still couldn't figure out what was going on. I looked at Calvin, who was still cuddling Calvin Jr. and then I glared back at Cristi.

"Somebody want to tell me what's going on?" I asked as nicely as I could.

"Oh, Calvin didn't tell you?" Cristi asked with a devilish grin.

"Tell me what?" I asked, meeting her cocky gaze straight on.

"Me and my son are moving in!" Cristi said with a triumphant smile.

Chapter Sixteen

Baby Mama Drama

*C*risti's statement actually caused me to laugh. Of all the things in the world, I knew that Calvin wasn't bold enough to move her in, so I laughed. Before long, Cristi and Calvin joined in on my laugher.

"Yeah, that's quite funny," I chuckled. "You got jokes."

When the laughter stopped, I looked at Calvin and the expression on his face turned from a grin into a look of nervousness.

"I am moving in with my son, and that's no joke," Cristi said firmly. "Calvin! I don't believe you didn't tell her!"

Calvin looked down at Calvin Jr., who was more beautiful than his pictures. The baby had a head full of hair and his eyes were narrow and sparkly. I noticed he even had dimples when he smiled back at Calvin. For a baby who had stopped breathing and who had been in an incubator for a week, he looked rather vibrant.

"Well, are my bags just gonna sit outside, Calvin? I had the cab driver to bring them to the door. The least you can do is bring 'em inside," Cristi said in an irritated street tone.

"Why didn't you drive?" Calvin asked, still cuddling his son.

"I told you my car in the shop," Cristi said. "You don't remember nothin."

"Naw, you said you had gotten it out," Calvin replied.

"No, I did not. You never gave me all the money to pay for it, remember? You know I been driving that rental car all week. And plus, I thought you were gonna let me borrow one of your cars!"

"I did not tell you that," Calvin said quickly.

"Oh, okay, now I'm just making things up. I guess next you're gonna tell me that you never asked me to move in."

"I asked for my son to move in, so I can help care for him, and you insisted that he can't move in without you. So I didn't have another choice," Calvin said, looking at Cristi and then at me as though I was supposed to understand. The more they talked, the more furious I became.

"Well, he is my baby, CK," Cristi said, crossing her legs.

"And he is my baby too," Calvin said calmly.

"So, que pasa? What's the problem then?" Cristi asked, throwing her hand in the air.

"Hold up, hold up, hold up," I finally interjected. "The problem is that three is a crowd and . . ."

"Four," Cristi interrupted. "It's me and my baby and you and CK, but you don't have to worry about us. You and CK can go on playing house like before. Hell, don't mind me!" Cristi giggled.

I didn't want to blow my cool, but I definitely felt like I was on the verge of losing it. Of all the ridiculous, stupid things Calvin had done, I never imagined he would move his baby's mama and their child into his house while living with me.

"So, I guess it didn't matter what I thought about this?" I said, turning to Calvin with a shaky voice. I was almost in tears.

Calvin looked at me with a frown, as though he was surprised by my disapproval.

"Shayla, what's wrong?" he asked as if he were clueless. "Cristi and I are just friends . . ."

"You said that when you got her pregnant!" I said in a cutting tone.

Cristi started laughing. "Oh, this is so cute. This is definitely cute." She stood to her feet and came towards me. "Baby girl . . ."

"I'm not a baby girl!" I said, smoldering. "My name is Shayla!"

"Well, Shay-la," Cristi mocked. "I do have CK's son and we had a pretty intense relationship, but it's not intense in that way anymore. It's past tense. I don't want him no more, so you don't have to be threatened."

"And I don't want you either," Calvin said in a high pitch tone.

"Well good, because I have a boyfriend," she said looking at me and then Calvin.

"Oh, that old Kermit the Frog looking punk?" Calvin said.

"He does not look like Kermit the Frog," Cristi shouted.

"The hell he don't," Calvin replied.

"Oh, you're just jealous," Cristi said and then she looked at me. "Is he jealous or what?"

I couldn't get any words to come out of my mouth. I knew that if I said anything my voice would crack. I was so enraged that I wanted to slap them both. My eyes batted as I tried my best to hold the tears back. When I felt a tear start to stream down from my eyes, I turned around abruptly and walked away from both of them.

"See there. You've already made her upset," Calvin said.

"I made her upset?" Cristi echoed. "If you had told her we were moving in maybe she wouldn't be upset CK. Give me my baby and go get my bags."

"You can get your own damn bags. I'm not your bell boy."

"CK, so you're just gonna let my bags sit out there in the cold?"

I couldn't take it anymore. I walked as quickly as I could up the stairs and into the bedroom. I ran into the bathroom, where I locked the door and put my back against the door, like I had been running from someone who had been chasing me. I slowly slid to the floor as I held my stomach, and I sobbed.

It took an hour before Calvin came knocking on the bathroom door.

"Shayla? Are you okay in there?" he asked in a concerned tone.

I deliberately did not answer. I had spent the past hour trying to figure out what I should do.

"Shayla?" Calvin said. "Shayla?"

I still did not answer. I was tempted to just pack my bags and go stay with Sydney, but the more I thought about it, the more I realized that Cristi should be the one leaving and not me. I also felt too ashamed to tell a soul that Calvin had moved Cristi and their son in. And since Sydney had gotten back together with Aaron, I felt like she didn't need me interfering with their relationship by moving in. If I told her about my situation with Calvin I was sure she would act like she was better than me and even self-righteous again. I was bewildered. I also couldn't believe I had not gone on my job interview. I really wanted to work, but I definitely wasn't gong to let Cristi Perez and her son get comfortable in Calvin's house while I was off somewhere working. Calvin had been paying my bills anyway. *Maybe going back to work is not such a good idea.*

"Shayla, open the damn door!" Calvin shouted, as I felt the door vibrate against my back from him trying to pry it open.

I didn't want Calvin to break the door down with me sitting in front of it, so I got up from the floor and flung the door open.

"What do you want?" I said curtly, as I stared into Calvin's eyes.

"Why didn't you answer me?" Calvin asked, with a frown.

"Calvin, move out of my way," I said, as I tried to walk around him. "I'm leaving."

Before I knew it, Calvin gripped me tightly around my waist and would not let me pass by him.

"No, you're not leaving," he said as he embraced me with a forceful, yet passionate hug. "You are not leaving me, Shayla, because you love me and I love you," he said with emotion.

I tried to push Calvin away, but his grip was too strong. "But I don't want Cristi here," I sulked. "We can't have a relationship with her here, Calvin."

I tried to bend down and release myself from Calvin's strong embrace, but he would not let go of me.

"Listen to me, Shayla," Calvin said. "Listen to me and stop fighting me. Just listen," he repeated in a raised voice.

I wanted to pull away from Calvin, but I knew that he wouldn't let me, so I stopped struggling, closed my eyes and listened.

"They are only gonna be here for a month," Calvin said carefully.

"A month?!" I said, as I opened my eyes to look at Calvin.

"Listen, please." Calvin said impatiently.

I closed my eyes again, not wanting to be taken in by whatever Calvin was going to say next.

"Shayla, my son almost died, but he's living. He's living, baby. And I want to do all I can to be the best dad I can be to him. Shay, my real dad wasn't around for me … and it almost killed me."

I opened my eyes to look at Calvin again. He loosened his grip around me. He looked as though he were in deep emotional pain reminiscing about his tormented childhood. He had the same expression he had on his face before sobbing about his son being in an incubator in the hospital. I felt his pain. When I searched Calvin's eyes I knew that I couldn't turn my back on him, but I pulled away and did just that. I walked away as my eyes burned with tears.

"Shayla, I promise they'll only be here for a month. I don't even get along with Cristi. I'm just looking out for my son," he said in a gentle voice. "They are gonna be downstairs in the basement and I hired someone to come over everyday to help them, so they won't be getting in your way at all. I promise, bae," Calvin said as he followed behind me.

I had a big lump in my throat and I had to swallow. When I did, I broke down and cried. Calvin grabbed me from behind, kissing the back of my head. He slowly turned me around to face him, and wiped my tears with his fingers.

"Stop crying," he said softly. "I don't want you to cry. I want you to be happy, Shay."

I fell into his arms and this time I held him tightly. I was scared. I was very scared. But I felt that Calvin had good intentions concerning his son. I just felt uneasy about Cristi's intentions.

I imagined her getting comfortable in the lower section of the house, and the thought of having to deal with her for a month made me feel nauseous. As I stumbled towards the bed, Calvin seemed anxious to comfort me and make sure I was okay. He picked me up and laid me on the bed and started massaging my back. His hands were strong and soothing against my skin.

"Take your dress off," he said, fumbling with my dress.

"Uh-uh," I said. "I don't feel good." I didn't want to be tempted to give myself to Calvin, although I was fragile. I knew that he would use my vulnerability to his advantage – as a weakness, and I didn't want to succumb to him so easily. But my body truly yearned for all of him. After Calvin massaged my shoulders and back, he drew close to me, positioning himself behind me. For the next 30 minutes few words were exchanged between us, but Calvin did inform me that he would be filming a Chunky Soup commercial with his mom in a few days. He told me that he had gotten the news yesterday. I was surprised he seemed so unexcited about the opportunity. I wondered if all the commercials, all the video shoots & television appearances, all the magazine covers and star treatment were getting old to him already. It seemed as if his son's illness had changed him in some way.

A few days passed, and surprisingly, Cristi had stayed out of my and Calvin's way. She and Calvin Jr. rarely emerged from the lower level of the house, and when I did see her, she was rather polite, although I often detected a sly smirk on her face that made me suspicious. At most times we would only say, "Good morning" or "How are you?" to each other. I even forgot she was in the house a couple of times, until I'd hear the baby cry or when Calvin would bring Calvin Jr. upstairs. Interestingly, as soon as Calvin Jr. would get too fussy, Calvin would take him right back to Cristi. Calvin never stayed in her presence more than ten minutes unless they were upstairs and Cristi rarely came upstairs. I thought that everything was going pretty good, until day four when things started to go sour.

I had not left the house for three days, unless I was with Calvin, but this time I had no other choice but to leave Calvin, Cristi and his son at the house alone. I was a tad nervous about leaving them, but I knew that I couldn't keep a watchful eye on Calvin and Cristi 24/7. Connie had driven to Atlanta and insisted that I meet her at Sydney's house for a day out together. I had not spoken to her in almost three weeks, so I wasn't about to tell her that I couldn't come spend the day with her and my sister because I had to watch my fiancé, his son and his ex girlfriend, who had moved in with us. I had missed my mom and knew that our distance was not good. Although she was very critical of my live-in situation with Calvin, I knew she also wanted the best for me. I figured Connie would ask me when Calvin and I were planning to marry. But Calvin and I had not spoken about being husband and wife in a while. At first I didn't know if it was a good idea to bring up marriage to Calvin while Cristi and Calvin Jr. were still there, but I wanted to move forward and plan my wedding. *I'm going to bring up marriage plans to Calvin tonight after I return.* In a way, I was looking forward to having lunch with Connie and Sydney and then going to the Mall of Georgia to shop. It reminded me of old times.

Sydney had been extremely exuberant since she and Aaron had gotten back together, but she remained humble. She said that she and Aaron were talking about having a fall wedding.

My day with my family went well. Although Connie quizzed me about my living situation and pressured me to move out if he doesn't marry me by my birthday, which is when I told her we'd be marrying. I kept my composure and just told her that I would indeed move out if I saw that he wasn't serious about marrying me.

"Calvin is just not ready for marriage though, Shay. You shouldn't have to pressure him either," Connie said.

"But he is the one who asked to marry me, Mommy. Why do you say he's not ready?"

"Honey, that boy is in the prime of his life. He's stringing you along," she said with a cynical expression. "He's a playboy. I don't want you to live a lifetime of sorrow and loneliness."

"Mommy, don't worry. Just leave it in God's hands, please."

Both Connie and Sydney seemed surprised by my comment, but I knew I had to say something to get the attention off me and my relationship with Calvin. I wanted so badly to invite them to Calvin's house, so they could see how large I was living, but I remembered that Cristi and her baby were there. *Damn Cristi.*

After a mostly pleasant day of hanging out with Connie and Sydney, I drove home in a bit of turmoil. The thought flickered through my mind that Calvin and Cristi were at the house having sex. I had not heard from him all day, although I had texted him a couple of times to let him know what I was up to.

Upon entering the house, I noticed an eerie quietness. Calvin's cars were all there, so I knew that he had to be around.

"Calvin," I called out nervously. "Cal-vin!" I yelled again, a little louder. Before I could get all the way up the stairs to the bedroom I heard someone's steps behind me.

"CK's gone," Cristi said.

When I looked around at her she was standing at the bottom of the stairway with a smile I couldn't detect. She had on Calvin's Versace robe that I had often worn around the house. She had on more makeup than I usually saw her wear. I wondered what she had on underneath the robe. I stared at her, wanting to ask, "Why in the hell do you have on Calvin's robe?" but I decided that particular question was secondary to what I wanted to know.

"What do you mean, Calvin is gone?" I asked.

"He won't be back for three days. He didn't tell you?"

"Excuse me?" I questioned, in a strained voice.

"He's gone to L.A. to film the Chunky Soup commercial and do a video with Beyoncé. I don't believe he didn't tell you!" Cristi added with a chuckle.

"Wait...wait...wait," I said. "He is gone to L.A?"

"Yeah. I don't know what kind of relationship y'all have, but y'all must not communicate at all," Cristi said.

"Look, Cristi, I don't need you to try to figure out what kind of relationship we have. We do communicate, and he did tell me that he was shooting a commercial. But he didn't say anything about shooting it in L.A. and he didn't mention anything about a Beyoncé video. Are you sure?" I asked, feeling quite annoyed.

"I am positive. He left, maybe a little over three hours ago. He should be landing soon, right? I'm sure he'll call me."

I was losing my patience with Cristi. "Well, this L.A. trip just came up suddenly, I'm sure," I said, turning away from her to go to the bedroom.

"No, he found out about it the morning he was over at my place when his agent called," Cristi said. "We had just brought Little C from the hospital. He has always known that the commercial would be filmed in L.A. and they worked with Beyoncé's people to get the video shot during the same week."

I looked around at Cristi, since it was obvious that she wasn't going to stop talking.

"Oh, really?" I said.

"Girl, that boy is a trip. He probably has some little side piece out there," Cristi sneered. "Do you trust him?"

I was shocked by Cristi's question and caught off guard by her directness. A part of me wanted to turn back around and ignore her, but another part of me wanted to continue talking with her.

"Yeah, I do trust him," I lied. "I just don't trust the side chicks. You know what I'm saying?"

"Well, it's not the side chicks. It's the hoeish man that you need to be worried about," Cristi said as she came up two stairs, as if she needed to be closer to me. "You might be better off with that guy you were with at Cheesecake Factory on New Year's Day, because CK is gonna give you grief. I guarantee it."

Once again, Cristi had caught me off guard and I didn't know how to respond. She seemed to be challenging me to get upset and agitated. I was definitely getting there.

"So, you ran and told Calvin you saw me with someone at Cheesecake?" I said calmly. "That was quite simple of you considering that you didn't know who he was."

"Oh, I know who he is," Cristi said strongly. "I'm not stupid. I keep up with the news. I saw his picture in the paper when they did a profile on his dad's business, the former football player and Rolls Royce man. His son is definitely fine, girl. Does he have any kids?"

She is really pushing it. I gave Cristi an intent stare. But I didn't want her to see me sweat. My heart beat fast.

"What's the point?" I said coldly.

"Ain't no point. I was just trying to make conversation, hon. Why you so touchy? You must really like the guy."

"I don't know what you're trying to find out, but I'm in love with Calvin and I'm marrying him."

Cristi bent over in laughter. For about thirty seconds I just looked at her as she reacted like she was in stitches. *Was it something I said?*

"What's so funny?" I asked.

"Girl, CK ain't gonna marry you," she said, with a smug smile.

"And why do you say that?"

"Cause he don't love you," she said. "He don't love nobody but himself. Plus, he ain't gonna marry somebody darker than him."

"You sound like a fool," I said calmly.

"I might sound like one, but you are one. A stupid fool at that. I'll always have power over CK. He'll always have me around. That's why I'm here now."

"Go to hell, bitch!" I said, and before I could even think about what I was doing, I had taken off my Gucci shoe and I threw it at Cristi. She moved out of the way, but it brushed her shoulder and landed at the bottom of the stairway. *Oh shit.*

"I know good and damn well you didn't just throw your shoe at me. I should come up there and kick your black ass," Cristi said, pointing her finger.

"Get your ass back downstairs where you belong!" I shouted. "You don't know who you're messin with." I felt totally out of control.

"Tu eres una puta y loca. You better be glad CK isn't here because he would beat your ass for throwing a shoe at me! He's not gonna marry you, you little black whore!"

I was quite stunned by Cristi's explosiveness and I had no clue what she had said to me in Spanish. I was also surprised by my own temper. I thought Cristi might come up the stairs after me, but instead, she picked up my shoe and walked away.

"Give me my shoe!" I shouted. But Cristi didn't say another word. I hopped to the bedroom and locked the door behind me. I drew a deep breath. I didn't know if Cristi would come up the stairs after me or not. *She is the one who is loca!* I then saw a note on the bed. I picked it up and read it carefully, trembling.

"Shay, I didn't know you were planning on being gone all damn day. I tried to call u on your cell and it went to voice mail and then I called your sister's but I guess she has changed her number. The location of the commercial got changed to L.A. and I have to be out there tonight! I'm staying at the Mondrian Hotel. I'll be under the name Sammy DoLittle. I'll call you once I land. Love, CKM."

"Yeah, right," I said and slammed the paper on the bed. I felt relieved that Calvin had left me a note, but it was obvious that the location of the commercial had always been in L.A. *Why couldn't he have told me?* I then figured he didn't tell me because he knew I'd ask to go with him to avoid being in the house alone with Cristi. He would have been right. I checked my messages, but didn't see that a call had come in from Calvin. I just sat on the bed feeling betrayed, once again. *Maybe Calvin does have someone in L.A., like Cristi suggested.* I was really angered that she had called me a black whore and had said that Calvin would not marry me. I was afraid of what Cristi would say or do next, but I sure as hell wasn't going to let her intimidate me. I kicked my one shoe off and leaned against the headboard in total frustration. I waited about 30 minutes and then I called Calvin's cell phone. It went to his voice mail.

"Calvin, call me as soon as possible. Everything is fine with Calvin Jr., but there is a big, big problem and I need to talk to you ASAP!" I left a message for Calvin. I then lie on the bed and flipped on the television. I was still fuming.

When I heard three knocks on the bedroom door, I was startled. At first I wasn't going to answer, but I jumped to my feet, walking towards the door in slow motion. I didn't know if I should grab a vase to protect myself from Cristi or what.

"Yeah?" I shouted, trying to have a tough tone in my voice, but truly feeling afraid.

"Shayla, it's me," Cristi said in a calm, soft tone. Her voice didn't give off any hint of anger.

"What is it?" I asked sternly.

"I need to talk to you. It's very important that I talk to you face-to-face. Could you please open the door?" Cristi whined.

I was apprehensive, scared and confused. I feared that Cristi might really do something crazy... like shoot me. She didn't sound angry, but I definitely didn't trust her in the least bit. I didn't answer her as long as I could and then I heard Calvin Jr. He made a squeal. The sound of his voice calmed my fears. *Surely Cristi won't kill me with Calvin Jr. in her arms.*

"Shayla, please open the door. I just want to say something to you," Cristi said. The baby let out a tiny scream. "Hush, baby boy. Mama's gonna feed you soon." Cristi said.

I took a few more feet towards the door and swung it open in a fast motion. Cristi stood in front of me smiling, with Calvin Jr. in her arms and my Gucci shoe in her hand. I was confused by her cheerful expression.

"Here's your shoe," she said gleefully. "These are cute. Where did you get them?"

I frowned at Cristi and took the shoe from her hand, ignoring her question. "Thanks," I mumbled, not understanding her personality change.

"Listen, I am so sorry for making you upset," Cristi said as she leaned her head sideways like a kid who had gotten in trouble. "I don't want to cause any problems, and I'm sure that it took a lot for you to have to deal with me and my son being here. So, please forgive me for being such a bitch," Cristi said as she let out a sigh. The tone in her voice sounded sincere, but something deep within told me not to trust her.

"I'm sorry for throwing my shoe at you," I said without much emotion. "I'm just a little tired and need some rest," I added as a cue for her to leave. Calvin Jr. was bright-eyed and smiling, and he was looking right at me. When I glared at him again, my heart started to soften. When he smiled, his eyes looked just like Calvin's. He even had Calvin's smile. He looked so soft and cuddly. To my utter surprise, Calvin Jr. reached out for me, almost throwing himself out of Cristi's arms.

"Oh, so you want your step mommy to hold you, hunh?" Cristi said. "You little rascal you" She then looked at me and gave me a twisted smile. "Take him, he's reaching for you," she insisted.

After dropping my shoe to the floor, I nervously reached for Calvin Jr. When I brought him closer to my chest, he made a "gah-gah" sound and seemed to get excited. His excitement caused me to laugh.

"Hi, handsome," I said softly. "What'cha doin?" Calvin Jr. continued to smile at me. He had the happiest face. A feeling of warmth and protection came over me. I knew that Cristi was staring at me intently, but I couldn't help but be taken in by Calvin Jr. To my surprise, he leaned his soft little head against my bosom. I melted.

"Ahhh, isn't that cute," Cristi said. "He likes you."

"He is so cute," I said, as I rocked him from side to side. Calvin Jr. suddenly raised his head and looked up at me. "Hi, sweat pea," I said, looking into his eyes. He was no longer smiling. He was now looking at me like he was just as enchanted with me as I was with him. And then he frowned, let out a sound like he was about to cry and reached for Cristi. *Ooookay.*

"Uh-huh," Cristi said as she pulled Calvin Jr. from my arms. "You're just like yo daddy. You little womanizer. You don't know which one of us you want," she giggled.

I didn't find Cristi's comment too humorous. In fact, it made me remember her cutting words earlier.

"Well, I need to get some rest," I said as nicely as I could.

"Shayla, please don't mention to Calvin that we had an argument," Cristi said with a serious face. "I promised him that we would get along. I do apologize."

I still couldn't figure Cristi out. I looked at her suspiciously. "Why do you have on his robe?" I boldly asked.

Cristi looked down at the robe, as if she had forgotten what she had on. When she looked back up, my cell phone rang. *Dammit.* But when I walked over to the nightstand and realized it was Calvin, I felt much better. Cristi just stood at the door, still looking at me.

"Hello?" I answered.

"Yeah, what's wrong?" Calvin said like he was out of breath.

"Cal-viiin," I said and looked at Cristi. Her eyes looked sorrowful.

"What's going on there?" he demanded.

"Oh," I stammered. "Nothing is going on." I glanced at Cristi, who had now walked all the way inside the bedroom with a smile on her face.

"Well, why did you need me to call so fast?" Calvin asked, seeming impatient.

"Oh, well, I ...I ... I just didn't know what was going on and . . ."

Before I could finish my sentence Cristi interrupted. "Calvin!" she said moving close to me. I looked at her like she was crazy. "Let me speak to him," she said reaching for the phone with a big smile.

"I'm speaking to him right now," I growled, feeling like Cristi was getting way too bold.

"What's going on?!" Calvin demanded. "Was that Cristi?"

"Yes, honey. That was Cristi, but everything is cool."

"Well, let me speak to her," Calvin retorted.

"Oh, okay," I said, annoyed that Calvin was asking to speak to Cristi. I handed the phone to her with an attitude and when she took the phone from me, she handed me Calvin Jr.

"CK Moore, what's up dog?!" she said, sounding like one of his boys. After a few seconds she said, "Aint nothing going on. We just sittin here chattin... and Jr. loves Shayla. She's cool peeps." Cristi looked at me and winked her eye. I rolled my eyes at her. "Yes, we are getting along fine, CK," Cristi continued. "Okay," she paused. "Okay. Okay, boy!" she hollered. "How many times are you gonna tell me. Hell, I ain't deaf." For a few more seconds Cristi just listened and then she burst into laughter. "CK, you are such a fool. Dejame! [Leave me alone]," she said in Spanish. "I'll talk to you later. Here is

your fiancé." She paused. "Oh, okay. He wants to speak to Jr."
She looked at me. "Shayla has him. Hold on." Cristi put the
phone to Calvin Jr.'s ear. "Say hi to daddy," she said. "Tell
daddy hi."

A smile came across Calvin Jr.'s face quickly and then
he practically screamed. I figured Calvin had said something to
him to make him react. "Okay, that's it," Cristi said as she put
the phone back to her ear. "CK, I'm gonna let you talk back to
Shayla, okay? I'll talk to you when you get back and stay outta
trouble," she said as she handed the phone to me and reached
for Calvin Jr.

When I took the phone from Cristi I held it to my chest
and gave her a look that I hoped she read to mean that I needed
her to leave. She smiled and sashayed off like she was queen of
the universe.

"Calvin," I said after Cristi left the room.

"Yeah, bae, what's up?" Calvin said. His tone was light
and gentle.

"Why didn't you tell me this commercial was being
shot in L.A.?" I scolded.

"What do you mean? I just found out. Didn't you get
my note?"

"Calvin I got your note," I said carefully. "But you
knew all along that this commercial would be shot in L.A, and
you didn't tell me, Calvin. You didn't tell me."

"Yeah, well you can believe whatever you want to
believe," Calvin remarked non-challantly.

"Oh, I can?" I said, knowing that Calvin wouldn't
admit the truth and feeling like he would turn things around if I
wasn't careful. "And when did this Beyoncé video come up?
You didn't tell me about that either."

"What?"

"Beyoncé. Are you gonna be in her video?"

"I wish. Who told you that?"

"So, you're not gonna be in her video?" I said. "Cristi
just made that up I guess."

"That girl stupid," Calvin laughed. "If I was doing a
video with Beyoncé, Jay-Z would have to worry, but hey, I've

got to go. I just got in the limo and I have to be on the set in an hour, so I'll call you later, aight?" he said in a rushed tone.

"Calvin?" I said softly.

"Yeah?"

"Can I come out to be with you?"

"Shayla, why would you ask me something like that?" he hissed.

"What do you mean?" I said, feeling unsettled.

"I'm out here shooting a commercial and I'm not gonna have time to do anything else, baby. You know that already, girl," he said.

"Well, can I at least order our invitations, so we can get married on my birthday? Calvin, I'm tired of waiting," I blurted out.

"You're tired of waiting?" Calvin questioned.

I sat on the bed trying to put my thoughts into words, but knowing that I couldn't say everything I wanted to say. "Calvin, I love you so much, and I really need to start planning our wedding. I just need some clarity from you . . ."

"Oh, so the ring isn't clarity enough?"

"Calvin, the ring is beautiful, but I need for you to be my husband. I want to be married to you, Calvin."

"Well, I want to be married to you too, Shayla, but right now, I'm out here in L.A. trying to get to a commercial shoot. So, let's talk about this when I get back home, okay?" he said gently.

I wanted desperately to talk about wedding plans with Calvin, but I knew from past experience that pressuring him would only make things worse.

"Okay, Calvin, but call me, no matter what time you get done tonight," I said. "Cause we just need to move forward."

"Okay," he replied calmly. "Gotta go, baby."

"I love you, Calvin."

"Love you too. Bye," he said and hung up quickly.

After hanging up a feeling hit me that Calvin did not intend on marrying me in May or anytime. The disturbing inkling sent a knot right to the pit of my stomach and I bent over in pain, feeling like the worst was yet to come with

Calvin. *What am I going to do?* I slid to the floor and prayed, "God, please help me."

Chapter Seventeen

Restoration vs. Desperation

The next morning I woke up feeling wiped out. My sleep had been interrupted several times throughout the night by what seemed to be creeping noises. But each time I had awakened and listened intently for any strange sounds, I only heard the ticking of the clock. I was definitely feeling paranoid. I even thought that Cristi had walked inside my room and was staring down at me with a vicious look. When I realized that it was only a bad dream, I got up and made sure the bedroom door was locked.

I was tired of my life being a bad dream, with only spurts of happy moments, and I wondered if God could somehow turn my life around. I had decided to attend church with Sydney, Aaron and Connie today. I needed to get spiritually fed and I was curious to see why Sydney's church drew more than 20,000 members and was called one of the fastest growing Mega Churches in Georgia. I had only attended church twice over the last year and my prayers to God seemed to be redundant pleas for Calvin to marry me. I had truly lost my spiritual spunk and could not relate when Sydney would talk about how "awesome" and "powerful" God was. *God doesn't care much about my sinful butt,* I figured. Sometimes I was too embarrassed to kneel in prayer – feeling like I was undeserving of good blessings. But all I wanted God to work out for me was to allow Calvin to become my husband and for our relationship to be less stressful. *That's not asking a lot, is it, God? Your Word says that all things are possible.* Today I wanted to be in church front and center. I was weary.

Before leaving the house for church, I decided to go downstairs to let Cristi know that I would be gone most of the day. I had not been to the lower level of Calvin's house since Cristi had moved in – not even to wash clothes. I figured it was best to avoid her at all costs, but today I thought I'd be friendlier. *I might even ask her if she wants me to bring anything back for her and Little C.* Cristi's downstairs arrangement gave her access to Calvin's movie theatre room, workout room, video game room, laundry room, mini disco, and a full kitchen. The bedroom she was occupying was one of the three elaborately decorated bedrooms on that floor. It overlooked the swimming pool and tennis court and even had a Jacuzzi tub just like Calvin's master bedroom. *Cristi is living too large for her own good,* I moaned to myself as I walked down the stairs.

"Cristi?" I called out, not wanting to frighten her by my sudden presence. "Cristi,'" I shouted again. I walked around the corner to her room and knocked on the door gently. "Cristi, I'm going to church and I'll be gone for most of the day," I paused. "I just wanted to let you know. You need anything while I'm out?"

Cristi opened the door in a slow motion, rubbing her eyes.

"What are you doing down here?" she growled. Obviously I had awakened her. Her expression was one of irritation. She was wearing one of Calvin's football jerseys.

"I just wanted to let you know that I'll be gone for most of the day," I said softly. I was a little confused by Cristi's grouchy attitude. "I won't be back until later today."

"Don't nobody care! I'm trying to get some damn sleep!" Cristi said bitterly and slammed the door in my face.

To say that I was pissed off would have been an understatement, but I swallowed, turned around and walked back up the stairs.

"Stupid hefer!" I groaned in a faint voice. I definitely needed to go to church before I was tempted to take my shoe off again and this time, beat her with it.

Once I arrived at church, I had no problem spotting Sydney, Aaron and Connie. They were standing by the water fountain just as Sydney had said they would be. I was running a few minutes late because the street leading to the church was a mile long with people trying to get inside the parking lot. You would have thought they were going to an R&B concert. Some were dressed quite casually in blue jeans. I was really surprised to see a few of the women dressed in club attire –

with spike heels and shorts skirts. *They must have come straight from the club.* I felt overdressed in my burgundy suit.

"I'm sorry I'm late," I said to Sydney. "I got caught up in all that traffic."

"Don't worry about it," Sydney said lightheartedly. "We just got here about five minutes ago. We're gonna have to go to the balcony."

"Really?" I said, not really understanding why Sydney's non-denominational church was so crowded. "Is this a special day here or something?"

"Nope. It's like this all the time," Sydney responded. "You want to get a visitor's sticker?"

"Oh, no. That's okay," I said and glanced at Connie, who was wearing the coat-dress Sydney and I had bought her for Christmas. She looked poised and young for her 51 years. She glanced at me and smiled.

"You look nice," Connie said grabbing my hand and squeezing it.

"Thanks," I said, returning the squeeze. I then looked at Aaron. "Hi, Aaron," I said.

"Shaylaaa," he said. "So glad you could come. What's been up?"

"A lot," I smiled as we proceeded to the balcony.

The choir sang two emotion-stirring songs. One was called "The Best is Yet to Come," and the other was "Wait on the Lord." The majority of the congregation stood to their feet, lifting their hands to the ceiling as the choir sang. Aaron and Sydney held hands and sang along with the choir and even to each other at times. Connie bobbed her head to the music, but remained seated. I just took it all in, feeling very unemotional, but actually wanting to feel something more. I started thinking about Cristi and how she had comfortably and slyly moved into Calvin's home with her son. I also thought about her strange disposition. *No wonder she and Calvin can't leave each other alone. They are just alike.* My mind definitely wasn't on the soulful gospel sounds coming from the choir.

Finally the pastor came to the pulpit. The congregation stood to their feet like he was a rock star. I stayed seated. For about ten minutes I tuned the pastor out as he began speaking, but I forced my thoughts to *be still* and listen to what he had to say when he said that God has a divine plan for everyone. He preached about Christ being number one and he said that putting another person or anything else before Christ would cause one to lose that thing.

"God is a jealous God and He won't settle for being number two in your life because you met some tall, dark and handsome man who makes your heart beat fast, ladies. And God is not going to come second to that fine woman you met either, men," the pastor said. "It's time to seek ye first the kingdom of God and His righteousness. No man and no woman can satisfy the thirst that only the Lord can quench. No job will give you the satisfaction only the Lord can give. He is the key to all your needs. He is your power source. Without Him, your life will be empty. He is the way, the truth and the light. How many of y'all know what I'm talking about?" The congregation clapped excitedly and some shouted "Hallelujah" or "Amen." I didn't move. I began to feel like someone had told the pastor about me as he went on and on about God never standing you up and never leaving or forsaking you, but that man would fail you every time. The pastor's voice continued to grow louder and louder. He said that God would make a way out of no way for those who are obedient to Him. He said that Jesus was a fortress, a rock, a healer, a comforter, a deliverer. Some women started getting happy – shouting. He also said, "But God is not gonna bless your mess. Come up out of that mess and let God take charge of your life."

I wasn't in the least bit convicted. I wanted to go home. *Home?* It hit me, at that moment that my living situation with Calvin, Cristi and Calvin Jr. was deplorable. *Do I really want to go back to that mess?* I began to tear up, not because of what the pastor was saying, but because I felt like I was losing myself to some force that had overtaken me. The force was Calvin Moore.

"God loves you," the pastor said as he was ending his sermon. "So, it's your decision. Today is the day of salvation. Now is the time to put God first and reap the enormous blessings of His kingdom. Make a new start with Jesus. Tomorrow is not promised. Today is your day. Be bold for

Jesus. If you've never accepted Jesus as your Lord and Savior, or if you already know Jesus, but you have backslidden and need to re-dedicate your life to the Lord, He is waiting on you. Come to the altar right now and give your life to the Lord. He stood for you, so get up and stand for Him and you'll discover your true destiny as a child of the King."

There was a part of me that wanted to run to the altar, but another part of me that did not believe that going to an altar could alter my life. I squirmed in my seat, but as if some force had control of my legs, I suddenly stood to my feet. When I stood, the resistance seemed to roll off me and I felt like I was taking a step towards my soul's happiness. I closed my eyes for a few seconds and I opened them again. Sydney took my hand in hers.

The pastor continued, "If you're in the balcony and want to make a new start today, come down the stairs and right this way to the altar."

I turned to Sydney and noticed that her eyes were filled with tears. "I'll go with you," she said softly.

The walk to the altar seemed to take forever, but once I got there my burdens seemed to lift off my shoulders, causing me to feel light and free. After the pastor had us repeat a prayer of salvation and re-dedication, Sydney embraced me.

"You made the best decision of your life," she cried. "The angels are rejoicing in Heaven."

I felt surreal as I embraced Sydney and cried tears of joy and relief. I felt exhilarated, like I was falling in love for the first time. My heartbeat escalated and a light seemed to surround my entire body. *This is a new beginning.* I felt born again. When the pastor came by to shake my hand, I trembled as he grasped my hand with both of his.

"This is your day, and the Lord is well pleased," he said sincerely.

I was tired of struggling and fighting for what I wanted. I was ready to surrender my life to God. I was ready for a change.

After a brief meeting for new members and converts the service came to a close, and reality sunk into my soul quickly. *What have I done?* I questioned my decision as Sydney and as

Aaron jumped around as though their favorite team had won the Super Bowl. Connie was excited too. She hugged me so tight that it hurt. Their excitement scared me. *What am I supposed to do now? Am I supposed to be different?* I quickly realized that nothing had really changed.

"Just take one day at a time," Sydney chimed seeming to sense my thoughts. "Everything will come together. Don't let fear creep in."

I was speechless as we walked to the parking lot. Fear was indeed starting to invade my mind like a wave. I didn't know if I could live up to my commitment to release sin from my life when I had gotten so comfortable living in sin. I wondered if there was any way I could ask God for more time, but I knew that I would at least have to try to do His will, since something more powerful than my own will had made me walk to that altar. *Maybe this same power will give me the strength I need to get my life in order. I surely hope so.*

After having dinner at Houston's and getting through the entire meal without feeling like the spotlight was on me, I told everyone that I needed to get home. Sydney and Aaron had talked about their wedding plans during most of the dinner and how they had started going to pre-marital counseling. *Goody.* Connie and Sydney disagreed about everything concerning her wedding. I was glad that they were arguing for a change and not Connie and me. Although I tried to engage in the conversation about Sydney and Aaron's big day, my mind was on the decision I had just made at church, as well Calvin and Cristi and Little C. I was eager to tell Calvin about my experience, but scared of what he might think. One thing was for certain. I wanted Cristi out of our home. I wanted Calvin to commit to God just like I had. I wanted him to commit to me more though.

When I returned to the house, Cristi was sitting comfortably in the den, eating popcorn and watching television. Little C was in front of her in his stroller. Cristi was still wearing Calvin's jersey, with what seemed to be no bottoms on underneath. I was rather surprised that she had made herself so comfortable upstairs in the family room. My first thought was to ignore her, but instead, I sat on the opposite end of the sofa beside her.

"How was church?" she asked, smacking on the popcorn like she had no manners. I eyed Cristi. She looked flawless. Her golden complexion and skin was supple and soft looking and her highlighted hair flowed down her back. Her nose sat perfectly between her big, dark eyes, her eyebrows were thick and perfectly arched, and her eyelashes had length that made her look doll like. At about 5 feet 9 inches, she had long legs, voluptuous, full breasts, although I didn't know if she had implants or not, a small waist and a firm, round buttocks. *She disgusts me.* When I looked down at her bare legs, I noticed a tattooed number on her lower ankle. It was number 85, Calvin's jersey number. *Well, I be damned.*

"What?" Cristi said, looking down at herself as if my staring made her uncomfortable. "Why are you looking at me like that?"

"Oh," I said, realizing that I had stared at Cristi a little too long. I turned my head to the television. "Church was fine."

"Could you do me a favor and watch Little C while I take a shower," Cristi asked politely.

I hesitated for a moment. "Well, yes, but . . ."

"But?" Cristi interrupted, frowning. "You know what... that's okay . . ."

"No. I was just gonna say that I need to call Calvin," I stammered. "I was just getting ready to go upstairs and call him."

Cristi frowned at me. "So, why do you have to tell me? So, he didn't call you back last night?"

"Was he supposed to?" I asked, getting defensive.

"I don't know!" Cristi laughed. "He is your fiancé!"

I felt intimidated by Cristi. "But you have his child!" I said as my emotions started to stir.

"You damn skippy! I do have his child. Does that make you uncomfortable? Are you jealous of me?" Cristi asked, wickedly.

"Give me a break!" I said calmly, but feeling myself starting to perspire.

"Well, you know that I will always be in Calvin's life," Cristi said as she swung her hair to the opposite side. "Can you handle that?"

"Handle what?" I asked in a sharp tone.

"That no matter what, even if you and Calvin do end up getting married, and I doubt that, I will always be in his life because I have his first born son." Cristi said as her eyes narrowed.

I wanted so much to scream at Cristi and tell her to get the hell out of my and Calvin's life, but I held my composure.

"Well, you might have his first-born son, but he loves me, and basically I'm the one sleeping upstairs with him," I said in a calm tone, determined not to let her get to me.

"And you don't think that I still sleep with him too?"

"Excuse me?"

"You heard me, right," Cristi retorted. "CK and I didn't get this baby boy by hunching on each other with our clothes on."

"You know, you are really trying to provoke me, but I don't have time for this stupidity!" I snapped as I stood to my feet abruptly.

"So, you're not gonna watch Little C for me?" Cristi asked with a smug smile.

"Hell to the no!" I said with indignation and turned to walk up the stairs leading to the bedroom.

"Well, don't get mad at me. I can't help it that you are sharing your so-called fiancé with his baby's mama. But I guess I'd be mad too if I were in your shoes."

I turned back around to face Cristi before reaching the stairs. "You know, I don't know where Calvin found a piece of trash like you, but I have more class than you could ever dream of having. And you might have his son, but I've got the ring and the man!" I flashed my eight carats at Cristi. "And you obviously don't have much respect for yourself because if you did, you'd realize that you can't win or trap a man by having his baby."

"So, you think that just because CK gave you that ring that you have him?" she laughed. "Girl, CK has given me plenty of bling. But he told me you couldn't have children, so I guess you'll have to learn how to deal with Little C and me and maybe a few other kids CK and I will have together," Cristi taunted.

"I can have kids. Who told you that lie?"

"You sure you can have kids? Didn't you lose one or two already?"

My stomach tied in knots and I felt enraged, but I stared at Cristi and silently counted to ten, which was a technique my mom had taught me to use as a child whenever I wanted to hurt somebody or say something that could hurt them.

"Whatever!" I said, as I turned around for the stairs again.

"Yeah, whatever!" Cristi uttered nastily.

I'm not gonna let this slut steal my joy. Cristi really did know how to push my buttons, and this time she had made me feel like I meant nothing to Calvin and like she had him wrapped around her finger. *And where did she get the idea that I can't have children? Calvin must have told her that I lost our baby.* Once I got to the room, I buried my head in the pillow and asked God to keep me from strangling her. As I expected, when I called Calvin in L.A. a few minutes later, he was nowhere to be found. When he finally called me back, it was 3 am. I had fallen off to sleep after locking the bedroom door, watching television and reading the entire book of Proverbs in the Bible. I called Tacara to see how married life was going for her so far. I also told her about my experience at church. We agreed to meet for lunch the next day. Talking to Tacara had always been comforting. I decided that I would confide in her about Cristi and her son moving into Calvin's home. I was looking so forward to getting Tacara's insight. She had wisdom beyond her years.

"You sleep?" Calvin stammered on the other end of the phone in the wee hours of the morning.

"Yeah," I said sleepily. "What took you so long to call me back?"

"I left my cell in the room. My publicist had me doing radio and television appearances all damn day, but I'll be home tomorrow night."

"Good, because I'm going crazy here with Cristi. She has provoked me, Calvin, and I'm not going to be able to handle her for a month. I just can't."

"I thought you were trying to get along with her," Calvin said.

"Get along with her? Calvin, that girl does not want to get along with me. She acts possessed by something."

"Ahh, come on, Shayla. You are the one who threw the shoe at her. You were acting possessed when you did that shit."

With suspicion and anger, I asked, "Oh, so you've talked to Cristi?"

"Yeah. I called this morning for you," Calvin said carefully. "She said that you had gone out to church and that you came downstairs and woke her and the baby up early this morning by screaming at her and then you slammed the door in her face. What was that all about, Shayla?"

"Calvin, I can't believe this. I did not slam the door in her damn face. She slammed the damn door in my face!" I protested, as I sat up in bed quite angry.

"Uh-huh. I know you, Shayla. You have a little temper. Why were you down there in the first place?" His voice was accusatory.

"Calvin, I went to tell her that I was leaving for church and she is a liar and you know that!" I snapped, not believing that Calvin was buying into Cristi's lies. "Cristi has got some real issues and I'm not gonna sit here trying to defend myself when you have said yourself that she lies. Calvin, I don't believe you are questioning me about her."

"It's just that you're not thinking straight and that bothers me," Calvin said calmly.

"I'm not thinking straight?" I exclaimed. "Cristi was the one telling me that you'll never marry me because I'm too dark and she said that she is still having sex with you, Calvin. She even made up some shit about you saying I couldn't have children. What do you expect me to do? Hunh, Calvin? Am I supposed to just smile and let her say anything she wants to me?" I said on the brink of tears.

"Naw, but you don't have to be throwing shit at her. She could have had Little C in her hands and if you had hit my son with that shoe, I would have been through with you. You're just not thinking, Shayla."

For a few seconds I was speechless. The conversation with Calvin definitely wasn't going well.

"Hello?" Calvin uttered after my silence.

"I'm here," I answered in a teary voice.

"Well, don't be pouting, Shayla, because you know you shouldn't have thrown your shoe at her. Cristi talks a lot of shit. Just ignore her, baby," he said.

"Calvin, I can't ignore her," I said with a trembling voice. "And it's obvious that you can't either, so I can just leave and let the two of you work things out."

"Hunh?" Calvin grunted.

"I just don't know if I can take her being here another day. Let alone three of four more weeks. And something tells me her month long stay is gonna be extended, and I just can't take it, Calvin," I wept.

"Well, Shay, I'm sorry you feel that way, but . . ."

"But nothing, Calvin," I shouted. "She is interfering in our relationship and she is evil and rude. I don't like her and she told me that y'all are still sleeping together, Calvin. Are you still sleeping with her?"

"Hell, naw. I don't believe you asked me that!" Calvin snapped.

"Well, I want to believe you, but it is so obvious that she is gonna go through great lengths to come between us. I don't trust that slut as far as I can see her!"

"Shayla, come on. Calm down. What has gotten into you? You don't have to be threatened by Cristi," he said.

"I am not threatened by her. Why would I be threatened by someone as ignorant and unclassy as her? I just don't think we should all be living under the same roof. Calvin Jr. seems to be doing a whole lot better now. Can't they move out, Calvin?"

"So, you want me to put my son out?" Calvin asked in a serious tone.

I paused hoping that the wrong thing would not come out of my mouth. "Calvin, I think Cristi and your son will be fine on their own. Can't you see what she is doing to us?" I said softly.

"You know what, Shayla," Calvin raised his voice in anger. "You knew when you started seeing me that other women wanted me, but I chose you, Shay. So why are you so insecure? I can't deal with your insecurity."

"Calvin, don't."

"Don't what?"

"Don't feed me with that insecurity stuff. You would make any woman insecure."

"Well, Cristi isn't insecure. And if I'm so bad and make you feel so insecure then why are you with me, hunh?" Calvin asked. "Can't you find somebody else who won't make you feel so needy?"

"Is that what you want me to do? You want me to find somebody else?" I asked.

"You know, at this point I don't care what you do. I'm just tired of you pressuring me, man. You are never satisfied."

"Calvin, I don't pressure you at all," I said calmly. "You told me that you wanted to marry me and now it seems like you're just pulling me along like a puppet on a string. Do you really want to marry me, Calvin?" I closed my eyes, fearing Calvin's response.

"You can't make me marry you before I'm ready, Shayla. Damn!" Calvin shouted. "I can't believe you are so desperate to get married to me. You are scaring me."

"Scaring you?" I said, feeling like Calvin was turning the tables on me. "So you are scared of marriage?" I asked.

"No, I'm scared of your desperation!" he retorted. "You are just desperate for me, man. This is ridiculous."

"Well, Calvin, I'll show you just how desperate I am," I said calmly. "I'm moving out because I can't take anymore of this. I'll just move out and we can work things out from a distance, okay?" My voice cracked.

"Okay," he said calmly. "But once you move out, don't think you gonna move back in. I don't play that back and forth shit. And I don't chase. I replace."

"Okay," I replied, already feeling a little torn, but knowing that Calvin wouldn't see things my way.

"So, are you moving out before I get back or after?" he asked, as if he were either excited about the idea or apprehensive.

"Uhhh, I'll probably move out in a couple of days," I said, trying to stay strong and not sob.

"Probably?" Calvin questioned. "Either you're gonna move out or you're not, Shay. I tell you what," he said and cleared his throat. "Just make up your mind by the time I get home tomorrow night. And if you decide to leave, just pack your shit before I get back, aight," Calvin said in a bitter tone.

"Okay, I'll do that, Calvin," I said sullenly and hung up on him.

By the time the sun peered through the window, I had only gotten about 30 minutes of sleep. I had prayed to God to help me to sleep and had read the verse in the Bible, "Come to me, all that labor and are heavy laiden, and I will give thee rest," but there was no rest for my weary heart. It was yet another night of tears and confusion for me. I regretted that I had not gotten a chance to tell Calvin about my experience at church, but something told me that it really didn't matter if he knew about my new beginning or not. After I got up, I pulled out my luggage in the guest room upstairs and started packing my clothes. But in the middle of folding a few pieces and putting them neatly in the suitcase, I pulled the clothes all back out frantically. "I'm not leaving!" I said over and over in tears. "I am not leaving." On top of not having anywhere to go, I still wanted things between Calvin and me to work out. I also didn't want Cristi to think that she had accomplished her goal by pushing me out of Calvin's house and out of his life. *I'm gonna stay and fight for my man.*

Lunch with Tacara at Café Intermezzo went fairly well. She showed me tons of pictures from her wedding and her Paris honeymoon. I held in my emotions and decided to only tell Tacara more about my decision to re-dedicate my life to the Lord, which she was elated about. When she asked me how Calvin and I were doing, I told her that we were fine, but that we sill couldn't decide on a wedding date. I had planned to tell Tacara about Cristi and Little C moving in and all the turmoil I had been experiencing, but Tacara's life seemed so perfect. She beamed with joy as she talked about her honeymoon, resigning from her job as a flight attendant, and being accepted into law school at Georgia State University. I faked it through our gathering and hugged her goodbye with plans to meet with her again in a couple of weeks. *Maybe things will change for the better for me by then.*

Calvin got home at 9:30 pm that night. It was sleeting outside and the electricity had just come back on, after being out for a couple of hours. It was already cold in the bedroom. I had not blown out the candles I had lit. I felt a tad romantic, but I was apprehensive about being intimate with Calvin for so many reasons. Plus, I didn't know what kind of mood he'd be in. I was glad that I had not seen Cristi the entire day. I noticed a woman in a black BMW come pick her and Calvin Jr. up before I left for lunch. I hadn't heard her return.

When Calvin walked into the room carrying his luggage in one hand and a Victoria Secrets bag in the other, the chill I was feeling turned into a warm feeling. He seemed surprised to see me propped up on the pillows. He looked at me with caution and then looked around the room, noticing the lit candles.

"The power went out," I said. "So, it's still cold in here."

I had on my red silk pajamas that were sexy, but not nearly as revealing as some of my other lingerie pieces. When Calvin looked back at me, his lips curved into a smile.

"What's up?" he said boyishly. I could tell that he was happy that I had decided not to leave. With one look at him, I was happy I decided to stay.

"Hi," I said in a faint voice.

Calvin dropped both bags immediately and walked over to me. He swept me in his arms. His mouth descended over mine and I embraced him tightly as we kissed passionately.

"Yeah, I'm desperate for you," I whispered in his ear as he planted kisses on my neck. "I am so desperate for you, Calvin Moore."

After we made passionate love, Calvin and I lay close to each other, but I felt a strange emptiness. I felt like I had already disappointed God. I also felt like my relationship with Calvin was peeling away at the core of my being. I wasn't sure who I had become and how much I'd be willing to compromise to keep him in my life. A tear streamed down my cheek and I pulled my hand out of Calvin's to wipe it.

"Are you okay?" Calvin asked.

"I'm fine," I whispered. But I wasn't fine. Despite the physical response of my body, I was torn between losing Calvin and finding myself.

Chapter Eighteen

Just Throw it in the Bag

The next day was one of the best days Calvin and I had shared together in a long time. We got up early and he suggested that we go to Chateau Elan for the day. When we got there, he treated me to a massage, a facial and a manicure and pedicure at the European health spa. We also tasted some of the different wines at the full production winery on Chateau Elan's property and had dinner with a USC alumni and former football player, Richard Elerby, who was about 10 years Calvin's senior. Richard, who brought along his wife, Diana, and I really enjoyed talking with each other. She was a spunky and witty with blond hair and bright eyes. While Richard and Calvin played golf Diana and I had a girl's day of pampering. For a little while I forgot that Calvin and I had this problem called Cristi. I wished that we could stay at Chateau Elan for a week, but Calvin said that we could only stay for the day because he had an important meeting early the next morning. I thought about telling him about my spiritual decision, but each time I went to tell him, I'd clam up. I didn't understand why I felt so uncomfortable about sharing my experience with Calvin.

When we arrived home from Chateau Elan, Cristi practically met us at the door.

"I'm glad you're back!" she said as she glared at Calvin and then at me. She was wearing a skintight black, mini dress and five-inch heels. She towered over me.

"Why?" Calvin asked.

"Because you are gonna have to keep Little C," she said, putting her hand on her hip. "I'm going out tonight."

"Where are you going?" Calvin asked as he walked past her.

"Out and about," Cristi replied. "What difference does it make? I'm grown, sexy and over 21. You don't need to be questioning me," she said and looked at me. "Hi, Shayla, how are you?" she said in a pleasant tone.

"I'm great!" I said and gave Cristi an even look and rolled my eyes.

"Well, I hope y'all didn't plan a romantic night, because Little C is wide awake and he needs the attention of his daddy and step mommy."

I ignored Cristi and continued walking to the stairway. I figured I'd let Calvin deal with Cristi. Little C was lying on a blanket on the floor in the family room. I ignored him too.

"Why do you have my baby on the floor!?" Calvin growled.

"I know how to take care of my own baby," Cristi said.

"But you don't need to be putting him on the floor, Cristi," Calvin argued.

"Don't tell me what to do, boy," Cristi said.

By the time I reached the top of the stairs, their voices faded. I wasn't up for hearing another Calvin, Cristi arguing match. I just wanted to relax and cuddle with Calvin and watch a movie in Calvin's massive collection. Calvin stayed downstairs for about 30 minutes, and then he came back up with Little C in his arms. I had changed into a leopard print night shirt Calvin had brought back from L.A., which was one of the lingerie pieces he picked up for me at Victoria's Secret. *Calvin can really be thoughtful sometimes.* When Calvin laid Little C on the bed beside me, Little C reached up for me with a happy smile. I swooped him up and tickled him and he giggled and screamed. When I looked at Calvin, his eyes glowed with pleasure. He sat on the bed and we both played with Little C like he was our child together.

"I can't wait for us to have our baby," Calvin said, as I was lifting Little C in the air.

I was so surprised by Calvin's words that I almost dropped Little C. "You didn't mean that," I said, as I cautiously looked into Calvin's dark, narrow eyes.

"Yes, I did!" he said convincingly. "I want us to have a girl, and I hope she looks just like you."

I shuddered at the thought of having Calvin's child, and I was stunned that Calvin was so comfortable with the idea.

"Calvin, I've got to tell you something," I said as I handed Little C over to him.

"Ahhh, hell. What?" Calvin asked with a frown. "Are you pregnant?"

"No," I chuckled. "I'm not pregnant, but I did re-dedicate my life to the Lord this past Sunday. I guess you can say I'm saved now."

"You're saved!?" Calvin said in a mocking tone. "Girl, the way you were giving it to me last night I would have never guessed that. What do you mean you're saved?"

I felt offended by Calvin's comment. I wondered had I confused him and even myself by being intimate with him last night.

"Calvin, I want to live a more Godly life. I went to the altar Sunday. I'm different now."

"So, you can't freak no mo?" Calvin laughed.

"Calvin, I'm serious!" I said getting annoyed. "Don't joke about it."

"Okay. Okay. It's just that I'm a little surprised," he scratched his head. "Why didn't you tell me last night?"

"I was scared," I said softly. "I wanted to be with you last night and I still do, but I want us to have God in our lives. Can you go to church with me Sunday?"

At first Calvin looked at me as if I had spoken a foreign language, but his frown dissolved and he leaned over and kissed me on the forehead. "I'll think about it, baby. I'll think about it," he said. He then looked at Calvin Jr. "Did you hear that Little C? Daddy's fiancée is a church girl now," he laughed. Little C laughed too and even screamed one of his loud screams. I wasn't too happy about Calvin's attitude. It was like he was taking my experience as a joke. *Actions speak louder than words though.*

Calvin and I watched one of the movies I had gotten and Little C fell off to sleep between us. At about 1am, I heard Cristi come in. Her heels were loud coming up the stairs. She pushed the bedroom door open without even knocking.

"Have you heard of knocking?" I said, sitting up in the bed.

"Knock?" Cristi said. "I don't have to knock. Give me my damn son!"

"Hey! Will you two cool it?" Calvin said. "You're gonna wake him up."

Calvin picked up Little C and handed him to Cristi, and she pulled the baby close to her and rubbed the back of his head. She then stared down at us as though she wasn't too happy seeing us in bed together. Her eyes looked evil and glassy.

"Close the door behind you, Cristi," Calvin said in a calm tone.

"Forget you, CK Moore. Just forget you," she said and turned around slowly.

"You back mighty early. Did you have fun?" Calvin asked in a lighter tone.

"I had a damn ball!" Cristi answered and turned around to face us. "And what about you, CK? Did you have fun laying up with your hoe and my son?"

"You are the hoe!" I screamed.

"Hey, Hey!" Calvin said, looking at me with a frown. "What did I tell you?"

"But you are just gonna let her call me a hoe?" I argued.

"But what did I tell you?" Calvin said. "Ignore her, okay!"

Cristi laughed and left the room without closing the door. I was glad that Calvin and I could finally cuddle the way I wanted to, but within minutes Cristi Perez was back in our room.

"What is it Cristi?" Calvin asked impatiently.

"CKaaaaa," Cristi whined. "I need you to unzip me. I can't get this damn dress unzipped."

"Well, how did you get in it?" I growled.

"Shhhh," Calvin hissed, giving me a scolding look. "Come here, Cristi. I'll unzip you. Hurry up though."

Cristi flopped on the bed beside Calvin and lifted her hair up in a sexy motion. I watched carefully as Calvin unzipped her dress down to the middle of her back.

"More, please," Cristi said. "More, Calvin."

"Aww, Cristi, that's enough. You have it from there," Calvin said as he sank back down in the bed. I was still halfway sitting up. I was livid at Cristi for asking Calvin to unzip her dress. *What is she trying to prove?* I wanted to slap her.

"So, you're not gonna unzip me more?" Cristi asked in a sexy tone.

"No," Calvin said curtly.

"What are y'all watching?" Cristi asked as she let her hair back down and turned her body to face the television.

"For Colored Girls," Calvin replied. "I'd rather be watching something else. By the way, you kinda remind me of that chick right there." Calvin was talking about Thandie, the feisty and highly sexual woman in the movie.

"But I'm cuter than her," Cristi said smacking her gum. "I liked this movie though," she said excitedly and leaned back against the headboard. "Have they gotten to the scene where she and her mama get into a fight?"

"Naw, not yet," Calvin answered.

"That's my favorite part," Cristi said. "Move over, CK."

At that point I was more shocked at Calvin for actually moving over. I burned with anger as Cristi got underneath the sheets beside Calvin, making herself very comfortable.

"I just want to watch until after that scene I like," she said as she looked at me and smiled wickedly. By that time, my mouth was hanging open and I could feel a rage coming on.

"It's okay, baby," Calvin said as he rubbed my hand underneath the sheet.

But it wasn't okay. Cristi had overstepped her bounds and Calvin had let her. I turned my head to look at the movie for a few seconds, trying to keep myself from cursing. *Count to ten, Shayla. Count to ten.*

"I forgot how comfortable this bed is," Cristi said and sunk down in the bed a little more, placing herself even closer to Calvin. To my utter astonishment, Calvin made more room for her and I noticed their feet kicking each other's between the sheets.

"Your feet are cold," Cristi whined.

"Yours are too!" Calvin grunted. "Hammer toes."

Like a mad woman, I grabbed the comforter and yanked it off the bed. I had had enough. I got out of bed shaking the cover and twisting my body from side to side. I couldn't take it anymore.

"Damn, yo girl got the exorcist or something," Cristi laughed. "Shay Shay gone cray cray."

I proceeded towards the door, as I heard Calvin say, "Hey. Where are you going with the bed spread?" in a clueless tone.

I didn't bother to look back at Calvin or Cristi. I walked around the bed and out of the bedroom.

"Shayla!" Calvin called out. "Bae, what's wrong?"

"Just let her go," Cristi added snidely.

When I got downstairs, I sat on the sofa feeling as though I had been in a fight. I wrapped the bed spread around my body and tried to get my bearings. I thought Calvin would come downstairs after me, but when an hour passed, it started to sink in that he wasn't coming. I cried. *I have to leave.* There was no question about it. *To stay would be to humiliate myself even more.* Being with Calvin had made me lose my sense of self respect. *But this is the last straw. I am leaving.* For a couple of more hours I rested on the sofa trying to figure out my game plan and hoping that Calvin would come downstairs to at least show his concern, but he never came. I knew that he kept a stash of money on him, so I decided that I'd take enough, as well as his American Express card, and go live in a hotel for a while, and then I'd have to figure out what I'd do next. I knew I had to leave though.

When I walked back into the bedroom, Cristi's dress lay on the floor near the bed and she was cuddled up to Calvin, with his back to her. The thought of them making love sent a deep pain down my side. I started packing my things quietly, but the more I looked at Cristi cuddled up to Calvin, the more frantically I packed. I opened drawers, throwing things into my suitcase without even folding them. I went into the other bedrooms and grabbed all my things, putting some into Calvin's Louis Vutton luggage. Lastly, I went into the bathroom and got my toiletries. When I went through Calvin's pant pocket and pulled out his wallet, I took the entire wad of money. I also found the American Express card, which was right on top of all his credit cards. I didn't care about Calvin discovering that I had taken his money and his credit card, that he made me give back to him after my spending spree in Vegas. I looked at Cristi and Calvin in bed and noticed that she had awakened and was staring at me. Calvin was snoring. He was a hard sleeper. I continued to pack my things, making sure I had everything. Each time I'd glance back at her, a look of satisfaction seemed to come across her face, so I figured she wouldn't wake Calvin up to tell him I was leaving. I hated her. I truly despised her, and I couldn't stomach her overt manipulation any longer.

When I got as many clothes as I could stuffed into the various suitcases and bags, I realized that I still had more clothes, new clothes and shoes that I had not packed. I grabbed Calvin's Gucci duffle bag from the closet and put the remainder of my things in it. Although I had turned the bathroom light on and was making more noise than I wanted to, Calvin still slept right through my packing. Even if he had awakened, I was determined to leave. *I don't have any other choice.*

When I walked by Cristi, putting my last piece of luggage down the elevator, which I rarely used, she had the nerve to smile at me. She had released her grip on Calvin to watch me pack and now she had a triumphant, "I won!" grin on her face, victory draping over her like a Super Bowl win. I shot my middle finger at her before leaving the room.

It wasn't until I checked into the Buckhead Ritz Carlton that I realized what I had actually done. A sense of freedom swept over me, but at the same time, I felt a deep sense of loss. I kneeled to the floor and balled my eyes out. When I counted out the money that I had taken from Calvin's pocket, I realized that it was way more than I had imagined. *What is Calvin doing with all this cash on him? $2,500 seemed to be an awful lot of cash to be carrying around,* I thought. But then again, Calvin was a big spender, always bragging about having "Plenty Money." I knew he'd be livid once he realized that not only had I left, but that I had taken his money and his credit card. I laughed out loud as I wiped my tears. *I don't give a damn.* As far as I was concerned, Calvin owed me for all the pain I had endured because of him. I felt a sense of strength like I had never felt before and my tears eventually dried up. Perhaps it was because I was all cried out.

After dozing off for a few hours, I woke up, not remembering where I was and what had happened. When it dawned on me that I was at the Ritz Carlton and that Cristi was at Calvin's, a sadness came over me, but I wrapped my arms around myself and just prayed for God to help me to be strong. I didn't know what else do but pray. I figured that things in my life had to get better from this point and that maybe my decision to move out would motivate Calvin to stop taking me for granted. And then, like a light bulb had come on, the thought of Diego entered my mind. In the wake of Little C getting sick, Cristi moving in, and all that had occurred over the last two weeks, Diego Jones had actually faded to the back of my mind. I remembered Diego wishing me the best when I told him I was marrying Calvin. "He could care less!" I said angrily. "Forget you too, Diego!" I said, yet feeling a deep longing for him. I just wanted to talk to him. "Why do you live in London?" I continued, as if Diego were right there listening. "I wish you were here, Diego. I wish you were here to comfort me."

I didn't know why I was getting all sentimental about Diego when my world with my fiancé was falling apart. I started to feel guilty for thinking about Diego, but I hoped that I would see him again someday. *And soon.* Out of pure spite, I called a customer service representative at Verizon and told her to change my telephone number. I figured that Calvin would eventually try to call and I felt that I would be weaker if I talked to him right away. My number was changed immediately. *I'm gonna fix him!*

After two days at the Ritz Carlton, I got bored. Even after going shopping and seeing three movies, I felt unfulfilled and unsettled. One thing I had discovered was that I didn't feel comfortable in my own company. There were too many voices telling me ugly things about myself. The most haunting thought was that I was a loser and that Calvin would never marry me, nor would anybody else. I even felt unattractive. I cried as I looked in the mirror at myself. *Not only is my face scarred, but my life is too.*

I had not told anyone where I was, but I had called Sydney, Connie and Tacara to give them my new number. I told them that I had been getting strange hang-up calls late at night. Neither of them seemed to suspect that something had gone wrong between Calvin and me. I guess I was becoming better and better at hiding the pain and faking it.

On the third morning of my stay at the hotel I decided to apply for a job at the Versace store in Phipps Plaza. To my surprise and elation, I was hired on the spot as a salesperson. The salary wasn't what I'd be making as a buyer at Saks, but the manager, Roberto, told me that I could make quite a bit of money on commission.

"You are so dashing!" he said. "I'm sure you'll be fabulous. Can you start tomorrow?"

I definitely wasn't prepared to start working, but I figured it beat being bored and feeling worthless. I started to miss Calvin painfully that night and the tears that I thought were all dried up came in like a flood. I never thought they would stop flowing, and the more I prayed for peace, the less peaceful I became. When I read the Bible and my tears started to soak the pages, I closed it and cried into my pillow. The thought that kept going through my mind was the ugly vision of Cristi and Calvin making passionate love and being happy that I had left. I wanted to call Calvin, even if it were just to hang up, but I knew that if I heard his voice I'd fall weak for him. I didn't know how I was planning to work at the Versace store tomorrow with puffy eyes. "Oh, God. Please let me sleep," I cried. I did not sleep at all.

My day at work didn't go as badly as I had expected. To have not gotten any sleep, I felt quite vibrant physically, after drinking a Rock Star energy drink. Roberto trained me on various aspects of retail duties and explained Versace policies to me. He also showed me the most popular Versace collections, and I helped him unpack a new shipment from Paris. I got excited looking through the new shipment of stylish clothes. Roberto and I "oohed" and "aahed" in unison. Roberto was Dutch and had moved to the States from Amsterdam five years prior. He hadn't told me much about himself, but I assumed he was gay because of his mannerisms, the way he swayed when he walked and his perfectly manicured face, with arched eyebrows. I took a liking to Roberto's warm and jovial attitude. His laugh was deep and cackling-like; bringing me to laughter each time I'd hear him, which was often. I made my first sale within twenty minutes of being on the floor. It was of a black, silk dress that sold for $10,000.

"Girl, you are good!" Roberto said, giving me a high five. "You are absolutely fabulous!"

I grinned, feeling proud of myself for a change. I realized how much I had missed the retail business. Clothes, accessories, fashion, color, style all brought a sense of freedom to my spirit. And working at Versace was the start of my new beginning in retail. Excitement oozed through my soul.

By closing time, I had made several more sales, totaling $20,000. Roberto did a dance, moving his arms and shoulders around in circles after we totaled up my sales for the day.

"Girl, you are the best!" he squealed.

"I am?" I laughed, as I watched him dance.

"Yes!" he said and spun around in a circle doing the dance. "You have sold more in a day than some people who have been here for years have sold in weeks!"

"Really?" I said, not believing Roberto.

"Honey, I'm telling you the truth. Where have you been all my life? And girl, I've been trying to keep my nose out of your business, but what lucky man put this rock on your pretty finger?" Roberto took my hand in his and gawked at my ring. "Lawd."

"Oh," I stammered. "Just this guy that I can't live with and can't live without," I said, feeling a pang of sorrow. "It's complicated."

Roberto looked up at me slowly, seeming to notice the pain in my voice. "Now, he is treating you right, ain't he?" he asked in a fatherly tone. "Cause if he ain't treating you like the precious queen that you are then we can't have that."

I chuckled as I slowly took my hand out of Roberto's. "Oh, he treats me good. He just has some issues to work out."

"Well, you let him work out his issues, and in the meantime, you can occupy your time here at the store. How would you like to be assistant manager?" Roberto asked in a serious tone.

"What?" I said frowning, not quite sure I had heard him right.

"I want you to be assistant manager," Roberto replied. "It's not like you don't have more than enough retail experience, and we were actually looking to hire and assistant manager in another two weeks. So, what do you say? You'll get a ten percent increase from what you started with today. Versace is a great store to have down on your resume as the assistant manager, girl. So, will you take the position?"

"Why, yeah!" I said excitedly. "I've never been hired one day and promoted to assistant manager the next day."

"Well, consider this your lucky day. I know with that rock on your finger you probably don't need this job, but it'll give you something to occupy your mind until your guy gets his issues straightened out." Roberto looked at me through the corner of his big eyes. "And plus, we get 40% off here."

"That's great! Calvin loves himself some Versace," I blurted out before thinking.

"Calvin? So, that's his name, hunh?" Roberto looked at me like I had said a bad word. "What does Mr. Calvin do, if you don't mind me asking? Yeah, I'm nosy."

"He plays ball," I said hesitantly. "Football."

"Wait a minute. Do you mean Calvin, CK Moore with the Falcons?" Roberto asked, as his eyes got even bigger. "Is that your man?"

I smiled coyly. Feeling a little embarrassed that I couldn't keep who I was dating from Roberto.

"Oh, my goodness! Did the CK. Moore give you this ring!?" Roberto asked.

"Yeah, the CK Moore," I said with a somber smile.

"Well, girl, you definitely don't need this job. When is the wedding? Oh my goodness, he is so fine. Wait a minute.

That was you on T.V. with him when he did that press conference, wasn't it?"

"Yep, that was me," I replied and looked down.

"Girl, you don't know how lucky you are. He is fine and rich. And I know some women and men who would do anything to be with him!"

"Well, he don't go that way," I quickly said. "He loves women . . . and women love him."

"So, you have to deal with a lot of women chasing after him, I bet?"

"Tell me about it," I murmured, not really wanting to be reminded of Cristi and all the women willing to do practically anything to get Calvin.

"Is everything cool though? You seem sad," Roberto said, searching my eyes. "You don't look happy, sweetie."

"Yeah, I'm cool. Everything is everything. What will be, will be. Ya know?" I said in a monotone.

Roberto just stared at me. "Unh-uh. Give that line to somebody else. I have a psychology degree," Roberto said.

I chuckled. "And what does that mean?"

"It means that I know a hurt woman when I see one. You want to talk about it?" Roberto asked soothingly.

"Not really," I said. But something about Roberto made me trust him. I felt as though he would listen to me without judging me, so I opened up to him telling him about all the things I had endured. By the time I finished telling Roberto about my relationship with Calvin and how he wouldn't set a wedding date and how I left him cuddled up in bed with Cristi, tears started to well up in Roberto's eyes.

"I'm sorry for all the ugly drama," I said, seeing that my sorrow had made Roberto's chipper attitude mellow.

"Shayla, what are you gonna do?" Roberto asked. "It sounds like you really love this guy or you wouldn't put up with that mess."

"I do," I started to tear up. "And I know this sounds crazy, but I miss him so much. I want to be with him – like tonight."

"Oh, God, Shayla. You've got it bad," Roberto said, as he sat down on a seat next to the register.

"I know I do, but how do I stop being a fool for love? I don't know how. I just don't want to lose him. He's the best thing that's ever happened to me."

"Well, sometimes you have to lose something in order to gain it," Roberto said.

"What do you mean?" I asked, not understanding where he was going. His words reminded me of something Tacara had said before.

"Sometimes you've got to risk losing what you think is a good thing to see if it's really meant for you. And if it's causing you that much pain, then you have to let it go."

"Well, pain is a part of relationships," I said, already wanting to justify Calvin's behavior. "And it's not like I've met anybody else who I would even want to date ... besides Diego."

"Now, who is Diego?" Roberto asked.

"Oh, just a friend," I said softly as my heart warmed. "He is this guy I went out with when Calvin and I were really on shaky terms." I paused. "Well, actually, Calvin and I had just gotten engaged, but he got arrested and I was really gonna stop seeing him. I had already told Diego that I would go out with him before Calvin proposed – before I got the ring."

"Hunh?" Roberto said, standing to his feet. "Oh, Lawd. This does sound complicated. So, do you like this Diego guy?" Roberto asked, seeming to become more interested in the conversation.

"Oh, my God, yes!" I blushed. "He is so polished and handsome and he is tall too, with these light brown eyes that just drew me in even more." I couldn't believe I was telling Roberto about Diego. "But he's in London."

"London!?" Roberto exclaimed.

"Yeah. And I don't even know why I'm telling you about him," I said, feeling embarrassed.

"Because you really like him, that's why. And you think there might be some possibility there. It's okay to like him. You can have feelings for two people. Obviously he left a good impression on you."

"Well," I stammered. "It's just that he seems more settled, but I love being with Calvin. I really am in love with him. But it's hard for me, because everybody is in love with Calvin. He's married to football, and his endorsements, and his baby's mama and his fans and his cars and I don't know if I will ever be a priority in his life," I said as I started to cry. "He has hurt me so many times."

"Shayla, I don't want to give you any unwarranted advice, and I know you don't want my opinion anyway . . ."

"No, that's okay," I interrupted. "Say what you want to say. I don't let people that I don't know that well offend me. Say what you want to say."

"Well, I just think you give too much power to your man. You need to start respecting yourself and then maybe he'll start respecting you."

"I respect myself," I said, getting more offended by Roberto's words than I thought I would.

"Do you?" Roberto said with a puzzled look.

"Yeah, I do. Calvin just needs me to be more secure. He needs me to take whatever he dishes out, and it's hard to do that at times. I really think he needs my unconditional love, but loving someone like that is hard."

"So, what do you need?" Roberto queried.

"Hunh?"

"What do you need, Shayla?" Roberto asked again. "Are you getting what you need with this high profile baller? I mean, aside from the jewelry and all the materialistic things I'm sure you get, are you getting what you want and need out of your relationship?"

I couldn't answer Roberto. As much as I wanted to tell him yes, I knew I'd be lying. I stared at Roberto feeling a deep sorrow for myself. Yes, Calvin had provided me with all the materialistic things I could desire, but when it came down to it, I wasn't happy. I felt empty.

"I don't really know what I need," I said in a shaky voice. "I enjoy all the things I do with Calvin though."

"But Calvin shouldn't be your life," Roberto said. "It's okay to not know what you need," he said, seeming to sense my hurt. He reached behind the register and handed me a tissue. "Most people who love the way you love, don't know what they need because it's usually about pleasing others all the time. You feel like if you could just be enough or take enough from a person, by giving your unconditional love, that they'll love you more. But that's usually not the case. They eventually end up hurting you even more. I've learned you've got to love yourself."

"And I don't love myself," I cried. "I don't."

"Well, at least you are admitting it," Roberto said. "Shayla, when you go home tonight, I want you to look yourself in the mirror and tell yourself, 'I am lovable,' okay? And you keep telling yourself that until it sinks in because you are beautiful, so don't let no man treat you like dirt, no matter who he is,"

I wiped my tears, but the more I wiped them, the more new tears flowed. Roberto's words had struck a deep cord in me. I had not opened up to anyone in such a long time and I knew that Roberto was speaking the truth to me.

"Come here, Shayla," Roberto said, putting his arm around me. He stood me in front of the full length mirror.

"What are you doing?" I asked, looking in the mirror and then at Roberto.

"What do you see, Shayla, when you look in the mirror?" Roberto held on to both of my shoulders, making me stand up straight.

"I don't know," I said with a slight chuckle. "I see a pitiful, lovesick girl who looks like shit right now."

"Okay, I want you to repeat after me," Roberto said.

"Okay," I agreed hesitantly.

"I am beautiful both inside and out," Roberto said in a strong mantra-like voice.

"I can't say that," I said. I tried to turn away from the mirror, but Roberto turned me right back around.

"I am beautiful both inside and out!" he said adamantly.

I sniffed, inhaled, and then exhaled. "I am beautiful both inside and out," I said softly.

"And I deserve a man who will love me and treat me with respect," Roberto said.

"And I deserve a man who will love me and treat me with respect," I repeated.

"I deserve the best because I am the best," Roberto said with attitude.

"I can't say that," I sighed.

"Shayla! Say it!"

"Damn," I stammered. "Okay, I deserve the best because I am the best," I looked at Roberto. "I'm not feeling this."

"Well, that's okay," Roberto said letting go of my shoulders. "You keep repeating that to yourself every day and you'll start feeling it. And do you know what will happen?"

"No, what?"

"You'll get the love you believe you deserve, because a man will only treat you the way you allow him to treat you," Roberto said as though he were my teacher.

"Well, I don't get it," I said. "What does this have to do with me leaving my man with another woman in his bed?"

"Girl, forget about your man and that woman for a minute and start thinking about yourself and your own feelings, okay?"

"And how am I supposed to do that?" I said. "It hurts so bad. I miss him."

"Well, that's normal. Just let yourself cry. Believe that everything will work out the way it's supposed to work out in time. Believe that you deserve the best and say, 'I'm not settling for less than the best.' Act like you deserve the best and your feelings will catch up with your actions." Roberto reached out to hug me. "Now, I'm gonna have to start charging you for this pep talk. Come on. Let's close down so we can get out of here."

When I got back to my room at the hotel, I tried to digest all that Roberto had said to me. I even looked in the mirror and chanted, "You are beautiful and you deserve the best," over and over again. But I did not feel it. I felt like crap. I decided to call Sydney to admit to her that Calvin and I were having a few problems. I asked her if I could move in with her for a couple of weeks. Sydney didn't ask any questions. She just responded, "Sure, you can move in," and told me that I had made a "wise move." She then informed me that Calvin had stopped by her house earlier in the day, looking for me. Of course my heart raced when she told me this news. Sydney said that when she told him that I wasn't at her house he asked if she had my new number.

"I knew something was up," Sydney said. "He had me worried for a minute, but I knew I had just talked to you about your new job and you sounded okay when I talked to you," she said. "Before I could really ask him anything, he just ran off and said he would catch up with you later."

When I hung up from Sydney, I lay on the bed, looking at the ceiling. I wanted so badly to reach out to Calvin. *I can't resist. I have to call him.* I picked up the phone in the hotel, not wanting Calvin to know my new cell phone number quite yet.

"Yeah," he answered in his usual, carefree tone.

"Calvin, this is Shayla," I said softly.

"Where is my money?" Calvin asked coldly.

"Excuse me?" I said, feeling puzzled.

"My damn money, Shayla. You took my loot and I don't appreciate that shit."

I couldn't believe it. Of all things, I definitely wasn't expecting "money" to be the first thing that would come out of his mouth. "So, is that all you're concerned about? Your money?" I asked as my heart sank.

"Hell, yeah. That's all I want. So, where can we meet so I can get my damn money?"

I held the phone in silence. I had a knot in my gut.

"Hello?" Calvin yelled into the phone. "Hello?"

I still didn't know what to say, so I began to cry.

"Shayla, what the hell is going on? Why did you call me?"

"Because my sister told me that you came by her house looking for me today and I thought you were looking for me because you loved me, Calvin - not because you want your damn money!" I said.

"Well, I want my money, okay!" Calvin said.

"So, you don't love me?" I asked. My emotions were going downhill fast.

"What's love got to do with my damn money? Was you thinking about love when you walked out on me the other night and took all my cash?"

"As a matter of fact, I was, Calvin. I was thinking about how much I love myself and how I deserve a man who will love me and treat me with respect," I said, using Roberto's mantra.

Calvin started laughing, which caught me off guard again. "Naw, you deserve a good ass kickin. That's what you deserve," he said as he continued laughing.

"You know what? You deserve the ass whopping. I hate you Calvin!" I said angrily, but not meaning my words.

"Well, thank you, but that still don't solve the problem of my money!"

I hung up on Calvin, furious at him for being so rude. But to my surprise, he called me right back – on the hotel line. *Damn Caller ID.*

"Shayla, I'm coming by to get my money, aight?" he said calmly, after I answered the phone.

"Why do you need this money so bad, Calvin? What's a couple thousand dollars to you anyway?" I asked.

"What's your room number?" Calvin asked.

I hesitated. *I've got to be strong. Lord, please help me to be strong.*

"What's your room number, Shayla?" he demanded.

"1020, but don't come by here," I said.

"Bye." Calvin hung up.

When Calvin knocked at my door 30 minutes later, a part of me was surprised that he had actually come, but I didn't know what to expect since he was so unpredictable. I opened the door slowly. Calvin had his arms folded across his chest and he looked at me with a look of authority.

"Pack your shit and let's go," he said with a stern gaze.

"I'm not packing nothing, Calvin," I said softly. "And if you want your money, here it is," I handed Calvin $1,500 of the $2,500 I had taken from him.

"You little thief," Calvin said as he took the money and pushed his way inside my room, closing the door behind him.

"You've got your money, so why are you coming in?" I asked.

"Get your shit together," he said, looking around the room. "Got my bags and everything. You little thief," he said. "Get all this stuff together and let's go."

"I'm not going with you, Calvin," I said. "I'm not gonna live with you and your other woman. I can't."

"Shayla, start packing your shit now," he said. "You are coming back to the house and we're gonna make it work."

"No, Calvin!" I said with force. "I am not going back with you. I'm gonna go stay with Sydney for a while. I cannot go back to your house unless Cristi is out."

"So, it's over between us," Calvin said as he came close to me.

"No, it doesn't have to be over between us, I just . . ."

"I'm not asking," Calvin interrupted. "I'm telling you it's over between us." He moved so close to me that I was afraid. His nose was almost touching me. "It's over. You understand?"

"Okay," I mumbled, looking into Calvin's pensive eyes. Calvin then threw the money up into the empty air, but he held on to the credit card. He turned around. As he walked towards the door, I wanted to ask him to stay so we could talk things out, but nothing came out of my mouth. He opened the door and it closed behind him. I sat on the bed, looking at the money he had let fall to the floor. I wondered if Calvin planned to come back. He never did.

Chapter Nineteen

Rock Bottom

Two weeks passed - fourteen long, tortuous days of inner turmoil and pain. I decided to stay at the Ritz Carlton a couple more days to give Calvin another chance to call. I even thought he might pop up at the hotel to try and reconcile with me, but when he didn't call or show up by the second night, I called him, only to hear Little C crying in the background. Calvin told me he was "busy."

"Okay. Well, this is my new number," I said softly. "I want to talk about things when you get a chance."

"What's there to talk about, Shay?" he asked.

"Us," I said. "We need to talk about where our relationship is going."

"It ain't going nowhere," he replied. "When you left this house, you made that decision."

And then I heard Cristi in the background. "What are you doing to my baby?" she hollered.

"Ahhh, girl. This boy all right," he said. "He just crying cause you pick him up all the damn time."

"He's crying cause he shit in his pants and you act like you don't know how to change him," Cristi ranted.

"You change him then," Calvin said, seeming agitated.

I wondered what part of the house they were in. *Is she in Calvin's bedroom? Has Calvin moved her upstairs now?* My mind burned with questions and jealousy as I listened.

"I got a new job at one of your favorite stores," I decided to tell Calvin, trying to keep him engaged in our conversation and wanting him to know that I was employed now.

"Where?"

"Versace," I said. "And I'm the assistant manager already."

"CK, could you go get his diapers downstairs?" Cristi said loudly. I figured she had to be sitting right beside Calvin for me to hear her so clearly through the phone.

"You go get'em," Calvin said.

"If you ain't gonna change him, the least you can do is go get the damn diapers. You sorry, man."

"Whatever," Calvin said.

"Hey, listen. You do sound busy, so I guess I'll talk to you another time," I said, hoping Calvin would tell me that he would call me back – or ask me to call him back.

"Aight, bye." Calvin hung up.

I was hurt. I had done so well without calling him, without hearing his voice, and now here I was feeling caught up again. *I'm not over him.* Even after standing up and repeating to myself more positive affirmations that Roberto had told me to say, I felt like crap. I didn't understand how I could feel so powerful by moving out of Calvin's home, changing my number and standing up for myself one week, but the next week feel totally defeated and at a loss. I felt like Calvin had turned the tables on me. It was obvious that my moving out had hurt him, but instead of doing the right thing by moving Cristi out and proving that he really loved me, he had chosen to make me hurt even more. *Just like Calvin.* But I still wanted to reconcile with him. Although loving Calvin had been more painful than it had been pleasurable lately, I still wanted to be with him desperately.

With Roberto's pep talks at work and by attending Bible study and church with Sydney and Aaron twice, I managed to gain some will power and not call Calvin for eleven days, and that's when I got the unexpected surprise that rocked my world.

I was re-arranging a display in the back of the Versace store and had only been open for about fifteen minutes. When I heard the chime go off, indicating that a customer had walked into the store, I proceeded to the front to be visible and to greet my customer. I was motivated to make a sell before Roberto came in at noon.

"Good morning," I said jovially, as I walked towards the front of the boutique.

When I walked far enough to get a view of my customer, my steps came to a complete halt and my heart almost stopped. It was Calvin, standing beside a very attractive woman wearing a short sweater dress and boots. Her sandy brown hair was thick and curly, almost looking like an afro – wild, yet appealing. Her legs were long, and she was curvy. When Calvin saw me staring at them, he turned in the opposite direction, like he didn't know me. He then grabbed the wild-haired looking woman's hand and said something to her. She giggled.

Calvin guided her over to the dress rack where he let go of her hand and went through the dresses, pulling one out that was long and sexy. He put it up to her shapely body and she shook her head like she didn't like the dress. Calvin put the dress back and pulled out another one that had a low cut in the back and sheer arms. She smiled and took the dress from him, seeming to like that one.

My head was spinning. I didn't know whether to choke Calvin or choke her. I couldn't get my feet to move for a few seconds, but when I finally did, I walked over to them. Calvin spun around, seeming startled by my close proximity. He looked at me like I was a stranger, as though he had never seen me before.

"Where is the dressing room?" he said as his eyes met mine steadily. "She wants to try on this dress."

I looked at him dryly, feeling injured by his disrespect. I was infuriated and shocked that he had stooped so low to hurt me.

"Ma'am, I asked where the dressing room is. My girlfriend, Toni, wants to try this dress on," Calvin said indignantly.

Don't stoop to his level. Don't do it, Shayla. Just walk away. Count to ten. But before I could count to five, I hauled off and slapped Calvin as hard as I could.

"What the hell!" Calvin growled, as he put his arms up while I threw several punches after the slap. It reminded me of New Year's Eve. Only this time, I wanted to really hurt him.

I hit him with my fist again and again. I then grabbed him around his neck and tried to choke him. I was going mad.

"Oh my God!" the woman screamed. "What is going on?"

Calvin pulled both of my hands from around his neck and shook me.

"Let me go, you son of a bitch," I panted wildly. Calvin held my arms tightly. His lips were tight and his eyes pierced into mine maliciously. I felt restrained by his hold on me, but I drew closer to him and kneed him in his groin area. He let go of me quickly and slumped over with a groan.

"CK, are you okay?" the girl asked, backing away with fright in her eyes. "I'm going to find security."

"Go!" I yelled. "Get security. I want him out of here, and you too, you slut!"

Stopping in her steps, the girl said, "Excuse me?"

"Yeah, I said it! Slut!" I snapped boldly. "Did you know he is engaged to me?" I shot my ring at her, thinking that it would give me leverage.

Her eyes grew bigger. Calvin limped over to her, still holding his groin area. A crooked smile came across his face. *Oh, so he's enjoying this.* I wanted to knee him again. He grabbed the girl's hand.

"No, we are not engaged," he said. "I tried to tell her it's over between us, but she keeps calling." He looked at me. "Stop calling me, okay?"

I tried to find anything I could get my hands on to throw at him, but all I could come up with was a magazine. I threw it as hard as I could. He caught it.

"Get out of here!" I yelled.

"Calvin, come on, baby. Let's go," Toni said, pulling on his arm.

At that moment, Roberto walked in. He looked at me and then at Calvin and Toni. "What's going on here?" he said, walking close to me.

"Roberto, get him out of here before I kill him," I said, trembling.

"Oh, so is that a threat?" Calvin barked. Toni pulled on his arm, urging him to leave.

"Get out of this store, you punk!" Roberto said in a strong voice.

Calvin burst into laughter. "Punk?' he said. "Man, who you calling a punk? You talking to yourself?"

"Man, I'm not afraid of you," Roberto said. "I will fight you."

Calvin cackled again. "Ohhh," he taunted. "I'm scared."

"CK, let's go, now!" Toni yelled.

Calvin glared at Toni and then back at me. "Okay, I'm leaving, but leave me alone, okay, little girl, cause I have a woman now and I just want you out of my life, that's all." He pulled Toni closer.

I swallowed and held my breath so I wouldn't burst out crying. I never imagined Calvin could be so cruel. The touch of Roberto's hand on my shoulder made me feel like I had awakened from a nightmare. But as much as I wanted the nightmare to be over, I knew it was real. Calvin strutted out of the store with his arm around Toni.

"It's okay, Shayla," Roberto said softly. He pulled me closer and rubbed my arm soothingly.

I pulled away from Roberto, feeling like my legs were about to give out. I ran into the stock room and fell to my knees sobbing frantically.

"Shayla . . . Oh my God, Shayla," Roberto said as he trailed behind me. "Shayla, don't let him get to you," Roberto continued as he got into the stock room. "He only did that to break you – to make you jealous. He is the one hurting, so he wanted to see you hurt. Get up, Shayla." Roberto grabbed my arms, trying to lift me from the floor. I continued to sob.

"Leave me alone," I cried. "Just leave me." I pulled away from Roberto and buried my head in my hands. I felt injured.

"Shayla, I don't want to see you like this," Roberto said. He touched my shoulder and squeezed it. "He's a dog, Shayla. You deserve better. Trust me, he's not gonna be blessed."

I wiped my eyes and lifted my head, staring straight ahead. "I can't believe he did this," I cried, feeling like a pathetic fool. I looked up at Roberto. "Is there something wrong with me, Roberto? What is wrong with me?"

Roberto stared at me like he was lost for words. He finally shook his head. "No. Nothing is wrong with you. There is something wrong with CK Moore. Shayla, you are too good for him. Get up, baby," Roberto helped me up as I started sobbing again.

"I hate him," I said, feeling weak and dazed. "I feel like he just stabbed me in my heart. I hate I ever met him."

"I know, but let God deal with him," Roberto said. "He will get his." Roberto reached out and embraced me.

"I've got to go, Roberto," I cried into his shoulder. "I can't stay today."

"Girl, I wouldn't expect you to stay after that," Roberto said in an understanding tone. "But are you gonna be okay? Please don't call him, Shayla. Just go home and pray."

The store chime went off again. For a second I thought it might be Calvin returning. I wiped my eyes again and tried to hold in my anguish.

"Stay here," Roberto ordered. He walked out of the stock room onto the floor.

I inhaled until I heard the voice of a woman customer asking Roberto about the new line of dresses. A big part of me wanted it to be Calvin coming back to apologize, but I realized just how far-fetched the idea was. I began crying again. Of all the times I had been hurt by Calvin, I had never felt as crushed as I felt now. I also knew in my heart that this was it for Calvin and me. *It's over.* He had forced me to let go by stabbing me and leaving me for dead. I figured it took the worst pain to help bring me out of something that was not good for me.

I grabbed my bag and walked out front. Roberto was still helping the customer. He glared at me as though he was surprised to see me emerge.

"I'm okay," I mouthed. I put my hand to my ear. "I'll call you later," I said softly.

"Wait," Roberto said to me. He looked at the lady he was helping. "Ma'am, could you excuse me for one second?"

"Sure," the lady said.

"Shayla, are you okay?" Roberto asked as he rushed to my side.

I couldn't help but give Roberto one of those "duh" looks. I could barely see his eyes from the tears invading my eyes.

"I'm sorry for asking that," Roberto said. "But are you gonna be okay? Shayla, please be careful driving home. I know you'll be okay. I've got faith in you." Roberto seemed distraught and clueless.

"I'll call you later, Roberto," I managed to say as I walked out the door as fast as I could.

When I got to Sydney's house, she wasn't home and I was glad. I cried for hours, trying to figure out why Calvin had been so cruel. Not only did I think about the way he had brought another woman, *some Toni*, into the boutique I worked, but all the hurtful and malicious things Calvin had done to me started playing in my mind. *The time he put you out of the car in Jamaica, the time he had another girl over and caused you such upset that you had a car accident and lost your baby, the time he was arrested for DUI and drug possession and had a stripper in the car, the time he promised to marry you in Vegas, but didn't show up, the times he'd flirt with other women in front of you, the time he moved Cristi Perez into his home without telling you and then allowed her to get in bed with you and him and snuggle up to him, the panties, the other women, the lack of respect ... the other women ... the lack of respect ... the other women ... the lack of respect. His cocky disposition.*

"God, I need to be set free," I lamented, thinking about how I might have allowed things to go from bad to worst. *Maybe I encouraged Calvin's disrespect by not telling him "enough" and ending our relationship a long time ago. Now I'm bruised and don't know if I will ever be the same again.*

When I heard Sydney come in from work, about five hours had passed since I had gotten to her house. I had cried for most of the five hours, and during the times I wasn't crying I stared at the ceiling, feeling like my life was over. It didn't surprise me when Sydney knocked at my door. I had told her that I would be working until closing.

"Shayla?" she said after knocking three times. "What are you doing home?"

Before I could tell her I wasn't feeling well, she entered the room. She frowned when she looked at me.

"Shayla, you've been crying. What's wrong?" she walked towards me and sat on the bed.

I didn't feel like lying to my sister. I sat up as my lips quivered. "It's over between us, Syd," I started to cry. "It's really over."

Sydney leaned towards me and embraced me tightly. I sank into her arms wondering how I'd get over the pain.

For seven days I did nothing but lie in bed and cry. My weight plummeted from 125 lbs to 117 lbs. Roberto had called every day to check on me, even twice a day sometimes, but I'd let his calls go straight to voice mail at most times. The last time I talked to him, yesterday, I told him I was just fine. I was growing tired of him checking on me and telling me to say all these mantras and positive affirmations that weren't working for me. When he asked me when I planned on coming back to work I told him that I would not be. After a long pause, Roberto said, "Okay, Shayla. I'll give you as much time as you need."

"No. You don't have to give me any time," I snapped. "I'm not coming back, Roberto."

"But Shayla, you've got to. I need you here. Don't let CK Moore ruin your life," he said. "Snap out of it."

I hung up on Roberto and he called back again and again, apologizing on my voice mail and telling me that he wasn't going to give up on me so for me not to give up on myself. I had no motivation to eat, no motivation to work, no motivation to do anything. *I don't want to snap out of it.* Depression was becoming my friend. My sorrow was overtaking me. The depression I felt inside my soul understood me. It helped me to block out the outside world. I felt hauntingly at peace in my sorrow. I didn't want to get out of bed. I knew that nothing was going to happen to make me feel better.

Things got worse. On the morning of my eighth day of blocking the world out and drinking only liquids and very little solid food, Sydney came into my room with some bad news.

"Shay, unlock the door. Unlock the door now," Sydney demanded. "Something terrible has happened."

I knew by Sydney's tone that she was distressed, so in my weakness, I got up and opened the door. Sydney clenched my hand and looked deeply into my eyes.

"Shayla, I know you haven't heard yet, but . . ."

"But what?" I screamed fearing something had happened to Calvin. I squeezed Sydney's hand tighter. "What?"

"It's Diego Jones dad," she said.

"Yeah, what about him?" I frowned.

"He and Diego's mom were in a bad car accident."

I snatched my hand away from Sydney. "What are you talking about? Where did you hear that?"

"It was just on the news," Sydney said. "It happened last night. Mr. Jones died and Mrs. Jones was airlifted to a hospital. I don't think she's doing too well."

"What?" I looked at her in disbelief.

"It was on Channel 2," Sydney said. "Shayla, you've got to get it together. Maybe you need to call Diego. I pray Mrs. Jones will be okay."

"Oh, no," I said shivering. Although I had not expected the devastating news of Clyde Jones' death and Claire being admitted into the hospital after a car accident, to be the thing that would save me from drowning myself in self pity and put me in motion, that's exactly what it did. If anything, I felt like I had to be stronger for Claire … *and for Diego.* Claire had inspired me so much with her words of wisdom when I was in Puerto Rico. *And poor Diego.* I wondered how he was handling the news of his father's death. After letting Sydney's words sink in for a while and deciding that I could no longer continue to destruct in self pity over a man who had obviously moved on, I called the Jones house and left a message with a woman for Diego to call me. I told the woman who answered the phone that I was a friend of Claire and Diego's and that I was sorry to hear about Mr. Jones' passing away. The lady on the other end of the phone said that she would leave the message for Diego and that he would be arriving today. "Please pray for my sister, Claire," she said. "She's in a coma."

After Sydney left for work, I searched the Internet for stories about the accident. It was my first time on the computer since I had left Calvin's house. AJC.com had a brief piece about the Joneses, saying that a drunk driver ran his car head on into Clyde Jones and his wife Claire as they were on their way back home from a reception. The story read that Clyde was killed immediately and that Claire was airlifted to a local hospital, as Sydney had stated, and that she was in critical condition.

"God, please save Claire," I prayed. "Let her live." In the midst of my Internet searching, I decided to pull up a web site that posted gossip about athletes, just to see if I could find anything new on Calvin. When I put his name in the search engine, I was horrified. I found pages and pages of new postings from women claiming to have been with Calvin intimately. There were even two women going back and forth, saying that they were pregnant by him. My eyes and heart grew weary again when one blogger's entry read that Calvin had put his fiancée out of his house and was now living with his baby's mama, Cristi Perez, who had been in his life for a decade. Some of the women who wrote about Cristi called her hood rat and very unclassy. *I know that's right.* One of the posts said that he was also dating a new girl named Toni, a model. I shuddered, remembering the day Calvin walked into the boutique with her. There was no reason for me not to believe all of the postings.

I waited to hear back from Diego, but the only calls I received were from my mom, Roberto and Tacara. By the time night time rolled around, I had heard more reports on the Jones' accident on the local news. The reporter stated that Claire was in intensive care in an induced coma at Northside Hospital, but that doctors said she was expected to recover. I didn't know if I should stop by the hospital or not. I wondered if Calvin had heard the news of the tragedy.

Within three days I had managed to gain back three of the eight pounds I had lost. My feelings about Calvin had turned from hurt to anger, especially after reading more gossip on the web sites. I decided that going to visit Claire in the hospital was the best thing to do. Of course the thought of seeing Diego excited me. I knew that it would be a bit much for me to expect to spend some quality time with him, but I really hoped we would get a chance to talk privately. *I want to tell him that I'm no longer with Calvin.* My heart beat faster as I thought about Diego. I knew that he would be sad about his dad's death and his mom's condition. *Maybe I can soothe his pain.*

I looked at my engagement ring and pulled it over my knuckle then back down again. *It's over between Calvin and me. Take the ring off then,* something told me. With that thought, I quickly removed the ring. I looked at it closely for a while. *I could probably open my own boutique if I sold this.* "Hunh," I grunted, realizing that selling my engagement ring just might be an option. *But I'm not gonna do that.* If nothing else, I wanted to keep the ring as something tangible I had gotten out of my relationship with Calvin. Of course I still had all the clothes, jewelry and some money too. *That dog.* I wondered what he was doing and how he had managed to start dating yet another woman when Cristi was still living with him. I wondered if Cristi had moved out. *But I can't worry about Calvin and his women.* I had to think about being there for Diego. *He's the man who needs me now.* And I needed him too. I stood up, walked to the bathroom and placed my engagement ring on the counter. "Lord, do I need him too," I murmured.

When I arrived at the hospital, to my disappointment, I was told that Claire was only seeing family members and that she had just regained full consciousness. I asked if Diego was there, but was informed that he had left the hospital a few minutes earlier. *Oh well.* I left a get well card for Claire and wrote in it, "I pray for you and your family. You're an angel on earth. Please get well soon."

By the next week, I still had not heard from Diego, but I knew I had to make it to his father's funeral. On the day of the funeral I got up with a refreshed, calm feeling. I had asked Sydney to attend the funeral with me, but she told me that she couldn't attend because she had an important litigation. The funeral was at 11am.

When I got to the church at 10:30am, the parking lot was already quite full, but I found a decent parking space right up front when someone backed out as I drove around. The church was large and beautiful with stained glass windows. I walked inside the lobby, where I signed the registry. A few people were standing around talking in soft voices and a middle-aged woman handed me a program.

"You can feel free to view the body before you're seated," she said softly.

The body? The thought of seeing Mr. Jones in a casket made my stomach feel like it was going to turn upside down. My eyes teared up as I walked down the aisle to view the body with several others. The church was almost full. I looked to the side and saw a few Falcons players who were seated together. My heart almost jumped out of my skin. *I wonder is Calvin here?* Mr. Jones had sold him a car since we met him in Puerto Rico. He had sold many athletes cars and did a lot of business dealings with them.

Diego and his immediate family had not yet arrived, but I noticed several rows roped off for family on the front, left side of the church. I finally got to the metal casket where Clyde Jones lay. He looked like he was sleeping. Although his skin was darker, he looked content, with a black suit on with a tie, and his hand crossed over his chest. In his hand was a wedding picture of him and Claire. I was compelled to touch his hand, but a woman came beside me quickly, invading my space. As I walked to my seat I scanned the room. Aside from the Falcons ball players, some sports announcers and a few players from other teams, I didn't notice anyone else that I knew. But there was a striking young lady on the row behind the family. She was crying. I figured she wasn't family or she would be coming in with the processional. I slid beside her as our eyes met.

"Hi," she whispered, wiping her eyes.

"Hi," I said back. *Maybe she's one of the relatives.*

When the procession finally began, I leaned forward to look for Diego. A certain rush came over me as he walked with his brothers and sister. Claire Jones wasn't present. *She must still not be doing too well.* Diego looked debonair and intact. He walked up to the casket and put his hand on his father. When he turned around, he looked in my direction, right at me. My heartbeat quickened. I smiled, but he just nodded his head, without an expression, and turned around as the rest of the family came in. I sat still through the hour long service as the girl next to me wept periodically. I gave her a few Kleenex.

After the service, everyone met the family in the church lobby. The family had formed a line and guests were shaking hands with all the Joneses, hugging them and giving their condolences. I was anxious to see Diego up close again. I knew he'd have to keep his composure and be cool about seeing me, but I felt that seeing me up close and getting a hug from me would definitely be a healing balm for him. Just as I approached Diego, a woman reached out to hug him, but Diego noticed me. He kept his eyes steady on me while he hugged the woman. He said a few words to her, but continued to look in my direction on and off again while he talked to her. I smiled coyly.

"Shayla," Diego said, once I was finally standing in front of him. His eyes were warm.

"Diego," I said softly, extending my arms to him. When we hugged, I felt wonderful. I held on to Diego tightly. I didn't want to let him go.

"I'm sorry I haven't called you back," Diego said, barely hugging me at all. "I was going to call you before I left to go back."

"Oh, that's okay," I said releasing Diego, sensing his distance. "I know you've been busy. I'm so sorry about your dad. How is your mom?"

"She's doing much better, but she wasn't well enough to attend the funeral," Diego said. "She had some internal bleeding and has a broken rib cage, but the doctors say she's going to pull through. Thank God."

"Good," I said. "I stopped by to see her, but she was only seeing family at the time. Do you think I can stop by to see her again soon?"

"I think she still just wants to see family for now, being that she's so torn up about my dad," he said. "Keep checking in on her though. I'm sure she'd love to hear from you."

"I definitely will."

I tried to search Diego's eyes, to get a hint that he was still feeling me, but I didn't pick up that vibe. Something was different. *Maybe he's just in pain.*

"Well, thank you so much for coming," he said cordially. "It's good to see you, Shayla."

"It's good to see you too," I said. "I'm sorry it had to be on such a sad occasion."

"Yeah," Diego looked down like he didn't have much more to say. "Thanks for coming," he said again.

Just like that? Something is not right here. I felt like Diego was pushing me away. I moved closer to Diego. "I'm no longer with Calvin," I whispered to him. "We didn't get married, so you don't have to be afraid to talk to me."

Diego's face looked flush. I felt stupid. *This is definitely not the time to tell him about my breakup with Calvin.*

"As long as you're happy, that's all that matters," he said. Right when he said that, the girl who had been sitting beside me crying in the church suddenly appeared.

"You okay, sweetie?" she said, rubbing Diego's arm. "You need me to do anything?"

My heart dropped.

"I'm fine, thanks," Diego said as he looked at her and she looked at him lovingly. They took each other's hand. She then looked at me.

"I'm Gabriella," she said, extending her other hand. "Diego's fiancée," she added as our hands touched.

"Oh," I said feeling like I had been stabbed again. "Oh, I…I…I'm Shayla."

"Shayla?" she frowned as if she should know me. "Have we met?"

"No. I'm a friend of Claire's," I said.

"And mine," Diego interrupted.

"Oh," Gabriella smiled. "Well, whoever is a friend of yours is definitely a friend of mine." She smiled at him. He smiled awkwardly.

I wanted to go run and hide. "Well, I'm going to get out of here," I said in a low tone.

"So, are you coming to the burial and then to the house?" Diego asked.

"No, I don't think so," I stammered. "I just wanted to come out and give my condolences to you and your family. I'll keep you all in my thoughts and call your mom at the hospital soon."

"Well, take care," Diego said.

"You too," I said. I looked at Gabriella. "Nice to meet you."

Chapter Twenty

Moving Forward

"The darkest hour is just before the dawn," Sydney said, embracing me. I had just told her about my surprise and hurt over Diego having a fiancée. "The Lord is getting ready to bless you beyond your wildest expectations, but He just wants you to be all His. He wants you to put Him first."

I didn't want to hear Sydney's words, but a flicker of hope came over me as she spoke. "For every pain and every loss you have experienced, God is going to restore you with something better. Even if it's not in the way you think or with the person you think ... He won't leave you broken like this, so be encouraged."

I had nothing to lose by listening to Sydney. I had hit rock bottom. *There is nowhere to go but up.* I didn't want to soak Sydney's dress with my tears, so I pulled back.

"But why is God punishing me, Syd?" I asked in bewilderment. "I've lost everything – Calvin, my job at Saks, Diego, and I don't even know who I am anymore. I've lost myself. How could a loving God allow me to hurt like this?"

Sydney looked into my eyes – seeming to search for words. She sank down on the bed and laid her head in my lap. "Shay, God didn't break up with you. He didn't fire you either. He won't ever leave you. He never ends on a negative note. It'll get better. I promise."

For three more days I allowed myself to mourn. I turned off my phone and secluded myself in Sydney's house, relapsing into my depressive state. The only time I came out of the bedroom was for a small helping of food and liquids here and there. But on the fourth day, something in my mindset shifted. It was like a sudden light came on. *I have to pull myself up or I will die.* And I wasn't ready to die. I wanted to live the abundant life that Sydney had said I could live. The first thing I

318

decided to do was call Roberto back. He had been calling me every single day, but I had not been answering my phone or calling anyone back.

"Hello?" Roberto answered.

"Roberto, it's Shayla."

"Oh my God, Shayla! I'm so glad to hear from you. Oh my God. How are you?"

"Not too good," I admitted. "But I'll be okay."

"No, Shayla. You will be better than okay. Please tell me you're calling to say you're ready to come back to work. I have a wonderful opportunity for you."

"Really? What's up?"

"I was asked to host a big fashion show at the mart – featuring top designs for the fall collection and I need someone to help me coordinate the fashion show. I told them that I knew the perfect young lady for the job."

"Oh, really now?" I said curiously. "How did you know that I know how to coordinate fashion shows?"

"You told me, remember? I guess you forgot. But when I interviewed you, you told me that you had put on a few fashion shows before. I know you can do it, Shayla. Please come work with me. I can't do this by myself."

"When is it?" I asked. There was a surge of excitement that came over me, but I didn't know if I had the skills Roberto expected me to have – nor the emotional getup that was needed.

"It's next month, May 25. I know that's soon, but if you come back to work, we can just plan accordingly and get this thing rolling. Some real big wheels will be attending. And several buyers from the major department stores will be there too."

"Did you say May 25?"

"Yeah, what's up? You already got plans or something?"

"No. It's just the day before my birthday, that's all," I said, remembering that I was with Calvin in Puerto Rico on my birthday last year. A quick memory of him giving me the heart necklace entered my mind.

"Well, that's great!" Roberto said. "We can throw you a party after the fashion show and you can start your birthday week off with a bang. So, when can you get over here, Shayla? I need you to be here at least four days out of the week. Can you do that for me? I really need some help and I've held out on hiring an assistant manager because I think you are cut out perfectly for the job. And if you coordinate the fashion show with me, there is no telling what opportunities will come your way. Pretty please, Shayla."

Roberto was definitely putting me on the spot, but a part of me knew that I had to do something or I would waste away in Sydney's house. She had not been hard on me about my depression, but she did tell me that I had to be the one to decide how long I'd allow my circumstances to get the best of me. Seeing her go to work five days a week, attend church, and spend time with Aaron, while having a vibrant attitude, made me want to acquire whatever it was that she had internally. But at the same time, I just didn't understand how I could pull myself out of gloom when the man I loved so much had dumped me and the man I saw as a potential mate had moved on and gotten engaged. *But I need to do whatever it takes.*

"Roberto, I appreciate you so much. I have been going through even more hurt since you last saw me. It's been tough."

"Really, Shayla. I'm so sorry. We can definitely talk about it."

"Yeah, I'll have to tell you everything when I see you. I've lost a lot of weight. I haven't been eating much."

"Well, come meet me and let's go have lunch at the Tavern in a couple of hours. It's on me. I'm famished and Darla should be able to hold the store down for a while."

"Darla?"

"Yeah. She's the salesperson I hired, but she can only work 20 hours a week and I still need an assistant manager and a fashion show coordinator for this big show. So, can we meet at 2 pm at the Tavern?"

I hesitated, wondering how it would feel to finally stop sulking and get out. "Yeah, I'll meet you at 2," I said.

"Goody!" Roberto exclaimed. "See you in a little while."

When I met with Roberto he immediately started talking about the fashion show plans, telling me I'd be responsible for casting the models, helping decorate the venue and publicizing the event. He told me I'd also be responsible for communicating with the designers to see which outfits they'd showcase.

"You'll be the host for the Celebrity Gifting Suite the day prior to the show as well," Roberto told me.

"I will?" I said, surprised that he was assigning me so many duties. He was yakking so fast that I could hardly digest everything he was saying. When I told him about Diego being engaged, he stopped to empathize with me for about five minutes. He put his hand over my hand and said how sorry he was, but he quickly added that the ideal man for me was out there somewhere. He said I had to concentrate on something other than having a man in my life.

"You've got to get your own life together, Shayla. Be the kind of person you wish to attract and then you will attract that right man," he said. "But you're not gonna have time for a man over the next month and a half with all we have to do. I guarantee you."

"But can you believe Diego is engaged?" I said, trying to steer the conversation back to my love life. "He had to get engaged over the last few months because when we went out, I don't think he was engaged. I know he wasn't. And Calvin hasn't called me since he came by the store with that Toni girl. I thought I might see him at Mr. Jones funeral, but he wasn't there. I've been reading all the gossip about him on the web. I think he has another baby. Can you believe that?" I sighed. "I wonder how he can live with himself. I thought he really loved me, Roberto."

Roberto wrinkled his nose. "He only loves himself, Shayla, and whoever ends up with him will have a lifetime of hell. You don't need that. Don't worry yourself about that CK Moore or Diego either. Just say, 'If someone walks out of my life, someone better is coming into my life.' You have to believe that and try not to look back."

"Well, it still hurts like hell. And those affirmations you say, don't work for me."

"Oh, they work," Roberto said. "Your conscious mind just hasn't caught up with your words yet. But they work if you keep saying them. There is power in the spoken word. Eventually you'll start believing what you say. What you put out comes back to you."

"Hmmm," I hummed. "If you say so."

"Okay, enough about that. Let's get to the store and start working on this fashion show. It's going to be incredible," Roberto said with excitement in his voice. "Trust me. You won't have time to think about those men much. Turn your pain into gain."

"Hunh?"

"Don't worry about it. Let's go."

For two days I worked at Versace, making high commissions. During my breaks and when customers weren't in the store, Roberto and I planned for the fashion show. He gave me a "To Do List" that had 10 tasks I needed to get done by the end of the week, which meant I had to take my work home. It wasn't such a bad deal since Roberto had talked to the producer of the fashion show, convincing him to pay me $5,000 as the assistant fashion show coordinator. I had not made any money in a while. I had put the money I had kept from Calvin in my savings account and had given Sydney $300 for letting me stay at her home for the month. She said she didn't want anything, but I didn't want to live with her, even if it was temporary, without bringing something to the table.

By the second week of being back at Versace I was so busy that thoughts of Calvin didn't overload my mind like they had when I was at Sydney's 24/7. My feelings were still hurt about his rude departure, but I had become more angry than hurt, which kept me from crying or feeling that gut-wrenching feeling, like someone had taken a part of my heart out. I was also hurt about Diego, but I tried to put him to the back of my mind as well. In the midst of making a few fashion show related calls, I decided to call Claire at the hospital.

"Claire speaking," she answered in a surprisingly vibrant voice.

"Claire? This is Shayla. Shayla Lucas. How are you feeling?"

"As well as to be expected. How are you, Shayla?"

"Oh, I'm okay. I stopped by to visit you a few days after the accident. I am so sorry about what happened. But Mr. Jones is in a better place," I said. It was the only thing I could think to say.

"Yes, he is," Claire said. "I'll be leaving the hospital by the end of the week. I would love to see you sometime soon after that."

"I'd love to see you too," I said. "I did see Diego and his fiancée at the funeral."

"Oh yes, he told me," Claire said. "Thank you so much for attending."

I wondered what Diego had told his mom about seeing me. "So, did Diego leave to go back to London yet?"

"He did. But he'll be back over the next few weeks."

"Oh, I see," I said. "I'm sure he's probably busy with his wedding plans and all. It seems like everybody is getting married except me," I chuckled.

"I don't think he's getting married anytime soon, but you just be patient. You'll marry the God ordained man for you when it's time."

I really wanted to ask more, but Claire moaned a little, as if she were in pain. I didn't want to push her to talk more. "Well, I will call to check on you again next week if that's okay with you."

"That would be great. Thank you so much and you keep your head up."

"Thank you. Thank you so much," I said. After hanging up, I felt soothed a bit, but I wondered why she said Diego wouldn't be getting married anytime soon. I just didn't understand how he could fall in love so quickly and propose to someone after our date on New Year's Day, although almost four months had passed since then. *Something is really strange*

323

about that. But people had been moving on with their love lives at a rapid pace and I seemed to be the only one experiencing a block in mine. *I just need to concentrate on this fashion show, like Roberto said, before I get depressed again.*

After calling to set up appointments with the designer's assistants to meet or have conference calls with them the following week, I got a call that came in from a private number. I answered.

"Hello? This is Shayla," I said, trying to sound professional.

"Yeah, what's up?" a smooth voice came across sounding like Calvin.

There was a thud in my heart. "Who's calling?"

"Oh, so you forgot me already?"

"Who is this?" I gulped.

"The love of your life."

"No, you're not," I said. "God is the love of my life."

"Oh. So, you don't love me no more, Shay. Come on, babe. It's been over a month since we been apart. I'm ready to kiss and make up. I miss you."

"What about Toni?" I said. "That's your new woman, right?"

"Ahh, Shay. I know I hurt you by bringing her up to the mall, but you knew that wasn't gonna last. Nobody understands me like you do. Plus, she and Cristi got into a fight. I thought she was gonna pull all of Cristi's hair out."

The nerve of him. "Do you really think that I'm gonna sit here and listen to you talk about your various women, Calvin? You have a real serious problem. You need counseling," I said calmly.

"Yeah, that's what I was calling to tell you. I started my mandatory counseling a couple of weeks ago and I wanted to see if you would go with me to my next session."

I hung up on Calvin.

He called right back, but as tempted as I was, I could not bring myself to answer the phone. He did not leave a message. *Who does he think I am, Boo Boo the Fool? I'm supposed to forget everything he's done to me, just like that?* I felt contempt for him. I also felt love for him, but I wasn't about to fall for his games anymore. *And then he had the nerve to mention Cristi?* I wanted to vomit. Instead, I directed my mind back to the tasks at hand – the fashion show. I wanted to help Roberto bring flair and glamour to the fashion show of the season. I still needed to call a few more designers to see which outfits they would showcase. I also had to help Roberto choose models from an open call tomorrow. *I've definitely got my work cut out for me. Calvin, I don't have time for your games.*

I guess when you transfer your thoughts to something other than your problems and concerns, something happens inside you – making your emotions go with the dominant thought. *Roberto is depending on me. I have to move forward and not backward by allowing Calvin's call to distract me.* I didn't know what it was, but I felt that my prayers and affirmations were starting to work a tiny bit. *I'm not going to continue going down a dead end road with Calvin.* After doing as much work as I could, pertaining to the fashion show, I called Connie.

"Hey, Mommy."

"Shayla Renee Lucas. How are you, baby girl?" Connie said.

I laughed. "I'm good for a change, Mommy. Guess what?"

"What?"

"I'm the assistant fashion show coordinator for one of the biggest fashion shows in Atlanta."

"Really? When did this happen?"

"Just recently. The fashion show is the day before my birthday, so I want you to come up and support me."

"You know I will. You sound really good, Shay, baby. I'm glad you are doing better. I was worried about you for a while."

"I know. I was down and out. But you taught me to always get back up when I'm knocked down, remember?"

"Yes, that's right. I'm so glad you remembered that. That's what your grandmother taught me. You're as happy as you decide to be."

I moaned. "I'm not really happy, Mommy, but I can't die in my sorrow either."

"No, you cannot. Don't ever let another person break you. If you give your power to other people, you will always be broken. Just believe that better days are ahead, no matter what you go through."

"I believe that."

After hanging up with Connie I realized that I had, indeed, been happier over the past couple of weeks by attending church on Sundays and by reading the Bible and other positive books. My confidence level had shot up and I really felt like I could cope. Of course I continued to read the gossip on the Internet about Calvin and his multiple women. The gossip was plentiful, but I tried to pretend he was a stranger, someone I didn't really know – so the posts wouldn't affect me as much. I even saw his number appear on my cell phone a couple of times after he made the initial call about me going to counseling with him. I had resisted calling him back. I was trying my best to guard my heart. I realized I had enormous support from those in my close circle. If it had not been for Sydney and Connie, Tacara, and especially Roberto, I would not be as hopeful as I was. I also thought about Claire's influence. I wondered how she could still sound so positive in the midst of the pain of losing a husband of 35 years. I lay on the bed, thanking God for my family and friends and praying that God would indeed bring the right man into my life.

For the next couple of weeks, my life was busier than I had expected. I was able to talk with many of the designer's assistants and I helped choose the models for the show. Roberto had invitations for the fashion show printed and sent to the A-listers of Atlanta and the fashion industry. I was thrilled to see my name on it. The front of the invitation read, *Roberto Eduardo Silva presents "Sizzle into Summer – Meet the Elite" Friday, May 25th 8:30pm-11pm at Americasmart.*

Once I opened the invitation it read, *You're cordially invited to Atlanta's most explosive fashion extravaganza ever, featuring top designs by Versace, Kate Spade, Sean Jean, Tommy Hilfiger, Dolce & Gabbana, Giorgio Armani, Yves Saint Laurent, Tom Ford, among other top designs. Come walk*

*the red carpet from 7pm-8pm. Fashion show begins promptly
at 8:30pm. General Admission- $50.00, VIP Admission -
$100.00. Dress Code- Chic & Stylish.*

And at the very bottom of the invitation was my name
in bold letters - *Official After-Party & Birthday Celebration for
Fashion Show Coordinator SHAYLA LUCAS immediately
following.*

One week before the fashion show, I got a call from
Roberto.

"Shayla, I know you've been working hard and doing
so well, but I'm getting ready to put a wrench in your program
right now."

"Oh, no. What, Roberto?"

"Sean Jean chose CK to be the celebrity model for our
fashion show."

"You're lying, right?" I said.

"I wish I was. They called me and told me that he
represents what their line is all about. Ain't that something?
Shayla, I wanted to tell them no, but I couldn't."

"That's okay," I said calmly. "I'll be okay, Roberto.
Calvin doesn't scare me anymore. I can handle seeing him."

"Shayla, are you sure? I doubt he knows you're
coordinating this show, unless you told him?"

"No. I haven't talked to him since he called me out of
the blue a couple of weeks ago. Remember, I told you I hung
up on him? Maybe he heard about the fashion show on the
radio, but I haven't spoken to him again."

"That's so good, Shayla. I'm glad you're being so
strong."

"I just don't want to hurt anymore, Roberto. I can't see
myself with an emotionally abusive man anymore and Calvin
was that to me. I even sent him his stuff back."

"You sent him what stuff back?"

"I sent him his designer bags I had taken from his house
when I left, the Louis Vutton and the Gucci. I had them
delivered to his house last week."

"Now, you are better than me. I would have kept those
bags, girl."

"No, you wouldn't have."

"Uhh-huu-unh."

"Well, I sent them back because every time I looked in the closet and saw those bags they reminded me of him and the pain I went through being his girlfriend and fiancée. Now, I'm just trying to figure out what I'm going to do with the ring he gave me."

"Sell it, honey! I bet it's worth a pretty penny. You should go to a jeweler to see how much you can get for it," Roberto said excitedly. "Unless you want to keep it?"

"To tell you the truth, I thought about selling it and opening my own boutique down the line," I said. "But that is so wrong, isn't it? To sell an engagement ring a man you still love gave you. But I'm definitely not giving it back. Not after all the pain I went through."

"I don't think it's wrong at all. Hell, if somebody gave me a gift and I chose to sell it, that's my business. Shayla, you sound like you are really over him."

"Well, I'm not over him, but I am done with him," I said. "Church has helped me a lot. I've learned that I have to keep the faith and believe that God has a plan for me. And you have helped tremendously, by saying all the positive things you say to me. I'm actually starting to believe that I deserve good love from a man who is going to commit to me wholeheartedly. You have really been a good friend to me, Roberto."

"You do deserve good love and commitment, Shayla, and that's what friends are for - to help you through the tough times. If you have a friend that's not encouraging you and who judges you, get rid of them. Who needs that?"

"I hear ya," I said. "Well, let's give Calvin one of the worst outfits we can find in the Sean Jean collection they sent us."

"Sounds good to me." Roberto said.

Chapter Twenty-one

Spotlight Reversed

$\mathcal{A}$ s the sun peered through the blinds, I felt like the day was going to be a good one. May 25th had finally arrived. I woke up exuberant, but anxious. Roberto and I had spent more than 12 hours a day working tirelessly on the fashion show for the last two weeks. I was ready to walk the red carpet in my red, sassy dress by Versace. The dress had a plunging neckline and back, a high slit, and flowed all the way to the ground. My silver Jimmy Choo sandals had diamond studs around the ankle and my diamond bracelet and chandelier earrings accentuated my look – making me look more like a model going to an awards show than a background fashion coordinator. I didn't want to overdo it, but I felt like being overdressed would definitely be better than blending in with the crowd in a blasé dress. Plus, Roberto and I planned to walk the red carpet together, and he told me to prepare to be interviewed and photographed by several reporters and photographers. I guess a little of Calvin had rubbed off on me when it came to flaunting. *Oh well.*

I was glad Calvin had not shown for the non-mandatory rehearsal for celebrity models two nights prior, but I felt tense about seeing him at the show. I figured he already knew I was helping coordinate the fashion show. His publicist, *some Gayle,* who he had newly hired since our break up, had sent over his measurements so that we could have two outfits he'd be modeling ready for him. *He'll probably have Cristi or Toni on his arm.* Shivering a bit, I wondered if I was really ready for what Calvin might bring. Whatever Calvin did and whomever he was with, I was determined to be strong. My mom, Sydney and Aaron, Tacara and Steve, and even Claire Jones would be attending in my support. When I called Claire she told me that she would be able to attend if the venue was wheelchair accessible. It was. I made sure that she'd be up front. It would be her first outing since the tragic accident. She was still recuperating, but said that she had made a lot of progress with the help of a physical therapist and her children. I didn't ask her about Diego, but I really wanted to. *He has a fiancée. I might as well forget about him.* I wasn't about to let anything spoil my first huge fashion show as a coordinator and my 27th birthday.

Roberto seemed mighty calm when we met at Americasmart three hours before the show. We had to go over the particulars and then planned to get dressed in our designated dressing rooms prior to the red carpet greetings. I noticed the suit with Calvin's name on it and the casual outfit we had chosen for him from the Sean Jean collection. There was nothing boring about either of the outfits, but they didn't have the flash I was sure he was used to having. He was a bold, colorful dresser. The Sean Jean outfits we choose for him to model were low-key, with shades of black and grey. Since he was such a big draw, we decided to have the Sean Jean line and Calvin be the finale of the show. "It's a good business move," Roberto had told me.

After the models started arriving and getting their hair and makeup done, I talked with Roberto about the order of the show. Some local celebs, a DJ from the local radio station, models and a few assistants watched me go over all the particulars with Roberto. A couple of models interrupted with questions about their outfits. Roberto would be hosting with one of the local newscasters, Angela Jamison. We went over the script with her. By the time I needed to get dressed, I still had not seen Calvin, although many of the celebrity models had come in – already having been on the red carpet. I got dressed quickly, knowing that Roberto would need me to be ready to coordinate the show. The makeup artist we hired applied my makeup to perfection and helped me put spiral curls in my hair. Just after I got dressed, a model squealed, "There's CK Moore." I tried not to look around immediately, but I casually turned my head to see him greeting a couple of the models.

"Shayla is going to give you your outfits, but we have a seat for you to watch the show until two scenes before you go on," one of the hostesses told him. "Or you can just stay backstage."

"Dayum," Calvin said when he approached me. "You look good as hell."

"Thanks," I said. I felt such love for him, but I did not like him.

"Give me a hug, girl. Don't act like you don't know me," he said, reaching out for me. When we embraced I felt a weak strength. "I love you, Shay," he whispered in my ear. "I'm sorry it didn't work out for us." I pulled away.

"Shayla, you ready to go to the red carpet?" Roberto interrupted, gently guiding me by my arm. "Glen is going to show CK his outfits and brief him about his turn and what he's to do. We need to get out there on the red carpet, so we can get back and be ready to start the show on time."

"So, man . . . you just gonna interrupt us?" Calvin said.

"Look, CK Moore, the only reason you're in this fashion show is because Sean Jean insisted that you be in it. Now listen, Shayla and I put this show together and we can have someone escort you out of the building if you get out of hand. This is not about you. It's about Shayla and me. It's about the fashions. You understand?"

Calvin laughed. "Man, that's not a warm welcome for a superstar. If you put me out, you're gonna ruin the entire fashion show."

"Let's go, Shayla." Roberto led me out so fast that I couldn't respond. He kept his grip around my arm tightly as we walked around the back, down the stairs and then back up the escalator. "Shayla, please just keep it moving. Keep it moving."

"Roberto, I am fine. You are the one freaking out. And you're gonna step on my dress," I said.

Once we got to the red carpet, cameras flashed and reporters held their microphones out to us.

"Roberto, how does it feel to host such a big fashion show with all the top designers?" one reporter asked.

"It feels wonderful. If it hadn't been for this young lady though, Shayla Lucas, I don't know if I could have pulled it off."

"So, we've seen a lot of celebrity guests and dignitaries come through on the red carpet, including football star, Calvin Moore. Aren't you engaged to Mr. Moore?"

When I looked up, I realized it was the same lady at the press conference who asked about racketeering, back in February.

"No, we're actually broken up," I admitted.

"So, how difficult is it for you to coordinate a fashion show with your ex fiancé modeling in it?"

"Not hard at all. I just saw him inside. Did you get to interview him?"

"No," she giggled. "He refused to give me an interview."

"And why is that? I can't see him turning down an interview," I said.

"Well, maybe it was because we had some romantic dealings," she said, moving closer to me. "Be glad you're done with him. I know a woman in Miami who just gave birth to his third child."

I was startled, but in a way I wanted to know more. "I'm sorry, but what's your name again?"

"Gloria," she said. "Here. Here's my card," she handed me a card that had her picture on it. "Call me and I can give you the scoop. I'm an investigative reporter as well as a stringer for the New York Post. I can tell you some things that would blow your mind. You are lucky you got out of that relationship."

I stepped back and looked her over. "Well, I've gotta go," I said. "Thank you."

Roberto was busy with another interview, so I walked down the red carpet not far from where he was, continuing to answer questions about the fashion show, but thinking about Calvin and this reporter. *So, she had romantic dealings with Calvin? Probably while we were dating, I'm sure.* But I wasn't sure if I would call her or not.

There was an uproar of applause when Roberto finally walked out with Angela to start the fashion show. I tried to keep my composure as Calvin stared at me while I gave the models their cues to go on stage. He seemed like he was in deep thought. Finally, when it came time for him to model, I had to notify him.

"Okay, Calvin, it's your turn," I said. "You're on."

To my surprise, Calvin grabbed my face and pressed his lips to mine. "Will you stop, please," I said, pushing him away.

Calvin released me and took a few steps back, staring at me with steady eyes. "You have to get out there," I said. "Go!" Calvin backed up a few more feet, giving me a reproachful look and then he turned around and headed to the runway. I watched from behind as the room full of people, 70 percent women, screamed as he walked down the runway. "Atlanta Falcons Calvin Moore is wearing a Sean John suit. And he is wearing it well, isn't he ladies?" The screams grew louder as Angela described Calvin's outfit. I wanted so badly to peep around the corner to see more, but I had to prepare my next model.

When Calvin returned backstage, he was laughing. I tried not to pay him much attention. "They loved CK Moore," he said, walking over to me. "The more they see me, the more they what, babe?"

I started to tell him the rest of his line, but instead I turned my back to him. "I've got to work, Calvin," I mumbled. At the finale of the show, Calvin sported a more casual, trendy outfit. The music volume grew louder as he strutted across the stage to thunderous applauds and squeals.

"Ladies and Gentleman I'd like to bring out the one other person responsible for making this show a success. She put in long hours and is really the key to this fashion show being a hit …. and that's Ms. Shayla Lucas. Shayla, come out here and strut on the runway," I heard Roberto exclaim.

I walked from behind the curtains beaming, as cameras flashed. I strutted to the end of the runway, seeing Claire Jones on the front row and some other familiar faces, Steve and Tacara and even Deidra, my former boss. I walked to the end of the runway as the applause grew louder when I purposely froze in a sexy pose and did my turn. I had practiced the turn several times in the mirror, so I knew I looked just like a professional model.

When I returned backstage, Calvin walked up to me. "You're going home with me, tonight, right, birthday girl?"

"So, you remembered, hunh?" I sighed. "But no. My family is here. Where is Cristi? You mean she's not here to support you?"

"Naw. She's not here. I put her out anyway – a few nights ago," he said. "She was too much drama. So, you're gonna move back in with me, right? That's what you told me."

"No," I answered. At that time Connie, Sydney and Aaron appeared backstage. They all hugged me with excitement. Calvin just stood there with no expression. None of my family spoke to him nor did he speak to them.

"Shayla, that was the best fashion show I've been to," Connie said. "I'm so proud of you."

"Go head, Ms. Shayla. Your walk and that pose at the end of the runway was awesome. You going places, girl," Aaron said.

"You worked it, girl. You brought the house down with this dress," Sydney said, leaning in to hug me. "Mrs. Jones wants to see you out there. I told her I'd come get you."

After talking with my family for a while, I headed out in the audience to greet Claire. She was wearing a turquoise dress and looked elegant, even sitting in a wheel chair. Her smile brightened when she saw me.

"There's the star," she said. "How are you?"

"What a delight to see you, Claire" I said. "I'm so glad you made it." I leaned down and hugged Claire.

"Before I forget, Diego told me to tell you hi," she said, smiling.

"Really? How is he?"

"He's fine. He hasn't made it back here yet, but he plans to come visit again soon."

"Well, tell him that I said hello." I said, not knowing what to say. I thought about the last time I saw Diego . . . and his fiancée. I really didn't want to ruin my night by thinking back on that. Claire introduced me to her sister, Carolyn, who looked a lot like her.

Not soon after the fashion show ended the DJ got the music cranking and my birthday celebration began on the main floor. To my surprise, Roberto rolled out a sheet birthday cake with two muscular male models by his side. The design on the cake was a picture of me walking on a red carpet with cameras surrounding me. Everybody began singing Happy Birthday to me. I glanced behind and saw Calvin signing a few autographs, but he was glaring at me in between autographs. He wasn't singing. He looked tense and worried. *He must be in shock about the attention I'm getting.* To my surprise, Deidra, my former boss, approached me after the birthday song and the applause.

"Shayla, congratulations," she said. "And Happy Birthday."

"Oh, my goodness, Deidra," I said. "You look great."

"And you look stunning," she said. "I'm so happy for you. I only want the best for you, Shayla." Deidre said, reaching out to hug me.

"I know you do," I said softly, returning her hug. "Thanks for your support. I really appreciate it."

The music was pumping so loud now that I could barely hear. The room grew more crowded as more and more people came up to me to congratulate me, to say Happy Birthday or just to chit-chat. Several strangers pulled out their business cards, telling me that they'd like to contact me about coordinating more fashion shows or modeling. Suddenly I felt a strong hand on my shoulder.

"Come here, Shay, let's dance," Calvin said, although there were several people still standing around me. "Come on," he guided me forward a few feet with his hand. "She'll be right back," he told the onlookers.

I walked a few feet with Calvin, then I stopped as I realized that I was allowing him to take control of me, like he had done in the past. I met his eyes. "I don't want to dance with you, CK."

"CK?" he said, frowning." Why you calling me CK? What's wrong with you?"

"That's what everybody else calls you."

"But you not everybody else. You my fiancée. Why aren't you wearing the ring, anyway? It would have set this dress off."

"I am not your fiancée, CK. Sorry it didn't work out for us."

"Why are you talking like that?" he frowned.

A couple of models came up to me while I was talking with Calvin. I had a feeling he might feel dissed and leave once I started chatting with them, and he did just that. "I'll talk to you later," he grunted and left abruptly.

The rest of the night, I enjoyed myself by dancing until my feet hurt. I even exchanged numbers with one of the male models, but I knew I wouldn't be going out with him, since he looked all of 18. When I got home, I fell on the bed, exhausted. But I was pleased that my fashion show had been more of a success than I thought it would be. I fell off to sleep, not worried about Calvin, but happy that I had experienced one of the best days of my life.

The next morning I got up and dressed hurriedly. I had told Tacara that I would meet her at her home for a girlfriends day out for my birthday at 11 am. It was 10:15. We planned to get together a couple of times throughout the month, but had not, so this was the opportune time to go see the additions Tacara had made to Steve's home since they had married and to celebrate my 27th. When I got to their home, which was a beautiful four-story home in the Sugar Loaf subdivision, Steve greeted me at the door.

"What's up, superstar?" he said. "That fashion show was off the chain. Sorry we had to run off after the show, but we really enjoyed it!"

"Thanks, Steve," I said.

"Tacara is still getting ready. But just make yourself comfortable." Steve led me into their spacious family room. "By the way, I'm so glad you broke up with that knuckle head, CK Moore, that I don't know what to do. All he was gonna do was bring you down."

"Well, it's not like I broke up with him really. He broke up with me after I moved out," I admitted. "I'm trying to move on with my life though." I looked down, feeling a lapse in my spirits as thoughts of my final night at Calvin's home flooded back to me. *Now why did Steve have to bring him up?*

"Don't worry. You'll be blessed with the right man for you soon," Steve said, slouching against the barstool.

"Well, no more athletes, and that's for sure," I said.

"Aww, there's nothing wrong with having an athlete," Steve said, rubbing his jaw. "Look at Tacara and me. I know there are a lot of ball players out there who cheat on their women – NFL, NBA, baseball players, hockey or whatever sport. We can be some selfish rascals," he continued. "Everything is given to us on a silver platter early in life. But there are some selfish and cheating-ass garbage men and blue-collar guys out there too. And some selfish doctors and lawyers who cheat for sure, and even some cheating preachers and deacons – you best believe. It's not being a ball player that makes the man cheat, it's the man's mentality and how he chooses to use or misuse his power. And yeah, there are more temptations out there if you're a high profile athlete, I'm not gonna lie, but don't think just because you met one cheating athlete that all athletes are the same. We're not. It's all about the inner man."

"I guess that's true," I said somberly while managing a small smile. I really didn't want to talk about men at all since I didn't have one. "I'm just trying to discover who I am right now though . . . and stay away from the Calvin Moore types."

"But I told you CK is all about CK," Steve reminded me. "I don't think he'll ever change."

"Maybe not," I sighed, annoyed by his words.

When Tacara came downstairs we headed straight to get a bite and then to shop. It was a good birthday, although I didn't spend it with a man.

The next day, I wanted to enjoy some me time, but when I woke up, after turning my phone volume up, I discovered that I had five missed calls. One call on my caller ID said Atlanta Police. It had just been placed, less than five minutes ago. I called quickly.

"Hi, did someone call here?"

"Yes. Is this Shayla Lucas?"

"Yes, it is," I stammered.

"Well, Calvin Moore gave us your number. He's been shot. He's on his way to Grady Memorial Hospital."

"Shot? What do you mean? Is he okay?"

"He was shot several times in the leg. He was still quite coherent. He was trying to drive himself to the hospital, but had to stop before making it because he was losing a lot of blood. He gave us your number to come pick up his car, but we're having it towed now."

I didn't care about Calvin's car. All I was concerned about was him. I hung up the phone and put on pair of jeans and tee-shirt and rushed to the hospital. I was hyperventilating as I drove past the speed limit. When I got to the hospital, Cristi and Calvin Jr., Toni, along with Norma Jean and Calvin's agent sat quietly in the waiting room.

"What happened?" I asked.

Cristi rose to her feet. "She shot him!"

"Who shot him?"

"Ro-shon-da," she said, pacing the small room.

"Who?"

"They got into some kind of argument after he went over to her apartment and she took a gun and shot him three times in the leg. Can you believe that? She shot my man."

"Who is Roshanda?" I looked around the room, seeing tears in Norma Jean's eyes. Tommy was comforting her. Toni's eyes met mine with a curious stare. She smiled hesitantly.

"She's his new girlfriend. Oh, he didn't tell you about her?" Cristi continued. "He moved me out for that skank. I told him she wasn't worth it. I told his ass. She's like 19 and doesn't even have a job. Talking about she was gonna win America's Top Model. Now her ass is gonna be America's Most Wanted."

I remained at the hospital while Calvin was in surgery. Instead of communicating with Cristi, I wanted to get all the details I could from Norma Jean. But Norma Jean was too distraught to talk. She held Calvin Jr. like he was her son. After about an hour of waiting around, the doctor walked into the room with a look of exhaustion. Everyone waiting scrambled to their feet. As his brows rose, I got a sinking feeling that his report wasn't going to be good. The doctor cleared his throat before speaking. "We were able to get the bullets out of his leg, but unfortunately it might have to be amputated if the infection doesn't clear up," he said sullenly.

"Nooooo," Norma Jean cried out while holding Calvin Jr. closer to her. "No, please save my son's leg. Nooo." The baby cried as he looked at Norma Jean.

"Oh, no," I trembled as Cristi grasped my arm, also sobbing. As much as I wanted to push her away, I couldn't. Toni remained silent, but her eyes filled with tears quickly.

"Stay calm. We'll have to see how things go. He lost a lot of blood and the bullets crushed his bone," the doctor explained. "We are going to try our best to save this young man's leg, but it is really bad."

The room, still filled with sobs and tears, felt cold and dark. I wanted to ask so many questions, but I couldn't get myself to speak. If Calvin lost his leg I knew he'd never be able to play ball again. *He'll never be able to do a lot of things again. And who is Roshonda?* In the midst of my pain, I decided to leave the room and call Gloria, the news reporter on the red carpet who supposedly knew the scoop on him.

"Hi, this is Shayla Lucas. Calvin Moore's ex fiancée. How are you?"

"Shayla, I am so sorry to hear about CK. It's all over the news. Is he okay?"

"We don't know if he'll be okay or not. His leg is pretty bad and he might lose it," I said hesitantly.

"Oh, God, no," she said. "I am sooo sorry."

"Do you know the young lady who shot him?" I asked. "Since you're a reporter, I thought you might know her."

"No, I actually don't know her, Shayla. I did hear that she is somebody that he just met recently. I don't know what happened. The details are sketchy, but I heard he went to pick her up at her apartment and they got into an argument about another woman or something and she threatened to kill him and when he went to run, she shot him. Is CK not talking yet?"

At that point, I felt like I was giving too much information to her. I didn't know why I had called her.

"Listen, I had a short-term fling with CK that lasted about two months. I didn't fall in love with him or anything, like the rest of his women, but I tried to help him and lead him in the right direction. I really did. But he would not listen and tried to get me fired from my job. A very trusted friend of mine told me that he was operating an illegal gambling business with some criminals and I did my research and found it to be true. He was betting on NFL teams with bookies and having people place bets for him. When I called him out at the press conference, I did it because I wanted him to think about what he was doing. I might have sex with a man, but if you're doing some illegal stuff, I'm not going to hide or ignore it. My father is with the FBI. CK needed to get out of that situation. And he did."

I was a little shocked, but not really. Calvin always said that he had other means to make money besides the money from football and endorsements. I never figured he'd allow himself to get involved in illegal gambling though.

"So, when did you have your fling with him?"

"I knew you were going to ask me that," she sighed. "CK and I had some dealings last year – right after the Super Bowl . . . after I interviewed him. We were only together about four or five times and I always made him use protection. He did say that he had a girlfriend though . . . and he mentioned you. But I knew there were many others. I already knew about Cristi and the girl who recently had his child in Miami."

"Now, who is she?" I asked. My stomach felt like it was turning upside down.

"I don't know her personally, but she filed a junction to have him do a DNA test, and the baby girl is his for sure. I think he worked something out with her, financially. Shayla, I'm so sorry to be telling you all this, but you need to know. There have been other women claiming to be pregnant by him too. There's also a woman in Dallas who had his child."

As strong as I had been, I began to cry. Although I knew Calvin had not been the most faithful boyfriend, I didn't suspect that he had so much more drama than met the eye. It made me feel sad. I couldn't hate Calvin though. He had brought a high into my life at times, something I had obviously been missing in my own life. I had forfeited my life for the excitement of his life, but just as things were starting to change for me, he was losing the thing that had drawn the excitement, his football career. I certainly didn't want that for him and I didn't know how he would handle that.

When I went back into the intensive care waiting room, Norma Jean was still crying and holding Calvin Jr. Cristi was talking to his aunt Natasha and Tommy and several players had come into the waiting room. Greg, a linebacker, asked everyone to come together and join hands as he prayed. He asked God to heal Calvin and to make him whole. After we sat around for about four hours, the doctor came into the room.

"We were able to save his leg," he said.

There was a sigh of relief in the room. I started crying again.

"But he's going to have to get a metal plate. It's going to take months for rehab and he won't be able to use that leg again in the way that he used to."

"So, what about his football career?" one of his teammates asked.

"Unfortunately, playing football won't be in his future. The leg was shattered, so we'll have to put titanium plating and metal screws in it and do some other things so that he can even walk again."

Everybody cried. *Just like that?* Calvin wouldn't be playing football anymore. I didn't know how he'd be able to handle that. *All this over a 19-year old he just met?* The doctor told us that Calvin was still sedated and that he did not suggest that we all stay to see him. I ended up leaving and deciding to come back the next day.

When I got to Sydney's I cried. My heart hurt for Calvin, but it also hurt because of all the things Gloria had told me.

The next day, I went to the hospital and one more girl was there, a pretty, petite girl holding a baby girl. She said the child was Calvin's. When I went into the room, there were people standing around him. I grabbed Calvin's hand.

"Shayla," he said.

"You don't have to try to talk," I said. "I'm sorry this happened."

I knew that all eyes were on me, but I continued to hold Calvin's hand. I sat in his room for a while longer and decided to leave.

Tears flowed again when I got home, but Tommy told me that Calvin's legs were insured. He also told me that the girl who shot Calvin had only known him a few months and that she was jealous and that he had warned Calvin about her.

When I got home, the phone rang. Versace wanted me to participate in the Paris Fashion Week. Wow. How could I think about going to Paris at a time like this? No, I wasn't Calvin's fiancée anymore, but I wanted to see his progress. And then I thought about all the girls who were already gathering in Calvin's room. How could I not think about going to Paris? I told the coordinator that I would be able to attend.

For two weeks, I called to check on Calvin, but the doctors said that he was having some emotional problems, so I decided that I would go back to the hospital to see exactly what was going on. Calvin looked at me strangely when I walked inside the room. He was chained to the bed. His mother was there and so was Cristi.

"Hey," he said with a frown.

"Hey, Calvin."

"Are you the cheerleader I ran into on the field? You're trying to sue me, aren't you?" he said snidely.

"Calvin, it's me, Shayla. No, I'm not trying to sue you."

"Oh, Shayla. That's right," he said, snapping his finger. "I remember you. Did you see my touchdown? I did that shit, didn't I?"

"Yeah, you were real good. You've always been good though, Smooth C."

"The mooore they see me, the mooore they want me," Calvin boasted. "I ran three kick returns for TDs and they act like they don't know who the best receiver in the NFL is. Are you kidding me?" he said. "But you got to throw the ball to me all the time and stop trying to run the ball though, man. I'm the runner. You gonna get hurt out there trying to run. Know what I'm saying?"

"Yeah, I know what you're saying, because you're the best wide receiver that ever was."

"You damn skippy," he said softly. "The best they ever had." Calvin slid back and closed his eyes.

I looked down, not wanting to burst into tears. Calvin didn't know who I was. Norma Jean had already warned me that his meds were causing him to hallucinate, but I didn't know if his delusions were because of the meds or if he was really losing it. It seemed like he had had a nervous breakdown. After the doctors told him that he almost lost his leg and wouldn't be able to play ball again Norma Jean said he cursed the doctor out and even tried to get out of the bed. From that point on, they said that Calvin had not been the same.

Chapter Twenty-Two

Paris Amour

W ithin five months I had been promoted to be the liaison between the New York managers, helping to get the new line of clothes in and ready for showcase. I was once again, a buyer, but this time, for Versace. I was also planning my trip to Paris for Paris Fashion Week.

Calvin was slowly going through rehabilitation, but his football career was kaput. The young lady who had shot him was found guilty of attempted murder and was sentenced to 25 years in prison. I called to check on Calvin periodically, but after still having to deal with his various women, including more of Cristi and now the mother of his new daughter, Briana, I decided to leave Calvin to deal with his own issues. I still loved him immensely, but I knew, even with him being half crippled, that women would always flock to him because he still had money – *for now*. I had learned that some of his finances were mishandled during his career, but the decision to insure his legs was one of the best ones he had made, although some thought he was being quite dubious at the time, after his Super Bowl win. "But if Troy Polamalu can insure his hair I damn sure can insure my legs," Calvin had said.

The time that I woke up and smelled the coffee – again – was when I went to visit him and there were two other girls also there, fussing over Calvin – not even Cristi. He laughed as they argued. He slowly came out of his delusions and hallucinations, but every so often he'd say something that would surprise us all, relating to football. He called me once asking me if I were going to wait on him after his game. I was stunned.

"No, Calvin. You don't have a game. What do you mean?"

"Oh, so it's like that, hunh? You don't want me now that I'm not playing ball anymore? Is that it?" he said. "You're just like the rest of them, Shay."

"What are you saying, Calvin? I love you whether you play ball or not. You know that."

"Oh, so you do still love me, don't you? I knew it. Why don't you just move back in, Shayla? I need you here."

Right after Calvin said that, I heard his baby boy cry . . . *or maybe it was his baby girl.* Whomever it was, it dawned on me quickly that he would still play with my emotions and that he wasn't about to commit to only me.

"I'm working on myself now," I said. "I'm not going to live with any man again before marriage. I'm sure your many women will take care of you."

"But they aren't doing me like you would do me, Shay," he said. "And you got to remember, I'm not just any man, so whenever you want to come back home, I'll move everybody out for you."

I thought briefly about what Calvin had just said. *He'll move everybody out for me?* Obviously somebody had to be living with him again for him to move them out.

"That's okay. Calvin. You don't have to do that for me," I said. "And I hope you get your life together. I'm praying for you."

"Oh, yeah?" he said.

"Yes. But I've got to go now. You'll be fine with all the love and support you've got in your life. I'll check on you another time, okay?"

"Okay, bae. Love you."

"Love you too," I said.

I was telling Calvin the truth when I told him that I loved him, but I also realized that loving him with all my heart, like I had done in the past, would be detrimental to my own inner spirit. I realized Calvin was incapable of loving anyone fully, although he used the love word quite flippantly. The shooting had caused him to re-examine some things in his life and slow down, which was an understatement, but even after he hit rock bottom, he was still Calvin CK Moore – a man who drew people to him with his charm and drama. It was his nature. His mom had also revealed to me that he had also been diagnosed with bi-polar disorder. *Why doesn't that surprise me?*

While I knew Calvin had his issues, I decided to go to counseling to help get a better grip on my own life and emotions. I was figuring out that I was the key to my destiny and I was learning slowly, but surely to build a life of happiness for myself. I had even rekindled a friendship with a high school friend who was also in the fashion industry, Jasmine Watkins. Jasmine had come to Atlanta from New York, and we hung out, had lunch and talked about everything from men to fashion. She was also meeting me in Paris. I couldn't wait to get there. I had heard so much about Paris Fashion Week.

I couldn't believe I had done so much in my career in such a short time. I had also gone out on one date with a new man, who was totally laid back and quiet, but I felt no chemistry and he seemed reticent, so I decided not to waste my time anymore after the first date. I had definitely felt affection deprived over the past 8 months, but I figured I'd be celibate instead of just getting my needs met by someone I didn't love and who didn't love me.

Just as I got on the train to concourse E at the Hartsfield-Jackson Atlanta International Airport, I felt someone looking at me. I looked up slowly and saw the face of Diego staring at me. For a minute, I felt like I was dreaming.

"Diego!" I said as my heart throbbed. Diego's mouth flew open, like he couldn't believe his eyes. "Oh, my goodness, what a surprise," I said, walking towards him.

Diego was still speechless. I looked around to see if his fiancée was by him. She wasn't. A warm smile creased his face.

Impulsively I ran into Diego's arms and we embraced. My roller board luggage fell to the floor, but I didn't care. I buried my face in his chest and reveled in the warmness of his strong arms. Diego did not draw back. He clutched me tightly and surprised me when he kissed me on the forehead. I felt warm and tender. When I finally looked up into Diego's eyes I noticed the way his eyes searched mine, seeming confused about the way I had just run into his arms. A quiver ran through me as he bent down to pick up my bag by the handle.

"It so good to see you," he said. "Please tell me you're going to be on my flight to London."

My heartbeat picked up. I was surprised by his words. His gaze was penetrating, as though he felt deep emotions, just like I was feeling.

"Unfortunately, I'm not," I said. "I'm going to Paris. It's actually my first trip overseas."

"Really?" he said. "And what is taking you there? Business or pleasure?"

"I'm going for Paris Fashion Week. I'm a buyer for Versace and I'm meeting some other buyers over there and a good friend from high school." I said. "So, you're headed back to London?"

"Yes, I am," he said with an enticing smile.

"I've never been to London. I hear they have a wonderful fashion week in February, so I was actually thinking about going there next year," I added.

"Well, you definitely should come to London," he said. "I won't move back to Atlanta until March, so that would be great if you could come visit before I move back. I can show you around and we can have some fun."

Wait. Doesn't this man have a fiancée? But I didn't want to ask him about her just yet. "Your mom came to my fashion show in May. I talked to her again a few weeks ago. How has she been?"

"She's really good," he said. "She told me that she attended your event. I asked her about you just a few weeks ago."

"Oh, really?" I said. "So, you're planning to move back to Atlanta?"

"Yes, indeed," he said. "I can't wait. I love London, but I'm ready to be home. I'm going to take over my dad's business with my brother Damian."

"Oh, that's great, Diego" I said.

"So, what time does your flight leave?" he asked. "Do you have time for a quick bite?"

I looked at my watch. "I still have an hour before I take off," I said. "I guess they'll start boarding soon though. But we can at least get some tea or something quick."

"Let's do that. Let's sit down somewhere and talk before our flights leave," he said. "I really can't believe I ran into you. I was thinking about calling you. I was definitely going to call you when I moved back to Atlanta."

"Really?" I said. "Was there anything in particular on your mind? I know that you and Gabriella are planning to marry, right? I think that's her name, right?"

"Yes, that's her name, but no, we're no longer together," he chuckled. "It was very short-lived. I'm sorry I couldn't talk to you more about her after my dad's memorial."

My heart leaped. *So, he's no longer engaged? Oh my God. Yes!* "Oh, we both obviously had a lot going on in our lives at the time," I said. "But I can't say I'm sorry that you two aren't getting married."

Diego smiled. "Everything happens for a reason."
When the train stopped at concourse E, Diego's phone rang. He looked down at it and smiled. "Guess who it is?" he said looking at me. I didn't say anything. "It's my mother."

"Hi, mom, what's up?" Diego answered. "Yes, I'm here. You're never going to believe who is standing right here beside me?" he said with excitement. "No, try again," he said. "Yes, you guessed it," he then hesitated. "No, she's going to Paris for Paris Fashion Week." . . . "Yep, that's what you told me. You want to speak to her? Hold on." Diego handed the phone to me. "It's my mom. She wants to say hi."

I got excited just thinking about Claire being on the other line. "Claire. How are you?"

"Ms. Shayla," Claire was laughing. "I can't believe you ran into my boy at the airport. How have·you been?"

"I've been well. You crossed my mind a couple of days ago and here I am, running into Diego out of the blue," I said. "What a coincidence."

"Well, nothing really happens by coincident," she said. "But I'm so glad you're traveling to Paris and I'm going to be looking for a postcard from you."

"I tell you what," I said. "I'll do more than a postcard. I'm going to come by and see you after I return and bring you back something special. How is that?"

"Okay, I'm going to hold you to that."

"Well, I'm going to let you speak back to Diego, okay?"

"You have a blessed flight and have fun, Shayla."

"Thank you."

When Diego took the phone back he told his mom that he loved her and that he'd be calling her tomorrow. He chuckled about something and said "I know Mom. I know. Love you too."

Diego and I decided to go to TGI Friday's. The hostess took us right to a booth, but instead of sitting opposite me, Diego sat on the same booth I was sitting at – moving quite close to me.

"I'm not invading your space am I?" he asked.

"Not at all," I said. "So, now tell me, what happened with you and Gabriella. Is she in London?" I figured I may as well get right to what I wanted to know. I needed to know his relationship status before allowing my excitement to reignite about him.

"Gabriella lives in New York," he said flatly. "We dated a few years back," he took a sip of the water the waitress had brought him. "She came to visit me during a tough time in her life and she was with me when I got the news that my dad had died. She took some time off and we flew back to Atlanta together. She was really helpful in my healing, although it still hurts to think about my dad. I still can't believe he's gone."

"I know," I said soothingly.

"But Gabriella and I realized about a month after my dad's death that our relationship wasn't going to work and we decided not to get married. She was dating a man in New York and they had taken a break from each other. When she came to London we thought that getting married would be the solution to the pain we were both experiencing. She thought she was still in love with me and I actually wanted to still be in love with her, after some disappointments. But it just didn't work out," he sat back in the booth. "I appreciated her for being there for me during a time of sorrow in my life, but we're not each other's soulmates. We both realized that after trying to have some kind of long distance relationship after she got back to New York and I went back to London," Diego stopped and looked into my eyes. "I had been wanting to call you, but I knew that you had been through a lot recently too. I thought about you everyday." Diego leaned closer to me, as though he was going to whisper in my ear. "Shayla, you are so beautiful," he said in a steady voice as he edged closer to me. He grabbed my hand under the table. "This is really strange for me, but my mom told me that I would run into you again soon. I didn't want to believe her."

My heart raced uncontrollably as Diego looked into my eyes. His eyes glistened. He seemed enchanted by me. The waitress interrupted our moment by asking if we were going to order anything from the menu.

"No, is it okay if we just sit here for a while? Both of our flights leave real soon," Diego said.

"Sure, that's fine," she said.

"So, you never thought you'd run into me again?" I said, thinking about Claire's prophesying nature and wondering what else she had told him about me.

"No, I did not," Diego said. "I mean, I wanted to see you again and when I saw you at the funeral and you told me that you were no longer with the football player, I was wondering what I had done by agreeing to marry Gabby. I felt horrible. I wanted to call you so badly."

"Oh, that's okay," I said. "I was a little shocked, but I handled it. That was a hard month for me – full of twists and turns."

"I am so sorry," he said.

"Why are you sorry?" I asked. "Remember, I was going to get married earlier in the year. I felt bad for telling you that. And as you know, that never transpired. It's completely over between Calvin and me."

"Oh, yeah? I heard about him being shot. Is he okay?"

"Other than him adjusting to never being able to play ball again and having slight hallucinations from time to time, he's okay. We're friends, but I have moved on with my life. I'm actually happier."

"You look happy," he said. "When I saw you for the first time, I was really drawn to you. I asked my mother for your number," Diego stopped to sip his water. "She told me that you were involved with CK Moore and that she had met the two of you in Puerto Rico or something like that."

"Yep," I said softly, not knowing if I should add more.

"Even though I'm not one to try to come between two people, I pressed her to give me your number, telling her I only wanted to say Happy New Year to you and she eventually gave it to me. She told me to be careful though." Diego stopped and looked at me. "I know you're heading to Paris, but if we don't make the most of this meeting, something is wrong with both of us. I want to stay in touch," he said. "I want to do more than stay in touch. I want to get to know you so much better."

I smiled. I wanted to be a part of Diego's life, point black. "That sounds good."

"Whoever ends up with you will be a blessed man," Diego said. "He will have a rare diamond."

"Is that right?"

"Yes, you're a precious diamond."

I was definitely enjoying this special moment with Diego Jones. I felt like he accepted me and understood me in some strange way and I was comfortable being near him. Although I wanted to stay and talk with Diego more, I glanced at my watch, knowing that I needed to get to my gate.

"I better let you get to your gate, before you miss your flight," Diego said.

"Well, that wouldn't be a bad thing if I could come to London," I said boldly. "But I guess I better go board."

Diego smiled, like he liked what I had said. He slowly moved out of the booth and took my hand. After he paid the waitress for our drinks, we walked to my gate, hand in hand.

Before I boarded, Diego kissed me on the forehead and hugged me again.

Once I got on the plane, my heart continued to pound. I couldn't believe that I had actually just seen Diego and that we had connected again. I wished that he were going to Paris with me. *Maybe I should have asked him how long it takes to get from London to Paris? It couldn't be that far.* Just as I was getting settled in my seat and the flight attendant came on the PA, I got a text. I looked down and saw that it was from Diego. It read, "You are so beautiful. You made my day. I can't wait to see you again." I almost melted in my first class seat. I texted him back: "I can't wait 2 see you again too. I was just thinking … is London far from Paris? Wish you could come visit me while I'm there." I waited a few seconds and then got a response back. "I will def look into it! Will call you when I land." I text him back, "That would make my week! Have a safe flight, Diego." He text me back, "You too, sweetheart."

I turned my phone off, but the thrill of excitement kept me from sleeping until the latter part of the nine and a half hour flight. The first half of the flight I utilized the Wifi access and emailed Roberto from my computer. We went back and forth via email as I told him about running into Diego. I also emailed Tacara and shared the surprise of running into Diego with her. I was looking forward to seeing my best friend from high school, but if Diego did make it to Paris, I knew that my time rekindling my friendship with her would be cut short. *I hope Diego comes. Oh, God, I hope he comes.*

By the time the landing gear hit the runway hard, I realized I had fallen into a deep sleep, yet it now was time for me to get up. I gathered my things and turned on my cell phone. I had gotten another text – from Diego. "I would love to come c u in Paris. Call u when I land." My heart leaped at the thought of seeing him again.

When I arrived at the Four Seasons Hotel in Paris, Jasmine had already checked in the room. I enjoyed seeing the sites on the way to the hotel, but definitely had a case of jet lag. I was anxious to hear from Diego once he landed. I wanted to call my mom and tell her what happened, but I realized my international plan for phone calls was quite expensive . . . plus, my mom didn't even know who Diego was. *So, I'll just have to tell her all about him when I return.* Jasmine and I caught up for about an hour and got a bite to eat. When we returned to the room, Diego called.

"Hello?"

"Shayla?"

"Hi, Diego. How was your flight?"

"It was a little bumpy and long, but I thought of you the entire time, so that made it better."

"I thought about you on my flight too. I fell off to sleep for about an hour, right before we landed," I said. "So, do you have to work today?"

"I actually do," he said. "But I was thinking I could take the train to come see you in Paris on Saturday. I know you're there for business and I don't want to interfere, but it would really be nice to see you again, especially since you're this close."

"How long does it take to get here by train?"

"About two hours," he said. "Or better yet, let me look into some flights. It's less than an hour to get to Paris by plane. That might work better for me."

"Whatever way you get here it would be great to see you," I said. "I'm going to find out the fashion show schedules later this evening and we can plan from there. I know you're probably not into fashion, but you might have to attend a fashion show or two with me Saturday evening."

"What do you mean, I'm not into fashion?" he laughed. "So, I don't have that fashionisto style to you?"

"You do," I giggled. "But I wasn't' sure if watching a fashion show would be something that would excite you."

"*You* excite me," he said.

Oh, my. Diego has got some smooth talk in him too.

"Well, that's good," I said.

"But I do like fashion, actually. It would be interesting to see a fashion show in Paris. You need me to get us tickets or anything?"

"Oh, no. My company sent me over here to attend these shows, so we don't have to pay for tickets. I have some all access passes."

"Okay," he said. "Maybe we can have dinner at the Eiffel Tower before the show and do something afterwards if that's okay with you. I really like Paris. It's very romantic."

The thought of being romantic with Diego made my heart warm. "Yes, I hear it is. I like what I've seen so far."

"Well, I know you need to get some rest and I don't want to hold you, so what about if I call you or text you later tonight to let you know my plans? How is that?"

SHAYLA'S CATCH

"That would work," I said. "I'll give you the details too, about all the shows and my schedule."

"Great!" he said. "Talk to you around 10 or so tonight then."

"Okay."

"Bye, beautiful."

I went to sleep for about four hours and then Jasmine woke me up and asked me to join her for a bite to eat at the café in the hotel. She hadn't changed much since high school. She was still petite and wore her hair very short. She had been valedictorian in high school, even studying engineering, but decided to go into the retail industry and now owned two boutiques in New York. We stayed in touch throughout the years, but over the last two years our friendship had waned, but I still felt the same closeness to Jasmine, although we had gone our separate ways. We quickly ate and went over to the Carrousel du Louvre, the venue where the fashion shows would be held and the epicenter of Paris Fashion Week. When I introduced myself to the hostess, she led me to the back of a big area where I was given my itinerary for the week and met with some executives for Versace. I was really looking forward to visiting the main showroom tomorrow.

The trends for the new season were bright and colorful. I watched show after show and took notes on what I thought were the most fashionable collections. Diego also stayed on my mind. I wondered what the possibilities might be with us. I was looking forward to spending some time with him.

When Jasmine and I got back to the room, I was exhausted, so I took a shower and fell off to sleep quickly. Diego's call at 10:05pm awakened me.

"Hello?"

"Hi, lovely lady,"

"Hi, Diego,"

"You sound really tired. You want me to call you back in the morning?"

"Oh, no. I can talk. Did you decide when you're coming?"

"Yes. I'm coming Saturday morning. I booked my flight to get there around noon and I'll leave around noon the day after. I got a pretty good deal through my travel agent." I could hear the elation in Diego's voice.

"I'm excited," I said.

Diego and I talked a few more minutes and hung up.

I had done so much during the week that when I woke up Saturday morning, I had minimal energy, but I was eagerly anticipating Diego's arrival. After taking a cab to the hotel, he called and told me, "I'm downstairs." My heart started pumping immediately. When I walked to the lobby, my eyes met Diego's. He glanced at me lovingly and kissed me on the lips. *Wow.* He looked handsome in blue jeans and a corduroy jacket. Once Diego got into his room he gathered me gently in his arms. His muscles were taut, making me feel protected. When we looked into each other's eyes again, he gave me a sexy smile. He had a glow in his eyes. Our first stop was to Cathedrale Notre-Dome de Paris. I had heard that the Cathedral had a lot of spiritual history and art, and I wanted to start off our site-seeing tour on a spiritual tip. Diego told me that he had seen many of the Paris sites, since he had been there several times, but he took pictures of me with my camera and with his and pointed out some of the sites to me like a tour guide. We walked for miles, hand-in-hand, checking out Notre Dame, the Eiffel Tower, and we ended up having dinner on the Siene River Cruise, which overlooked Paris. *Quite romantic.* All through dinner, Diego gazed at me with a desire in his eyes. I was intrigued with him as well. By the end of the evening, Diego suggested we take a horse driven carriage back to the hotel. Excitement twirled through me when he guided my chin to him and gave me a soothing, kiss on the lips.

"Are you good?" he asked after the gentle kiss.

"I couldn't be better," I said as my heart fluttered.

When we got back to the hotel, we went to our separate rooms, with plans to meet again in 40 minutes. When I saw Diego again, he looked dapper in a blue cashmere sweater, a black jacket with double zippers and black slacks. *Stylish, indeed.* I put on a military style black dress with long sleeves that was cut right above my knee and a defining belt and black high-heeled pumps. Diego and I held hands as we walked into the venue where the fashion show was being held. I squirmed a bit when we passed a Sean Jean ad with Calvin on the billboard just as we were about to enter the auditorium. *Oh no. I don't want to be reminded of him.* Diego seemed to notice that I had seen Calvin's picture as we slowly walked past it. He guided me gently into the room.

After the fashion show, we headed straight back to the hotel in a cab. I ached to be near him throughout the night, but I knew that I would need to resist. He must have felt the same way – like he needed to call it a night before something else happened that we couldn't take back. When he walked me to my door, he took my hands in his, and pecked me on the lips.

"I'll call you in a few minutes . . . when I get to my room, okay?" he said huskily, with a look of longing, but reticence.

"Okay," I muttered. Diego then pecked me several more times on the lips. After the third peck, he kissed me deeply, thrilling my every sense. Chills swept over my body. But Diego must have known where to draw the line. He stepped back suddenly.

"If I don't go now, I'm gonna want to make love to you," he said grasping my hand. "And once I make love to you, there's no turning back. I'll want to wake up with you the next morning and the next morning and the next. I wouldn't want you to leave, going back to the states, and not be able to have you again."

I wanted to surrender to Diego and let the next morning take care of itself. *Is he testing me to see what I'll say or is he making the decision that we should put love making off?* His eyes, heavy with desire, questioned me like he was waiting on my response. "Well . . . we'll have more time together," I said and leaned into Diego's shoulder. "I've enjoyed you so much," I said as I held him. He drew me closer and kissed me on the forehead.

When I walked inside the room, I dropped my purse on the floor and fell on the bed, feeling overwhelmed.

"You okay?" Jasmine asked, looking at me with an upward brow.

"No," I muttered. "That man does it for me. He is so tempting."

"Well, why are you back in here then? Shouldn't you be in his room? You may as well give him some. You know you want to."

"It's too soon for that though," I said to Jasmine. "I'm trying to start off a relationship without letting sex guide me, but allowing God to guide me."

"I understand totally," Jasmine said and smiled. "Plus, if you give it up too soon, what will he have to look forward to?"

The hotel phone rang, startling me. Jasmine answered. "Hold on one sec," she said. It was Diego.

"Just wanted to make sure I'm gonna be the last thing on your mind before you fall off to sleep," he said.

"Oh, you don't have to worry about that. You're gonna be the last thing on my mind tonight and the first thing on my mind when I wake up."

When I looked at Jasmine, her smile was big. "Ooooh," she said with a giggle.

Diego and I talked until falling asleep on the phone. I had managed to get undressed while I was talking to him. I heard Jasmine's snores ten minutes into my conversation with Diego.

The next morning, my cell phone rang. It was Diego.

"I was going to call your room, but it's off the hook," he said. "I think we spent the night together on the phone," he chuckled.

"Oh," I said, looking down at the hotel phone on the floor. "I guess we did."

Diego had to leave the hotel at 9:30 in order to get to the airport for his flight, but I wasn't ready for him to leave. But I knew that if he stayed another night I might not be so strong.

"I want to see you again," he said before getting into the cab. "When can I see you? You said you're coming over for London Fashion Week in February, but I'm not going to be able to wait that long. I'm coming home for the holidays – not Thanksgiving, but Christmas."

"Oh, that would be great," I said.

Diego leaned down and tasted my lips. "Okay, I'll call you when I land," he said.

On my flight back to Atlanta a few days later, thoughts of Diego Jones took over my mind. I didn't know what was next for us, but I felt something I never imagined I would feel for any man. The intensity of my emotions, mixed with a peaceful knowing that Diego was just as enamored with me and would do me no wrong, was something I had not felt while with Calvin. Wrapping my blanket around my shoulders, I closed my eyes and reminisced about my time with Diego in Paris. *The best is yet to come.* I just knew it.

Chapter Twenty-Three

The Ultimate Catch

iego and I spoke with each other almost everyday for two months after my return to Atlanta. Past romances, old hurts, to our dreams and hopes for the future all were a part of our long conversations. The Christmas season was here again, and I was looking forward to spending more time with Diego. He was taking a flight in from London on Christmas Eve. I couldn't wait to see him.

The two months had been long and hectic for me. I had worked long hours at Versace, and I was also putting my business plan together with hopes of opening my own boutique in the coming summer. A few talks with a savvy financial planner and attorney that Roberto had introduced me to assured me that opening my own clothing store was worth the investment. I made the decision to continue living at Sydney's until her wedding next October. Since she refused to take more than $300 a month from me, I had high hopes of having enough money saved up to put down on a swanky boutique in Buckhead or Atlantic Station. I was still contemplating selling the ring that Calvin had bought for me, but instead of just selling a whopping $850,000 ring, I thought I'd give Calvin a call and at least tell him about my plans. *It's the right thing to do*. I gazed at the sparkling ring after dialing Calvin's number.

"Hello?" he answered.

"Hi," I said. "Happy Holidays." I had not spoken with Calvin in about three weeks. I had been checking on him periodically, but had long come to the realization that having a committed relationship with him was never going to happen. I was glad I was over him.

"Yeah, Ho, Ho, Ho! You calling to tell me you want to come back to me for Christmas?"

"Nope," I said. "I just want to talk to you about something that's really been on my heart. I want to get your opinion."

"Yeah, go ahead."

"I'm opening a clothing boutique next summer and it's gonna cost me a pretty penny. I want to own the shop, and I'm trying to do it without getting into a lot of debt."

"Dayum, Shay. I ain't playing ball no more. I can't afford to open a boutique for you."

"I'm not asking you to, silly. I just wanted to know how you would feel if I decide to sell this engagement ring you gave me. I need the money, you know. The ring is beautiful, and I'll always cherish it and what we shared, but I've moved on with my life."

"No, you haven't," he said cockily. "You still love me, and you'll be coming back to me, Shay."

"Okay. Whatever you say, Calvin. But seriously, would it make you feel bad if I sold this ring? It would be for a great investment – my own boutique."

"Hell, I don't care what you do with that ring. It's not like I paid for it, but you can still get a lot for it though."

"What did you say? You didn't pay for it? What do you mean?"

"Shay, you know I gots people in high places. The jeweler worked out a deal for me in exchange for something I worked out for him. That ring was a tradeoff."

I was dumbfounded. I couldn't believe Calvin was actually admitting to me that he had not paid for the eight karat ring and that he got it through some tradeoff *–probably some crooked deal.* "So, I see," I uttered, trying not to get angry. "You didn't even pay cash or do credit for the ring? So, that's why it was so easy for you to put it on my finger. It wasn't valuable."

"Hey, girl, I did pay for that ring . . . just not with cash. And I put that ring on your pretty little finger cause I thought I was gonna marry you. But you didn't want to be married, Shay. You couldn't hang."

"No, I could not hang," I said. "I don't think you understand the pain you caused me. Obviously you have not changed either, Calvin!"

"What I gotta change for?" he said. "I'm a good man. Who I need to change for?"

"You need to change for yourself. Sometimes you can be so cold and to tell you the truth, you didn't have to tell me that you didn't really purchase the ring."

"Oh, so you want me to lie? Is that what you want me to do?"

"Well, you are so good at lying about everything else. I didn't have to know you did a tradeoff with a crook to get a ring for me."

Calvin began laughing. "You are something else, girl! You are something else! But I did hear about a store that went out of business in Atlantic Station, and I was actually thinking about buying the property myself and turning it into a strip club," Calvin stated.

"Yeah! Sounds like something right up your alley," I remarked.

Calvin started laughing again. "I'm just kidding, girl. You still love me, don't you? You wanna come back home?"

"No," I told him quickly. "Not at all. In fact, I'm dating someone and I'm happy."

"Oh, really? Who is he?"

"You just worry about opening your strip club and all your miscellaneous women."

"I don't have miscellaneous women, babe, but you shoulda known that I wasn't ready to get married. I ain't gonna marry until I'm like 35, and I'm gonna be faithful to my wife, for sho. She's gonna have herself a good catch."

"Oh, yeah?"

"That's right. That's right."

"Well, I wish you had told me that you didn't want to get married until you were like 35."

"I was gonna marry you in Vegas, remember? But I got reinstated to the team. I don't know why you didn't understand that."

"Yeah, don't remind me, but all things work together for the good."

"What you mean by that?"

"Obviously, it just wasn't meant for us to be together. By the way, you didn't tell me that you have two or three babies and a couple on the way. You had better watch it. You do know you can go broke from dishing out child support, don't you?"

"Shii'it. I ain't going broke. I'm about to sign a deal with these movie people to do a documentary on my life. I ain't going broke at all. And I only have two kids. All that shit you be reading on those gossip sites is false. Why do you care anyway? You got yourself a new man, right?"

"You are exactly right," I proudly stated. "So, I don't know why I'm on the phone with you. It's my ring now, so I can do whatever I like with it. Goodbye, Calvin."

"You sure you want to hang up?" he said. "You know you gonna be calling me back. You can't help yourself, Shay. You love me."

"Okay. Whatever you say, Calvin. Goodbye and have a Merry Christmas."

"You too, baby doll. I'll see you soon."

"Bye."

I was livid. Even though I knew deep down inside of me that my relationship with Calvin was over and done with and I was looking forward to developing a new relationship with Diego, it still hurt that Calvin was so callous about what we had shared and didn't really value me. I picked up the ring and swirled it around my index finger. *And here I was thinking he had spent $850,000 on a ring for me.* He was still egotistical and selfish, even after almost losing his leg. *I guess he'll be like that for the rest of his life.* And then for Calvin to have the nerve to say that he is a good catch. *Please.*

I thought about Calvin for about two more minutes then I decided I couldn't allow my conversation with him to ruin my day or slow me down, so I put the ring back in my jewelry box and went to join Sydney as she and Aaron prepared dinner.

The next morning I rushed to get dressed and to look my best. Diego was arriving on an afternoon flight, which only gave me more time to get excited. I was picking him up from the airport. *I'm so ready to be in his arms again.* It was amazing how much we had shared on the phone. We had gotten to know each other a lot better. Our mutual connection was stronger than either of us ever expected.

While waiting for Diego to call from his cell phone, I parked illegally by the airport curbside and hoped the police would not ask me to move. Within three minutes of my wait, Diego showed up. He dashed around to the driver's side of my car, and before I could get out, he was trying to open my locked car door. As soon as I unlocked the door and stepped out, he lifted me in his arms and kissed me passionately. I didn't care who was watching. I kissed him right back and wrapped my arms around him. Neither of us let go. We swayed from side to side in each other's arms – reveling in the moment. Diego drew back to get a good look at me.

"My Shayla," he said. "I missed you." Then he drew me close again and we hugged some more.

I stepped back. "Let's get in the car. We are blocking traffic," I said giddily, euphoria filling me.

With Diego in my car, I could hardly drive straight. His presence filled me with excitement. In blue jeans, a charcoal wool jacket and a burgundy scarf around his neck, he looked so handsome. He smelled just as delightful. I tried not to appear too jittery, but my palms were sweating in my gloves. As I drove away from the airport curbside, Diego put his hand on my knee and squeezed it. It was comforting to have him near me again – touching me again.

When we arrived at the Joneses house, I wasn't surprised that the home was just as exquisite as their home in Puerto Rico. Diego proudly introduced me to everyone by saying, "This is my girlfriend, Shayla." Claire Jones just smiled, almost seeming to blush while Diego introduced me to his family. I spent the next few hours stuffing myself with gumbo, laughing with Diego and getting to know his siblings, Claire and other family members. When I had to excuse myself to go into the bathroom, I was surprised when Diego snuck in behind me and grabbed me around my waist. Like two teenagers experiencing puppy love, we kissed several times and hugged each other.

"From the first day I saw you I knew you were the one," Diego confessed tenderly.

"Is that right?" I said, quivering, before he planted another kiss on my lips.

I told Diego that I had promised my sister that I would make it to her Christmas Eve dinner party even if I got there late. He agreed to go with me. It was 9 pm when we finally arrived at Sydney's home, and everybody had already opened their Christmas gifts. This year it was only Aaron and Connie present, so it was more intimate. I could tell that Connie liked Diego from the beginning. She had a sparkle in her eyes, like she was excited for me. Aaron and Diego hit if off immediately. Aaron and Sydney decided that they were going to see a late movie. Diego and I just found comfort in sitting in front of the Christmas tree, holding hands. Our bodies automatically gravitated towards each other like magnets. He stroked my hair as I relaxed in his arms. As Diego drew me closer, he put his lips against my ear and spoke so faintly that I could barely hear him, but hear him, I did.

"I love you, Shayla," were the three words that were music to my ears.

My voice was too choked to speak, but the sensations in my body spoke volumes. Diego lifted my chin and kissed me. *Maybe he already knows I love him.* I shuddered when I felt his body harden, but I knew that it wasn't the time or the place. *Not yet. Not at Sydney's house.* We had already talked about putting physical intimacy off as long as we could. I wanted to wait, but I also ached for him. *Plus, he's the one, God. He says I'm the one.* Before things got too heated, Diego stood to his feet and put on his jacket. *Dang.* I truly didn't want him to leave.

For the next week, companionship was non-stop between Diego and me – dinner at the finest restaurants, a mountain climb, movies, and even a night of dancing.

By the time New Year's Eve rolled around, we decided to bring it in together, in church. It had been a wonderful, romance-filled week for us and we wanted to both give thanks for all our blessings through the year. Before we went to church, Diego stopped by to pick me up for dinner. My mind raced back to last year's happenings, when Calvin had come over and proposed and how I had gone out with Diego the same day. Little did I know that the year would be filled with so many ups and downs and that I would lose someone I thought I loved more than life itself. But I gained someone even better for me. *I really want things to work out with Diego,* I prayed as the New Year came in. I had heard that people come into your life for a reason, a season or a lifetime. I was beginning to believe that Diego had come into my life for a lifetime.

On New Year's Day, right after Diego finished sampling the brunch I had prepared, the doorbell rang. I looked through the peep hole and saw the person I least expected to see. Calvin! *No! This can't be playing out again, on the first day of the New Year.* I opened the door and he limped over and gave me a hug. I lightly hugged him back.

"What are you doing here?" I asked. "I have company."

"Oh, yeah?" Calvin said. "Who?"

"My boyfriend," I said softly. "Diego."

"Diego?" he repeated and boldly walked inside as if he needed to see him to believe it. When Calvin saw Diego sitting on the sofa, his eyes widened. "What's up, man?" he asked in a curious manner.

"Yeah, man. What's up?" Diego said in a street-wise voice that I wasn't expecting and stood to his feet. They gave each other a handshake, and Calvin looked at me as if I needed to introduce them, so I did.

"Calvin, this is Diego. Diego Jones," I said cautiously.

"Where do I know you from, man?"

"Diego is Clyde Jones son," I blurted out.

"Oh, yeah. I knew you looked familiar," Calvin continued to stare at Diego suspiciously. "I met you before, haven't I?"

"I think we met once, but it was a long time ago - at the Rolls Royce dealership," Diego recalled.

The room grew quiet for a moment. I didn't know what to say next. Calvin was staring at Diego now with pensive eyes. He had his cane in one hand and a gift in the other. *This is really strange. Oh God, this is really strange.* I felt a bit of compassion for Calvin, but I wondered what trick he was up to now. *And what is the gift for?* I had already told Diego about my occasional conversations with Calvin. I had told him that he had moved on and so had I. I didn't want Diego to read anything more than friends into Calvin's surprise visit.

"So, Calvin, we haven't spoken to each other since right before Christmas. Did you have a good one?"

"It could have been better?" he said blandly. "I just thought I'd stop by to bring you a gift. I wanted to get it to you earlier, but you know how I am. Better late than never, right?"

I didn't know what to do or say when Calvin handed me the perfectly wrapped gift. I took it hesitantly. Diego reclaimed his seat on the sofa. Trembling, I slowly walked across the room and took a seat next to Diego.

"Sit down, man," Diego said.

Calvin took the seat directly in front of us. He rubbed on his chin. His eyes were downcast. I felt like something strange was going on with him.

"How is Little C?" I asked as I toyed over the gift, not really wanting to open it in front of Diego.

"He's good," Calvin answered. "He asked about you."

"What?" I laughed. "So, he's talking already?"

"Yep," Calvin said, staring in my eyes. "Go ahead. Open your gift."

I took another look at the gift, feeling quite awkward. I then looked at Diego for approval. "Go ahead," he said softly.

"Calvin, I wasn't expecting anything from you," I said, tearing the paper off the gift. "I've moved on with my life. You know that."

"I see," he nodded and looked at Diego.

Once the paper was off the gift box, I opened it. To my surprise I found a key inside.

"What is this, Calvin?" I asked, taking the key in my hand. "What is this?"

"It's the key to your own clothing store," he said proudly. "It's located off Atlantic Station Drive. Remember the property I was telling you about that was going out of business and was up for sale? Well, I bought it and I want you to have it."

"What?"

"I care about you, Shay, even though you have moved on," he said and glared at Diego. "I bought you a boutique, okay? And I don't want anything in return. All you gotta do is move in . . . into the boutique, that is. I arranged everything where all you'll need to do is pay the utility bills. It's just something to repay you for all the pain I caused you."

I was still looking at the key, speechless. "Calvin, who . . ."

"I know what you're thinking. Come on, Shayla. It wasn't a trade off or a dirty deal. I'm a new man now. Believe it or not."

He really did know what I was thinking. I was wondering what Calvin had done to get the boutique and why he was giving this key to me now. *I can't fall for this. Not when I've been blessed with the man of my dreams.*

"Calvin, I must say I'm flattered. I just can't take this key. I can't accept this."

"Why?" he questioned. "At least go by and see the place. It's really nice. I know you got a new man and all. You mind that I bought her a store, Diego?"

Diego looked at me and then at Calvin. "Yes, I do mind," he said directly.

"Oh, and why is that?" Calvin wanted to know.

"Because Shayla and I are together now. She's going to be my wife, and I don't want her taking any sympathy gifts from an ex boyfriend just because he messed up. If she wants a boutique I will buy it for her."

I was shocked, to say the least. *I'm going to be his wife? When?* I started to say something, anything, but Calvin spoke before I could get my words together.

"Man, please. So, your pops left you with a lot of money, huh? I heard he was a billionaire. So, the loyal son steps in and takes over his dad's business and now you think you can just buy my girl?"

Diego surged to his feet. I didn't know if he was going to hit Calvin or what, so I got up from my seat and scooted in front of Diego.

"Calvin, don't. That was very rude of you," I said. I then turned to face Diego. "Diego, can I speak to Calvin alone, please."

Diego didn't say a word. He just stared at Calvin with ferocious eyes. He then looked at me. "So, you want to talk to him alone?" he asked as his eyes questioned me even more.

"Well, no. It doesn't have to be done that way," I said, seeing that Diego wasn't all pleased with my asking for a moment alone with Calvin. I faced Calvin. "Calvin, here is your gift," I handed him the key, the box it came in and the wrapping paper. "Thank you, but no thanks. I'm saving up to get my own store. I don't need a man to rescue me."

Calvin stood to his feet. "Oh, Snap. When did this happen? The damsel in distress doesn't need a man to come to her rescue. Are you sure?" Calvin started laughing.

"Man, it's time for you to leave," Diego said.

"I ain't ready to go," Calvin said. "I came over here to claim what's mine."

"Nothing or no one over here belongs to you, man, so just leave," Diego insisted, taking a few steps forward. "Take your cane, your gift, and get the hell out."

Diego surprised me. I didn't know what to say. At the same time, a frightening feeling came over me. I knew that Calvin wasn't one to back down. But now Diego seemed just as hard-nosed.

"Calvin! No, wait a second. I have a gift for *you*," I told him. Diego looked at me somewhat perplexed. "I'll be right back, babe," I assured Diego.

"Oh, so you got a gift for me? Cool! Unlike you, I don't turn down gifts."

"Just stay right there," I walked away hoping that the intense exchange between them wouldn't escalate before I could return from the bedroom.

"You ain't goin to get no gun are you?" I heard Calvin say as I hurried out of the room. "I'm not up for no violence today. I'm already one leg down," he muttered.

When I returned, they were still standing face-to-face, looking at each other as if they were getting ready for a boxing match.

"Here you go," I said, coming between them and handing Calvin the engagement ring. He took a long look at the ring, but he didn't take it. "Here, Calvin. Take it. I don't need it anymore. I don't know if it was ever mine in the first place. Please take it."

Calvin reached out and slowly took the ring from me. "Ahhh, now you wrong for that! You know I got this especially for you cause you wanted to marry me so bad," he said snidely. Calvin then turned to Diego. "Man, she been begging you to marry her too?"

"Get out, now! Or do you want me to throw you out?" Diego said sternly. Calvin took a few steps forward, as if he were challenged by Diego's words.

"Calvin, please go," I begged as my anger rose. "Goodbye!"

"Well, can we still be friends?" Calvin asked with a smirk.

"No, Calvin. We cannot! Just go!"

Calvin poked his cane around on the floor like he was doing a dance. He then slowly walked towards the door. Both Diego and I followed him. I could almost feel Diego's tension. I knew he was angry. When Calvin opened the door I had a feeling he would do or say more, and he did.

"If you ever change your mind you know where to find me. You gonna think about me every time you with ole boy. There's nobody else like me," he boasted.

"Thank God there isn't." I exclaimed as I slammed the door in Calvin's face.

I turned to face Diego. He still looked quite tensed, so I leaned into his chest and embraced him. He held me gently while massaging the back of my neck.

"I'm sorry," I said softly.

"Look at me," Diego said. When I looked into his eyes, Diego looked tender and warm. "There is nothing to be sorry for," he said cupping my face in his hands. "Don't apologize for his stupidity. I already knew he was a fool when he didn't marry you when he had a chance. But one man's loss is another man's gain." At that moment I knew Diego was everything I had ever prayed for. Diego then planted the most passionate kiss on my lips. Our kisses grew more and more intense as he gently stroked his tongue along my parted lips. I wanted all of him. I didn't want to live a day without him.

Epilogue

As I heard the traditional wedding song, I took a step forward to enter the church sanctuary. I was looking forward to spending the rest of my life with the man of my dreams. Walking down the aisle to meet my soul mate was a dream that had finally come true for me. I gracefully took small steps down the aisle in my white, asymmetric neck-lined, mermaid, floor length gown. My uncle Martin escorted me down the aisle. I was happy. I glanced from side to side, smiling and truly grateful for my more than 200 guests as they stood in my honor. Most of them had expressions of awe on their faces. I wore my hair in a high bun, which was accentuated with white roses in the back. I felt like a princess. The closer I got to my groom, the more I realized I was marrying my knight in shining armor. *Wow*. He looked like a stallion in his black and white tuxedo attire. As I got closer to him, he shifted his weight from one side to the other. Sydney, my maid of honor, had tears in her eyes. I couldn't believe I had actually beaten her to the altar, but I was looking forward to celebrating her union with Aaron in a couple of months. My bridesmaids, Tacara and Jasmine, were teary-eyed as well. When I finally reached the altar, I turned to my right to see my mother who was also shedding a few tears.

"Who gives this woman to be married to this man?" the pastor asked.

"Her mother and I do," Martin exclaimed.

I smiled as my beloved took my hand in his. "I love you," he whispered. As I looked into his eyes, I could see a look of longing. I allowed him to lead me a few steps forward.

My thoughts went back to when Diego had proposed to me. It had been three months since he moved back to Atlanta. I was surprised and overcome with joy when he got down on one knee at the Atlanta Botanical Garden. We savored every moment as we enjoyed the Atlanta skyline and the most enchanting displays of tulips and daffodils. Steve and Tacara were on the outing with us. They were in on Diego's plan to propose to me. I knew nothing about it, so I was surprised when Diego asked me to be his wife. That day was one of our most memorable days together so far. I didn't know I could feel so much love. As we cuddled in each other's arms, his warmth and gentleness penetrated my soul, and his passion left my head spinning. We set a date the very next day, so for the last three months, all I had done was plan my wedding.

I had not heard a word from Calvin since he came over on New Year's Day. I had read, via web site reports and social media, that he was being sued by Tommy Daniels, his agent, for not paying for some sort of services he had rendered him. That was truly a surprising read, but then again, it wasn't. His relationship with Tommy had been strained for quite a while. I also heard that Cristi had, indeed, moved back in with him after he was shot, but that his home had recently gone into foreclosure. Diego and I had closed on our three-story home in an upscale neighborhood in Roswell just last week. I was ecstatic that God had brought the right man into my life so I could know what true love really is. I had found God and my own inner strength to know that no matter if a man was in my life or not, I could still be happy.

After Diego repeated his vows, I repeated mine: "I, Shayla, take you Diego, to be my lawfully wedded husband, to have and to hold from this day forward, for better or for worse, for richer for poorer, in sickness and in health, to love and to cherish; from this day forward until death do us part."

My better half slid the beautiful platinum diamond band on my finger. I was still wearing the 5 carat diamond he had specially designed for me. The ring was a symbol of his commitment and undying love for me. I slid his ring over his knuckle, telling him the same. I felt like I was at the top of the highest mountain. We then moved over to the unity candle and lit it. When we moved back to the altar, the pastor gave us a more serious talk about sharing a life together. He told us that we would have to be committed to loving each other through the highs and lows of our lives, and that with God in our lives, all things are possible. He then said a prayer that seemed to take forever, although it was only about two minutes.

Finally, the pastor spoke the words I had longed to hear. "By the power vested in me, I now pronounce you man and wife. You may kiss the bride."

My Diego gave me a loving look, leaned in and planted the sweetest kiss ever on my lips. He kissed me again and again, until our guests applauded. "I love you," he said. "Oh my God, I love you."

"I love you too," I said softly. I was so overjoyed.

"Ladies and gentlemen, I present to you Mr. and Mrs. Diego Jones," the pastor announced.

At that moment I felt a lightheaded rush, like I was going to faint. But before I got weak in the knees from the overwhelming joy I was experiencing, my husband took my hand and gently brought my arm through his. I felt a sense of security by his strength and touch. Diego looked at me and winked. We then walked down the aisle, overjoyed to start our new lifetime journey together.

THE END

Sonya Jenkins is a versatile entertainment journalist, actress, author and publisher of WWW.SONYASSPOTLIGHT.COM. For more than 20 years Jenkins' coverage of celebrity profiles has included personal interviews and articles on Beyoncé, Eddie Murphy, Vanessa Williams, Don Johnson, Halle Berry, Tyler Perry, Wesley Snipes, Billy Dee Williams, Xernona Clayton, Danny Glover, Bishop T.D. Jakes, Whitney Houston, Grant Hill, Evander Holyfield, Stevie Wonder, and several others.

Born in Atlanta, Ga., Jenkins began her journalistic endeavors while in high school where she became editor-in-chief of the school newspaper. Jenkins studied Communications at the University of Tennessee where she received a Bachelor of Science degree in Communications with an emphasis in journalism. Her work in the University's journalism department for three years and as a sports writer for *Smokey's Tale Magazine* (for the University of Tennessee) piqued her interest in sports writing. During her early twenties, she was nominated an Outstanding Young Woman of America, and worked as an intern/production assistant at "Entertainment Tonight" in Hollywood. Jenkins gained a wealth of knowledge about television production and the entertainment industry that has proved beneficial in her career.

In 1990, Jenkins became a regular contributor to *Upscale Magazine*, where she soon became *Upscale Magazine's* first entertainment editor. Jenkins' responsibilities included writing cover stories, editing and writing news for the entertainment column, and covering entertainment events such as the NAACP Awards, The Grammys, The Soul Train Awards, and press junkets around the world. Jenkins has also written free-lance articles for *The Atlanta Voice, The Atlanta Tribune, The Atlanta Metro*, and *The Tennessee Tribune* newspapers, and *Sophisticate's Black Hair, YSB, Contemporary, Atlanta Christian Family, Excellence, Black Elegance, Gospel Today, Urban Influence* and *Belle* magazines. In 1996 the Atlanta Association of Black Journalist nominated her for a Pioneer Black Journalist Award for her outstanding work as a writer.

In addition to Jenkins' print writing, she created the weekly industry news segment for "Entertainment Atlanta" – dubbed the first entertainment news program in Atlanta. Jenkins' debut on-air interview for "Entertainment Atlanta" featured actress Elizabeth Shue from feature films "Back to the Future" and "Leaving Las Vegas." During the historical 2000 presidential election, Jenkins worked as a video journalist for CNN's world headquarters in Atlanta. She also created a newsletter, *Sonya's Spotlight & Spotlight Entertainment* in 1994 and re-launched it as a colorful print magazine in *2002*. In 2003 Jenkins transferred *Sonya's Spotlight* to *Season* magazine. She covered national entertainment news and wrote cover stories on Beyoncé, Mary Hart, and Jessica Simpson. Jenkins on-air coverage has showcased one-on-one interviews and red carpet coverage at The Trumpet Awards, which she has covered since its inception. Jenkins has also transferred Sonya's Spotlight to the Internet in 2007 with *Sonya's Spotlight* Web Magazine, WWW.SONYASSPOTLIGHT.COM. In 2013 Jenkins was a Trumpet Awards Foundation Honoree for their annual High Tea with High Heels event, honoring a select group of distinguished women. Jenkins is also a member of the Atlanta Press Club.

SHAYLA'S CATCH is Jenkins' first novel (published in March, 2014 via Amazon-Kindle) of many more to come. Jenkins also recently re-ignited her acting career – an aspiration since childhood. She has worked for and made appearances in SELMA, Tyler Perry's A MADEA CHRISTMAS, "For Better or Worse," "The Haves and The Have Nots," Lifetime TV's "The Trip To Bountiful," and "Marry Me," BET's "Let's Stay Together," and "Being Mary Jane," and several other films and television shows.

View Sonya Jenkins' Web Magazine at
WWW.SONYASSPOTLIGHT.COM

Made in the USA
San Bernardino, CA
28 April 2015